1001

Persiranian Stories

of Love and Revenge

1001

Persiranian Stories
of Love and Revenge

Yahya Gharagozlou

Cover and interior artwork by
Parinaz Eleish

Book design by
Clare Wolfowitz

ISBN 978-0-692-79509-5

Blackeyes Press
Boston, Massachusetts

To a far more interesting family than any fiction can convey.

Acknowledgements

Books often have birthing problems; 1001 small and large problems plagued this one. Its healthy delivery was made possible by a creative editor, a believing agent, and numerous patient readers. Any remaining defects can be traced back to the progenitor.

I would like to thank Clare Wolfowitz for editing the manuscript and helping with all the details analog or digital; but more importantly for her unswerving support. Thanks to Steve Kasdin from Curtis Brown, Ltd., for the phone call one afternoon, asking to represent me. Thanks to Candace Cheatham, editor at Kindle Nation Daily, for spreading the word through the newly built alleys of our digital age. Thank you, Claudine Holdgate, for sitting permanently on my shoulder, proofreading anything I commit to computer memory. More thanks to Ali Rahnema for knowing everything there is to know about 20th century Iranian history; Babak Veysi, the Frenchman who corrected my French; and Soad Kousheshi, for teaching me the rules of Belote.

Finally the largest thanks to all the readers who acted their part: Parinaz for reading like a loving wife, Hazi for reading like an elder protective brother, Mahmood Nobari for reading like a best friend, and my two darling Ahari cousins Nader and Nargess for reading and beating the bushes for publishers; and to my two daughters, Leila and Homa, for just being.

Table of Contents

Genealogy of the Poonaki Family

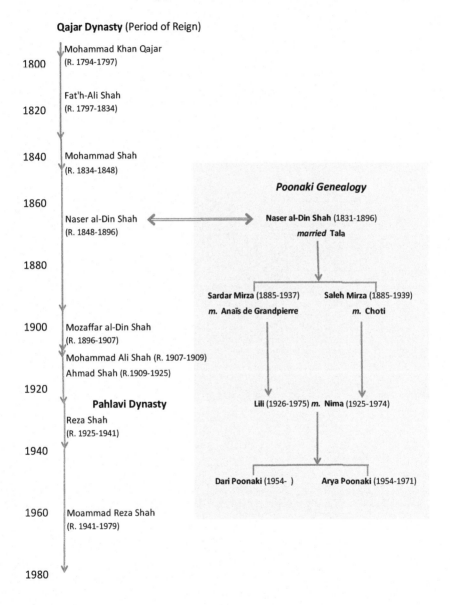

Qajar Dynasty (Period of Reign)

1800 — Mohammad Khan Qajar (R. 1794-1797)

1820 — Fat'h-Ali Shah (R. 1797-1834)

1840 — Mohammad Shah (R. 1834-1848)

1860

Naser al-Din Shah (R. 1848-1896)

1880

Poonaki Genealogy

Naser al-Din Shah (1831-1896) *married* Tala

Sardar Mirza (1885-1937) *m.* Anaïs de Grandpierre   **Saleh Mirza** (1885-1939) *m.* Choti

1900 — Mozaffar al-Din Shah (R. 1896-1907)

Mohammad Ali Shah (R. 1907-1909)

Ahmad Shah (R.1909-1925)

1920 — **Pahlavi Dynasty**

Reza Shah (R. 1925-1941)

Lili (1926-1975) *m.* **Nima** (1925-1974)

1940

Dari Poonaki (1954-)   **Arya Poonaki** (1954-1971)

1960 — Moammad Reza Shah (R. 1941-1979)

1980

Preamble

1. The Fat Storyteller Tells the Story of the Story

Lord of heaven and earth, thank you for
hiding these things from those who think
themselves wise and clever, and for
revealing them to the childlike.

— *Psalms* 8:2

"*Bismillah-e-Rahman-e-Rahim*, in the name of God the merciful and the compassionate: should He deem me deserving of one more hour of breath, then I, your true servant, Abol-Hassan Hekaiatchi, will narrate to you, honored ladies and gentlemen, the trials and tribulations of Rostam and Esfandiar. Yes, you know the story, you have read it. Please excuse my impertinence, honored ladies and gentlemen; you don't know the adventures of the mighty Rostam until you have heard them from your humble servant's lips. A telling story is in the *telling* of the story."

That's how my Baba would begin any one of thousands of tales, all neatly pigeonholed in his brain. A whisper might catch the ear; a wink would share a secret; a lift of one bushy eyebrow would invite their curiosity: with a thump of his silver-clad stick his listeners were brought to the rigid attention; a puffing-out of his voluminous cheeks, and they felt the fear of the Almighty. He threw that deep, powerful voice around the room, and the audience needed to be reassured that this was only a story. My Baba was a master storyteller.

All that is in the past. Now that he has returned to my dreams, those warm loving memories are being washed away by this new entity, whose resemblance to

13

my father is as deep as that of a man to his own shadow, formed at the midday prayer.

I can't vouch for the incorporeity of a ghost, still less of a ghost in a dream. But ever since Baba's ghost decided to invade my dreams, lodging a little way into the auricle of my left ear, no amount of washing in the morning rids me of this imagined stubborn grainy residue, a hangover from my vivid dreams.

From these dreams, buzzing like a fly held in a fist, he endlessly admonishes me, as well as my blessed mother, his second wife, and the entire living world. He links his misfortunes to the behavior of his offspring— meaning me, his only son. He reproaches me for his massive coronary, which killed him in twenty minutes flat fifteen years ago, and even blames me for his ghostly existence in my dreams—a direct result of my activities over the past five or six years.

"These days even the dead seem terribly misinformed. What does my father know about our times? All he's privy to are my nightmares, and God knows they are tame compared to my waking hours. All he remembers are the Friday prayers, followed by the smell of kebabs smoking in butter-drenched pilafs; the water pipes gurgling around the tea-room; the tinkling glasses and saucers of vinaceous tea. What does he know about the breakdown of respect?

Do you hear me, my darling Baba? We are in different times. Yet you keep after me relentlessly. I, alive and in ruins; you, wide-awake from eternal sleep, living vicariously through my subconscious, reminding me night after night of my responsibility to the Creator —repeating over and over what you drilled into me when you were flesh and blood:

> The storyteller who goes to his grave with an untold story destroys a universe. He has committed genocide; he must face his maker on the day of reawakening.

Here, now, I will repay my debt. I will tell my story—
though not quite the way you trained me to tell it. A
story you, my darling Baba, have half-followed in my
dreams (mixed with celery, yogurt, and the softness of
skin). Nine nights of storytelling overwhelm my
dreams.

I know our origins with the Almighty, the special
consideration He feels for us yarn-spinners. When the
All-Knowing blew life into the storytellers' clay, he
gave us freedom of imagination and made us responsible
for our creations. Still, the compassionate, in His infinite
wisdom, felt for our plight and commanded Gabriel, the
angel of death, thus:

"I have cursed man, the storyteller, with an excess of
imagination. Hence, in his last moment, *you* shall bear
witness to the untold creations of his mind. I shall treat
these as my own. Those he takes to the grave, he shall
answer for them on the Day of Judgment."

Tariq-e-Sabbar, the fifteenth-century soothsayer
(known as Blackeyes), describes the fate of the talented
storyteller Rumi (not the poet): for seven consecutive
years, with Gabriel at his deathbed, Rumi recounted tale
after tale as he emptied his crammed imagination. In all
that time Gabriel, trapped and transfixed, couldn't
recover a single life on Earth, such that old women with
tumors the size of ripe figs writhed in pain, unable to
die. On battlefields, mutilated bodies twitched in search
of their missing limbs. At the bottom of the ocean,
drowned sailors, bloated like the throats of bullfrogs,
gaped hopelessly for air. Organic matter refused to
decompose. Food became scarce. Firewood couldn't be
found despite the cold winters, for the cut trees
remained green as cucumbers.

Rumi, at heart a compassionate man, at last
blasphemed. Before his storytelling was finished, he was
moved to utter a final "Amen." As punishment he was
turned into a parakeet, to wander the world over,
uttering nonsense until the end of time. From that day

forth, the parakeet became the symbol of all story-tellers—not a symbol of repetition (as many assume), but a sign of warning and responsibility.

Trained since the age of three to become the greatest storyteller of this benighted country, I now am reduced to scratching with graphite on machine-pressed woodpulp to tell my story, in this small, stinking room I inhabit on top of Mammad-Ali's grocery store.

Still, a great improvement over my former quarters. You remember the cross-eyed Mammad-Ali, whose grocery store was just two blocks from the tearoom. How we neighborhood boys mocked him by pointing at objects on the shelf behind him, watching him scramble from shampoo to soap as he tried to guess our intention. He is the only soul who has shown me kindness since I walked out of prison—oh, yes, my Baba, prison. Mammad-Ali has become a sugar daddy of sorts to your son. I live with the smells of saffron, fenugreek, sumac, turmeric, cumin, and dill weed. I hear from morning to night the commissary demands of the neighborhood wives. I can see our tearoom from the grease-covered window. Every morning, I have strong tea with *lavash* and feta. For lunch, Zahra, their daughter—cross-eyed like her father—brings me rice and *khoresht*. And at night, they send up whatever they leave uneaten. He has given me a roof over my head, and he has given me time. I am thankful for his large and small kindnesses. He, in turn, thanks you for favors done in the past.

Let me warn you, my darling Baba, that should you, by chance, stumble across a crusty dream filled with written words, you must forgive my cowardice. The written word is just a substitute for memory, a catacomb; the treasures it holds must be brought out with the buzz of vocal cords and a twist of the tongue. I hear your voice (God bless your buzzing soul). "Where are the grimaces in the written word?" you used to ask. "Where is the cadence of a well-chanted poem, or the modulation of a well-performed war cry?" Until the day the winds change and our tongues are free to flutter anew, writing must serve as a down payment. In this country of ours, wagging tongues have been placed on the list of endangered species, and we don't want to end up like the Caspian tiger. Despite my fear of turning into a gibbering parakeet, I hope to redeem myself in your noncorporeal eyes, so that you can return to the resting place you so desire.

Let me first, then, set down the strange circumstances by which I came into the possession of this strange tale, and the promises I made to a madman.

2. The Omniscient Narrator, Creator of the Fat Storyteller, Tells His Story

"Vengeance is mine, I will repay," says the Lord.

Romans 12:19

Dear Ms. Vakil,

I don't consider myself a vengeful person. Even if I were, I am in no position to punish anybody. And I certainly don't believe in the pen-is-mightier-than-the-sword nonsense. The pen serves merely as a tool, marking credits and debits in the ledger of life. I will let the Lord take care of the rest.

To have chosen a childlike simpleton to narrate the story as my avatar preserves the age-old tradition of telling stories through an innocent—and, more practically, gives me legal protection in a country that adheres to the letter of the law. Rest assured, he is not decorative. I will not entirely abandon you to him nor let him wallow endlessly in a world of make-believe.

It has been many years since you approached me, acting as volunteer editor of the newly conceived *Encyclopedia Persiranica*. If I remember correctly, it was at the Qajar Conference held at the Copley Place

17

Marriott in Boston. You asked me to contribute an entry on my family, the Poonakis.

How delicately you tried to hurry me along by pointing out that the letter P would come not sixteenth, as in the English alphabet, but third, as in ours. I remember how your left heel tilted back and your right hand unconsciously chased your Hermès scarf (a small token to the Islamists) all the way to the back of your head, slipping against your blue-black hair. I swear I heard the electricity crackle. You looked so young that I asked if you attended a local school. Today you would have taken it as a compliment. Instead you told me a tad impatiently that you had just finished your dissertation at Edinburgh. You took my refusal to participate in the project with a sideways bite of your lower lip and thanked me. From the paucity of your letters I daresay we are well past P.

I saw you enter the Charles Hotel in Cambridge a few months ago. You looked womanly, more harried, still energetic. You pushed the revolving door from the lobby like a prisoner making an escape. You looked creamily rich. We, the moneyless old money, notice such distinctions by the smallest accoutrements. Your vintage Hermès *sac à dépêches* was a dead giveaway. I can't say I recognize your name as one of us. *Us:* a strange pronoun, meant to be inclusive, and yet we use it always to elevate ourselves into more elite company. Please don't take offense. I am not, and have not been for some years, in any position to be snooty. You are a historian and familiar with the Thousand Family nomenclature. I count *à peine* forty families left—all intermingled and cozy. No denying we are an endangered species. But are we worth saving? I haven't seen any groups in Orange County holding posters in our support. The ASPCA should be involved, for there has been plenty of cruelty in our benighted country, but that has not been exclusive to us. Neglect will take care of us; in time there will be little reason to hunt our not-so-shiny pelts.

Years have passed since your request. But writing something on my family has never been far from my mind. More than thirty years have passed since our revolution. The regime has worsened in its brutality and corruption. You can appreciate my reluctance to set down details of a family that believes in the separation of mosque and state—as opposed to the philosophy practiced by the current regime. I needn't dwell on the fate of the Indian writer whose book brought down the wrath of the Muslim world through the condemnation of one old man. I enjoy my modest cup of tea. I hate to imagine it upset by ignoramuses. Nevertheless, I will set down the history of this family. I have taken a few necessary precautions which I present to you as entertainment, a who-done-it, or, more accurately, a who-wrote-it plot.

I brought home from Best Buy a brand new computer, an enormous monitor, a laser printer, and all the necessary software. I felt like a knight putting on his armor before battle. I promise you historical gossip that will make your jaded colleagues turn suitably green. I promise you scorching cruelty mingled with loveless and lovely love. But more important to you, I promise you original historical goodies. I will need time to unroll my weightless memories. Persist, Ms. Vakil! I am not a likeable sort but I should be able to convince you we live in a world that would judge me perfectly sane compared to the madness that has taken over my tragic country.

As foreign names cause difficulties for readers at the beginning of these enterprises—remember Tolstoy's first fifty pages?—I will take the more modern option of rolling the credits right away instead of taking a bow when all is said and done. In any case, I prefer film to theater.

How can one describe the Poonaki family tree? An hourglass: identical twin princes stand as its pillars. One of them marries an aristocratic French beauty and has a daughter. The other marries (his third time) his secretary's fiery sixteen-year-old daughter and has a son. These cousins marry to produce a pair of sterile twin boys, ending the Poonakis in three generations. A genetic palindrome.

Immediately, you can place my twin grandfathers in the historical milieu you know so well. The royal twins' father was Naser al-Din Shah, the fourth monarch of the Qajar dynasty, who ruled for fifty years, contemporaneously with the English Victoria. Like her, he had an era named after him: the age of Naseri. He spawned the boys in 1885 in his harem with the daughter of his bootmaker, after a summer afternoon stroll, at a few strokes (so to speak) past three o'clock. The royal bootmaker came from Poonak, a village not far from the capital. Much later, when last names became obligatory, under the all-powerful Reza Shah, my monozygotic grandfathers registered the name Poonaki as our patronymic: a gesture of humility, because taking the name of a village for a last name was more in the tradition of peasants.

Saleh Mirza, known simply as the Prince, stands as the more famous of the twin princes. He had three wives. The first wife, the Shah's granddaughter, was a great match built on his prestige. Serious in all aspects of life including his philandering, he spared no woman who came within his range. It was the young, third wife, known as Choti, who shattered his heart but produced his only son: Nima, my father.

My maternal grandfather was the Prince's twin brother, Sardar Mirza, who remained willingly in his brother's penumbra. An elegant, jovial man, he suffered terribly at the hands of Mohammad Ali Shah, the twins' crowned nephew. Sardar Mirza came as close as any man to being executed during the tumultuous years after the 1906 Constitutional Revolution. I plan to restore his reputation with a good dose of literary sunlight, as an important figure in the Revolution. He married a French countess who gave birth, also belatedly, to my mother, Lili.

My parents, Nima and Lili, were thus twice cousins; they were born a year apart, in different continents. They married after the Second World War. Like today's celebrities, they shone brightly for a time. Their marriage would be eight years old before they gave birth to us, the second set of Qajar twins. They named my brother Arya and me Dari. The practice of family intermarriage is common, and I admit that our genes are as cross-wired as any; they could probably fit snugly in a single chromosome without loss of information. We could have been perhaps a degree tighter, but my brother and I are merely fraternal, rather than identical, twins. I am happy to announce that we were born without superfluous digits and with no hairy appendage attached to our coccyges.

Historians have used this compact genealogy of the Poonakis as proof of Qajar degeneracy. Ms. Vakil, please ignore facile theories linking family intermarriage to some manifest genetic failing. Social taboos notwithstanding, the congenital risk from incestuous procreation doubles only if some latent defect already exists.

A colleague of yours has made the case for a pathological oligospermia, or lack of motility, in our family. Knowing of my paternal grandfather's philandering coupled with our family's low birthrate, I concur. After handing my silicone collection condom to the leering male nurse, whom I swear had his tongue pressed into his cheek, I learned that my own count did not come close to the required 20 million sperm per milliliter. I mention this humiliating diligence of mine to demonstrate my sincerity in searching for a truth that transcends the facts.

As young boys, my brother and I saw Gregory Ratoff's *The Corsican Brothers* at the Alborz Movie

House, which showed old double features. Have you seen it? Douglas Fairbanks Jr. plays Siamese twins, separated as infants by one Dr. Paoli. When Mario's neckband is choking him, it is Lucien's crying that alerts the household. It is this sensibility that gives rise to so many sympathetic-twin stories. One child weeps from the pain of the other; twins separated at birth are reunited in adult life only to discover common accidents. In our case, when one of us cried, the other giggled. Our bookend twin grandfathers could not have been more different: they loved one another deeply, even though they lived apart most of their lives.

How I love H. B. Warner as Dr. Paoli, bracketed by the adoring Monsieur and Madame Dupré, when he says, "I have separated their bodies—" (here, the camera zooms in on his genteel, silvery goateed head as the orchestra swells and subsides, like acoustic quotation marks) "—*but what of their souls?*" The doctor's distant gaze contemplates a dark future. Even with the ridiculous Farsi dubbing, you can imagine the effect on us: twin boys sitting in the dark movie house, seeing one Douglas Fairbanks watch the other Douglas Fairbanks die.

I have read your article on my twin grandfathers in the *Encyclopedia Persiranica,* and I can't fault the facts. You are right. Who am I to argue? They were born on the third of August, 1885. One held a number of important cabinet positions; the other wrote essays and articles on modern early twentieth-century painting. But what of their souls, Ms. Vakil? What of their souls?

Before the rolling credits fade, one last character deserves to be named. Professor Dal, the famous surgeon and our step-uncle, lived in our home on and off for most of our lives. The Prince had adopted Professor Dal as a child, when he still thought himself infertile. He acted as a supportive elder brother to my parents during difficult times.

To protect the names of the guilty, I take the pivot of this particular universe and rotate it a few degrees. I call this special country Persiran. It exists in parallel to your objective country, but I live in it more comfortably than I could there. Even so, here they speak the same Farsi as you speak. My country contains all the same cities. The same crude oil bubbles out of the same fields. The wrestlers wrestle with the same grace. As in your country, our wolves are smaller than those in northern Europe. Tempted as I might be to blot them out, Persiran tolerates even the same clergy. I can see only one difference. *My* country has room for me, the last Poonaki standing.

Ms. Vakil, I can confirm that I am in possession of a valise full of correspondence between my princely grandfathers. I would guess that a history professor these days would kill or maim a human being—and surely any of her colleagues—for original manuscripts never seen or touched by greedy hands. I promise that the documents will be ample payment for your patience and your diligence. They belong to the objective country you try to document so lovingly. This valise contains information that goes back to the creation of our constitution; it must be like discovering new letters from the signatories of the U.S. Constitution—if not a Washington or a Madison, perhaps from a young Charles Pinckney. Ms. Vakil, I have researched your background thoroughly. Your small publishing house in Tehran has put out quality work. Your precarious position at the university attests to your integrity. The papers will be yours in due course.

Do not be angry with me. I remember you in my mind's eye as not only lovely but also intelligent and resourceful. Use our story with caution. My only request is that you deal with the history of the Poonakis with the same energy you showed that day in pushing your way through the revolving doors of the Charles Hotel.

3. The Fat Storyteller Picks Up the Story Where He Left Off

"They have forgotten nothing, and learned nothing."

—Abbas Milani, *The Shah*

Thirteen years have gone by since the glorious Islamic Revolution. My grandfather, Karim, played his part: during the revolutionary years, he stopped reciting the legendary tales of the Shahnameh and instead regaled the tea-house clients with political news from newspapers: unlike them, he could read. Since those days, war has brought misery to everyone.

Only a few months ago I sat in our tearoom, Baba— *your* tearoom, passed on to me when you passed on— and wailed at my misfortunes. I cursed my luck, unaware that there are no limits to man's fall. Forty generations of storytellers precede me; I could name and number five of them as I sat in that decrepit tearoom. Yet I, Salman Hekaiatchi, direct descendant of the mighty Ferdowsi son of Hassan, grandson of Karim, the incomparable storyteller of the court of Qajar, had been reduced to serving tea in my own establishment. I, who spent his childhood dandled on the knees of the aristocracy, I am now ordered around by that despicable pirate Hamid, who calls himself my business partner. This self-righteous ass, of uncertain parentage, calls my tearoom a "sanctuary"—where "an honest man can obtain, without daily harassment, his narcotic."

Our tearoom, which now smells like urine, was built by the great Karim; the Golden Tea Room was famous for its mosque-like gold cupola. Now the gold has peeled away. The throne of the Grand Bazaar, once the sitting room of princes, cabinet members, and rich merchants, has now turned into a meeting place for dealers, murderers, Afghanis, Palestinians, addicts, and any other imaginable lowlife. As a child I ran around benches covered with Kerman carpets, where the most respectable people sat listening to your declamations. Waiters expertly swirled the charcoal pack in dangerously wide circles to make it glow. They delicately deposited each light-as-a-feather charcoal on the well-packed, precisely moist tobacco in each waterpipe. At the center of the room, an octagonal stone piscina tiled in lapis lazuli splashed clear water from a lazy fountain. The water overflowed into an elaborate, majolica-tiled, cobalt-blue gutter. You, my Baba, used the fountain as a rhetorical device—now an endless sea, now a back-crushing waterfall.

Today the piscina is a chipped pool of brackish water covering grimy, cracked tiles. Hamid and his band of jackals use the pool for their self-righteous ablutions before their prayers with Niyyat in the corridors of the tearoom. As they finish their prayers, they look over their left shoulders, not as a symbolic act—looking toward the angel recording their wrongful deeds—but to check how many customers are waiting.

How I'd love to dream of this abominable, nefarious, reptilian Hamid, whose like has never before crawled upon the surface of this earth. That dream would be for *your* benefit, my Baba, to show you what your generosity has produced: Hamid, the boy you bought from some peasant family to work for you, now rips to shreds the hand that fed him. How hurt I felt—for I knew. I knew, Baba, that you did not consider me worthy of our family's name. I knew that you did not think that I could carry on our family tradition. You wanted a good looking boy, and I did not fit.

But no matter how hard I concentrate, I end up dreaming only of indulgences: of little meat-filled pies, overripe figs, cream puffs so light they could levitate— and, yes, of women. Women parade through my dreams—clad, semi-clad, naked, all unmolested—yet any sign of my arousal sends you into a rage that can only be soothed by my sudden awakening.

If I could plan my dreams, I'd show you how Hamid has claimed to be your son, denouncing his own father as a cuckold and his mother as a tramp. Tell me it is not true, my darling Baba. Without compunction he admits to being a bastard. And a bastard he is. But *your* bastard, Baba? With this pronouncement he has claimed half my inheritance, half my tearoom. And who's to deny the claim of a Revolutionary Guard?

Hamid, along with half a dozen of his cronies, moved into his new headquarters the day after I received the revolutionary court order. To add insult to injury, he asked—no, ordered—me to demonstrate my storytelling skills. Keeping revolutionary dogma alive, I was ordered to replace every shah and prince in the tales with the heroes of the revolution. Replace Keyumars, the first Shah of the world, with the Imam; gift the albino Zal, the legendary Persiranian warrior, with the name of some white-haired Ayatollah.

Hamid would begin the show. "Now, my friends, we are in for a delicious treat, a story from my portly partner, the storyteller. Come over here, Salman, and let me show you off to our guests." Hamid would sweep one arm out in a grand gesture, while keeping his other hand on my shoulder.

I lowered my tray, the silver tea service clinking. I stepped toward Hamid, my eyes on the floor. "He tells stories as well as he eats, and you can see he is magnificent at eating." Hamid pinched the belly that sagged over my sash. The guests laughed, and one—a man called Abol, with broken black stumps for teeth—called out, "Portly, my ass, this boy is as wide as he is tall."

Another said, "I hope his words flow out as well as his food flowed in."

Laughter sounded all around, amid the tobacco smoke so thick it hid the ceiling. Hamid intervened. "Ah, friends, shame on you, making fun of our storyteller."

He paused with a comic's timing, then added, narrowing his eyes: "That job is entirely mine."

I swallowed and remained silent. Hamid's cat-like eyes showed that he was not yet done with me.

This was a schoolyard humor that I had thought was behind me. Hamid and his repulsive friends pinched and fingered me, making lewd weighing gestures near my chest to suggest large breasts, until my voice hit the high note of upcoming tears. At this, Hamid would affect a piratical jump from his throne into the middle of the room and, with mock seriousness, remind everyone in the tearoom of our steadfast partnership. How dare anyone berate a partner of his? He'd admonish every individual present in the room by name. From all corners, people would then direct at me mock apologies, punctuated with small snickers. The laughter became deafening.

These people, the pathogens of my society, found the tearoom a welcoming environment in which to coalesce and multiply. Drug dealers trafficked openly, even arraying their products on the tables and loudly underbidding one another. Once I might have enjoyed the sweet smell of opium wafting from the rooms behind the main hall—discreet, private rooms reserved for the wealthy men of the Bazaar. Who would deny a few men the chance to while away a few hours in relaxation, gossip, and complaint about their wives? Times have changed. Afghan gun traders were selling Kalashnikovs for the price of a few grams of hashish, right there, in your tearoom.

One week, on the day we received our supplies—when Hamid would certainly be at the tearoom—I entered my former office, three steps up in the corner of the main hall next to the entrance. My approach was to be an attitude of bonhomie, so as not to produce any ill will between partners. I explained to him the history of the establishment, told him about the people who used to frequent the place, and finally pointed out the illegal activities going on right under his nose. He lounged behind my mahogany desk, nodding in agreement. "I am shocked at what you are telling me," he said. "Let me get this straight. You are saying that my good friend Ismail deals in opium?"

I nodded my head vigorously. "Yes, yes! And Ahmad, right in front of me, sold three Uzis to the two Palestinians you brought with you the other day, and—"

"That's not possible. It can't be." His handsome face twisted in a disbelieving grimace. "We must immediately put an end to this business. What a fool I have been not to have seen this before. Let's go out there, you and I, like the two partners that we are, and clean this place out. What do you say?"

"Like the two partners that we are," I whispered. I would have followed him to the source of the river Euphrates. Hamid opened the door to the office and gestured for me to precede him down the stairs.

The geography of the tearoom had not changed a great deal. Men sat in a large circle around the room; the benches were now covered with rough carpets that you wouldn't use for saddling a donkey. The main change was the addition of Hamid's gaudy, gilded chair that he had acquired in one of his raids on wealthy homes. He never used the benches again. He liked the Western style—and the fact that everyone lounged around him.

From the office door, I could see the faces of half the clientele, and the backs of the other half. I stepped proudly out of the office, about to descend the steps— and Hamid's heavy army boot delivered to my backside the most painful kick of my life. I flew down the steps, crashed into two benches holding four customers, and ended up in the filthy green water of the fountain, breaking two of my teeth on its spout. The roar of laughter rose and fell like an ovation after a great performance. Hamid, still standing in the office, shut the door on his own laughter. Smarting from the humiliation, I was sitting in the four-inch puddle and feeling my lips and teeth when the door to the office opened again. Hamid's voice called my name in the most natural tone, as if nothing had happened. He ordered tea. On cue, the clientele began shouting at me to fetch them tea, as if the job had been invented for me.

From that moment my duties became apparent to everyone, myself included. I had been turned to a common servant. Baba, I know you wonder why I did not stand up to him or complain to the authorities. As I must remind you, we live in different times. Hamid has the local authorities in the palm of his hand. Better to be a living servant than a dead proprietor.

4. The Omniscient Narrator, Creator of the Fat Storyteller, Intrudes as Promised

> *"Houses have crumbled in my memory as soundlessly as they did in the mute films of yore."*
>
> — The Stories of Vladimir Nabokov

My brother and I were born on the tenth of January, 1954, seconds apart, mimicking Esau and Jacob. Jacob, you will remember, followed Esau out of the womb with his hand on Esau's heel. They were twins like us, non-identical: the Bible tells us that one was hairy and the other smooth, one was canny and the other simple. When we came out, one was weak and sickly and the other strong and healthy.

I entered this world the color of one large bruise, as I experienced my first choking—hardly an impressive debut. My father named me Dari. Behind me, my brother, Arya, took advantage of my labors to slip and slide out with ease, a trait he displayed all his life. His name—a conceit of my father—captured a lingering 1930s racial reading of our Aryan heritage.

There were physical horrors in store for me. You have by now noticed my love of movies: I imagine a metallic blue camera lens approaching our country house from the air, shooting from a helicopter. The windows of the house tinkle gently with the draft from the helicopter. A shot of the power generator suggests the real reason for the vibration, and at the same time indicates the rural surroundings. Neat touch. It's a one-story house. In the living room a weak bulb breathes in and out, an optic metronome, as the generator throbs. In the corner of the room, two babies lie wrapped in identical cribs, like open-faced mummies. The camera focuses on a tear in the mosquito netting over one of the cribs. The director underlines the importance of this tear with solemn, repetitive drumming. Something is wrong. We dolly in. A gray tail is seen resting easily on the side of the crib. A murmur of horror ripples through the audience. What is this movie called, *A Rat in the Crib?*

We cut to the bedroom, a sensual shot of the mother while she dreams. The audience knows it's a dream. The setting is surreal, with dull-colored geometric shapes filling the background. The mother's eyes are closed, one arm across her brow: the music speeds up, as the rat is seen at work. The mother continues to dream, while the rat gnaws at the baby's cheek, moving toward his right eye.

Now we see the night watchman approaching the room: Gorbun-Ali, a giant Turk from Azerbaijan with soft white skin and blue-black eyes. At 70, he hops along with the help of two old crook-handled canes. Can a one-legged man tiptoe? Let's say he can. The music chases itself higher and higher. The rat hears a sound and, as it lifts its ugly head to listen, the director zooms in on its bloodstained front teeth. Then the head of the guard's cane catches it in one hard, sweeping motion.

The scream of a dying rat is re-created in the studio, without much conviction, by speeding up a tape of human laughter. The watchman has saved the baby.

The other baby sleeps soundly. No stories to relate of twins' empathy.

This accident, my munched face, disfigured me for most of my childhood. It began near my upper lip and spiraled toward the outer part of my right eye. As I grew, the change of bone structure helped, though my face still shows a slight asymmetry. You have seen me, Ms. Vakil. I hope you agree that I don't cut too shabby a figure.

Though my birth certificate asserts that I am fifty-eight years old, I consider myself to have been born sixteen years after the biological event. I imagine that some god, probably Aeolus—a figure like one of those painted by Botticelli in the cornices of the Sistine Chapel, with cheeks impossibly puffed up—must have placed my mother's navel delicately in his mouth, like the knot of a birthday balloon, and slowly expanded the amniotic membrane outside her body to engulf us, even as she gave birth to her darling boys. This comes close to describing how my brother and I saw the outside world for those first sixteen years. Each year, another deep sigh from our guardian Greek god expanded the balloon around us until one of us—and only one of us—pricked it, and went to join the insipid society of other men.

No manmade law could have stopped the two of us from our single-minded pursuit of each other's destruction. Twins: either hairy or cunning. A biblical wink to the slow reader forewarns evil coming to the hairy fellow. Poor hairy fellows. It is what makes the Old Testament bigoted. In fact, our twinned intentions toward one another were symmetrical, our behavior toward the outside world mere tactics to gain advantage, until one of us should come out the winner. I won.

→ Dari ~ 56 yrs old

I do miss him. Forty-two years later, like a gymnast waxing nostalgic about her past performances, I reflect with longing on those sixteen years. I miss the purposefulness of our existence. Sometimes even today, I find myself plotting and planning, immersed in a way of life now meaningless. The intensity of our life was so savagely vibrant that, simply by closing my eyes, I can transport myself to the Poonak Valley, where we spent so much of our boyhood.

Our country home, with its flat modern architecture, sat posed on the western side of the Poonak Valley, like a green wart on the side of the dusty eponymous village. Our house looked east toward the city of Tehran. Even then, the city on the other side of the gulch sat beneath a permanent mass of menacing smog. I am told little remains of the gardens that stretched, interconnected, for miles northward as far as the village of Farahzad. Miles of poor, suburban travertine houses with inadequate water and sewage systems have replaced them. The village has in fact joined the Tehran suburbs. Today the house serves as the offices for the administration of Beheshteh Zahra, the city's graveyard.

Can these petty officials even imagine our lives in those days? My mother's open-air lunch parties, where the women, slathered in expensive suntan lotions, tanned themselves in their frilly sixties bikinis. The men sat in the shade of the oak trees, taunting each other over endless games of backgammon, the tumbling roll of dice on the wooden boards helping create crescendos of racket and hilarity. And all through the day you could hear the constant noise of ice, clinking in tumblers of gin and tonic. Tehran in those days offered an uncomplicated, comfortable urban life. There was one small store on Shahreza Avenue where my father bought French and English magazines. An overstuffed shop called Bonami on Ferdowsi Avenue provided all the un-Islamic charcuterie my mother's heart desired.

I am not sure I can be fair to my father's and mother's memories. How can a child be? He might experience a few rebukes and later recall his parents scolding him all through childhood; or he might dismiss a traumatic experience, so as not lay blame on a guilty parent. My strongest memories of my parents are from the sixties. My childhood distortions do not fit the description others give of my mother and father. I remember her only as a mature, older woman. We, like all the Poonakis, arrived to adorn the middle age of our parents; we were never children of young couples. I cannot associate my mother with her youthful pictures. The short-haired, chin-jutting rebel of a girl was by then transformed into an elegant *seizième* Parisian. More French than Persiranian, she carried her elegance with ease. In the fifties and sixties, we imitated everything foreign; an original foreigner carried much cachet, and my mother was the real thing. To our culture she conceded only her blonde hair, which she colored to a soft reddish brunette to lessen the stares in the streets. She saw herself as a Catholic, thanks to her mother's insistence and her father's active disregard for anything religious. To her, religion was less about God than about the culture surrounding it. She liked everything Catholic and disliked everything Islamic— again, not the religion but the culture. She spoke Farsi fluently, with a French accent that had the effect of the accordion used in movies to establish "Frenchness.' She developed a biting wit. Like many intelligent foreigners, as a guest of our country, she could see both the forest and the trees. Years before, in the sixties, she had predicted the revolution. Every time she saw the young Shah's helicopter fly over the city to his palace, she'd comment to the guests—all courtiers, for by then my father was a close confidante of the Shah—"How we all depend on the flawless service of a few mechanical parts."

She lived only half the year in Tehran, the other half in Paris. When she was in the house, we spoke French

1001

more often than not. I can put her squarely in your imagination, if you, like everyone in this world, have watched *The Sound of Music.* No, Ms. Vakil, I am not thinking of Julie Andrews, that peasant nun who steals the heart of Captain Georg von Trapp. When my brother and I saw the dubbed movie (including the songs) and first caught a glimpse of Baroness Elsa Schraeder, played by Eleanor Parker in her two-piece orange Chanel suit with the elegant polka-dot silk-shirt, we turned to each other in giggles and exclaimed "*Maman!*" My mother's wispy, circumflex eyebrows were, of course, more questioning; her pupils had a tincture of green, as did my father's eyes; her body was thinner, not quite as womanly as Elsa's; her laugh was almost manly—loud, with occasional unladylike snorts. But from that point on, the movie made no sense to us at all. Why would an aristo throw over a woman with so much grace and humor for a bandy-legged, manipulative, guitar-playing nun? A *noblesse oblige* fling, in some Austrian auberge or haystack, would have been understandable. There was nothing to dislike in the Baroness: even graceful in defeat (as my mother would certainly not have been), her glittering diamond earrings twinkle in sympathy with a not-quite-dropped tear. Something I never witnessed: my mother's tears.

My father, in his middle age, seemed to me a pathetic hanger-on at the imperial court of that youthful parvenu, Mohammad Reza Shah: only the second Shah of the Pahlavi dynasty, but the last of the Shahs, ending an empire of twenty-five hundred years. What a weight to take to his grave!

I have since softened my opinion of my father, a handsome and elegant man, popular with all who came into contact with him. He feared no one. Fearless, not brave: lacking fear as an innate characteristic. Early in his youth, he spent some time in the army. During his life, he worked for only a few years. He followed Montaigne's rule for living nobly: "You and your descendants must engage in no trade and pay no taxes for at least three generations." He gave his allegiance to a mediocre king who himself understood nothing of loyalty. I recognize now that my father was a Lancelot born a few centuries too late. His type wears the nonchalant pose of the heroic, not easily mimicked or packaged by our marketing gurus. Our century, our society doesn't require Lancelots. For the last century, the Persiranian government has been chock-full of the Talleyrand type: malleable, compromising, conspiratorial, unprincipled—that is, without ties to principles. In a perfect Darwinian world, as Lancelots and Talleyrands are born, the times will select those that fit the occasion. The overuse of Talleyrands, in our history, has left little room for the Lancelots. My father was ill-suited to the world of petty rivalries and brutal politics. He waited for the heroic time when *all* would be asked from him. The problem was that no one ever asked. He fit the Churchillian adage of being born to success but doomed to failure. Without any epic battles to fight, the drip, drip, drip of ordinary life destroyed him. I knew my father only during this last, dripping phase.

Ms. Vakil, I don't have to tell you how the smog and the urban sprawl have advanced, in their democratic fashion, to connect and cover all the towns and villages around old Tehran. *The Economist* cites Tehran as the smoggiest city in the world. Close to forty thousand people die there from pollution-related illness every year. But in those days, on a spring day, a half-hour traffic-free trip from the center of the city to Poonak meant you could see a clear starry sky at night, smell the harvest and the fresh dung of sheep and cows in daytime, hear the sound of the river below. In summer, the river left behind in its dry bed large boulders to serve as our make-believe castles and fortresses as we played with the boys from the village of Poonak. The primitive irrigation system, the source of all the peasants' brawls, watered all the hardy fruit trees in the valley: the Siah Mashad cherry trees with their pornographic red twin cherries, whose stems any boy worth his salt could tie in a knot with his tongue; the walnut trees, which blackened our hands for months after school started; and the red and white mulberry trees, which we and the village boys fiercely (and class-consciously) raced up, to shake the branches for the village girls beneath, who held blankets fireman-style to collect our treasure.

And always there stood, on the highest and thinnest branch, illuminated by the last rays of the sun, Hamid, the son of the *kadkhoda*, the village headman. He was more beautiful than handsome, still a mere boy, with his filthy bare feet and toes clenched like a parrot on a perch, his black eyes sparkling as they signaled his victory. Hamid, who became the friend of one twin and the lover of the other, would never side with either of us; but he paid the price of a guilty bystander.

The First Night
0001

The Fat Storyteller Discovers His Septuagenarian Scheherazade

[handwritten: 70-79 year old] *[handwritten: Queen Consort from 1001 nights]*

"You think," said the Other, "that a name should economize description rather than stimulate imagination?"

— H. H. Munro, *The Complete Short Stories of Saki*

Just a few months after the kick that sent me sprawling into servitude, Hamid—this so-called revolutionary guard, local committee man, son-of-a-jackal—decided, without my knowledge, to take full control of my tearoom. Why, you might ask? Apparently, other forces had taken an interest in the tearoom. The local Mullah Haj Rajab had begun asking awkward questions. Never lacking ingenuity where profit was concerned, the unscrupulous Hamid devised a plan to get rid of me altogether. *[handwritten: All ties to father]*

What had I done to deserve this misfortune, except to be an obedient son? Hadn't I learned by heart, with all my heart, thousands of lines of poetry? Hadn't I rubbed my Baba's feet when he came home exhausted?

It was the day before Norooz, the New Year. Hamid hadn't been around for a few weeks. The teahouse derelicts were in a good mood, and business was hopping. I had just emptied a basin full of brown dishwater into the gutter in the back alley and was about to return to the tearoom through the back door when I heard someone calling my name.

Coming towards me was a small figure clad in a black chador, one corner of which she held between an even set of teeth, to prevent the veil from slipping off her head.

"Mr. Hekaiatchi," she said between closed teeth, in a low, timorous voice. "I am your cousin. Your brother sent his regards and asked if there was any work you could give me in the tearoom."

41

"My brother?" I asked.

"Hamid Hekaiatchi," she said, sure of the effect.

I had forgotten that Hamid had used my last name since he had established you, Baba, as his father.

"I will work for modest wages."

"You will have to," I said, trying to be authoritative. "How old are you?"

"Seventeen." And with that, the chador slipped off her head with a faint electric crackle like silk on silk, revealing a face like the moon, two charcoal eyes aglow in a perfect round face, and the beginnings of a portentous swell on her chest. The chador was back on in an instant.

"You may begin early tomorrow morning. You'll work in the kitchen."

"Thank you," she said. "Hamid said to tell you that he'd be grateful to you in the future."

When I look back, what a lark it all must have seemed. What a joke! "Grateful to you in the future," she had said. What a consummate actress. There was indeed plenty of work in the kitchen, but little of it was done by her. In a matter of days, her chador became only a frame through which she exhibited different parts of her body—a womanly thigh, a girlish calf, a milky chest, all shown as if accidentally to provoke my desire.

She had no shame about bringing her charms to my attention. I might reach for a rag that had fallen on the floor, and Fatmeh's ankle would be there for me to see.

"Do you always stare at girls so insolently, Mr. Hekaiatchi?"

"I beg your pardon." My face burned.

She laughed without mirth. "Put your eyeballs back in your head."

I held up the towel as evidence of my innocence. "I meant no offense."

"Your eyes find me a hundred times a day. I can feel it, even when my back is turned." She raised the chador several more inches to scratch her calf, complaining of non-existent mosquitoes.

"It will not happen again." How did her beauty affect me so?

"Not for at least ten minutes, is my estimate." She turned away with her impudent laugh.

I admit that her looks and, yes, even her connection with that rascal had me fooled. In my own defense, it was glands, biology, and nature that were the real culprits. For no matter what state I am in, or what foul circumstance has darkened my mood, the sight of an attractive girl makes me feel half my weight. What is the origin of this uncontrollable desire? Simply, remarkably, embarrassingly, twenty-nine years of virginity. I, Salman Hekaiatchi, after twenty-nine years of travel, education, and refined upbringing, have yet to experience the folds of a woman. An oversight, it might be said, that could be easily fixed by a quick visit to one of the whorehouses in the now defunct New-City, the old red light district of Tehran. Not quite. Virginity is only a symptom. → Eluding to what? Specifically.

I was in one of those bouncy, half-my-weight moods when I walked into the kitchen. Fatmeh, the girl, was squatting on the floor in the kitchen near the outside door in the traditional position of all washerwomen, her skirts pulled all the way up to her thighs as she washed my clothing in a large basin. I watched her for a while from inside the doorway. Magnificent femininity: this was no ordinary washerwoman. She panted from the exertion of scrubbing; strands of hair coiled over her flushed face; her naked feet, pointing outward, pinky-red from the water, were planted wide apart, showing the curves of her thighs. As she scrubbed, her arms stretching up and down the serrated washing board, I couldn't help but notice the oscillating rhythm of her ample backside and think of performing an unmanly act of love that I could only complete by rolling myself underneath her like an eager car mechanic. Conscious of my stare, she looked aside as she rubbed the sweat off her face with the back of her hand and caught my desire transparently reflected on my face.

"*Azizeh-del*, darling, if you want to get between my legs, just say so," she said in a hard, crass tone, without a trace of her accustomed shyness. Then, to my absolute astonishment, she coolly pushed the tub to one side and used her palms to slide her body backward nearer the wall; she lay back, her head awkwardly against the wall. With a lithe wriggle, she pulled the folds of her skirt all the way up to her hips. Her bare thighs made a milky heart against the brown stone floor, and then she bent her knees in the air and opened her legs: there, in a yawn, her matted, ageless vagina waited patiently to swallow me in one slippery gulp. She put her finger to her nose, hushing me, and with the other hand, like a traffic attendant, motioned me forward. "Come on, then, get your fill, and hurry before someone comes in."

"My God . . . my Lord," were the only words I could repeat over and over. Flabbergasted and hypnotized by this pilose cyclops, I fumbled, approached, and fumbled some more. The heavens had opened, and they beckoned me inside. Never giving a thought to the customers waiting for their tea, I fell with all my weight in front of her on one knee and then laboriously lowered the other. I reached furiously into my pants to produce the perfect piece to that heavenly jigsaw. It had hardly been exposed to the open air when, like a cheap water pistol, it emitted four squirts, all over her legs and clothing. Just as in my few visits to New-City, my premature overexcitement at the sight of a woman's nakedness prevented me from finding asylum within her body. My knees slowly separated, and there I remained, while this whore-child produced from deep in her throat a woman's mocking laugh.

"That was easy," she remarked. Getting up with a bounce, crying now and screaming for justice, she ran into the tearoom. In the buttoning of a fly, the kitchen was filled with people accusing, cursing, screaming, slapping, and pinching. I have never been able to understand the reason behind pinching as a show of force, but ever since I reached my present size, people have pinched me in times of violence. Grown men grab my flesh and twist it, as if to satisfy themselves of my reality.

An ugly crowd for ugly times. Energized by my high-pitched squeals, it was giving me a good beating. I crawled halfway under the table to protect my head. For once my body mass was of some use, as shield to my internal organs. A couple of men pulled uselessly at my legs. As the kicks and punches increased in number, I found myself, to my surprise, looking forward to my own demise. In a systematic beating there comes a moment of lucidity just before unconsciousness. I was reaching that stage—and suddenly, I burst into laughter.

Taking their sudden silence as my cue, I let out another, lengthier explosion of high-pitched laughter. At this outburst, the beating stopped. More people began pulling at my legs to drag me out from under the table. Somehow it had dawned on all of them that they were in the presence of a madman. I continued to laugh assiduously, leaving little doubt about my state of mind. I assure you it was no easy act, as four or five men pulled me up. They escorted me to the basement with a few salutary kicks and slaps to the back of my head. They threw me into the dark cellar where I landed on a mountain of coal. Someone shouted upstairs to call the neighborhood committee. Now I sat in the dark. I could see only the door, framed by a thin, fading rectangle of daylight, interrupted by its hinges. Hours went by. The tearoom emptied. I could no longer hear the muffled din of customers above. Finally I heard the key turn in the lock. The authorities—three of my "partner's" cronies—looked inside with some trepidation. Each invited the others to go in and fetch me. I immediately increased my cachinnations.

(I can smile now, as I sit in my cozy room above Mammad-Ali's store, remembering the three boys, barely eighteen, looking into a dark, dirty coal room and trying to discern a *man* in the incoherent mass sitting on a pile of coal. My high-pitched laughter reverberates in the empty basement.)

The three discussed their orders. They pulled straws. They dared each other. They argued— but Imam Ali himself couldn't drag these boys into the coal room to come after me. I wasn't in a mood to cooperate until I heard them discussing their options.

"Why don't we shoot him right where he is?"

"Agha Hamid told us to take him outside the city."

"I say we shoot him right now and drag him out to the car and dump him later."

It was time for me to reduce their options, and live to fight another day. Covered in soot, arms stretched out as if to hug the world, I exited the room, letting out an operatic laugh. The boys pulled the safeties of their Kalashnikovs, ready to slay a fairy-tale monster, the repulsive mother of the ogre Foolad Zereh. Ignoring their threat, I moved toward the stairs. The three of them—their guns pointing entirely out of fear, as in a scene from a Hollywood movie— followed me upstairs.

It was late at night; the stores of the great Tehran Grand Bazaar had rolled down their corrugated steel shutters. Only a few Afghani sweepers still worked with a concentrated diligence. The three guards shoved me into the back of an old, off-white Rambler with slippery, plastic-covered seats. All three sat in the front seat. We drove west, out of the city. I recall passing the unfinished urban apartments of the old Shah's regime, God bless his soul. We drove past the airport and headed toward the town of Karaj on the old road known as Jadeyeh Ghadim-eh Karaj. The purple shadows of the mountains on our right moved passed us like an unending convoy train. The driver turned left onto a small dirt road; the mountains cleaved away and disappeared in a wheel-spun storm of dust. In front lay a flat terrain lit by the hard light of the moon. In the middle of nowhere, there appeared under the headlights broken brick walls adorned with faded, salmon-colored advertisements for lipsticks and pressure cookers. I continued my laughing until the driver took a sharp right onto an even smaller dirt road.

Now I began crying and laughing alternately as I realized how close I was to being granted an audience with my maker. I am embarrassed to say that both my bladder and my sphincter lost control and did their part, leaking urine and fecal matter in small panicky spurts, no matter how hard I tried to contract my anal muscles. The boys in front began sniffing the air with the confused look of tracker dogs, silently questioning each other's body control. As the smell filled the small space in the car, it dawned on them that this was not the result of a small indiscretion, one where everyone accuses everyone else of being responsible. Finally they looked at me. I was prepared, with my most dazzling smile plastered over my face.

They pulled to the side of the road and, praise be to the Lord, started to discuss the situation. The gist of their talk was religious: should they kill an insane man? Thank God, superstition doesn't spare the criminal mind.

After some time they headed back toward the city. An hour later, all of us close to suffocation, we arrived somewhere in town, a few blocks (I realized) from the British Embassy. We stopped in front of a pair of wrought-iron gates guarding a large house surrounded by a spacious garden. The driver prodded at the horn a few times. An old, sleepy man—no doubt the gardener or the doorman—opened the gate with difficulty. We drove along a path around the house and parked under an awning over what was once a magnificent door, into which some ignoramus had cut a rough opening to install a smaller, metal door. The driver renewed his short bursts of honking. The door opened and two men in white walked out. A third man appeared close behind them, still putting on his white shirt.

The driver jumped out and kissed the half-dressed man on both cheeks. They whispered; we could hear their soft laughter. I was out of steam; fortunately, the two guards sitting in the car were satisfied with my imbecilic smile and closed eyes. The driver came back and, not wanting to come closer than was required, prodded me out of the car with his Kalashnikov. He pushed me over to the first two orderlies in white, who quickly stepped back, shocked at my appearance. The driver, glad to be rid of me, simply jumped into the car, grabbed his nose with his thumb and forefinger, shook his head in mock horror, waved a nonchalant adieu to his friend, and drove the car out of my life, as the sun shone wan and silvery against a pearly sky. Maybe I should be more thankful to these guardians of the revolution for sparing my life, against the orders of that murderer, Hamid. From where I sit today, safe, roofed, and being taken care of by the more than ample Zahra, I treasure those tiny moments. As I stood covered in black soot, caked shit, and a mixture of piss and sperm, the brave, bearded children of the revolution, for the second time that night, dared not approach me.

Outside the unknown house, the orderlies cleaned me off with a garden hose. Complaining all the while that I had delayed their morning prayers, they escorted my wet, shivering, and tired carcass inside. I read on the plaque affixed to the small metal door that I was the guest of the Martyrs Foundation for Mental Health. We walked through several corridors, passing clean, well-lit rooms on either side. The rooms had been repurposed to "take care" of traumatized war casualties, men who sat on their beds looking outwards with their hollow, brutalized gaze.

I squelched my way down the corridor in my wet shoes, and we arrived at a desk next to a door. The orderly picked up a set of large keys on a heavy ring and opened the door, which led to a staircase heading down. Below, we entered a tenebrous corridor with cells on each side. One bare sixty-watt bulb hung from the ceiling. We stopped at the fourth cell door on the left. One of the orderlies began unlocking the complicated door, twisting the rough iron keys in the two huge, rusted padlocks, making sure that the clanking sound of the horizontal bar and of the padlocks against the door echoed loudly through the long, high-ceilinged corridor. Finally he pushed open the heavy door. Instinctively I leaned back against the other two orderlies. They saw this sign of my resistance and instantly, in unison, swung me inside like a sack of rice. The door closed with a bang. The padlocks clicked shut.

In the dark, my head cocked, my ears pricked, I waited like an animal. I could hear the rhythmic breathing of another being. I was convinced that I had been put into this cage with some crazy beast, and that the guards from a vantage point outside were watching and betting on how long I would survive the ordeal. When nothing happened, reason slowly returned: I was probably sharing a cell with some poor creature in the same situation as myself. People were brought to this asylum to be taught a lesson. In all probability, they would release me in the morning and tell me that in the future I should watch my step.

I began to recover my mental balance. As my eyes grew accustomed to the dark, I discerned high on the opposite wall a small, rectangular window framing a milky dawn. I could feel the floor, covered with straw. I quietly moved away from the metronomic breathing to sit in the opposite corner, under the window. After a while, as my courage returned, a paralyzing fatigue set in. I stretched out flat on a thin mattress that felt to me as comfortable as the fluffiest down-filled bedding. I fell into a deep sleep.

My thoughts were not unhappy ones. It had been the most eventful day of my life. A jailbait daughter of Eve had almost had me within her, a mob had nearly torn me apart for rape, three young Muslims had debated shooting me in the middle of nowhere, and now, labeled a lunatic, I was sleeping in a cage with some wretched animal. Here was much to tell, and brag about, for the benefit of future listeners in a tearoom owned fully by me.

The Narrator Ends Up at the Same Place as His Fat Storyteller Only Ten Years Earlier

"The enormous condescension of posterity"

— E. P. Thompson

Today I live in a world devoid of all the pleasures granted me by birth. In my latest career, I write technical software manuals for a Boston tech firm. Perched on a hill in Waltham, I watch as if through a martini glass the endless traffic on Route 128, blinking red taillights snaking like dragons in a Chinese carnival. I spend hours with engineers, writing the safety and legal warnings that no one reads, essential to soothe management sensibilities and support the legal community's way of life. I respect the corporate world, as the true successor to the feudal system of which I was once a beneficiary. The trivial difference: the powerful today rely on legal means to pass their wealth down the generations, rather than on our well-worn *blue genes*.

I labor away in a comfortable-enough cubicle, a cocoon assembled by my employer to show his care for my well-being. I say this without a trace of irony. The fuzzy walls of the cubicle, a mixture of nylon and high-content wool, harbor a corrugated cardboard septum that traps all sound like a Cadillac muffler. All objects are arranged ergonomically. The monitor, on an articulated arm, pours its light through four layers of molecularly bonded optical coating, protecting my eyes from the emission glare. A padded and contoured wrist support next to the keyboard disperses weight to soothe my carpal tunnel and my trapezius muscles. The floor mat has a decal promising that the variable terrain will cause my feet to angle, thus stimulating a network of veins circulating blood up through my legs to my heart.

A few simple, useless objects, like the fat Montblanc fountain pen on my desk—the same one that my forgetful father always left uncapped, lying on an open page in his *petit salon*—function for me like little time machines. Like that well-known cut, where the murderous prehistoric bone morphs into a Pan American spacecraft. The mere existence of this pen effortlessly transforms my Waltham office into our city mansion in its walled garden, during the last few days of the not-so-*ancien régime*. I had lived five happy years: my brother's shadow no longer weighed on me. The petrodollar flowed freely; the country, through an orgy of construction and industrial growth, had improved more quickly than at any other time in the last two millennia. There were no obvious reasons to look for a mass uprising.

But a year earlier, a year before the grand theft of the country I so loved, I had witnessed directly in front of me a lowly mullah slap a blameless policeman who stood guard in front of the Carpet Museum uptown. He accused him of keeping the museum open on a Friday, the Muslim Sabbath. Nothing about that scene made sense to me. I grabbed the mullah's hand to prevent another slap. The short mullah turned to me, his eyes mean: "Agha will take care of *all of you* when he comes back." I interpreted Agha to mean the hidden Imam. I laughed, and behind his back I rotated my index finger a few times, pointing to my head, to indicate to the policeman that we were dealing with a cracked buffoon. Who is the cracked buffoon now, Ms. Vakil?

February 1, 1979. This date stays with me. The swimming pool stands half-full; a cool wind pushes the large planks, used as de-icers, sending them thudding quietly into one another. In the greenish water beneath, necklaces of frog spawn gently undulate. Daily, the crowd outside my garden walls marches down Ferdowsi Avenue. It senses our total capitulation. Hypnotically the marchers chant the name of an old man that few of us had heard of just a few months back. I hear on the radio that an Air France flight has touched down in

Mehrabad Airport, bringing to our city the "light of our lives." He is to deliver to us *la dolce vita*, not in paradise but right here on Earth. He plans to go directly to Behesht-e Zahra—the city cemetery.

I dressed in appropriate garb to pass as one of the *peuple*. Not a necessary precaution. Plenty of well-to-do fools sauntered on the street in a strangely festive mood, hand-in-hand with all classes of people, like the Jews in 1478, welcoming the Tribunal of the Holy Office of the Inquisition. I took a taxi to the cemetery, through the crowd that gradually impinged on the traffic. At the railway station, I walked toward Yadavaran Road. The crowd thickened dangerously, mostly shantytown dwellers, with very few villagers and peasants. Some patronizing fool of a Western writer would later write that they displayed "an incomparably more profound" straightforwardness. I saw only knife-wielding, depraved gutter fighters, strutting amid the truly, deeply, no-light-in-the-eyes ignorant. The crowd walked and propelled me forward. Waves of chanting recalled a soccer match, though I could not make out the words. I slipped into a small grocery shop to buy a coke from the diminutive, bearded, cross-eyed man behind the counter. As I stood drinking it, watching the crowd pass by the door, a small trap door in the ceiling of the shop opened and two little boys' heads shouted down to their father, "Agha Joun, Agha Joun, the Imam is coming!" The man walked toward the ladder and then hesitated when he saw me standing at the front of the store. I offered him ten toman if I could join him on the roof. With a flick of his arm, he slid closed the corrugated tin shopfront, plunging us into instant darkness. In the square hatch of light, the shopkeeper was now hurrying up the ladder. I climbed behind him to the second floor, emerging among neat sacks of guni. Stepping out through a window at the far end, he pulled himself up onto the roof, with me close behind him.

It took me no time to get accustomed to the winter light. Around us, there were not many buildings but brick pits and shanty towns on the dry, flat, desert-like terrain. We were not alone on the roof. People stood on other roofs or hung precariously on the electric poles or sat on tiny ledges in the broken walls. Beneath me I saw something that defied belief: humanity as an organism, a collective devoid of individuality; a mindlessness that western witnesses would describe, again and again, as an "organic plebiscite." Far up and down the street flowed this liquid, a river of heads. The chanting undulated high above the crowd. Far to my right I saw a convoy of eight vehicles slowly parting the crowd on Yadavaran Street. A blue-and-white Chevrolet Blazer approached with two young men perched on its roof, the cynosure of the surrounding creature with the million eyes. Hundreds of motorcycles and their toxic blue exhaust plumes threaded playfully around the convoy, and the horns of unmoving cars built a solid wall of noise around it all.

And then, chopping through the bedlam, came the sound of a helicopter rotor. We all looked up to see a UH-1 Huey approach to land on a promontory off the road. Five hundred yards out from the helicopter, and just a hundred yards from us, the Blazer stalled and stopped dead. Next to the driver sat a figure unmistakable with his signature beard. I could see clearly his son as well, in the back seat, leaning forward with the face of a man in a silent movie: a caricature of witless terror. As the crowd pressed in on the car, Khomeini attempted to open the car door in a kind of panic. The driver rose to the occasion, on his greatest career drive. (He would later be one of the founders of the Revolutionary Guards and, as head of the Mostazafan Foundation, inheritor of millions of dollars of public money.) Now, he simply prevented the "Imam" from opening the door and from certain death. He had no control of the car but kept pointing to the helicopter.

The crowd understood and attempted to push the car, but the steering gear must have failed and the car veered to the right. I heard the repeated cry of "Ya Ali," an invocation for help from the Prophet's successor (his son-in-law and cousin), the standard Shi'a invocation before any physical effort. And now the car indeed inched forward—off the ground. The crowd had *picked up* the two-ton car and were carrying it toward the helicopter, by now sitting on the ground. The theatrics, I knew, would only enhance the dawning legend of the upcoming Islamic Republic. All, all was lost.

On the twelfth of February, a meeting of three four-star generals, eighteen generals, four division commanders, and two admirals ended with an announcement of the armed forces' neutrality in the conflict. After thirty-six days in office as the last Prime Minister of the Persiranian monarchy, the courageous and rational Shahpour Bakhtiar disappeared from view, whereabouts unknown. (He would be beheaded, no less, in a suburban Paris apartment, a few years later.) Khomeini installed Mehdi Bazargan as Prime Minister: "Through the guardianship I have from the Holy Lawgiver, I hereby pronounce Bazargan as the ruler, and since I have appointed him, he must be obeyed. It is a government based on Sharia." Then, a few lines later, comes this elegant refinement of the divine right of kings: "Revolt against God's government is a revolt against God. Revolt against God is *blasphemy*." Let me ask you, Ms. Vakil, what part of these perfectly logical sentences did the intellectuals running gaily about the street not understand? Not one of them thought to object to this hijack of a promised democracy. Our 1906 revolution was peopled by individuals; what I witnessed that day was a brain-laundered crowd, incapable of judgment, welcoming the second coming.

Watching, we all knew it was just a matter of time before they came for us.

On April 1, a bright and soft spring day, by popular vote, the new theocracy replaced 2,500 years of monarchy.

Soon enough, I hear it arrive at my doorstep. I hear the bus roar up the street toward my gate. Wheels screeching, it pushes on through: the gates spring open, bounce against the walls, and slap the sides of the bus as it roars into the courtyard and lurches to a stop. A mocha-colored Mercedes with tinted windows. I step behind a geranium plant.

With a hiss the door opens. Three boys jump out, armed with Uzis—made in Israel, though they miss the irony. (Only culture breeds irony; these boys will need a few more generations.) Wearing fashionable rather than religious week-old beards, they stand dramatically, eyes narrowed, alert to danger lurking behind any tree. And then—appearing in the door of the bus is my childhood friend, Hamid. I have not seen him since my brother's death, four years earlier. He wears brown brogans, Western blue jeans, and a red cotton shirt with the tails hanging out, except where a revolver is tucked into his trousers.

His face has lost its delicate beauty, replaced by a more geometric bone structure. His eyes still retain their almond shape. He holds a sheaf of documents, mouth turned sharply down, eyes flaming with purpose. He points the documents at me like a weapon. "By Ayatollah Khomeini's decree this house and all its contents are henceforth the property of the Islamic Republic of Persiran to use as fit for the good of the people of this neighborhood. Also by the same decree, the owner, one Mr. Poonaki, is under arrest, accused by a number of witnesses of practices unbecoming of Islam." He shows no acknowledgement of our friendship. It's all business.

I leave the protection of the geranium plant. One of the boys immediately moves in on its blue Lalejin ceramic pot and viciously jabs at it with his gun, so it shatters. "Stop that immediately," Hamid shouts at the boy, who swallows a self-satisfied smile.

A crow flaps its wings to rise lazily from a tree in a corner of the garden and hover back on the branch. Behind the bus, a tobacco-brown dog runs past the gate. I learned later that Hamid, a mongrel himself, had joined the Revolutionary Guard just moments after he learned that the Shah had fled the country. "You will sign the consent order forthwith."

I read the decree. The Ayatollah—who could scarcely have known of my existence—has signed in his own hand the warrant for my arrest and the seizure of my home.

I hold out a placating hand, seeking reason. "Hamid, this is surely a mistake. My family has lived in this house for three generations."

I see him bite down; red crescents appear at the corner of his mouth.

"How come he knows your name?" one of the boys asks.

"You have taken tea with my mother and father," I whisper, with greater care. "Surely—"

Before I can say another word, Hamid's gun swipes across my left cheek. I land on the gravel; Hamid pulls me back up. I try to straighten my spine, the pain makes me stagger. He smells of lye soap.

Hamid shoves a pen under my nose. "Sign it."

All will be made clear, to me and to you, Ms. Vakil. In the end, I signed over all my wealth—houses, land, bank accounts, and cars. The signing is an Islamic nicety for Muslims involved in grand theft. All my property, and that of many other prominent families, was already forfeit, by an act of the parliament that week. Nevertheless, our jailers paid strict attention to moving the loot from the *haram* to the *halal* column on God's balance sheet. The owner's acquiescence is achieved in time. Mine came after nine days—and let's not forget the nine nights.

Hamid, an insider, a respected revolutionary guard, arranged my release. He drove me to the airport the same day I signed the documents and handed me a passport with all the required stamps. I had chosen Boston as my final destination, because my family had an apartment and a modest bank account there. In the course of a few days, I would wear the label of *immigrant.* Imagine a tightrope walker who performs tricks a few hundred feet in the air. He hears the drum rolls. He looks down. To his surprise, the circus staff has removed the net. This is my definition of "immigrant."

Recounting my sixteen years of gestation requires no madeleine to conjure memory. Our efficient psychic laundress irons our memories smooth, or else we would all suffer the fate of Borges's character, Funes the Memorious. In my case, the laundress could do nothing about the rips and tears in the fabric of our being. So it is settled. This tale will be about rips and tears. I will not tell my story to a jury of readers, only to reveal myself at the end sitting in a maximum-security prison cell, waiting to receive a lethal injection. The statute of limitations has long since passed. Nine candlelit nights, spent imprisoned in the basement of my own house, served to remove all particles of privilege from my life, as effectively as a fine-meshed sieve.

"It's a true story," an elderly lady warbles to her husband as they leave the cinema. I make no such claim. The idea for the structure of this story came from my cubicle mate, a Russian programmer named Alex. (We work in teams of two: programmer and writer.) He noticed on my desk a copy of *The Book of the Thousand and One Nights* (in the admirable French translation of Dr. J. C. Mardrus).

"That book," said Alex, "has the coolest *operating system.*"

"How so?"

"Look how many stories you can plug in, nested and all. So simple. Scheherazade is the kernel, letting the hardware and software communicate. Clearly, the stone-hearted king is the hardware."

So it is that I have used the oldest storytelling structure in existence. I still need 1001 nights to spin my yarn—but expressed as a binary number. The truth will surely shake our genetic branches more viciously than we ever shook the mulberry trees in Poonak, though presented in layers of gauzy fiction. Let its fruits fall where they may.

The Second Night
0010

The Fat Storyteller Wakes to Discover the Professor

"Omne ignotum pro magnifico: everything unknown passes for miraculous."

— Sir Arthur Conan Doyle,
The Adventures of Sherlock Holmes

The next morning I awoke to ululations. Disoriented and unsure of my location, I sat up to see an old man standing in the center of the cell. The morning sun filtered through the small window, creating a corridor of silver dust motes while illuminating this decrepit, hoary man. His bald dome was decorated with a semicircle of long, white hair that hung down to his shoulders. A dirty loincloth partly concealed his delicate frame and heavily wrinkled skin. His back, when he turned, showed two nasty, festering wounds. His face seemed to converge on the lower mandible, as if gravity had made the bone and muscle flow to their lowest equilibrium. Except for the light blue eyes and milky skin, I might have taken him for a mad fakir from Hindustan. More astounding were his actions: every few seconds, he threw his head back and began growling like a dog. The growl was followed by a howl. He paid no attention to my presence, and I did my best not to intrude. Some howls later, an orderly opened the small porthole in the door and looked inside.

The old man stopped screaming and turned his head. Then, with no warning, he shouted at me:

"What am I?"

"What was that, sir?" I asked

"What. Am. I?" he articulated.

"I . . . I don't know," I stammered, not knowing what to expect. He removed his loincloth and ceremoniously revealed a small penis resting on ridiculously large testicles, putting me in mind of a turn-of-the-century bicycle.

"And now, can you not see what I am?" he asked, as if the removal of the loincloth could reveal what was inside his mind.

"No, sir." I tried to avoid antagonizing him any further. Clanking noises announced that the orderly had decided to come in.

"You fool," he scowled. "I am an *oil well*, don't you see?"

An endless unlocking procedure was followed by the clanking of the cumbersome horizontal bar. I resisted the temptation to scream for help.

"Of course I do," I responded.

"Shut up, you fat oaf, and watch." He began urinating in my direction. The flow would have drenched me even more from the bladder of a younger man. Finishing, he turned one-hundred-eighty degrees and, to my horror, I could see his defecation oozing from between flaccid buttocks. The door opened at last to admit a large, hairy orderly. The old man, now in a frenzy of waste production, set his arms akimbo, threw his head back as if in victory on the battlefield, and started to spew a thick lava of vomit.

The muscular orderly waited patiently, his hairy arms crossed across his white overalls, and gave occasional short encouragements. "That's right, Professor, get it all out, bring the price of oil down. Yes, that's good, old man, a little more now." When it was over, the orderly approached the exhausted man from behind, picked him up in a bear hug, and, as if lifting a child, carried him screaming out of the room. Left behind in the cell was yours truly, praying to the Almighty for kindness and pity. The irony of my own performance the night before was not lost on me—but this old man operated at a different level. That he could shit and vomit at will to convince his captors of his insanity gave some hope that he was in fact sane.

This first unnerving meeting with the man I came to know as Professor Dal—the witness, as his name implied—did little to prepare me for the second. That afternoon, the same meaty orderly, accompanied by a much smaller, weasel-like colleague, brought back the old man, drugged and asleep. They threw him on the mattress like a sack of rice. They also brought along a mop and a bucket of water mixed with some noxious disinfectant.

I started negotiating for my release. By this time I had dropped all pretense of insanity. I begged to be released and not to be left alone with this maniac in his drugged stupor. I explained that I belonged to the *Bazaary* class and posed no threat to the Islamic Republic. No amount of tears or supplication worked. To humiliate me further, as I knelt prostrate before the meaty orderly, the weasel sneaked up behind me and gave me my second-ever kick in the ass and sent me sprawling, face-first, into my cellmate's dirt. They ordered me to clean it up; they expected the cell to be cleaner than my mother's bedroom. "And I know about your mother's bedroom, because I have been there," said the hairy orderly, holding up his left arm as if checking his watch and pumping his fist back and forth, in a crude representation of what he would do to my dear departed mother. They left in uproarious hilarity.

I cleaned the mess, and here the straw came in handy. Thoroughly dejected, I began to think about supper. Somehow, throughout my life, no matter what the crisis, my appetite has never diminished. I could easily, at one sitting, consume two chickens, a panful of rice, and a half-dozen eggs and wash it all down with a jug of *doogh*—that lovely, creamy mixture of peppered yogurt and water.

I lay there impatiently and waited for food. I tried mentally rehearsing the sins I had committed in my life and found that none deserved this severe a punishment. Finally our jailer brought the food—the same grotesquely hairy man: his beard line reached above the cheekbone and formed a right angle where the nose met the eye socket. I wondered if the man ever slept. When I saw the size of my portion, I couldn't hide my disappointment. The orderly flashed a set of cavernous gums.

"What's the matter, you don't like our food? The doctor suggests a strict diet for you. We are concerned about your body as well as your mind."

"No doctor has come to see me. Can I see a doctor?"

"I am your doctor. I am advising you that you need to lose that disgusting flesh you have hanging from you."

It had become apparent that my release would not be negotiated with this animal. I wanted to encourage a visit from a real doctor. I wisely held my peace until the orderly left, then gulped the broth ravenously. I chewed the stale bread, after wetting it in the bowl of water. In the blink of an eye, I made the whole disgusting mess disappear. Only then did I realize that, in my haste, I had eaten the old man's share as well. For the next two hours, I lay petrified on my bed, holding my eyes almost shut so as not to appear awake, and praying he would remain dead to the world until the next morning, when I could offer to share my breakfast with him.

In this agitated state of mind I fell asleep. In my sleep I dreamed that the hand of God descended from the sky. He laid his flat palm over my entire back, each digit the size of the butane tank we used for my stove in the tearoom. It blessed and caressed me. It applied gentle pressure on my back, at first like my dear mother's massages when she woke me to get ready for school. Then the pressure increased. One of the fingers curled around my body and covered my ribs on the left side. I dreamed a series of painful pokes, as if the Almighty were mightily displeased with his servant. I swam toward consciousness through several layers of sleep, coming up to the surface for air. At first I thought it was a visit by Bakhtak, the ogre who often visits me after a large meal. I uttered my special short prayer for the occasion and tried to go back to sleep.

My prayer did little to make the pressure go away. Besides, I recalled that I had hardly eaten a morsel of food. I became mindful that Bakhtak must have thinned out considerably; he had become much bonier.

"Baba, is that you?" I didn't feel a tickle in my ear either. Spiraling through degrees of wakefulness, I felt the unmistakable poke of a metallic object in my side. It was a forceful poke. It hurt.

"Quiet down or I'll stab you this instant." It was the old man. The voice and intonation had changed. The intention was criminal, but the voice was that of an educated man, the tone ruthless. He had climbed on top of me in my sleep and was about to murder me for broth and stale bread.

"Sir," I pleaded. "It was an honest mistake. You may have my share of the food tomorrow. Please spare me."

"I said, quiet down," he insisted. "The food is unimportant. You and I have much to talk about. To be exact, I have much to say and you have much to hear." The voice, calm and measured, should have been reassuring, but fear continued to paralyze me. Not for one moment did I consider trying to remove the old man from my back—though a shudder of my body would have thrown him halfway across the cell. The pitiless voice kept me as still as my trembling body allowed. Whoever this man was, there was no hesitation in the voice. He would have pushed his knife into me without hesitation. That object was continuously applying pressure on one of my higher ribs, close to the heart.

"Who are you, and what are you doing here?" I pleaded.

"All in good time, but can I trust you to remain still and listen to me?"

"Yes, but please get off my back."

Then a startling transformation took place. The voice changed in timbre and tone. Now a wise old man, he spoke to me kindly. Gone was the underlying threat. "No, dear boy, I can't do that. We need to form one silhouette. The guards often check through the peephole. I have made a straw man of myself." He smiled at some inside joke. "I must be in contact with your body so that I can tell how much time we have left. And since you can't sleep on top of me, I must sleep on top of you." With this, he removed the pressure of the knife, which turned out to be a spoon-handle. He made himself comfortable on top of me, lying supine on my back to stare at the ceiling and crossing one leg over the other knee.

What did this madman want from me? What was it that we were to do together? For an instant I feared some sexual intent, but quickly dismissed the thought. He spoke evenly.

"Look here, boy, do you know who I am?"

"An oil well?" I asked apprehensively, fearing a repeat of the previous morning's spectacle.

He snickered into his hand like a girl. "My name is Professor Dal, the letter Dal, Dee, the initial for my first name, but most people call me *Arbab*, boss, because I used to be the big boss at the hospital. The name stuck." He did not explain his strange behavior of the morning.

"The *surgeon*?" I asked, incredulous. "The same Professor Dal who was the Shah's physician?" This man, my cellmate, had been the most prominent surgeon in the country until a few years before the revolution, with a career spanning half a century. He was an aristocrat, hobnobbing at the royal court. But later, during the oil boom of the seventies, he became vocal against the cartel and fell from grace, almost disappearing from view.

Over the next eight nights, Professor Dal recounted the story of the Poonakis, a family that had lasted only three generations. He told me of the twin princes—the devoted founders of the family—and of their twin grandchildren, whose lives were spent in hating one another. These stories were incredible: they had a chimerical quality, which at the time I put down to Professor Dal's state of mind.

Each night, after our evening meal of broth and bread, the Professor crawled over to my mattress and, without the slightest hesitation, climbed on top of me, made himself comfortable, and began telling his stories. At times these seemed merely the spewing words of a raving lunatic, who found my body a softer mattress than his hard pallet. Other times they were the sage words of a wise man, the straightforward recital of tragic and savage incidents. I marveled at his vocal acrobatics, able to bring to life each character—man, woman, child.

That first night, as I shifted my large frame to accommodate the weight of his bones, he said calmly, "Stop fidgeting, kind boy. We only have eight nights to tell our full story."

"How do you know that? Did you hear something from the guards? Are they going to let me out? They are, aren't they?"

"Quiet, boy. I want you to meet Tala, the Shah's umpteenth wife."

The Professor Tells the Story of the Young Princes

*"Wednesday I think. Thursday I enjoy.
Friday I play. Oh unhappy Saturday: my
legs are bleeding from the strokes of
cherry-tree branches."*

— Persiran nursery rhyme

All stories are stories of conception. In the West, they are called love stories. To arrive at the surgery room where the difficult twins were born, I need recount only four previous conceptions. Let me tell you about the opportunistic Tala—daughter of the royal bootmaker, Shah's concubine, and mother of the royal twins.

In her old age she wore flowery housedresses, her white hair, hands, and bunioned feet all smeared with an overabundance of bright orange henna. She talked incessantly and acted as if she were still sixteen years old, elaborating with enthusiasm every detail that had excited each of her five senses in the early years of her life. Tala was a high-fidelity instrument that recorded and played back her first sixteen years. She eventually died in midsentence, describing a pair of earrings worn by one of the harem eunuchs.

What thoughts must have gone through young Tala's mind, as she gazed through the intricate fenestrations of the harem walls into the palace garden? We see, with her, the flowered plots, hyacinths and narcissi. Some with a single blossom, a badge of azure; or a ring of creamy white petals encircling a grainy golden cup, damp with dew. Marble pools disperse water from wide fountains, like waves of molten silver. The schools of gold-finned and silver-finned fish storm across their pools, as one mind and body. All, lovelier than her dreams.

The daughter of a bootmaker, just sixteen years old, she was in her fourth year of concubinage. Now she was ready to receive, for only the second time, the king of kings, the monarch of all Persia, in the same room, his Room of Delight. Rich carpets, rugs, and rare brocade draperies luxuriated in shades of deepest red. Plush velvet and cashmere cushions, embroidered with pearls, leaned against the walls. Tiny mirrors cemented into the walls glittered like precious stones, framing hunting scenes depicted in oils. In the center of the wall behind her, a single canvas portrayed His Majesty the Shah, the lord and master of the harem, at age nineteen.

Tala was ready. Her body had been rubbed lightly with *sadri*, a special perfumed rice. Her lips were colored red with powder made from a rare insect found in the dried mud at the outer rims of the desert. She had dressed in the latest fashion: the thick, flounced tutu had been introduced into the harem by the Shah himself, after seeing ballet dancers perform at the opera house in Paris.

The city resonated with the sound of midday prayer. It was time. She bared her heavy breasts. She picked up a pair of copper tongs, cupped her left breast, and placed the nipple between its jaws. She pinched lightly. Then, in a quick, downward motion, she crushed the tissue. Pain blurred her vision. She let out a soft moan. She examined the bruised nipple, now standing erect, bulging, the color of a dead calf's tongue. Satisfied with the result, she placed the tongs on her right breast and with trembling hands repeated the process. The pain made her fall back on the cushions. The Shah, she knew, loved thick nipples.

No sacrifice was too small or too great. She still had her childhood memories: sucking on small chunks of sugar wrapped in dirty muslin; the salty taste of her mother's finger with its tiny scrap of opium under the nail, lulling her to sweet sleep; the well-modulated voice of her father shouting at her to come down from the roof. Tala, "Gold," they called her, on account of her straw-yellow hair. Indeed, she owed her new wealth to the random genetics of her golden hair, both on her head and, even rarer, elsewhere. You could say that the famous Poonakis were able to keep three generations in luxury thanks to the color of Tala's pubic hair.

She was twelve when her father gave her away. On a Wednesday, her mother walked her for the first time to the bathhouse. When they returned she found the house filled with trays of delicacies: fruits ripened to perfection; nuts of every kind—walnuts, almonds, pistachios—filling half a dozen elaborate trays; boxes of honey-nougat and pistachio-nougat stacked neatly in a corner; plain toffees; toffees filled with nuts; fondants shaped like half-moons; Turkish delight. There were sweets she had never seen before—peppermint lumps decorated with gold leaves, boiled sweets that stuck deliciously to her fingers. It all felt like an adventure. What child would not see the bright side of this bargain?

The next night, she was brought into this very room at Golestan Palace, the Room of Delight, to await the Shah. At twelve years old, her dozing mind had drifted in and out of imaginative nightmares. Her mother and aunt had painted for her a bizarre picture of men's absolute right to insert into her body a part of their bodies without her complaint. She had never seen, or heard anyone describe, a penis. A silky prepubescent tuft of yellow hair had recently covered her vulva.

The Shah came in late. She awoke to see his rough outline quietly undressing. Her first clear sense of him in the bed was a heavy, clinging odor of briny sweat. He entered her scrawny body unceremoniously. Her yellow hair, her only claim to distinction, mattered little in the dark. She bled excessively, which disgusted him. They replaced her immediately. She understood the look of pity on the faces of the other concubines, even years later.

During the next four years, she shared in the harem life of deceptions, insults, gossip, and intrigue. Eunuchs, chamberlains, pages, courtiers, guardians, door-listeners, sorcerers, interpreters of dreams, starred and star-crossed victims, and professional witnesses—all maneuvered around one another in this complicated universe that revolved around the schemes of concubines, this tiny independent city within a city. Each with her own system of intelligence, the concubines plotted and counterplotted. The elders backed their favorite young champions. Their means were various, their objective the same: to bear the Shah a son—a son whose claim to a share of the Shah's patrimony would guarantee his supporters a secure and comfortable old age. These were truly the most refined and dangerous politicians of the realm.

Tala survived the years of plotting. The women, except for a few foolish youngsters, grew to respect her as a worthy and dangerous rival. Soon after that first failure, she began to plan her readmittance to the Shah's chamber. Under her own strict discipline and scrutiny, she developed into a desirable woman. Never allowing herself to become fat or thin, she kept herself at the difficult stage of skintight plumpness, a perfect feminine roundness. She oiled and rubbed her skin every day. She wore the thick veil outdoors, to protect her light skin from the heat and dust. On this day, all her efforts would be handsomely repaid.

That morning had been her first triumph. When the shrill, panic-stricken voice of the eunuch Djavaher ("Jewel") announced the arrival of the Shah, the women, as always, came running from all directions. Tala stood in the corner, looking up. The Shah emerged on his balcony above the well-paved courtyard. Walking down the stairs, he looked majestic: black bobbed hair; a long nose; a dashing, dagger-like mustache. Only his eyes—sleepy, mud-colored, and hidden under drooping eyelids—showed a man long at odds with his own overabundance.

He wore a white linen shirt and a padded coat of thin cotton wool, quilted with silk thread, and over that a light blue coat, tight at the waist, with pointed cuffs lined with cashmere and a narrow border of rare brocade. He had thrown over his shoulders a long orange cape lined with the finest sable, the hundreds of small fluffy tails forming its fringe.

As the Shah reached the bottom of the stairs, the women, already kneeling, bowed their foreheads to the ground. Djavaher, stout and fussy, jumped down from the balcony into the courtyard. He knelt and kissed the Shah's hand in a state of devotional enthusiasm. The Shah smiled beneficently all around, gently nodding his head. In the shadowed corners of the courtyard, the reflections from the large diamond on his Persiranian lamb hat jiggled wildly.

Before the chief eunuch could finish his welcome, there was a new commotion, as the black eunuch Djohar ("Ink"; he was rumored to be an Abyssinian prince) arrived like a whirlwind. He had the shaved head and smooth, black body of a pugilist. Djohar claimed to be a descendant of the Prophet, destined to be the last of that line. Pushing through the small herd of women, he announced that the queen, Ghamar-ed-Dowleh, the Moon of the Empire, was ready to receive. With Djohar on one side and Djavaher on the other, the Shah walked across the yard, smiling at his prostrate *houris*. He climbed the marble stairs at the far end of the courtyard and disappeared behind a growth of jasmine, into the small tent-like structure set up on the queen's balcony.

Well aware of the rigid social hierarchy and of their own place at the bottom of the ladder of influence, the women sat in their places. None was jealous of the

Queen. They stared at one another insolently—some emboldened by their corporeal beauty, others by their distinguished ancestry. All waited for the Shah to emerge from his cultural visit: the Queen was well known for her literary and poetic talents.

The Shah liked discretion. Having made his choice before entering the queen's chamber, on leaving it, he would give a brief nod toward the desired girl. The women kept their eyes lowered as a sign of respect: their faces must show no expression that could question the Shah's choice. Only the eunuchs would follow the Shah's gaze to pinpoint the fortunate woman; later, they would discreetly inform her of her luck.

For four years, Tala had planned for this day. The month was at its most propitious. She well knew that the Shah had not chosen her; he had shown interest in another concubine, one with the body of a supple boy. Tala stood apart from the other girl. To the end of her life, a grainy, coquettish laugh arose from deep in her throat when she recalled the scene. If questioned, Djohar—for the price of half of Tala's dowry—would himself apologize to the Shah for the error. After all, there were many such afternoons; one small mistake did not displease the Shah. And Tala would not disappoint.

Ensconced in the Room of Delight, she still had work to do; no detail was left to chance. Tala ordered the sweets and the sherbet to be brought in immediately. Two young and pretty servants came in with colored glasses and a decanter of sherbet. As soon as she was alone, she quickly flicked open the stone on her ring. With a steady hand, she poured the powdery contents into the decanter. She knew the risk. Anyone caught adding any foreign substance to the Shah's food or drink faced a painful death. The peasant girls now returned with trays of honeyed pastries; they exited with blushes. Supremely victorious, Tala basked in the sound of their giggles.

The powder, a fertility potion made by Sarah, the Jewess sorceress, contained, among other ingredients, crushed pearls, a certain grain of spice not unlike pepper, a few hairs of the upper lip of a live leopard, and the navel of a gazelle, cut immediately after an attack by a lion. The sorceress had uttered talismanic words, while the powder dried under the spell of five moons. And Tala sat, patiently awaiting her master.

She heard his footsteps. A loud sneeze stopped him in his tracks: a sneeze is a bad omen, a divine warning to abandon any present enterprise. Tala scoffed at the insult. Imagine someone trying to stop her with that nonsense! It must have originated from one of the young concubines; they all knew the Shah's religious zeal. She leaned back on the cushion, listening for a second sneeze, the divine signal to resume. Soon enough, she heard the footsteps of the Shah approaching the door—thanks to the virtuoso performance of the professional sneezer she had thought to hire.

Tala gave birth to a pair of twin princes on August 3, 1885. The Shah named them Sardar Mirza and Saleh Mirza. The twins, the only pair at court, had a special place in his heart, and so he allowed them the honorific Mirza, "Prince." (In a redundant Persiranian manner, the title Prince is also added before the name.) Unusual problems attended the birth. At delivery, Tala suffered a mild stroke that affected her memory: from this point on, she would only clearly recall her life before the pregnancy, sixteen years that would be repeated in her mind again and again.

The two princes, Sardar Mirza and Saleh Mirza, grew up together until the age of eight, surrounded by the womenfolk in their father's harem at Golestan Palace. Identical twins, they grew up inseparable. When they were four years old, their nurse found them in their shared bed caressing, smelling, and licking each other's heads like cubs in the wild. They felt no guilt, but the ignorant around them frowned on this behavior, and the twins spent their childhood evading plots to separate them. According to the rules of harem politics, full brothers always stuck by one another against half-brothers; half-brothers had each an array of mothers, servants, and eunuchs fanning enmity against the others.

The boys were given lessons in French, English, mathematics, and gymnastics—not by a *monsieur* or a *mademoiselle*, as tradition demanded, but by an English tutor, a Mr. Wilfred Sparroy (who did, however, fully in keeping with tradition, teach their lessons in French). A jovial man, he had also taught the Shah's grandchildren, offspring of his eldest son, Zell al-Sultan. Zell al-Sultan was the twins' eldest brother, fully forty years their senior. Mr. Sparroy had an atrocious French accent; the English, in their conceit, believe that foreign languages should be spoken with as English an accent as possible. Throughout his life, Saleh Mirza would say *parlay* for "talk," *brou-ee* for "noise," and *un oaf* for "an egg."

Saleh Mirza, a serious boy with unusually developed powers of concentration, was interested in politics. He read and translated meticulously, from either French or English, every newspaper he could lay his hands on. That he achieved so much in politics—known by all as "the Prince"— was a testament to his brilliance: a Qajar prince (it was said) had less chance than a donkey-driver of becoming prime minister. (Indeed, most fields of activity were closed to a royal prince.) His brother Sardar Mirza, a merrier, happy-go-lucky child, turned out to have a linguist's facility.

Each year, the different tutors gave a progress report on the Shah's children. The Shah himself, Naser al-Din Shah, the Pivot of the Universe, would attend the report reading with enthusiasm, inviting a number of other notables—foreign scholars, missionaries, and resident consuls—to join him. Outdated mural maps of the world, made in Germany some twenty-five years before and presented by Mr. Hoeltzer of the Indo-European Telegraph Department, were rolled out in the courtyard for the occasion. A dais was set up for the day-long event with a circle of chairs on it, where the few foreigners would sit alongside the Shah. Everyone else stood in a semicircle behind the Shah's chair, heads slightly bowed, arms crossed against the chest.

The boys, five to sixteen years old, kneeled in turn on the small, square cushion placed directly in front of the Shah. With their heads bent under their tall astrakhan hats, they stared straight at the ground. Deemed small adults, they wore no special children's clothes, no sailor suits or lederhosen. They wore the traditional overcoat of Persiran cashmere, with a straight military collar. The coat, buttoned only at the neck, fanned open in front, cinched tightly to the waist, and then fanned out further like a pleated skirt reaching just below the knees. The open front allowed the bold to display a purple, brown, or ruby undercoat of silk or velvet. Shoeless, the kneeling boys wore baggy white socks, almost hidden by the coat's folds.

The reading of the report had about it a touch of the Olympiads and even a trace of dueling. It could set into motion complicated political eddies that spun through the harem, as the details of the event were later recounted by the favorite eunuchs, as if in sports commentary. During the day itself, the solemn atmosphere would give way to mayhem as the boys competed: they gave dueling poetry recitals; then, chalk in hand, they raced to complete arithmetic problems on the stones in front of the dais. Little boys holding strings stretched their arms across the maps, the sides of their faces touching the brownish, elevated mountain ranges, unable to reach the target city—and thus failing in the attempt to determine the distance between the specified foreign capital and Tehran, the center of the universe. The foreign consuls tested the children on their language skills, while the tutors (most of them French) fumed at their own legations when they marked down a favorite prince. Throughout the ordeal, the Shah pointed and smiled, complimenting and berating his children according to his strong prejudices. The winner received a gold coin, accompanied by a round of kisses from all notables around the dais. A loser or two might risk a bastinado, often meted out by the tutor or the eunuch.

Naser al-Din Shah, the Pivot of the Universe, attended the last report reading of his reign on April 30, 1897, just one day before a bullet from an ancient revolver brought his life to a close, and with it the forty-eight years of the eponymous Naseri era—a cataclysmic change, comparable perhaps to the transition from the Victorian to the Edwardian era.

Then in his sixty-fourth year, he leaned that day more heavily than usual on his cane. A lifetime of twenty-course meals had not punished his figure terribly: he had the habit of chewing, tasting, and enjoying morsels of food before spitting out most of what was offered. The characteristic Qajar bedroom eyes, which would become even more pronounced in his son, gave him a regal chin-up posture—of necessity: to see better from underneath his drooping upper eyelids.

On that day Sardar Mirza and Saleh Mirza, the two twelve-year-old princes, vied for the best spoken and written French against three of their half-brothers, including two who were much older than they. It was the peak of spring. The shallow channels circling the courtyard ran full of burbling spring water. Monsieur Rocha, the consul from Rasht, was in attendance. His use of some French *argot* confused many of the boys as well as Master Sparroy himself. Sardar Mirza won the verbal test handily on the strength of his superior pronunciation, despite his tutor's English-laden French. Saleh Mirza, on the strength of his superior intellect and hard work, beat all the others in grammar. Now, as they sat for the dictation, Monsieur Rocha read aloud one of La Fontaine's fables. In a loud and clear voice he repeated didactically each phrase, in a rhythm drearily familiar to any victim of the French educational system. Concerned for His Majesty's patience—the Shah was easily bored—the tutors hovered over their charges' shoulders, alert to the first sign of misspelling. These sudden-death dictations never went beyond a few sentences.

Monsieur Rocha grandly pronounced the title of the fable: *La Grenouille qui veut se faire aussi grosse que le Bœuf,* "The Frog Who Would Make Himself as Big as a Bull." First to fall victim to ignorance was seven-year-old Ahmad Mirza. In due course, this young prince would become a regular guest of Franz Joseph I; nevertheless, the proverbial frog, a spelling horror in French, defeated him early. He was eliminated with little fanfare; his young age begged the audience's indulgence.

Next to fall was Mohammad Reza Mirza es-Saltaneh, a handsome fourteen-year-old prince with eyebrows that showed no punctuation between them. In a leap of imagination, he attempted to distract Monsieur Rocha with a princely command to repeat himself more clearly—adding, for the benefit of the audience, that he couldn't understand this man's regional accent. Taken aback, Monsieur Rocha turned toward the audience. Seizing his opportunity, the Prince lip-mimed an appeal to his tutor behind the consul's rigid back, seeking the correct spelling of that bovine at the rear of the title. The tutor, angry at his presumption, stared stone-faced. The consul's repetition of the word was of little help; either you knew the smooching French diphthong or you didn't. As the offended tutor grasped the Prince's ear in a mean pinch, hissing over and over the word *crétin,* the Shah—followed, with some hesitation, by the rest of the company—burst out laughing. He rather favored Mohammad Reza Mirza.

81

This roguish young prince would in time become a good friend and a good elder brother to the twins. A frequent presence in the Poonaki house, he was later kept ever-present in the daguerreotypes arranged on top of the grand piano and on the small mahogany side tables. In honor of this dictation mishap, his brothers nicknamed him *le Bœuf.*

Monsieur Rocha now began to recite the fable: "*Une grenouille vit un bœuf, qui lui sembla de belle taille.*" The three remaining boys chewed the ends of their freshly cut wood, writing utensils, twisting in agony. The tutors quickly zeroed in on the results: the sixteen-year-old Nosrat al-Din Mirza—another victim of Mr. Sparroy's Franglais—had transformed the word *taille*, "size," to masculine neckwear by spelling it *tie*. He nevertheless went on to become a fair painter and a musician, as well as a good companion to Sardar Mirza during their adult years in Paris.

Monsieur Rocha continued the recitation for the remaining two contestants, the twins: "*Elle qui n'était pas grosse en tout comme un œuf/se travaille, Pour égaler l'animal en grosseur.*" Here, Saleh Mirza decided out of brotherly love to give his brother Sardar Mirza the prize, a decision that would have far-reaching consequences in their lives. He pretended to be another victim of the French diphthong and of Franglais, producing instead of *un oeuf* ('an egg'), *un oaf.* Thus, his darling brother got the gold coin and had his lips kissed by their royal father.

♆

Sardar Mirza did not have much time to rejoice in his schoolboy victory. The very next afternoon, the ululation of the harem could be heard from every window of Golestan Palace. An advance guard had brought word that the Shah, his father, had been shot after prayer at Shah-Abdol-Azim Shrine, but he had not died.

1001

Let me give you a few strokes of paint to color your history book. Here sits the still-virile Shah inside the great mosque, four miles outside Tehran, holding the same posture as at the report reading the previous day, leaning on his silver-encrusted cane. A rivulet of sweat escapes the royal forehead, to be dabbed away by a handkerchief-bearing servant. It is hotter than yesterday; the mosque, further south than the palace, is less protected from the sun. Nevertheless, the prayers at the famous sanctuary always leave him pleased with his own piety. Complying with tradition, he now intends to receive petitions in person.

Watch now as a man of average height—thin, wearing a poor man's clothes and wrapped in a tattered blanket—approaches the Shah of Shahs, just as he completes his prayers. As with all assassinations, people will marvel at the coincidences that brought about all the necessary conditions for the act to succeed. For instance, this is the first time a crowd has been allowed to remain inside the mosque while the Shah prays.

Mirza Reza Kermani, not to be confused with Mohammad Reza Mirza (Mirza at the end only denotes a prince; otherwise, it is just a name), carries a sheaf of paper that looks like a petition; it hides his rusty gun underneath. He looks modern in his disheveled, proto-terrorist garb: a thin, white turban, like a series of handkerchiefs knotted at the corners; an unkempt beard, perhaps a bit too well tended for an illiterate. His eyes are close-set. With his delicate, dark, bony fingers curled on the trigger, he approaches confidently, never in doubt. He fires point-blank: three shots around the heart. In fact, the Shah's real heart, his favorite wife Jayran, has long been buried, thirty-seven years ago—indeed, just a few gravestones away. Again, people will marvel at the coincidence.

Mirza Reza represents the liberal view of society. He later stated, "I had a chance to kill him before, but I didn't because the Jews were celebrating their picnic after the eighth day of Passover. I did not want the Jews to be accused of killing the Shah." Yes, certainly a liberal view. By August, a mere three months hence, he will hang in public for two days as an example for all to heed—though not, as we see in hindsight, an effective deterrent.

Cool, always cool, the Premier drags the Shah's body into the carriage. His full name is Ali Asghar Khan Atabak, but all know him as Amin Soltan; he will serve a full nine years as premier. He talks loudly, for all to hear, addressing the Shah as if he has somehow escaped with his life. "Your Majesty, let us go back to the palace. Your shoulder is grazed and needs attention." In the carriage the dying Shah gurgles, "If I survive, I will rule differently." With that, he plunges into an irreversible coma.

The Premier straightens the Shah in the carriage, holding up the royal sleeve to wave at the crowd—even getting the Shah to nod to the crowd by pulling the hair at the back of his head. Poor Amin Soltan cannot know that a similar fate awaits him, too, to be shot in front of the parliament by the anarchist Abbas Agha. But that is nine years in the future.

The Premier sends advance guards to Tabriz, the seat of the Crown Prince. Then he dispatches couriers to the foreign embassies to garner support for the Crown Prince. This presence of mind, and loyalty, makes his reputation; he will keep his job for most of the new Shah's reign.

The Shah is dead. Long live the Premier?

The Shah died that night at the palace. No one is informed that night: the Crown Prince—the second-eldest surviving son—will succeed, now to be called Mozaffar al-Din Shah. But he must first receive the support of the Russian and English delegations. The eldest son, Zell al-Sultan, will not accede to the throne, as the issue of a non-royal mother; the Qajar dynasty required a prince to have royal blood from both progenitors. Four elder bothers have already died, and Mozaffar, though Crown Prince, was never one of his father's favorites. Still, he has followed tradition by waiting for his crown for as many years as it takes, far from the capital in the city of Tabriz.

The ululations in the harem turned serious: hundreds of women were desperate to know their fate. Most of them would be married off to men in the commercial class. As with buying a celebrity's car, there was no stigma attached to marrying one of the Shah's wives or concubines—rather, it conferred bragging rights. Women with children would be given a stipend.

To the twelve-year-old princes, the new Shah—their second-eldest brother—seemed like their grandfather. Twenty-five years in waiting, at the age of forty-four the new Shah looked anything but new. His upper eyelids, drooping heavily, resembled small tortoise shells sliding back and forth in his skull. A deep furrow etched his forehead, half an inch above his eyebrows. He wore two long white mustaches, like brooms zapped by static. Wan and sick, he looked prematurely old and spoke with a heavy Turkish accent. He was outwardly kind but quite uncaring.

Within a month, he took a twin on each knee to explain to them their future. They were to inherit the village of Poonak, with all its lands and income, in perpetuity. The land and gardens of Poonak would support the family in relative comfort for years to come. Today, Poonak is integrated into the city of Tehran; at the prices of today, their land would be worth over a billion dollars. Their mother, Tala Khanum, received a small annuity and went back to live with her father.

The Shah turned slowly to the Premier standing behind him, who now handed the Shah a royal decree wrapped in a gauzy gold ribbon. "Which of you is

Sardar?" the Shah asked gently. *"Ah, je vois que votre français est excellent."* Sardar's chest puffed up like a young dove's at the Shah's commendation. "We will be sending you to France to study with Monsieur."

He then turned his head, like a slow turtle. "And you can only be Saleh Mirza?" He smiled tragically at this triumph of logic. "You, my boy, we are told, are an excellent scholar. You will study with us here at the palace and then matriculate at the Dar ul-Funun." The polytechnic institute trained the upper-class youth in medicine, engineering, military science, and geology.

A few strokes of the pen had decreed that the two brothers would not see each other for ten years. They never forgave the Shah, or his court, for this forced separation.

Sardar Mirza always maintained that his trip to Europe resembled a dream. He'd dream that he lived deep at the bottom of the sea; dream-logic explained the absence of oxygen. In a race to reach the surface, he would kick-swim toward the hazy light. He'd wake up gulping for breath in his Paris bed. Then the mechanical noises in the street, the smell of the bakeries, the sound of spoken French, all marks of a steady civilization, would calm him immediately. He loved being in Paris.

But the journey to Paris did resemble an ordeal of swimming underwater, toward the bottom. The route to Europe took months—to Tabriz in the north of Persiran, via Qazvin and Zanjan; and then to Odessa, and on to Europe.

They started on a cold, sunny morning. You could see the snow sparkle miles away on the Alborz Mountains. Gray landscape would be their scenery for the next one hundred and fifty miles, all stone and wet earth, dotted here and there with scrub. Of the twelve gates of Tehran, they chose the Qazvin gate, to cross the high Persiranian plateau. In keeping with the ancient tradition of accompanying a respected traveler some of the way, Sardar Mirza's brother and ten horsemen were to accompany them all the way to Qazvin on a sad, two-day ride. The two young boys rode hand in hand while two slaves held their horses and pulled them in tandem. Their heads just visible between the twitching ears of their mounts, the twins cried inconsolably, openly, without shame.

Their fourteen-year-old brother, Mohammad Reza Mirza es-Saltaneh—the famous Le Bœuf—rode behind on his own horse. He had now come of age; his newly crowned brother had entrusted him with the Crown Prince's official seal, to carry to Tabriz and present to the new Shah's own eldest son, Mohammad Ali—now Crown Prince in his turn. Despite the vast age differences between the Crown Prince and his brothers, the twenty-four-year-old Crown Prince would awkwardly call these three young royals "uncle."

Qodrat, Sardar Mirza's personal servant, followed a few lengths behind, as he would remain at his side throughout his life. He pulled his long, black beard over his eyes to hide his tears. The Armenian factotum, Simon Khan—a trusted and trustworthy *hamekareh*, a jack of all trades—had been given responsibility for the safety and wellbeing of the three princes. Thin, tall, and ascetic-looking on his gray steed, with his back held as stiff as a ladder, the Prussian bearing was belied by the fatalistic outlook of the soft brown eyes. Born in Odessa, he was fluent in French, Russian, Persiran, and Turkish (as well as a number of dialects), and he peppered his speech with salty phrases in all of these tongues. He had straddled East and West all his life—and he would die at the hands of the Turks during the Armenian genocide.

After a full day's ride, they spent a miserable night at their first camp. Despite the cold, the wind carried a fetid smell of decay as thick as the soles of their leathered shoes, permeating the camp and robbing them of appetite. The hungry howling of jackals and the piteous braying of a stranded donkey in the distance kept them awake most of the night. The donkey's cries filled their ears with a pleading sound, rising and falling through the hours of darkness. Hadn't the Prophet said that the braying of a donkey confirms the presence of Satan nearby?

Up at four in the morning, they used dirt to make their ablutions and quickly said their prayers. After tea, feta, and bread, they were on the road by five. The smell worsened as they rode west, and the braying became louder. They used their shawls to wrap their noses and mouths. Three miles on, they found the source of the unbearable smell—an open grave, where the peasantry would dump their old animals. The entire column of riders gathered around the natural dugout to see the hundreds of donkey skeletons at different stages of putrefaction. The only donkey with his skin intact was lying on his side halfway down the slope. He was still breathing. Simon Khan, the factotum, looked at the rider next to him and flicked his index finger across his own throat. The rider unsheathed a knife, swung his leg around the saddle, and jumped to the ground in one smooth move. The rider inserted the knife straight into the soft neck below the muzzle and pulled it out in one smooth motion—no cutting. The ass gurgled and sighed once.

They arrived at the outskirts of Qazvin in the dead of winter, at the setting sun, and approached the city through its outlying gardens and groves. To the boys, accustomed to the palace and its gardens, this was a miserable terrain of twisted, naked woodlands; nothing indicated that Qazvin was once the capital of the Safavid Empire. Hundreds of spindles of smoke, curling among the sparse trees, indicated where peasants were burning cow dung to stay warm. The royal party passed into the town along narrow alleys covered with frozen mud and snow, their horses' hooves echoing like stone crushing stone. This ancient capital had none of the wide streets built by their father in Tehran; it looked as though Genghis Khan might have passed through only a few months ago. Mangy dogs, their emaciated bodies covered with festering wounds, halfheartedly chased the procession of horses and mules. As they rode toward the bazaar, the town showed a modicum of life. Small workshops were lit by weak lanterns, throwing long moving shadows of the owners as they rushed out to beckon the rich horsemen to enter.

Late in the evening, they at last entered an elegant vestibule that opened onto a large yard, well lit by torches. Four balconies faced the courtyard, and chambers with small verandas surrounded the whole. This was the newly built Sa'd al-Saltaneh caravanserai, the largest caravanserai in the empire, decreed into existence by their father and built with only the most expensive bricks by the governor of Qazvin—what passed for a grand hotel in those days. Servants appeared from every corner and ran to greet them. The party would occupy three of the *hujrehs*, or guest suites. All the rooms were constructed three feet above the courtyard. Inside the rooms, comfortable bedding had been spread on the floor; a felt skullcap, a comb, and a toothbrush had been placed on each pillow. Used though these items were, they preceded by seventy years the baskets of fresh toiletries offered in the bathrooms of our Marriotts and Hiltons.

The travelers felt a sense of order returning to their miserable lives. The next morning, after a good night's sleep, they ate a breakfast fit for three princes. Spending their last day together, they washed and relaxed in the Sadieh Bathhouse behind the caravanserai. And it was there, with the help of their older brother, that the twins hatched a bold plan to extend the accompanied part of Sardar Mirza's trip, all the way to Tabriz. Scrubbing the dirt from their skin, they asked each other why they could not travel together as far as Tabriz. As the servants poured the clean hot water over them, they asked, "Who would be harmed?" Tingling under rigorous rubdowns, they considered the solution. Wasn't Le Bœuf planning to return to Tehran, after handing the seal to the Crown Prince? Couldn't Saleh Mirza then return with him, after a few weeks of rest in Tabriz? They well understood that disobeying the Shah had consequences. The twins cared not a hoot, as long as they stayed together.

The day belonged to the brash Le Bœuf, whose sense of adventure was matched by his native cunning. It never entered his brain not to take the opportunity to outsmart the next fellow: today he would be called a practical joker. As they drank icy water and sweated the last of the fatigue from their bones, Le Bœuf told his young brothers not to worry and to leave it all to him.

His first act, after their morning at the baths, was to ask his servant to summon a professional letter writer to his room. Letter writers were easy to find, behind mosques and official buildings. They set up shop on the street with small wooden boxes displaying samples of their handwriting. The samples were an unnecessary formality, provided for the illiterate to examine like first-time buyers in an art gallery. Le Bœuf demanded the best calligrapher money could buy. The prize proved to be an old man who looked like an Indian maharishi with a toothless, tongueless, gummy smile. Forty years earlier, the governor had ripped out his tongue for some minor infraction. The calligrapher sat cross-legged while Le Bœuf dictated the letter.

To Their Highnesses Mohammad Reza, Saleh, and Sardar Mirza, my inestimable uncles:

In the name of God and his infinite kindness: we welcome our uncles to the city of Qazvin. We have sent our courier to meet you and convey our warmest greetings. We await your arrival in Tabriz with much anticipation. Having never met our twin uncles and having heard much about how inseparable you are, we would not wish to receive the sad half if we could have the happy whole. We shall expect your presence at court by the end of the month. Signed and sealed by the Crown Prince.

Ah, that seal, that would seal their fate as well. After the old letter writer left, Le Bœuf unwrapped the intricately sewn cloth with its velvety inside to reveal the royal seal. The silver surface of the seal had etched on it the smiling royal lion holding the sword, the strangely irregular sun rising behind it. He used a candle to warm the yellow wax. With his tongue licking his lower lip, he affixed the seal to the letter, and smiled.

The more difficult step was to find a suitable person who could act the part of courier. Again, Le Bœuf sent out his servant, this time to look for a *luti* near the bazaar. Forerunner to the English "lout," the *luti* combines chivalry and chicanery in varying measures, depending on his character. The Prince, always comfortable with this sort, spent the afternoon interviewing promising candidates. He found what he was looking for in a muscular Turk, who came with a propeller-like black mustache, a manly stance, and minimal riding skills. The man maintained an infuriating grin at his own cleverness.

With a few choice words, the Prince wiped the grin off the Turk's face. His lack of riding skill, however, was problematic. The man flopped on top of a horse like a straw figure. He decided to have him walk the horse into the caravanserai. The fourteen-year-old Prince spent the rest of the evening dressing the man and teaching him how to bow and proffer the letter. As Tabriz was the country's most Turkish city, the man's accent worked to their advantage. The Prince paid his "messenger" liberally, making sure he understood that once the deed was done he needed to disappear for a few months.

Before dinner, as Le Bœuf and Simon Khan were smoking their evening *ghalian*, sitting on a Baluchi rug on the veranda, they heard the messenger shouting in the courtyard with just the right note of urgency.

"For God's sake," said the Prince, acting more bored than irritated. "Let the man know I am sitting right here and tell him to stop shouting my name. Bring him to me."

The man played the part convincingly enough. Le Bœuf broke the seal, read the message, and passed it languidly to Simon Khan. "This should make the boys happy."

Simon Khan read the short missive. He looked mistrustful. "The Shah's orders are the Shah's orders," he said quietly. "They cannot be reversed even by the Crown Prince." Le Bœuf sat stunned. Simon Khan had swallowed the bait; what he was questioning was the Crown Prince's authority to countermand his father.

The messenger stood with eyes downcast, as he had been trained to do earlier that day.

"You are right, and sagacious to boot, Simon Khan," Le Bœuf piped up. "It does put us in an awkward situation. Do we arrive with just one prince, crying his eyes out? It seems to me we are displeasing one of our masters. From what I hear, our nephew, the Crown Prince, takes offense much too easily."

Simon Khan brooded for a bit. Then, to answer Le Bœuf's question, he posed a question of his own: "Your Highness, would you mind if I kept the letter in safekeeping, to answer any questions of impropriety that may arise as a result of flouting the Shah's orders?" Poor Le Bœuf was loath to hand over the evidence of misusing the seal, but he had little choice.

"Simon Khan, you may keep it as long as it serves you."

"Thank you, Your Highness. I will also have the escort return to Tehran. I will write a letter to the court minister informing him of our intention to take His Highness Saleh Mirza to Tabriz. I will let them know that while Sardar Mirza and I will continue to Paris, Saleh Mirza will return with you in a few months' time—if, of course, that is agreeable to you." Even the clear certainty that the day of reckoning would come did not lessen Le Bœuf's pleasure in telling the boys this good news.

In the next four days, they traveled northward, one hundred twenty miles to Zanjan. The three princes were now accompanied only by Simon Khan, Qodrat, and five riders; all shared the twins' high spirits, full of laughter and joy. The young princes looked no further forward than the next ten days of riding together to Tabriz.

As they moved north, the light gray colors of the flatlands changed to greener, more elevated scenery. If the events that followed had not blighted the memory of those four sunny, glorious days, the twins could have feasted for years on the details of that passage: Simon Khan and Qodrat teaching them how to hunt; learning to maintain a horse's trust when dismounting; chasing hare into the brush. And there was always Le Bœuf's horseplay—literally. Early one morning, he crept beneath the horses' bellies and loosened the saddle straps of the guards' horses, so that, mounting simultaneously, the five guards fell to the ground in unison; everyone, including the guards, laughed uproariously. In the afternoons, three of the guards would trot ahead with the mules to set up camp. By the time the rest arrived, a skinned deer or a few plucked pheasants would be roasting on a hearty fire. At night they would sit around the fire and listen to Simon Khan describe faraway places like Odessa and Erzerum. He told them of the Tartar tribes riding in the Caucasus and the Turkish *bashi-bazouks*, plundering the countryside when he was a boy.

Years later, in Paris, Sardar Mirza purchased a portrait of a *bashi-bazouk* by Jean-Léon Gérôme, to hang in his bedroom at the Hotel Lutetia. Picasso might tease him about his romantic notions of the Orient; but more than most—certainly more than Picasso—Sardar Mirza could accurately measure the distance between romance and reality.

Tanned, healthy, and full of talk, they entered Zanjan on the fourth day. Zanjan had had its troubles with their father since it became a center for the Baha'is. Viewing the spread of the Baha'i movement as a threat to the dynasty, the Shah's premier had put a number of people to death. It was deemed prudent, then, as their small procession crossed the city's twisted alleys at midday, for the ceremonial front guards to refrain from shouting the arrival of the princes. They stayed the night at the Sangi caravanserai.

Starting out the next morning toward Tabriz was a foolhardy plan, beginning a journey of one hundred eighty miles amid flurries of snow that stuck to their eyelashes. Maybe Simon Khan felt the animosity of the Zanjan populace, or maybe they were in thrall to the convivial mood of the last four days—but they continued. The day turned colder, the clouds grew thicker and more ominous. They trotted briskly enough to cover thirty miles that day, seeing ever fewer riders and fewer men walking the road.

Snow and rain alternated all through the day. They spent a cold night, damp seeping into their bones. It was nearly impossible to keep their fire burning with any heat.

The next morning they made good progress, but that afternoon the gusts whipped the snow with such fury that the riders felt they were entering a tunnel of needles. Their faces raw, they huddled on their saddles, wrapped themselves in shawls, and rode close together, the guards encircling the boys' horses and the pack mules. No one voiced aloud any fear that packs of wolves or jackals might attack an isolated animal.

By six that evening they could not see two horse lengths in front of them. Simon Khan ordered the group to form a circle and to force their mounts to lie on the ground in a circle around them. He tied the animals' front and back legs and covered the nervous beasts and their riders with traveling rugs. The two brothers huddled next to the warm, yielding stomach of one of their horses. They ate dried bread and fell into a deep sleep.

At around three in the morning, Simon Khan woke everyone up in the dark. "Your Highnesses, we need to get the horses moving or they will freeze." Inches of snow had settled on the camp, but the wind had finally stopped: the frenzied flurries of yesterday had given way to large, patient flakes that settled demurely on the ground and muted all sound. The men untied their horses' legs. On Simon Khan's signal, the snow-covered camp abruptly came to life. The horses, startled at the whistling and tugging of the riders, rose in that awkward way that horses stand up, shaking the snow off of the heavy rugs. The men began packing the mules.

Their pace on the third and fourth days was slow but deliberate. It snowed all day and night, never relenting until the afternoon of the fourth day. They stopped often to let the horses rest; the beasts tired easily, plunging their legs unceasingly into and out of snowdrifts. They camped at an abandoned farmstead, and Simon Khan ordered the men to make a shelter by tethering the black tentcloth to its derelict walls. They cut pieces of the mud walls to make crude, slow-burning bricks from their straw. Simon Khan knew they had to pick up the pace. They had brought food for five days and were running low: all that remained was dried bread and some figs. He estimated at least three more days of travel. The responsibility of the princes' safety weighed heavily on him.

The next day they woke again before dawn to bitter cold. Both boys' faces looked pinched and thin; their elder brother was in no better shape. The landscape, still purple in the waning moonlight, was unenticing: an untidy wilderness lay ahead of them, an unending vista of barrenness behind. A cacophony of jackals disturbed the peace; and distant silhouettes on the circular horizon were a sharp reminder of the presence of silent wolves. The horses shifted their weight on the thin, crunchy layer of icy snow, with the sound of dozens of crisp apples being bitten into all at once. The sun came up orange-colored, without heat, but soon it brightened into a chilly, sunny day.

Before noon they reached a shallow frozen river. For no reason at all, the sound of gurgling water beneath the ice revived them. Water ran along the shores of the river, splashing against the smooth pebbles, appearing and then disappearing under the ice. At this sign of life, after days of riding in the snow, Simon Khan celebrated privately. He believed they were now northwest of Hashtrood, a region of eight rivers running north-south. That meant the riders could reach Tabriz in two days. In the distance, among a few hovels near the frozen river, Simon Khan thought he could see some animals wandering about. He ordered the group to quicken their pace.

A pack of jackals sat in the middle of the river on the thicker ice, busily pulling at a carcass, probably the remains of a wolf kill. The sound of the horses did not disturb their feeding until the party was on top of them. The jackals now scattered, but they held their ground at a distance. Sneering suspiciously, bloody muzzles low to the ground, they watched the riders from a hundred yards downriver. The remnants of that feast would haunt the memories of all three boys for the rest of their lives: the half-eaten bodies of a woman and her two children, frozen to the ice, shamelessly exposing their insides for all to see. The cadavers lay supine, stomachs torn open and emptied as in an anatomy class, their extremities gone who knew where, their very faces chewed clean.

The horses circled awkwardly past the bodies. Beneath the clomping of their hooves on ice and snow, the muted river gargled. The jackals growled, in the distance. The men had eyes only for the young boys, whose silent tears lay frozen on their snowburnt cheeks.

They spent their coldest night yet. Simon Khan and Qodrat sat up all night, the boys sleeping between their legs, swaddled in the rugs and any other wrappings they could find.

Sardar Mirza coughed all night and awoke in the morning with a low fever. Simon Khan and Qodrat well understood the gravity of the situation. Every one of the escorts would be severely punished if any harm should come to the royal princes. Qodrat asked the feverish Prince to ride with him, but the boy refused. As always, they started out while it was still dark. Simon Khan pushed the horses even harder, well knowing that after a trip such as this they would be worthless in the bazaars of Tabriz.

An hour into their march, the horizon now streaked a dull red, Sardar Mirza's horse fell behind by twenty yards. He was accompanied by only one other rider, hanging back behind the column. Three wolves came out of nowhere to attack both horses simultaneously, light gray wolves who made up for their slight size by their quickness and strong jaws. The two thrashing horses, in a whinnying panic, ran into each other, nearly bringing both riders down.

The first two wolves focused on the guard's horse. The guard shouted for help and kept his head. Drawing his sword, he sliced at one of the wolves: it had bitten the back of his saddle and was suspended in the air by its own locked jaws. The sword ran across the wolf's muzzle, head, and left eye, producing a satisfying yelp. But continuing its trajectory, the sword now cut deep into the leg of the guard's horse, just above the stifle joint. The wounded horse lunged in pain, trampling the second wolf, which was trying to get a grip on the horse's smooth belly. The horse fell on top of the wolf, and the guard went flying into the deep snow on the ground. The wolf managed to squeeze out from beneath the horse and quickly scurried off.

The other riders had turned and now watched in horror as the third wolf bit deep into the hock of Sardar Mirza's horse. Simon Khan pulled out his gun and pressed his horse into a gallop. Sardar Mirza's horse, whinnying in pain, tried to disengage the wolf, kicking fiercely backwards again and again, with Sardar Mirza holding tightly onto his saddle. The wolf had bitten deep and would not be shaken off. Sardar Mirza would have been thrown but the traumatized horse suddenly gave up the fight. It sat back on its hind legs looking philosophical as the wolf tore viciously at it, head jerking left and right. Weakened by fever, Sardar Mirza gripped the saddle but was slipping helplessly backward. As Simon Khan pulled beside them, he shot the wolf with one hand and grabbed the boy with the other—just as the horse finally collapsed to the ground.

The two horses were bled to death using the same technique as had been used for the abandoned donkey. The twins now rode with Qodrat and Simon Khan. The coolheaded guard received a gold coin for his bravery; with his arm in a sling, he rode Saleh Mirza's horse. Sardar Mirza shook uncontrollably. Qodrat wrapped him as warmly as possible and held him in a tight bear hug as they rode together. The next day they reached the wide highway to Tabriz, just as the noon call for prayer sounded from the mosques of the city.

The city of Tabriz—known as Dâros-Saltaneh, "the abode of the kingdom"—once housed half a million people, as well as 300 caravanserais and 250 mosques, until it was devastated by the earthquake of 1780. It was now a flourishing city of 150,000. It was nicknamed the Fever-Dissipating City for its healthy climate, situated on a plain between rows of barren hills.

Simon Khan ordered the two guards to ride ahead to perform the traditional shout, "Make way, the princes are coming"—enforcing the warning with blows of their rods. Simon Khan wanted to get to the palace as soon as possible. They could already see the thick-walled Arch of Ali Shah, visible from all approaches to the city.

The travelers headed toward the oddly named Summer Palace, where Crown Prince Mohammad Ali had established himself that very winter. The palace, built in the southern part of the city, sat on seventy-five acres of gardens (inexplicably named the Northern Gardens). This fortunate location spared the travelers from having to cross the city. They approached through the entrance gate, a handsome brick arch, from which a long double avenue led to the palace. In front of the majestic fountain stood a group awaiting their arrival. Le Bœuf, tired and cold as he was, began to sweat: the time of reckoning was close at hand.

As the tired horsemen arrived at the fountain, Qodrat handed Sardar Mirza to a servant, who put him gingerly on the ground. Heedless of the horse's height, Saleh Mirza swung his legs to dismount; Simon Khan caught his arm in time to lower him carefully or the Prince would have fallen on his face. Saleh Mirza ran to hug his brother and whispered to him over and over again that all was well. Nearly unconscious, his brother hardly heard his words.

A tall, foreign young man stood in front of the waiting group: dressed in traditional tutor tails, and clean-shaven but for the immaculately barbered mustache curled to a thin perfection. He spoke to those gathered behind him without turning his head. "What they say about the Highnesses' dedication to one another is true. Our French-to-be Prince looks under the weather, *n'est-ce pas?*' He spoke with an atrocious Russian accent. This was twenty-three-year-old Seraya Shapshal, known to the Persiran court as Shapshal Khan, born in Bakhchysarai in the Crimea; a Karaite Jew, he was the Crown Prince's personal tutor. In less than ten years he would exchange his tails for a court minister's uniform, when his charge would be crowned. He emanated menace toward the young princes, speaking to Simon Khan over the boys' head with obvious contempt.

"Let's first clarify your situation, Your Grace. I cannot think of any circumstances under which the famous Simon Khan might disobey His Majesty's direct orders." He paused ominously. "We received an angry and confused telegram last week, from His Majesty's minister."

Simon Khan, not knowing the full extent of the situation, answered with the simple truth. "When I received the Crown Prince's order, I assumed you had cleared it with Tehran." His innocence pained Le Bœuf, standing behind the two boys, his hands on their shoulders.

"What order?" Shapshal Khan rolled his eyes and stretched out his hand. "The telegraph did mention an order from the Crown Prince. We have looked through all our records. No such order was sent to you."

Now Simon Khan drew the forged order from inside his jacket. The confusion on Shapshal Khan's face as he read the order gave Simon Khan confidence to look around, offering the boys a reassuring smile that stabbed at Le Bœuf.

"I wrote it myself—" he blurted out loudly, "—to keep my brothers together for a while longer." No need to let the charade continue; it was too painful for everyone involved. "Simon Khan knows nothing. I have the Crown Prince's seal, with our brother's compliments. I used it to fool everyone."

Simon Khan's smile froze and his face lost all color. "Your Highnesses—" he began to sputter.

"I asked him to do it," Saleh Mirza volunteered. "We just wanted to see Sardar Mirza off in Tabriz."

"Mais c'est charmant ça! Tant de courage," Shapshal pronounced. "Such charming courage. Now that that has been made clear, if Your Highnesses would follow me, the Crown Prince awaits you in the reception room, in the interior court." Simon Khan made to follow, but Shapshal stopped him with a curt gesture. "The Crown Prince wants to see his uncles in private."

"The boy is sick, and the other two are near exhaustion," Simon Khan whispered in the Russian's ear. "Let them rest first."

"That is up to the Crown Prince, Your Grace," said Shapshal Khan.

Shapshal and the three princes walked to the large interior court lined with flowerbeds. They entered a circular building with a marble fountain in the center, its bowl emptied for the winter. Shapshal knocked at the door of the reception room. Someone said, "Enter," in Turkish. They walked into a small room adorned with paintings of the foreign envoys who had visited Tabriz. The walls and ceilings were covered with tiny pieces of mirror. Standing behind a bureau, the Crown Prince looked younger than his twenty-four years. On each side of his puffed-up chest a matrix of medals adorned the smart black military uniform; nevertheless, he had the look of those spoiled, overweight adolescents who can be seen today in the malls of Dubai. He looked angry, though the drooping mustache and the pouting lower lip, much like a little boy about to cry, made it seem less serious.

The Crown Prince listened while Shapshal Khan whispered the circumstances. The court minister in Tehran had sent a number of telegrams in search of explanations, accusing the Crown Prince's court of incompetence. But now the Crown Prince's mood improved. He talked to the boys at first in Turkish. Seeing that they did not understand, he switched to the Turkish-accented Farsi they all understood.

"Welcome, my uncles," he said. "Before putting this incident behind us, we need to let Tehran know that you have arrived. Thanks to God, you are alive. I hear you had a trying trip. We will need to clarify to our father and friends in Tehran the circumstances leading to this use of our seal, you understand. And we have a small problem. Once we send the telegram to Tehran, they will invariably ask what punishment I have decreed for this instance of *lèse-majesté*. We ask you, why wait for the inevitable question? Don't answer, because we have often asked the same question of ourselves, and we come to the same answer each time. Let's not waste a telegram. Let us mete out your punishment quickly and be done with it." He rubbed his hands, satisfied that all angles of the problem had been addressed. "We will witness the *bastinado* outside, immediately," he instructed the tutor.

"Your Highness," Le Bœuf began. His words came tumbling out. "The young princes had nothing to do with this. A *bastinado* could kill him"—he pointed to Sardar Mirza, who swayed, leaning on his brother. "Look at him, Your Highness. He is burning with fever."

"Don't overdramatize," the Crown Prince replied. "Take your punishment and be done with it. But then we want you and your brother to leave us immediately to go back to Tehran. We don't want to see you around our palace again."

The cruelty of this new order took a moment to sink in. Besides the danger of the *bastinado* for Sardar Mirza, to force the others—in January!—to repeat the trip they had just experienced could mean death for both Le Bœuf and Saleh Mirza.

By the time Shapshal escorted them outside, a crowd of courtiers had gathered in silence. This vicious punishment was one practiced regularly by the courts, the government offices, and the schools. The practice did not necessarily diminish the person being beaten; it had been meted out to ministers and premiers, who would then return to their duties. But to beat three princes of the realm at once was unprecedented. A strip of ground had been cleared of snow. Silk carpets lay on the ground. All respect was shown to the rank of the victims.

The three boys lay next to one another, a few feet apart. Sardar Mirza fell asleep—or passed out—immediately, lying with his hand outstretched in his twin brother's hand. Saleh Mirza, in the middle position, kept his head turned toward his twin. After this day, it would be ten years before he saw his brother again. The princes' feet were bared, and a man with a thin waspy waist asked their pardon. He placed a bamboo pole under all six feet, beneath the ankles. He placed another bamboo pole of similar size on top of their ankles. He then firmly tied the two ends of the bamboo sticks, so that the feet stuck out between the sticks.

They waited this way for about ten minutes until the Crown Prince emerged, followed by Shapshal Khan. No speeches. There were around forty witnesses, among them Simon Khan and Qodrat—the latter using his beard to collect and hide his tears. The Crown Prince made a sign, and two muscular servants picked up the bamboo poles and raised them from the ground, so that the six soles pointed to the sky. Three mustachioed men picked out three long sticks from a bundle on the ground. They whipped each stick in the air with a deft wrist movement, listening for the pure note with heads on one side, like dogs before a hunt. A pure note meant no internal cracks. Once each had found his perfect stick, two of them took their places on each side, to flog sideways at the feet of Sardar Mirza and Le Bœuf. Another placed himself in the middle, to lash out the length of Saleh Mirza's feet—a more difficult position that needed care not to break the toes.

It was the twenty-eighth of January, 1896, a leap year, a Tuesday. It was late afternoon and cold. The soft northern light lent the scene a tragic atmosphere. Three strong arms stretched up into the air, and three sticks came all the way back past three men's shoulders, bouncing gently with their own weight. The men waited for the Crown Prince to give the final nod. The young princes' frozen, reddened soles were about to get skinned. Later the Shah, a fleetingly kind man, was genuinely incensed when he heard of the princes' treatment by his eldest son. His anger lasted a day.

Saleh Mirza and Le Bœuf were escorted out of the city the very next day, not knowing whether Sardar Mirza would survive. It would be days before they could walk. At the end of each day's riding in the fierce cold, servants carried them from their mounts to the camp, a bitter humiliation for Le Bœuf.

Saleh Mirza barely survived the trip back to the capital. It took months to restore him to health. He survived by feeding on his hatred and anger, rehearsing bitterly every moment they had spent in the company of the Crown Prince. He would mature into a taciturn character who saw life as a series of random events to be borne without complaint, a man with a strong moral structure. He believed that his travails had prepared him some day to redress injustice through the exercise of power—though it would be many years before he understood what that power was.

Sardar Mirza also nearly died. He lay in bed for weeks with the doctors in attendance. The Crown Prince, fearful of the consequences, kept his illness a secret. Astonishingly, Sardar Mirza emerged from the ordeal with a *joie de vivre* that lasted him a lifetime. He seldom placed himself in situations where life could deal him a bad hand, believing that, by steering cleverly, he could avoid life's blows. From this philosophy he also developed a habit of not thinking too deeply about the past. Beauty attracted him. Ugliness repelled him.

After Norooz—the first day of spring—Simon Khan, Qodrat, and Sardar Mirza began their journey toward Paris. They would take what was then the most direct route, crossing the Caucasus and the Black Sea to Odessa. From there the railways would give them many ways to reach Paris. Thin and drawn, the Prince had lost his boyishness, but his eyes still brimmed with humor. The Crown Prince, feeling an improbable smidgen of guilt, had agreed to send an accompanying guard as far as Urumiah. There they engaged a coach-and-six, upholstered in thick, cherry-colored, buttoned leather, to travel the three hundred fifty miles to Tiflis. The carriage, essentially a house on wheels, had a large box reserved for the ladies and a smaller one for the male passengers. Simon Khan sat in the male section, but the Prince rode on top of the carriage next to the Cossack driver, a Taras Bulba type who wielded his whip as if signing historic documents. At every stop, this driver would invite all kinds of men to punch him in the stomach; he laughed aloud at everything Sardar Mirza said, though he understood not a word.

With the return of spring, the cold now merely refreshed Sardar Mirza. Thanks to their triple-crown *podorozhnaya*—the Russian license that gave them priority for fresh horses at every stop—they made great time covering the three hundred fifty miles, most of it through Russian territory. They traveled via Julfa, entering Russia via the rope ferry across the Aras River, and headed toward the ancient city of Nakhichevan and on to Tiflis.

At night they stayed free of charge in the two-room Russian post-houses. Newfangled English-made iron telegraph poles accompanied them all the way to Europe, courtesy of Messrs. Siemens, who bore some responsibility for the princes' punishment in Tabriz: the new system conveyed messages with such efficiency.

They arrived in Tiflis at midday in a torrent of rain that turned everything to mud. The Kur runs through the city, dividing itself to create an island in the middle. Water had washed over the bridges in the fog-drenched afternoon; the population in the streets went about their business. In any other city, a royal traveler might have gone directly to the palace of Grand Duke Michael as an honored guest. But the people of Tiflis harbored great reservations about the Qajar dynasty: only a hundred years earlier, Agha Mohammad Khan, Sardar Mirza's ancestor, had sacked the city and demolished all its churches.

The city, famous for its sulfur baths, was divided into colonies. The Russian colony with its large buildings lorded over the Oriental section. Outside the city, 150,000 Russians bunked in barracks on the hillsides: a show of force to all the Caucasian minorities, though directed mainly at the Turks farther to the west. Throughout the city the travelers glimpsed the colorful uniforms of Russian Cossack officers.

The Arabic name for the Caucasus is Jabal al-Alsun, "the mountain of languages." In Tiflis you could hear them all. Ossetians spoke to Tajiks in a muddled Farsi. The Mingrelian beggar snubbed a handout from an Abkhazian refugee. The intellectual Talysh, over a shared hookah, encouraged his Lezgian brother to resist the Russian tyranny. Peasant Tartars bought silver-stamped daggers from Persiran merchants. German millenarians argued about the second coming of Christ with the Greek Orthodox. Animated by the fervor of a family feud, Talmudic Jews fought anti-Talmudic Jews. Turks narrowed their eyes at Armenian shopkeepers with a deep distrust that would one day blossom into bloodlust. And the hotel-owning French competed with stiff-collared English diplomats to dominate the rest.

Simon Khan, now in his element, made straight for the American store and purchased some newly introduced, off-the-rack suits that required only the smallest of adjustments. He bought a trunkful of Western clothes for them all: white starched shirts, waistcoats, silk socks, shoes, and a pair of galoshes each. Sardar Mirza, a born dandy, would later recount with peals of laughter their first Western shopping spree; the notion of wearing off-the-rack American suits would astonish his aristocratic French friends.

Simon Khan lodged them at the Hotel de Londres, to catch the train to Poti the following day. This hotel, the first European-style hotel Sardar Mirza had ever experienced, introduced Qodrat and him to the concept of modern plumbing. Bathing in a tubful of water occasioned murmurs of disgust at wallowing in one's dirt, and no amount of coaching could persuade either of them to sit on a toilet seat. For the rest of their trip, they squatted on the seats of various hotel toilets without allowing any part of their bodies to come in contact with the porcelain. (Later, of course, Sardar Mirza would have to deal with the smirks of the other schoolboys—nothing like peer pressure to encourage a change of habit.) During dinner, no amount of aristocratic bluff could evade the difficulties of eating the *potage du jour* with an actual spoon. Simon Khan's task was far more difficult than Professor Higgins's assignment—to convince his pupil to lower his standards and eat with utensils.

It rained all night. In the morning the foot-swallowing quagmire in the streets required either bare feet or galoshes. Dainty women dressed in European-style dresses, their faces covered in the *hijab*, hopped on the backs of strong Albanian water-carriers to cross the street. Men lost their shoes with the sound of a champagne cork. The Prince and his companions rode a phaeton to the railway station, a monumental building set miles outside town, a harbinger of massive Soviet architecture. On a number of occasions Simon Khan scattered a few worthless coins to induce bystanders to push the large carriage wheels out of the mud.

The train had begun running to the Black Sea port of Poti twenty-five years before; it had not changed much since. The Prince sat next to the window in the first-class compartment, staring at the scenery with the eagerness of a boy watching television. His eyes, unused to the color green, marveled at the beech and pine forests interspersed with well-cultivated fields bursting with Indian corn. The deep valleys filled with fruit trees and ferns, the mounds of thistles decorated with their red and bruise-colored berries, all marched past his eyes, changing height and size as they magically moved up and down at the same speed as the train.

In 1897, the port of Poti, built on marshland known for its flies and frogs (an English pub perhaps, The Frog and Fly?), had much in common with American gold rush towns circa 1849. The city's famous mayor, Niko Nikoladze, was in the early stages of rebuilding Poti, and the town had an unfinished look. They stayed three days at the Hotel Jacquot (barely tolerable) before boarding a flat-bottomed steamer to take them to the river mouth, and then another steamer for the five-day trip around the Black Sea to Odessa. A few of their fellow passengers from the train accompanied them for this part of the journey. Two Russian generals, four or five rich Turkish merchants with their red fezzes, half a dozen English diplomats, and a French aristocrat with his wife and three daughters, all settled into the first class cabins on the upper decks, where our Persiranian prince was berthed, along with Simon Khan. The second class, consigned to the boredom of the bourgeoisie, was where Qodrat was relegated, along with the other servants and nannies of the first-class passengers, when they were not attending to their employers. On the lowest deck, in third class, a multitude of diverse ethnicities milled around in confusion, surrounded by their makeshift luggage. An uneasy sea could quickly soak them to the skin.

Few places display the mixture of Eastern and Western side-by-side as do the ports around the Black Sea. Nevertheless, strict separation existed. The Europeans considered the Persiranians—the Orientals—savages in need of Christian enlightenment. Simon Khan understood this well and continued to teach the young prince Western ways of behaving, to diminish his chances of embarrassing himself in the dining room.

The steamer started its five-day tramp to Odessa by rounding the Abkhazian coast. Seen from the portholes, the big timber forests sailed uniformly by. Simon Khan spent the afternoon walking the decks to meet some of his fellow first-class passengers. "I am His Royal Highness's secretary. Forgive the interruption, but His Royal Highness would consider it an honor if you would join him at his table for dinner." The Prince, as the brother of a king—a duke, in the terms of the English peerage—had the prerogative to invite any of his fellow passengers to his table. To refuse would be *lèse-majesté*. Of course, the fact that the Shah had perhaps dozens of children and brothers might undercut the comparison a little. Simon Khan took advantage of this confusion to bolster Sardar Mirza's position at every turn.

In choosing dinner companions, Simon Khan sought out the most fluent French speakers as well as those who would be most agreeable to his ward. He had noticed Sardar Mirza's lack of hauteur and saw it as a distinct disadvantage. Today we interpret hauteur as superciliousness; but a measure of loftiness, Simon Khan firmly believed, was necessary in a royal personage. It established the distance necessary to forbid any questioning by the common man.

Simon Khan chose Pyotr Alexeyevich Krasnov, a hearty graduate of the Junker Infantry School in St. Petersburg who wore a chestful of medals from the Crimean War, along with his neurasthenic wife. Simon Kahn also befriended another passenger, a stuttering young English secretary by the name of Mr. Scott, whose superiors had discovered that he had a French mother. Hoping to repair his damaged career, he was then traveling back to England to make a good marriage. (Years later, Mr. Scott, as a middle-aged bureaucrat assigned to the Tehran Embassy, would be of great help to the twins.)

Simon Khan made a far more momentous decision that day: he extended a dinner invitation to one Monsieur le Comte de Grandpierre, who was traveling with his three daughters, prettily arrayed in muslin and lace. Each of the three young ladies would meet her future husband during this pleasant Crimean trip. The eldest, Catherine, a voluble fourteen-year-old, had met on their way to Odessa an Italian aristocrat: though one of the rare Italian aristocrats who was not a pauper, his lineage lacked the clarity required by Monsieur le Comte. The second daughter, Régine, thirteen years old and the prettiest of the three, would meet (in Yalta) a Volkonsky from the famous Russian family—but he too was deemed ineligible, having indeed been made a pauper by the Russian Revolution. And twelve-year-old Anaïs de Grandpierre would marry Sardar Mirza twenty-six years later, after meeting him again at a party given by André Gide; the unlucky count would oppose this match as well, to a wastrel Oriental. All three daughters eventually eloped, allowing *le tout Paris* to speak of poor old Monsieur le Comte as their own King Lear.

The steamer's first-class dining room, outfitted in mahogany, leather, and brass, held six round tables—five smaller ones surrounding the largest like the petals of a flower. The tables were set with pink, hand-painted Sevres plates depicting the French countryside, layered in threes with their soup bowls on top. The Baccarat cut-glass stemware danced its reflections on the Gorham's silver settings. A glistening black piano the size of a swimming pool served as a mirror for the glittering chandelier.

Did the two twelve-year-olds, at this initial meeting, experience love at first sight? Self-consciousness prevailed, though each of them had an intense (if not painful) awareness of the other's presence. Sardar Mirza sat almost silent in tie and tails; the soft hair on his face and arms shone a dusty gold, his hair jet-black. Anaïs was a wispy, elegant girl, with deep, round eyes that expressed a heartbreaking sensitivity. Sitting properly—her long legs crossed, one foot hooked behind the other—she, too, said little. Nevertheless, over the next few days, the two would establish a bond strong enough to survive years with no contact.

The Comte offered a short, Germanic bow to Sardar Mirza, who acknowledged it with a practiced gentle recognition. The future father-in-law then introduced each of his daughters by name. Sardar Mirza welcomed them with a few of his best sentences, as if repeating the-rain-in-Spain-stays-mainly-on-the-plain. Mr. Scott did the same, but with a pronounced stutter that the children witnessed with horror, as if watching an exhausted runner limp across the finish line.

General Krasnov, unconcerned with ceremony, greeted the young prince with some affection: he slapped him on the back, winked, and even made a coin disappear behind HRH's ear, to the delight of all the children. Sardar Mirza laughed aloud—and then quickly restored the inscrutable royal countenance he had practiced at Simon Khan's behest. Thanks to such breaches of etiquette, the dinner thawed, and Sardar Mirza's sphinxlike pose disappeared, never to return. Simon Khan and the rest of the adults, grasping the situation for what it was, allowed a degree of latitude normally reserved to the first days of summer vacation. The general recounted so many amusing stories that even the Comte joined in with a few of his own, making his daughters exclaim, "Papa!" in delighted disapproval. So began five days of adventure, camping, and picnics, with expeditions into port towns, countrysides, and palaces with endless corridors.

Their first stop was Novorossiysk, on the northern coast of the Black Sea, just then celebrating its first anniversary of Novorossiysk's designation as the official capital of the Black Sea Governorate of the Russian Empire. The fireworks in the port enthralled them all. The Comte remained aboard, watching them from the ship. The city's brass band played some loud and indistinguishable martial songs as the crowd's approving roar greeted each brilliant spattering of the dark sky. Sardar Mirza and the three girls weaved among the crowds, with poor Qodrat following as best he could in their wake. The three young ladies were in the charge of Mademoiselle Marte, the French governess—who divided her attention between Mr. Scott and Simon Khan, despite the latter's disapproval of her reckless and lovely laughter.

The children gave the slip to Qodrat and Mademoiselle without even trying. Large as a giant, his black beard reaching his belly, Qodrat drew the attention of the crowd, who made it hard for him to pass through. The three girls and Sardar Mirza found themselves a perch on a sea wall, far from the noise. The girls removed their shoes and socks and had Sardar Mirza do the same. Naked feet dangling, they shrieked every time a large wave hit the wall, the foam climbing like an ominous shadow to spatter and tickle their feet. Sardar Mirza's attention never wavered from Anaïs, the quietest of the three sisters. The attraction was understood: the two older sisters never interfered. They all enjoyed that evening together—but Anaïs de Grandpierre and Sardar Mirza enjoyed it more.

At noon the next day, the steamer anchored at Kerch, a small though ancient village only eighty miles up the coast that formed lying between the Black Sea and the Sea of Azov, the shallowest sea in the world. But the girls had received a tongue-lashing from the Comte, for disappearing so thoughtlessly and worrying Mademoiselle Marte—and for this crime, much to Sardar Mirza's disappointment, they were now restricted to the steamer.

There was no question of punishing the Prince for his own delinquency. Mr. Scott, an excellent tour guide, invited Sardar Mirza and Simon Khan to accompany him to the Kerch hilltops. There they saw breathtaking views of Asia and Europe in their eternal geological embrace, and, closer by, the ruins of the ancient acropolis where King Mithridates committed suicide rather than surrender to Pompey the Great.

Dinner that evening was followed by games of Messenger Boy, Ludo, and Snakes and Ladders, restoring peace between children and adults. The next day, a warm rain kept everyone inside, as the steamer made its way toward Yalta on the Russian Riviera. From there, the group planned to cover the 35 miles to Sevastopol by land, much to the delight of the children. The steamer would pick them up 24 hours later.

Simon Khan had made sure to forward Sardar Mirza's itinerary to Yalta, to the Crimean office of the Grand Duke, without specifying in his telegram the age of his highness. The reply he received, however, conveyed regret that the Duke would not be available—

and still more regret that the Grand Palace at Livadia was closed for repair. The Grand Master of Ceremonies instead offered His Royal Highness the hospitality of the small palace at Livadia, known as the Maliy Palace (where Czar Alexander III had died, three years earlier). For how long, the Grand Master wished to know, would His Royal Highness take residence?

Cutting its roaring engines, the boat churned into Yalta's newly built artificial harbor at around three in the afternoon, to the accompaniment of hundreds of squawking gulls. A warm drizzle made an oil painting of the landscape. Deep in the background, through layers of fog, lay the Crimean Mountains. Nestled in a ring of verdant hills, Yalta had captured the hearts of three successive czarinas since the reign of Czar Alexander II, gradually transforming itself from a lethargic village to a summer resort.

Two imperial landaus stood in the shade of the cypress trees, awaiting the party's arrival. In their festive holiday mood, they chose to leave the landaus to the general's valet, along with Qodrat and Mademoiselle Marte. (Poor Mr. Scott had fallen ill and remained on the steamer.) The rest of the group walked the three miles to Maliy Palace, their voices echoing loudly from the woods on each side as they climbed the winding, hilly road in a light drizzle. A thin veil of fog hung around the cedars, pines, and wild chestnuts. Lower down the sloping mountainside, the sea gently washed the rocky shores, again and again.

Monsieur le Comte spoke of a new sparkling wine produced on an estate only a few miles down the road. The three girls, wearing the white sailor costumes just then in fashion, made quick sorties into the forest to pick mushrooms, berries, and flowers. Sardar Mirza joined them, no longer self-conscious: in those few short days his French had improved. The general played the clown, wearing one of his wife's silk scarves around his head while gallantly holding an umbrella over hers.

One by one, the chirpy conversations quieted to silence. Coming up from the rear, the general called loudly to his wife, who merely smiled and motioned for him to look up.

Embraced in gentle swirls of mist, there stood Maliy Palace, glowing in the late afternoon. It resembled a colossal Spanish galleon with an enchanted forest woven around her. Green vines and tangles of clematis, mixed with roses, wisteria, and honeysuckle, had crawled through the geometric wooden fretwork that covered the light pink walls. Fussy ornaments and decorative pilasters gave the building a frail, lived-in look. Water was gurgling down all the gutters that day. Low in the southern sky, shards of crimson light broke through the clouds, penetrating the thick oaks and chestnuts and turning the hundreds of windowpanes into arrayed sheets of fiery copper. Half a dozen giant cypresses stood guard, taller than the palace itself. Islands of shrubbery appeared among sunken rose gardens; the thickets of laurel, myrtle, rhododendron, and curious herbs lent the air a redolence of pine, mint, lime, and vetiver.

Cossack guards in long blue coats and bearskin hats had gathered the group's sparse luggage from the imperial landaus. Five of them now stood at attention in front, awaiting their arrival. A frail, stooped, tall, silver-haired man dressed in tails pushed past the guard and moved toward the guests. Bred over generations to glide silently on smooth marble or parquet floors, he trod uncomfortably on the gravel, with exaggerated care. Now he lowered his head in a simulacrum of a bow to the Comte: his natural stoop limited the extent to which he might bend his arthritic body.

"Welcome, Your Highness, to Maliy." Long attuned to any hint of diplomatic *faux pas*, the steward needed only a slight movement of the Comte's eye, with an accompanying discreet cough, to swivel smoothly in midsentence toward Sardar Mirza.

"I am Ruslan Papkov, the royal butler, at your service. Your Highness, may I tonight also introduce to you Count Volkonsky, who is also a guest of His Majesty the czar?" Sardar Mirza gave his casual acknowledgement—painstakingly learned—that all the arrangements suited him. The three girls, safely shielded from the butler's view, smirked at both of them.

"*The* Count Volkonsky?" asked Comte de Grandpierre.

"The *young* Count Volkonsky, sire."

A third son-in-law for Monsieur le Comte, in the space of a fortnight.

They would meet him at dinner—a shy, slight, fifteen-year-old noble, wearing spectacles. He had opted to stay at the palace instead of following his father on a week-long hunting trip. He had little trouble fitting into the group, having already caught the eye of Régine, the prettiest de Grandpierre sister.

Following Papkov inside, they found a children's paradise. The marquetry on the floors, made of well-oiled contrasting woods, was perfect for skating in woolen socks. Room after room was filled with overstuffed sofas covered in cretonne and chintz, chairs in lace-patterned silks decorated with moiré ribbons, and mahogany desks inlaid with gilded leather and burdened with neatly stacked, unread books. There were wood statues of laughing, turbaned black slaves carrying plates of food; gold clocks supported by intertwined Greek wrestlers; and bronze mythological characters caught at the midpoint of their human-to-animal transformations. Chaotic objects were strewn about pell-mell on large and small tables: multi-jointed silver fish, porcelain frogs, ceramic Staffordshire greyhounds, glass knickknacks of every shape. Heavy silver daguerreotypes, so thickly arranged that each overlapped the next, showed three generations of royal children catching butterflies, rowing boats, or posing *en famille*. In short, each room was a family room in the Victorian home of a particularly well-to-do man.

Papkov himself was a greater surprise. All evening, he recommended games with a twinkle in his eye. In his lifetime of serving Czar Alexander III, he had witnessed the most undisciplined family life in all the European courts. The unassuming czar was simple in taste; he and his Danish czarina, who had grown up in the least pretentious court in Europe, encouraged freedoms among their children that shocked the Russian aristocracy. A somersault or two had even been seen at court.

The maids and servants welcomed this newly arrived group of children with pleased indulgence: the palace had felt like a morgue since the death of the old czar. (The Comte, General Krasnov, and Simon Khan paid a price for the general lack of structure, enduring a less-than-mediocre evening meal. Cooking had not in any case been a priority for the old czar, and now the butler had simply replaced the late chef with a cook hired from an inn in Yalta.) After dinner, Papkov suggested a game of hide-and-seek. General Krasnov, in his usual cheerful mood, volunteered to be "it.' As the children scattered in all directions, Krasnov promptly took his seat in the living room to enjoy a cognac with his companions, while his wife chided him for tricking the children.

"Pyotr, you cannot leave them out there all night."

"Ninety-eight," the general yelled. "Oh, my dear, you forget," he murmured, sotto voce. Turning his head once more toward the staircase, he hollered, "ninety-nine"—and again whispered to his wife: "All the fun is in the hiding, no?" Then, the grand finale, he bellowed: "One hundred!"

Sure enough, the young Volkonsky had followed the pretty Régine down a hallway. Catherine, feeling older and not up to playing, sneaked into the library to read. Anaïs and Sardar Mirza had tiptoed up the narrow staircase and raced through the upstairs corridor. Darting into a corner bedroom, they failed to notice the black ribbon pinned to its door. Moonlight from the tall windows filled the bedroom where Alexander III had succumbed to chronic interstitial nephritis a few years before. The white walls and polished parquet floors reflected a creamy blue light.

The two children whispered and giggled as they looked around. Next to the overstuffed armchair where the czar had spent his last minutes, a white cross marked the floor. The cream-colored cashmere blanket used by the czar had been folded there lovingly. A small Napoleon III chandelier hung from the ceiling, faceted with black silhouette portraits on ivory and adorned with four dangling velvet tassels. Two oak-carved miniature armoires, resembling medicine cabinets, were attached to the walls. The French windows opened to a small balcony that looked out over the Black Sea.

Anaïs walked to the cross on the floor, and then, with a glint in her eye, asked Sardar Mirza to come and stand in front of her. They stood silently for a minute, subdued by the moonlight spilling over them and the cross. She whispered to Sardar Mirza, "You will marry me when we are older, *n'est-ce pas?*"

"*Oui,*" answered Sardar Mirza. All the prepubescent tensions of the last days drained out of them. They might have been (as they would be some day) a middle-aged couple in love. Like all lovers, they would relive the moment of this unconventional proposal. Anaïs de Grandpierre, later known simply as the Countess, never forgave the destruction of Maliy, supplanted by the neo-Renaissance Livadia Palace with its Florentine towers, host to the Yalta Conference.

1001

Just in that enchanted moment the doorknob creaked, making them run behind the czar's capacious bedroom chair. For those interminable seconds before the door opened, the two experienced that delicious fright known by all children the world over. Then they heard the kindly voice of Ruslan Papkov:

"Children, Your Highness, may I be so bold as to request that you find a more suitable hiding place? The empress would be angry indeed, if she learns that I have allowed anybody in this room, even such distinguished guests as yourselves."

⚘

They set out for Sevastopol, and the steamer, early the next morning—a bright, sunny day. The imperial carriages had been put at their disposal by Papkov, and, as they began to move, the visitors waved with enthusiasm at the farewell party arrayed in front of the palace. Papkov smiled. The young Volkonsky looked forlorn. The maids waved handkerchiefs. The guards showed no emotion.

They kept the sea on their left, choosing the coast road to climb 2000 feet through lush subtropical vegetation. The children were dejected, anticipating the end of their adventure. That evening they sailed toward Odessa, the steamer's final destination. As the sun set under a cobalt sky with a few cloudy flourishes, the white churches and houses of Sevastopol, though battered, were bathed in pink. It looked lovely—if anyone had cared to look.

In Odessa, the parties separated. The general and his wife remained in that city for the final month of his life. The Grandpierre family continued to Trieste and then Venice, to return in late August to Paris. Mr. Scott was bound for London. Simon Khan, Qodrat, and Sardar Mirza boarded a train to their final destination, the Gare du Nord in Paris. We will wait twenty-six years for the betrothed couple to meet again; Mr. Scott will meet both of the twins within ten years.

At this point the Professor fell silent at last. I felt him float away. I dreamt of the two princes. In my dreams I mourned their separation.

The Third Night
0011

The Not-So-Omniscient Narrator Intrudes
Again and Again

*"It can't be helped, I prefer my vices to my
friends."*

— Marcel Proust

Dear Ms. Vakil,

Your suspicious questions warm my heart. You are
genuinely interested: it appears, as they say in my
adopted country, that I have hit a home run. Both my
grandfathers played roles in the Constitutional
Revolution that will make you proud. You dropped—
for a brief few sentences—your veil of courtesy to
question, maybe too sharply, the authenticity and
provenance of my documents.

Let me assure you that the historical documents in
my possession are not a mere fictional device. They
were stored in my paternal grandmother's house. You
know from your own research that Prince Saleh Mirza,
my paternal grandfather, had three wives. The first
wife, was, like him, a descendent of Naser al-Din Shah—
a granddaughter of the Shah. Our family tree resembles
an ingrowing toenail. I do not have to remind you of the
science regarding inbreeding. The second wife, a
woman of good family, was invisible to all, and I will not
mention her existence again. The third wife, Choti,
needs no introduction to you, Ms. Vakil, as she is famous
in her own right. Her role in our lives, brief though
monumental in its consequences, has never been fully
revealed; clickety-clack, out comes the first skeleton.

I met her, for the first and only time, the day
Khomeini returned from Paris. I had just returned
home, dejected from the synchronized hysteria of a few
million people, when my Bengali servant ran out all
aflutter, talking in his mix of pigeon Farsi and English:
"Mr. Poonaki sir, Mam come to the house. She push me
sir. She sits *patisaloon*." By now an expert at decoding

the man's argot, I understood that some woman sat waiting for me in the petit salon where I had my office. I opened the door to see a figure standing with her back to me, admiring on the wall a custom jigsaw puzzle of my French maternal grandmother.

"Except for that," she pointed to the jigsaw, "little has changed." The woman turned to face me: a compact, thin woman of seventy, white hair à la brosse, wearing a severe grey tweed ensemble like a British matron of the twenties. Not a trace of humor in her face.

"Can I help you?" I asked.

She came over and, to my surprise, took hold of my face with both hands, angling her head back to better inspect me. "You are a copy of your father," she said. "Maybe a bit thinner. What on earth did you do to your face?"

I pulled my face back abruptly. "What I can do for you, madam?" I dislike people referring to my defacement.

"Nothing whatsoever. I am your grandmother, and I wanted to take a good look at you. You have turned out all right."

And that is how I met, for the first time and only time, the infamous Jaleh Darbandi, nicknamed Choti by my grandfather. Her father, a school teacher (and later my grandfather's secretary), had filled her head with ideas of democracy from his experience of the 1906 Revolution. As a teenager, she earned a reputation for wearing a *hat* beneath her veil. And when, in 1936, the autocratic Reza Shah forbade women to wear the veil, she walked out in the street that day—shoulders back, not an ounce of self-doubt—with her thick, brown waves of hair blowing in the wind. It almost caused a riot. One of the clerics mentioned the incident in the parliament, with a reference to Caesar's wife. She later cut her hair short and left my grandfather abruptly, when my father was only eleven years old.

"*Grandmother?* Aren't you supposed to be living in Moscow?" An unabashed member of the KGB, she held (I understood) a teaching position at Lumumba University in Moscow. Thanks to Nima (her son and my father), she had managed to escape with her life during the Azerbaijan fiasco in 1946.

"Well, plus ça change, plus ça change," she replied. "We have a new situation. That blood-thirsty Shah can no longer do us harm. These asswipe mullahs can't tell their right hand from their left. We are finally ready to run the country. *It is only matter of time before we inherit the earth!*" And in two shakes of a duck's tail, she had turned our reunion into a political morass, championing the discredited Marxist remnant.

I must have protested, because the next moment I felt a sharp slap. "Just like your father—a monarchist to his dying day!" Her eyes blazed, almost feverish. By god, this woman could have been Colonel Klebb, the SMERSH agent in the James Bond movie *From Russia With Love,* played (for keeps) by Lotte Lenya. This woman was no different than the religious zealots out there. Her eyes, bird-like, jittered around my face.

"Does it work?" I asked.

"Does what work?" she spat.

"The slapping. Because you are going to have to slap *a lot* of people to have them buy into your righteous ways."

She laughed; under the desiccated exterior, I caught a glimpse of her former youth. My father had talked about Choti's physicality—but I hadn't expected a frontal attack from an old woman I had known for only a few minutes.

We made peace for the next hour or so. I showed her the gazebo-cum-house behind the main house, where she had lived as one of three wives of my grandfather. It had stood unoccupied for close to forty years. My grandfather had willed it to this woman standing before me.

From the day she left, the fully furnished house had been cleaned daily, as if the mistress of the house was expected any moment. My grandfather's practice was to spend one night of the week with each of his wives. He kept the habit, spending the third night—always a Thursday night—alone in Choti's house. If he brought a gift for any of his wives, he brought one for her and placed it in the empty gazebo, even years after she had left him, creating no end of jealousy and talk by his two wives. They could not compete with her memory.

Choti laughed at all the artifice. "Did he really think I would come back? *He*," pointing around, "all this was stifling. I couldn't bear it. *He*," she again pointed with both hands at the heavy furniture, "all this was my way out." She defended her cynical opportunism: "He got a bargain. I gave him *me*." A suggestive gesture of both hands indicated her lower body. "And of course, I gave him his only son, your father."

To her, preserving the little house intact was a ridiculous act of folly. Not a moment of sentimental reflection crossed her mind. Later that evening she left the house through the back door—a habit from years of being on the run, probably the way she left forty-three years before.

A couple of years later, at seventy-four, Choti died in Evin, the famous Tehran prison—unrepentant, and no doubt with a clear picture of how the country should be run. A Russian spy, one Vladimir Kuzichkin, had revealed to the British a list of Soviet agents in Iran. She would have been outraged if her name had been omitted. The British, forever loyal to their tradition of duplicity, passed the information to the Islamic Republic.

Imagine: giving an old woman over to this regime. She did better than I, who lasted only nine days and nights.

My three paternal great-grandmothers' houses were close enough to the main house that the sneeze of Gorbun-Ali, the main house's doorman, could be heard. They were identical: three large, two-story gazebos, hexagonal, facing the main building, with full-length windows on both floors. Each house had a long, narrow garden in back with a door opening to the back street, giving its occupants private access.

The two remaining wives died within three months of each other; their two houses were boarded up and never lived in again. Over the years, the houses were used for storage, but in my time there, even that practice had ceased, and the buildings had deteriorated beyond salvage. The insides smelled musty. I remember large wooden crates sitting in the middle of the room, packed with large, expensive furniture, all abandoned. A few smaller, cheaper settees lingered nearby with their upholstery and springs exposed, rotted by water and consumed by termites. The paneling had splintered. The windows, all broken, had been boarded up with wood and brick. Crumbling plaster from the ceiling threw a gauze of dust over everything.

Everything: Closets filled with half a century of mildewed clothing. Hatboxes strewn about, some empty, others holding unworn hats with complicated netting. Stacks of trunks and suitcases, filled with gold-braided court uniforms, morning coats, and wedding suits. Tuxedos, once shiny and black, were now maps, traced with soft contours of milky mold. More: Walking sticks, ceremonial swords, yellow-hued daguerreotypes; papers, notebooks, and camera equipment spanning decades of technological breakthroughs—timers, flashes, light meters. There was even a German Luger. The abandoned houses were a paradise for exploring kids.

The third gazebo, the one I had shown Choti, I finally boarded up a few days after her visit, and just before my arrest. I used well-worn rather than new boards, to match the other two.

I had arranged, through a so-called friend of the family, to use the diplomatic pouch of the Spanish consulate to send out two suitcases of documents, as well as two Qajar paintings that by themselves would have made unnecessary my consignment to technical writing. The suitcases, deemed worthless, only arrived in Boston a full ten years later—well after the time I first saw you. The paintings never did. Somewhere in Alicante, a thieving consul undersecretary is lying to a roomful of friends about how he met some art dealer on Manouchehri Avenue during the last days of the Shah and purchased for nothing (*para nada*, giving a Spanish shrug) these two treasures of Qajar portraiture. How the suitcases made their way to me at last I cannot reveal. It would expose an innocent man to needless danger.

To give you some confidence, I have mailed to you the letter that Le Bœuf forged and sealed with the Crown Prince's stamp. I think you will agree that our old street scribe was not a bad calligrapher. Consider it a crumb marking your path to academic fame.

My grandfathers' correspondence, while they grew up, contains much of interest about their childhood experiences and establishes their separation as *the* momentous event in their lives. Saleh Mirza has written factually and with little emotion about the horrendous experiences of their trek to Tabriz—but only after reaching middle age. A less faithful correspondent than his brother, he wrote letters more or less monthly.

Sardar Mirza wrote weekly and extensively, detailing happy memories of his journey from Tabriz to Paris and his eight-year stay in the city he considered the love of his life. His letters—at least, those in my possession—refer only once, and only in general terms, to their experiences before Tabriz. His travel from Tehran to Tabriz, he says, narrowed his senses down to a point (a dimensionless entity, in geometry) so that he remembers nothing. But, in reverse, the geometric point then splits itself into a wider and wider bombardment of the senses, from the beauty of civilized society everywhere he looks. That uncomfortable, even harrowing journey has become an adventure that recolored his life with vivid memories. One gets the feeling that he had read Gogol. He remembers Poti—a filthy, disease-ridden hole—only as a place where the sound of frogs kept him awake all night. Had he perhaps developed a selective memory, that filtered out or ignored anything unpleasant? Or was this merely the Persiran custom of not telling a loved one anything disagreeable?

The brothers' letters spare us any account of the beating. Yet their separate lives begin with that brutal shower of sticks on their bare feet: they both see this moment as the pivotal point of their lives. This is when we can peel the two boys apart as individuals, as life exacted a harsh physical price. The hormonal chemicals that coursed through them at that moment burned a deep groove that transformed them into two unique individuals, men who—though still wholly loving one another—would later act so differently during the Constitutional Revolution. Ms. Vakil, I want to help you reconstruct the long-forgotten reputations of these two historical figures, figures your profession has for too long dismissed.

Traveling westward had a momentous effect on a young boy: those carriages, steamers, and trains served almost as time machines. Modernity leaked eastward from the West at a geologically slow pace, keeping the population beyond the Caucasus isolated to a degree that is difficult to comprehend: the first trains would arrive in Tehran a quarter of a century after Sardar

Mirza's journey to Paris. From his privileged position, the young Prince at first presumed that such a remarkable conveyance was at his personal disposal. The discovery that train travel was in fact available to *all manner of people* thoroughly cracked his model of the universe. Sardar Mirza's transformation from young Eastern potentate to budding Western gentleman began in Tiflis, with this trenchantly distressing observation.

The Prince now questioned another bedrock assumption. Could it be that the Qajar dynasty, his sacred provenance, was merely a historical curlicue? In these new lands, ordinary people's everyday surroundings surpassed anything he had seen at his father's great palace. A childhood managed by ignorant women and eunuchs had taught him that he lived in the greatest empire man had known—but at every stop from Tiflis to Paris, the evidence of his own eyes confounded this worldview.

In Paris, speculation gave way to capitulation. Nothing could have prepared him for Paris. Everything he knew crumbled away—the self-aggrandizements, the ignorant suppositions, the flattering lies. Never an envious boy, it was not in his nature to assume that the riches of others would detract from his own well-being. Indeed, in some circles he would come to be known as the Democrat Prince.

Sardar Mirza arrived at the Gare du Nord in 1897, at the height of *La Belle Époque*. This was a shocking and frightful, joyous and exuberant time, when the legacy of the French enlightenment—of revolution and anticlericalism—inspired all forms of art, entertainment, and literature. The "winds of beauty," *les vents de beauté*, wafted his soul upward like a kite.

Much later, he brought his ten-year-old daughter, Lili, to see Monet's *Boulevard des Capucines*, the masterpiece that captures so perfectly the throbbing energy of the cafe crowds. He tried to explain how all this had struck him when he first arrived, how the busy Parisian thoroughfare—with its horse-drawn omnibuses, the patiently waiting crowd of passengers— had contrasted with the forlorn, impoverished streets of Tehran. Lili of course could not understand; she had yet to visit the old country.

When he first arrived, everything excited his voracious brain, though his letters to his brother only complained of schoolwork and "tedious old men" teachers. At first he wrote in Farsi, salted with French idioms, but switched to French at around the age of fifteen. He wrote and wrote, detailed letters to his brother. And his brother read and read, hungry for every detail set on paper by his darling twin.

Paris was then in the grip of the cult of "the right to be lazy." The cabarets were packed every night, as singers, poets, and storytellers spun their yarns around the dispossessed, prostitutes, and rogues of the city. The *Folies Bergères* had democratized the café-concert, offering novel forms of amusement to all classes. At roller coasters, racetracks, wax museums, and music halls, the elite disported itself alongside the general populace.

Indeed, along the *grands boulevards*, any random swath of the streaming crowd appeared richer, better dressed, and more elegant than anything encountered in his father's palaces. "Our palace mice are poorer than their church mice," he joked to his brother. Sardar Mirza could not comprehend the West's exaggerated notion of oriental riches. All forms of transport fascinated him. When the metro opened, at the turn of the century, he made Qodrat take him again and again, despite Qodrat's fear of this underground monster.

The Dreyfus Affair dominated everyone's lives. He wrote his brother detailed accounts. Like many aristocrats worldwide, at the start of the affair he believed in Dreyfus' guilt. His slow evolution to believing him "not guilty" left him forever distrustful of his own kind—a possible clue to his later actions, during the Constitutional Revolution in Persiran.

Another flash of understanding occurred when, at the age of fifteen, he attended the 1900 Universal Exposition. He disliked the spectacles—the grand Ferris Wheels, escalators, talking film, Campbell's soup, nested Russian dolls. What stunned him was the exhibition of French painting. For the first time, France gave official recognition to one of the greatest movements in the history of art. After years of abuse and neglect, the Impressionists—Manet, Pissarro, Renoir, Degas, Morisot, Monet—saw their works hung next to the traditional masterpieces of the nineteenth century. This exhibit electrified and dazzled Sardar Mirza. Lacking artistic talent, he nevertheless wanted to be part of this movement—to support it, promote it, write about it. Thereafter, painting would never be far from his mind.

By the age of seventeen, he had visited the pleasure sweatshops with little enthusiasm: he admitted to his brother that he suffered terribly from post-coital depression. He sampled absinth and opium with a more sustained eagerness. He bought a bicycle and developed a passion for it, frequenting the Vélodrome de la Seine on Sundays. You get the idea, Ms. Vakil. Sardar Mirza wallowed in *gauloiserie*, never to emerge from its waters.

Let me transition, gawkily, seventy-five years and throw open the windows of the chalet and hang out the duvets for a good airing. I've told you that I spent nine days in the prison that had been my own house. What I have not made clear is that I shared that prison with my Uncle Dal, the famous surgeon. He had been among the people getting off the bus, the day of my arrest. I spent nine days sitting in a cell in the same house where he was also imprisoned.

With his iconic bald egg-shaped head and his teeth like planks, the man who had brought me into this world stepped stiffly off that bus and appraised the house with a nostalgic air. He acknowledged me with a strong embrace. He had loved my father like a brother (they were in fact adoptive brothers). But ever since the first time he set eyes on her, he had loved my mother like no sister. Uncle Dal now entered the main house like a man returned to the throne; he would live there for the next ten years, never to leave it. For a short period, the Islamic Republic of Persiran used my house, the Poonaki residence, to hold important political prisoners. Then, on June 28, 1981, the People's Mujahedin bombed the headquarters of the Islamic Republic Party, and seventy-two Islamic worthies gave their lives happily to reside in heaven. This presented an existential threat to the newly named Islamic Republic of Iran, which in turn produced a great gush of political prisoners; the Poonaki residence was no longer adequate, and Evin, the notorious Tehran prison, received the overflow. My house was transformed from a prison to an asylum, and Uncle Dal smoothly navigated the transition of roles.

My uncle had in fact spent his childhood in this house. My paternal grandfather, Saleh Mirza—the Prince—had adopted him on a whim, because he liked his fair coloring and because he was childless at the time. Uncle Dal grew up bright, modest, and knowing; liked by everyone, quiet and kind, he never hurt a soul. He had thick blond hair and blue eyes, with a thin, equine face which God had drawn in perfect symmetry. His looks ensured him the unquestioning respect we invariably accorded to foreigners (however much we may have hated them as a group).

My grandfather sent Uncle Dal to Germany for his education, at a time when few Persiranians did so for their biological children, let alone for an adopted child. (Later, in the thirties, the Prince again sent him away to protect him from the political atmosphere under the erratic Shah, Reza Pahlavi.) The move to Germany coincided roughly with the birth of Saleh Mirza's only son, my father and Dal's new brother. Uncle Dal felt with bitterness that he had been exiled, denied his place in the household in favor of the new arrival. Completing high school in Germany during the rise of the Nazis, he sympathized with the Nazi movement, as a reaction to the all-too-evident colonial aspirations of the English and the land-grab of the Russians. He then completed medical school in Germany and stayed there till the end of the war, practicing his vocation on the endless stream of injured soldiers. The war scrubbed him clean of any youthful enthusiasm for ideology. He returned home to a warm welcome by my parents, who loved him dearly until their deaths.

Our uncle joined the court as a friend of Mohammad Reza Shah, the last monarch of Persiran, having treated his wounds after an attempted assassination in February, 1949. Uncle Dal joked with the Shah that his hat had greater need of attention, as it had taken the first three bullets before the fourth entered the Shah's cheek and exited through his upper lip. The fifth injured his shoulder; the assassin's gun jammed on the sixth bullet. The Shah used this pretext to amend Article 48 of the Constitution, giving himself the power to dissolve the Majlis—a first step toward amassing total power. A fair enough exchange for his unwanted set of false teeth. The event earned our uncle a permanent seat at the table—by which I mean the Belote card table. Uncle Dal never took advantage of this privileged position, except, once in a while, to urge the Shah to soften some punishment of the opposition.

Uncle Dal had some rare gifts. At medical school in Berlin, his manual detection of tumors had become legendary. His sensitive hands competed with the best X-ray technology of the time. Too thick for a surgeon, his hands touched, cajoled, and massaged flesh until they felt cells gone awry. He'd immediately advise surgery. Those who looked for a second opinion often faced a difficult choice: the second opinion invariably contradicted Uncle Dal, the Professor, for lack of adequate detection systems. Those who did not follow Professor Dal's diagnosis often ended up with an advanced or inoperable tumor.

The birth of the next set of twin boys, my brother and me, marked a turning point, when Uncle Dal attended the birth as a medical observer and friend. Remarkably, we infants emerged immersed in a "black viscous liquid." As a trained researcher, Professor Dal immediately collected a sample of the fluid for laboratory analysis, and to his surprise, the material was eventually pronounced Grade A Persiranian crude oil. The medical personnel in the delivery room—the surgeon on duty, Dr. Malik; the gynecologist, Dr. Rasekh; and two nurses—all noted the presence of some dark material, though (they said) the Professor exaggerated the amount. All of them expressed relief at the test results: clearly, someone had introduced a quantity of oil into the antiseptic environment of the delivery room. The orderlies responsible for maintaining cleanliness were accordingly disciplined.

A few months later, Professor Dal noticed the dark texture of my mother's milk. He even observes in his notes the iridescence of a pale rainbow on the surface of the contaminated milk. And, while playing with the infant Dari, uncle Dal became drenched with black urine. Convinced that the Poonaki body could manufacture oil, uncle Dal became strangely erratic.

Dear Ms. Vakil, what can I say? I am not introducing a García Márquez character: we are narrating fact-based history, not magical realist fiction. A sensitive man, hammered by the war, returned home to great professional success but with a precarious hold on reality. His mind remained in a delicate balance.

Possibly the sight of my mother's open thighs as she gave birth brought to his mind, in the most physical way, her eternal inaccessibility. Maybe the fifteen hours of this difficult birth made him hallucinate gushes of oil.

Possibly his diagnosis of tumors also began to leave reality behind. Indeed, he diagnosed cancerous cells earlier and earlier in each patient who entered his small office. He recommended surgery wholesale to man, woman, and child—anyone who passed through his sensitive hands. By the mid-sixties, newspapers had begun to speculate on his competence. He chose to retire without fuss. He almost abandoned his luxury duplex apartment downtown, preferring to stay with us; he was given a permanent room that we called *Uncle's room*. We saw him only at nights, as (like a vampire?) he disliked coming out during daylight. No, his room was not in the attic. And no, I have no memory of him acting crazy.

Six thousand miles away, and almost twenty-five years ago, night covers the land of a thousand and one nights. The Persiran/Iraq war has ended. My frightened Storyteller picks up his story.

The Storyteller Eyes the Professor with Suspicion

"...the stars,
That nature hung in heaven, and filled
their lamps
With everlasting oil, give due light
To the misled and lonely traveler."

— John Milton

My darling Baba, your seat lies vacant; in these times there are certain advantages to not living here on Earth. Perhaps Almighty God has seen fit to equip you with corporeal eyes, as you hover to witness the destruction wrought by this longest of wars. Maybe you employ *my* eyes. But then, with all respect, dear Baba, how could you and I see so differently?

The war has ended. By suing for peace, the old man—by his own admission on the radio—has drunk from the poisoned chalice: not a very a potent brew, since he continues to live happily in Jamaran. Through eight years of trench warfare with our neighbor, our troops have hopscotched through minefields. They breathed the stench of nerve gas. They ate and shat in their dusty trenches in unimaginable heat. On cue they ran out in waves, to be slaughtered by an entrenched enemy. I am told that a million people died. Why, Baba? To what purpose? A madman launches by stealth a cynical war, to recapture the glories of the seventh century and a dollop of oil. For six more years a stubborn old man refuses peace, because he yearns to set the clocks back to the same bloody century.

Baba, I am not talking about you. I am talking about the *other* stubborn old man, who has brought us to this sorry state. No respect. No laws to speak of. No respect even for their own laws. Look at what that rascal Hamid has gotten away with, with never a peep from the

137

authorities. Did they ever *ask* how he came to own the most famous teahouse in Tehran?

Everyone lives in fear. I have not set foot outside Mammad-Ali's shop since I left that prison they call a madhouse, that madhouse they call a prison. You call me a coward? Baba, have you forgotten that Mammad-Ali's shop is only two blocks from the teahouse? I can see the back door of the teahouse from my front window, through the broken shards of a white fluorescent letter (shaped like a drawing of a woman's breast, a semicircle with a dot in the middle—the letter *N* in our script). It is Mammad-Ali's store signage, mounted on the window of the second-floor storeroom I call home. They would see me step into the street, even dressed in a black chador.

I asked Mammad-Ali to visit the teahouse to conduct a reconnaissance. He reported that the enemy was entrenched and living in filth, though the end of the war has slowed their arms business.

"What can I tell you that I would not tell your father?" Mammad-Ali lamented. "These rascals have dulled the sparkle of life. They have destroyed beauty, music, poetry. They have destroyed our country." I didn't know Mammad-Ali could wax poetic.

I will bide my time before making a move. Meanwhile, let me keep my promise to my master, my *arbab*, the mad witness, my Professor. Let me continue with my story.

ℨ

I woke to Professor Dal's screams. There in the natural light, wearing only his loincloth, he screamed with his head thrown back, like an old wolf howling at an imaginary moon. His upper body was zebroid, bruises circling his torso making a light-and-dark moiré. I faced him in the middle of the cell. I winked and nodded, now an accomplice to his absurd foolery. He acknowledged nothing, however.

"What am I?" He resorted to his old question. I felt annoyed at his perseverance.

"It's me, Hekaiatchi," I whispered. "The guards are not around. What are we doing? Do you want me to howl too?" Slowly, like a kung fu master, he shifted to face me and, in the same slow motion, lifted his hand high while I watched, an idiot's smile on my face. Reaching its apex, with no warning whatsoever, the hand made a lightning descent to deliver the hardest slap I had ever received in my young life. Only the mass of my body kept me from pirouetting to the floor. I felt a crick in my neck and tasted blood in my mouth. Gingerly I ran my tongue around the inside of my left cheek, and it felt like chewing gum mixed with cookie crumbs.

"What am I?" he repeated.

"An oil . . . an oil well?" I asked. I waddled as fast as I could toward the door and screamed for help.

Professor Dal reenacted exactly the scene of the day before. Removed his loincloth and began producing copious amounts of waste. The guards arrived and removed him for the rest of the day. I cleaned the mess as best I could, happy to have seen the last of him.

Late in the afternoon, they returned him without explanation. I begged the guards not to leave me alone with this madman. They laughed at my hysterical fear of an old man weighing barely a hundred pounds. He slept well into the night. Though I tried to stay awake, I too dozed off.

I woke with a jerk to find him straddling my stomach. He still smelled faintly of vomit.

"Wake up, my bag of feathers. The night is young, and I have much to say. We must speak of the agonies of birth and the manias of motherhood and the sex lessons of our protagonists." Just like that, he became the same lucid old man he had been the night before.

"Get off me," I barked. "I don't want anything more to do with you and your craziness. Go back to your corner and let me sleep."

"But, dear boy, what's the matter with you?" He sounded genuinely concerned. "I thought we had left all that nonsense behind us. Come, turn around and let me lie on your back."

"But this morning you slapped me and pissed all over me. *Who are you?*" I snorted.

'That is exactly what I am about to tell you."

He began to tell me his own history. This was wise: my Baba used to say that the narrator must first establish trust, not to be thought a gossipmonger or a charlatan.

The Story of the Professor

"There is nothing either good or bad, but thinking makes it so."

— Hamlet

I will bring to life, on this heavenly back of yours, the lives of many. Details that I had no business knowing were told to me, at all times: when women gossiped in my presence as if I were their son; when hard-drinking princes exposed state secrets as if I were their brother; when opium-smoking servants divulged information as if I were their ward. But my own threadbare story cannot be checked. I will give you the barest of details, for it is not my own story that is of interest. Still, you need to understand the character of the witness if you are to believe him.

I can recount the circumstances under which my mother was rid of me, since Prince Saleh Mirza has repeated them to me on a number of occasions. "The Prince," we call him, for in a land of a thousand princes he stands out as the most able. On one balmy winter day, I learned abruptly, brutally, that I was the illegitimate son of the World War I German spy Wilhelm Wassmuss. Wassmuss would deny this, even more brutally, when I visited him in the thirties, aged sixteen and on my way to Germany to become a surgeon. By the time I met my alleged father, our own Lawrence of Persia, all his derring-do was behind him. A few months later, he would die in Germany, a bitter man.

The Prince wrote my name on the nineteenth page of the Koran as Davood (to be shortened for the rest of my life to the initial Dal, the letter "D") Wassmuss, son of Wilhelm Wassmuss. I knew little of my last name until the age of eleven. I had been delivered to the mansion as an infant, along with a story written on a few sheets of paper in a woman's hand—an educated hand. The papers had been pinned onto my coverings with little protection, and by the time I had been cleaned and swaddled, they were thoroughly soiled.

Because I resembled the Prince in coloring, he adopted me. In this part of the world, people have a preference for the paler skin. As you can see, my pliable one, my skin had the amber hue of a fine scotch; my hair was the bright yellow that a child would use in drawing the sun, a source of pride but also a mark of my foreignness.

For eleven years, I occupied a special place in the household. I slept in the main house, in my own room. The Prince told me only that the woman who handed me in was not a beggar; I knew little more until that day in summer, with the Englishmen present.

In 1905, the Russians and the English had divided the country into "zones of influence." The Russians ached to seize outright the northern provinces; the English longed to own the oil that bubbled up like a spring in the southern provinces. But at that time, during the Constitutional Revolutionary years, the Great Powers maintained a thin pretense of Persiran's independence. "In diplomacy, the agreement to *pretend* to accept something can, over the years, harden as solid as the Great Wall of China," the Prince counseled. "Hold on to it like your life depends on it. In our case it does."

Ten years later, in 1915 (the year of my birth), the English and Russians were now allies (never a good thing for us), engaged in a desperate existential war with Germany. They had dropped any semblance of diplomacy. We, the Persiranians, were miserable pawns in a European conflict. The Allies warned us against displaying any sympathy toward the Germans. As I sit atop of you seventy-seven years later, our history in that period can be summed up as a begging existence. Juvenile administrations, always seeking permission, came and went: their survival depended on divining the minutest intentions of each of the Allied embassies. Conspiratorial plots simmered in every corner. The Allies were credited with superhuman control over human events.

These were difficult and lonely years for the Prince. He had been married to his second wife for three years—still without issue. The tittering talk at the court questioned his manhood, despite his well-earned reputation as a mass fornicator. This sober man, resembling Cato the Younger, believed in a chain of tradition that included his sexual pleasures as a right. Once, no more than five years old, I sat on his knees playing with his green beads in the small garden of our city residence. He waited for his afternoon tea, his permanent frown captured in the hurdles of wrinkled skin on his forehead. His secretary (also my elementary teacher), a thin ascetic man of forty, had placed a tall, red accounting book on the table, preparing to walk him through the details of some land-swap.

A fleeting figure along the garden wall, some distance away, made the Prince lift his head. A pleased curiosity smoothed his forehead. "*Dokhtar, dokhtar*, you, girl, come here!" he shouted in his *basso profondo*. A thin, reedy girl, maybe thirteen years of age and quite filthy, walked over with her head high, not in the least intimidated. An eraser rubbed anywhere on her skin would have produced shavings of dirt. I knew her to be the same secretary's daughter. The Prince put his hand in her shirt and felt for her budding or nonexistent breasts. She made no movement to stop him, staring him in the face unashamed. A cough by the secretary prefaced the awkward introduction: "Your grace, my daughter Jaleh." Not a trace of awkwardness by the two staring parties. The Prince wetted his thumb to rub the dirt from around her mouth. Her thin, taut lips resisted the rubbing. I saw the incarnadine redness of the inside of her mouth as she bit his thumb with the quickness of a mongoose—a warning bite rather than vicious. He drew back his hand reflexively. Thumb to mouth, he twisted his head back up at his secretary, with a look of "What's this?"

The poor man was clearly appalled. "Your grace, she takes after her dead mother, God rest her soul. The woman had a camel's temper." The Prince returned his attention to the girl, who had lost interest and was tracing her finger around the embossed lettering of the accounting book. The Prince, quick as the same mongoose, slapped the back of her hand hard; it was her turn to withdraw her hand, outraged at being outsmarted. Frightened, I burst into a fit of crying. The Prince emitted a howl of laughter, causing a murder of crows to flap to a different branch. He kissed the top of my head. He had enjoyed himself. He dismissed her with a wave, no doubt to her father's chagrin. "Master Secretary, you need to give your daughter either a good beating or a thorough wash." Another burst of laughter and a heavy handed caress across my head to quiet me down.

"Your highness, she has an aptitude for books. I have taught her how to read."

Before the Prince could return to the account book, the secretary asked if he could have Choti join my lessons. The Prince grunted approval, though his mood became unaccountably a little darker. That is how I came to know Choti. Mark my words, my comfy airbag, that bite, that bite in 1920, was the birth of the modern woman in our unenlightened country. But I stray—and you wobble too much. Stay still. I want to introduce myself properly.

The Prince had told me little of how he came to adopt me. But he was always respectful in talking of my mother. This is the story he told me.

"One day, during the years I was the governor of Fars," he said, "a lady in rags approached my horse at the governor's gate. I could see that she had been brought up properly—she didn't walk to the middle of the street like the other beggars. On the sidewalk, she extended a baby to me, like a votive offering. I could not see her face, under her worn but high-quality chador. The baby, wrapped papoose-style, looked like a European child—white, blue-eyed, with a shock of blond hair sticking out of the head wrapping. "Your Highness, take your son." I admit that when she said that, the people around quieted down, for our coloring matched—and quite honestly, not knowing who stood underneath the chador, I myself had a moment of doubt." Here he would let loose the abrupt guffaw that delighted everyone.

"She sensed the tension and immediately added, 'Your Highness, I make a present of my son. He will serve you as your slave, if that is your wish.'"

He related all this, but I believe that this memory of his had borrowed a great deal from the wrenching letter he shared with me that haunted me all my life. I might question the Prince's timing, for the tender age of eleven sounds rather young, were it not for the second blow he dealt me right after I had finished reading the letter.

We sat in our country garden in Poonak, at lunchtime. (For one last time, I permit myself to use the possessive pronoun in relation to the Prince and his estate.) A weak sun and a balmy wind gave everything a buttery feel, and the small walkways around the garden gave off a slight smell of fresh mud after the morning rain. The sluices controlling the feed from the large reservoir had been opened, and their overeager streams surged through our gardens to quench the fruit gardens in the valley below.

The Prince sat as usual on his straight-backed chair. Forty years old, he had snow-white hair and a short, grizzled beard that the genetic salt shaker had sprinkled a few times more than the pepper. He had taken up the use of a sturdy walking cane, which he held upright between his knees. Watching the activities in the garden, he leaned forward and propped his chin, almost prayerful, on his thick hands covering the curve of the handle, with the concentrated gaze that unnerved those around him. (In fact, the Prince was severely myopic almost his whole life. When he finally acquiesced to a pair of spectacles, he was startled to see stars in the night sky; he had been near-sighted for so long that he had no memory of them.)

That day, he called for me in a voice loud enough to carry all around the garden. I ran to him with the enthusiasm of a hound, lacking only the thumping tail to underscore my complete devotion. Two Englishmen sat at the table with him. Mr. Scott I knew well enough, as an attaché at the British Embassy. He and the Prince had been friends from the glory days of the Constitutional Revolution. The Prince introduced me to his companion, a Mr. Nicolson. He wore a brown three-piece suit that appeared to be made of burlap. His tie was knotted so tightly that I credited it for his slightly protuberant eyes and his startled look.

"Mr. Nicolson," the Prince announced, "this boy has been under my protection since his birth. I can assure you he is *not* a German today." Not understanding the significance of his denial, I started to laugh.

I cannot say why the Prince chose that time, in front of two English diplomats, to hand me my mother's letter. He looked at me with detachment. "Boy, I have something here for you to read." He had dropped the possessive pronoun: an immense drop in my social status. "*My* boy" translates to "son." I doubt I caught just then the subtlety of this change, but I have had years to replay his exact words.

The letter itself pierced my little heart. Badly stained with baby shit, it related my mother's sad story. She wrote:

1001

I, Zoleikha [the last name is omitted as indecipherably soiled—not as a literary device for anonymity], set down the following account of myself so that my son will not go forth into the world without a name and so that those who read my story will take pity on my son. Let God be my witness that all that I have written is the truth as I know it in my heart. I write by dipping into my China-ink-soaked cloth my galam, made of wood cut narrow by myself, as my tutor had taught me. I was beaten senseless after being thrown out of my father's house. They beat me to induce an abortion. You held on tight, son. I hope you prove to be the fighter your family has been.

I will not waste ink on writing down the travails of my trek to Shiraz. Nor will I detail my months of surviving on the streets of Shiraz. Sometimes people fed me out of pity; other times I had to resort to the basest of survival techniques open only to us women. Tomorrow, I shall take my baby to the governor's house. I hear a Qajar prince of great reputation has come to us. I want nothing in return for my baby. Life has nothing left for me. Gold would only prolong my miserable life.

My son, we belong to the Tangestani tribe. We came from the village of Dilwar, known for its pirates. Yes, son, your grandfather was a pirate of great renown and courage. I will not sully my father's name any further than to say that I feel every ounce of shame I have brought down on him. I deserve his wrath. If not for you, I would have shown him my mettle by ceasing to exist. Once I have you safe, I will follow the path to honor. He trusted me with every ounce of his being. He had me learn reading and writing when he could do neither. Not one woman in our midst could read. He used me as a messenger early to send messages to his pirate captains.

When Dilwar, where I was born, was bombarded by the British on the pretext of arresting my father, my father escaped and moved what was left of his life—and us—to Bushehr. There, we came to live in the house of the honorable Rais Ali, the Tangestani chief.

147

I saw the German Wassmuss for the first time two years after the dastardly act of the English, when my father, brother, and I traveled to Shiraz to meet him under the protection of the governor of Fars, only a few months after the start of the Great War.

We arrived on a sunny winter day. The cool air, like an angel's breath, had our niqāb flaps resting lazily over our faces. The large house was bustling, preparing for the visit of both Rais Ali and the governor. In the courtyard, a large European, dressed like a Persiran lord with a pistol in his belt, ordered the servants about in fluent Farsi; I assumed the man to be a God-fearing Muslim. I learned later that Wassmuss had converted to Islam as had the entire German nation; my brother tells me he heard the German Shah speak through the wireless, telling of his joy when he found Islam. Thanks be to God! My soul trembles at the thought of a kafir, an unbeliever, touching me.

As we crossed the yard behind Wassmuss, he turned abruptly and ordered me to get on with the cleaning of the andaruni, ready for the honorable Rais Ali's womenfolk. I was embarrassed by the mix-up: I was no servant. He noticed my Arab garment. He moved toward me and repeated his order in perfect Arabic. At that moment a soft gust of wind lifted my niqāb and showed him my amused smile. He stopped midsentence. Like the shadow of a bird flying overhead, a confused smile crossed his face.

I grabbed down my niqāb and explained quickly in Farsi my relation to the coming party. He knew all about my father. He immediately lowered his gaze and apologized again and again, ordering the servants even more sternly to make our rooms ready and comfortable. I tried to explain that we had come to help with the arrangements, but he would hear none of it. He displayed such courtesy and civility that no one believed him a European.

Rais Ali, my father, and my brother arrived in the late afternoon. Wassmuss welcomed each of them with a thoughtful pishkesh, a present. They talked for two days. The honorable Rais Ali, may God protect his soul, had sensed the aligning of the stars. He had dreamed of throwing the English yoke from our backs and letting us walk once again as proud Arabs and Persiranians. What better time than when the yellow dogs were at each other's throats? The governor, Mukhbir-al-Saltaneh, also a British foe, encouraged us all to band together and push the enemy into the gulf. Wassmuss, weighed down by more gold than the Shah himself, promised us all kinds of material support. To his credit, he kept his word throughout our struggle.

For the next six months, they used me to convey the British positions to Rais Ali and Wassmuss. I could leave Bushehr without suspicion: no one suspected that a woman could be trusted with such delicate missions.

Wassmuss moved his headquarters twenty miles outside Bushehr. I traveled to him two more times: once to let him know that rifles had not arrived, and a second time to let him know of our imminent assault. By the time I went back to Bushehr that last time, I was full of him—and of you, my son. I didn't know about you yet. I planned to go back to Shiraz and become one of his wives. He, of course, had to disappear when our assault failed. The British are still chasing him.

My son, you cannot comprehend the heat in midsummer in Bushehr if you have never experienced it. During the day, no one can stay out under the sun. Even us, born here, will bleed from nose and ear before long. We could only operate under the cover of night. We attacked them an hour before dawn. They did not know our strength. We surprised them. My father's brother attacked them, and he gave me the following account:

"I lay in the groves face down and dared not lift my head. British bullets flew in a swarm inches above my scalp, cracking the air and whistling eerily. 'Come with me,' Rais Ali called, and he pushed himself up from the mud and charged the sepoys, carrying his rifle across his chest. More bullets whizzed overhead. Next to me, Farhad, my courageous nephew, lifted himself from the mud. His naked feet sloshed as he ran after the commander. A bullet tore at his neck, speckling me with blood. He kept going. I intoned a prayer and pushed myself up, racing after Rais Ali. A bullet nicked my thigh, but I charged. We all screamed at the top of our lungs. In the ensuing gun battle, we killed three of the enemy and wounded scores more. We pressed our luck by attacking the British Residency. The English, from their high vantage point, rained hundreds of rounds of bullets on us. A second stray bullet pierced your brother's skull from behind his ear."

Rais Ali later presented my brother's cadaver to my elderly father and asked his pardon for failing to protect his son. That night we washed my brother's body. With my own hand, I gave him his Hunut: I applied fresh powdered camphor to his forehead, his palms, his knees, and his big toes. I put the wajib part of the loincloth from his navel to knee. I sewed and knotted the full cover of the kafan at the top and bottom. Within three hours, we had buried your uncle.

The English surprised us by landing forces at Dilwar, south of Bushehr, early in the morning, when the heat could be tolerated. From the ship they lobbed firebombs on innocents and indiscriminately killed women and children. My brother's wife and his two children—your cousins, not yet five years old—were slaughtered. They joined their father's grave before sunset. My father has sat immobile for months, as if each of the dead represented one of his limbs. The men from the village fought bravely, but the incessant machine guns proved overwhelming. They destroyed our birthplace.

We kept on with our attacks on Bushehr night after night. The English dogs resupplied the port from the sea. We were powerless to stop them from the seaside. They sat high above us. They broke our will when they lit the night with their small, sun-like machines that followed our men no matter where they ran. One of the roaming lights caught Rais Ali full in the face. I am told he smiled as the bullet caught up with his destiny. He joined the Almighty without a word of complaint.

The fight continued till late summer, when the British destroyed the villages of Zanganeh and Halileh.

Long before, we had lost our will to fight. Now the infidel, dirty English are once again masters. My father remains in mourning. Son, if I have any advice for you, it is to distrust all that is English. I trust your welfare to the Almighty. Live a life of honor, my son.

My fluffy one, you can imagine that, at the age of eleven, this letter affected me considerably. A young boy dreams of an imaginary mother every night of his life. He then receives, out of the black, as it were, a letter addressing him directly as "son." Worse still, in the letter she describes her ultimate sacrifice in giving her child a comfortable life.

The Prince watched me read the letter, his chin still resting on top of the cane. I picked my head up and stared into his bloodshot eyes. I wanted to tell him that the letter changed nothing. I wanted to tell him that I would always consider him my only father. He didn't let me talk. He leant forward, coming close to my face.

"Do you understand the import of the letter, boy?" he asked.

Hardly comprehending, I nodded.

"Good." He turned to his visitor. "Mr. Nicolson, my young ward here is a legitimate Persiran national. Contrary to all rumors and appearance, he is not German." I felt even then that some agreement had been made among the three men before I had arrived at the table. They nodded and asked not a single question.

The Prince, his arms locked stiffly on top of his cane, got up without waiting for the servants to assist him. "Hear me all!" he pronounced, in a voice that echoed all around the denuded, wintry garden. Everyone working there stood up straight to listen. "The Almighty, with a little bit of help from my wife, Choti," he smiled as if to himself, "has seen fit to finally bless me with a child." The dogs barked a few times, and the whole household rushed out. A few snot-nosed peasant boys ran to spread

1001

the news, and their fathers came to give congratulations, pausing from their labors in the gardens below. The two Englishmen muttered inanities like, "Well done, old boy." The Prince, ready for all eventualities, distributed coins to all and sundry from a feminine red velvet purse. In the confusion, few would notice my expression, a pale imitation of joy. The Prince noticed; he seldom missed a nuance. Yet no kind word was uttered to soothe my wounded feelings.

Still distributing the coins, the Prince asked a question in his stilted French, though both the diplomats well understood Farsi. "Mr. Nicolson, I hope your audience with His Majesty went well yesterday."

"Tolerably well. He was full of praise for Your Highness."

"Would you make a wager with me?" the Prince asked. Mr. Nicolson, a soft, civilized man, smiled and shook his head gently. No diplomat would take that bait. "What odds would you give that I will see my child grow up to this young man's age?" He pointed towards me with his cane. Even with my scant French tutoring, I somehow understood the question.

"Your Highness has a strong portfolio in His Majesty's new government," Mr. Scott purred.

"Mr. Scott, you and I indulged in a fabulous feast in our youth. We would let *le diable* caress our buttocks, if only to sit at that table again."

I remember little else from that afternoon.

Over the next five years, the Prince dispensed his patriarchal privileges, rooted in time-honored tradition. He continued to treat me with fairness, and, yes, kindness—the kindness shown to a friend's son. Never again did I sit on his knees while he chatted with guests; no more did I feel his casual caress on top of my head as he crossed a room. The Prince's natural neglect eroded my standing in his household. Guests to the house

152

would previously have prattled polite nonsense on greeting me, but now they passed by stone-faced. Small slights by the servants flowered into the ultimate slight: I had to endure their pity.

Choti's new status, as mother-to-be, was all the more difficult to bear given our own long association. For four years, she had shared my lessons under her father's tutelage, essentially in the position of a mendicant (not that you would know it from her manner). Her father, at least, showed me the deference reserved for a prince-in-waiting. Choti soon grew into a striking woman, impossible to ignore. She did not wear any headdress in my presence; I was but a boy. She held herself erect, as if watching the world from a height. (Later in life, her straight, almost boyish carriage would serve her well, wearing disguises when in hiding.) She had a birdlike quickness about her. The pupils of her eyes had an uncomfortable jitter. The birth of Nima made an awkwardness that never allowed us to establish a warm relationship.

In one afternoon, I had lost a family. My childish imagination rushed to repair the palpable damage by building on those few soiled pages a new, if intangible, family structure. I placed Wassmuss, the distant adventurer, in the middle of my new world, a world in which he would one day show up to claim me. I saw him as a Sinbad, impossibly perched high on the yard of a lateen sail in a ship something like a dhow—but larger, much larger, swaying high in full pirate gear and ordering his loving, piratical in-laws to make good speed, for they needed to rescue me.

I don't want to give you the impression that I transformed into a milksop Cinderella sitting in the attic, communing with rats while being atrociously mistreated. Ah, you don't know who Cinderella is, my ample comforter? From your story, I would say she is someone much like you.

My education continued with the same severity as before. Yet I gained some freedom to explore on my own. As I matured, I began to grasp that no ship would arrive to rescue me by sailing miles inland; I understood that I would need to do some work on my own behalf. My interest in all things German grew in tandem with my commitment to finding my new father. This was duly noted; a German tutor appeared at the house. The Prince worked in mysterious ways.

The arrival of a foreign tutor stirred the social semaphores to action, cushioning my social freefall. Herr Lorentz, a dapper young man dressed always in a sober dark suit, arrived every day at around two o'clock. He spent three hours with me. I always tried to keep him longer, but after my lessons he tutored Choti for two hours, always accompanied by a chaperone. The mildest-mannered of men, generous and considerate, he tried to instill in me a love of literature. Specialization had not yet made its mark on the twentieth century. He was the last of the polyglots with an encyclopedic knowledge of Persiran, having studied the *Persiranistik* field from the Avesta to the Kurdish language, including the history of religion and culture. By the time he arrived in Tehran, he had traveled the valleys of the upper Oxus, recording the ancient languages he came across.

He stayed with us for two years, during which he tried to convert me to the European humanistic tradition. He made me read Goethe: briskly patrolling the table where I sat, he would hold the book at arm's length and move his pince-nez back and forth to focus on the letters. He corrected my pronunciation with the patience of an old nun; he patted my head like a pet when I did well. At the passage where young Werther and Lotte read the poems of Ossian, his eyes would tear up.

Herr Lorentz's deep learning in Persiranian history and literature did not interest me. My hunger for all that was German left no room. The Prussian chancellor Otto von Bismarck had captured my imagination: it was enough for me that Queen Victoria had called him the bitter enemy of England. Herr Lorentz, tut-tutting mildly to express his horror at my militaristic leanings, would change the subject to Rilke's poetry, hoping that modernism would be more to my taste. I preferred to dissect modern history, waxing heatedly on the unfairness of the Versailles treaty. Choti, in the other room, spent her time with Herr Lorentz reading Marx and Engels, which displeased him even more than my naïve enthusiasms for the German military.

I developed a great affection for Herr Lorentz: he changed the course of my life by suggesting that the Prince send me to school in Germany. Though he may have deplored my narrow interests, Herr Lorentz had a high opinion of my ability to soak up knowledge. The Prince agreed at once. Probably it solved a problem; perhaps it salved his conscience. Herr Lorentz wrote to his alma mater, the Berlinisches Gymnasium zum Grauen Kloster, to recommend me highly to his old headmaster (who happened to be his uncle). Meanwhile, I hatched a private plan to seek Wassmuss in the south, where the newspapers had recently reported his presence.

I had by now matured into—why be modest, my springy one?—a fine-looking young man. I drew stares wherever I went. Five-foot-ten, I was considered tall and well made. My blue eyes and light hair, combined with my dusky coloring, made me look like an exotic animal in this land of black hair and eyes.

My last visit with the Prince took place in the week before I left. Evidently, he awoke one morning to slap his forehead and reproach himself that he had forgotten to discuss with me the birds and bees. I tell you, my wide hippopotamus, having lived for seventy-five years I still cannot untangle the mystery of the Prince's relation to me—whether he loved me, or saw me as an amusement, or as an albatross hung around his neck. In any case, no boy ever experienced "the talk" the way I did. He did it in his usual way—direct but unorthodox, and in a bathing house.

In a world gone private, I still long for the rituals of public bathing, as practiced religiously every Thursday night to prepare for our day of rest. I loved the hard scrubbing dealt by the professional washers, wielding their prickly loofahs until tiny, doughy rolls of dead skin and dirt adorned our bodies. Scalding water poured from large ewers, again and again, washed away the scurf and left our skin flushed and smooth. We whiled away the time discussing politics, telling jokes, or horsing around, splashing water at each other; we walked outside wearing fresh clothes and smelling of rosewater, our fingertips wrinkled with whorls of spare skin. The world looked fresh and clean.

I rarely accompanied the Prince on his bath hours. Whenever I did, he listened to me patiently and questioned me on my academic progress. He always had a few friends with him, in addition to the host of servants and washers. I welcomed his invitations: the outing invariably included exceptional sweets, sherbets, and tea. When Ali-Akbar, his manservant, gave me the message that day, I looked forward to the usual ritual.

But entering the bathhouse, I found the Prince without his usual entourage. He was accompanied only by Ali-Akbar, who stayed by the door, as well as a professional washer whom I had not seen before—a tall, thin, hollow-chested man with a skeletal face, dotted with the pox, and lugubrious eyes. The thin cloth of his reddish-brown wrap went twice around his lean hips.

The Prince, a hefty man by now, sat on the tiled platform: small granny spectacles on his meaty nose, his head large and oblong beneath the short, white, nearly invisible hair. He ordered us to be washed thoroughly.

The man did so without comment. As we were being washed, he observed that he had neglected some important aspects of my education. Misunderstanding his meaning, I assured him that even though religious study had not been my strong suit, I had made considerable progress in the subject since we had talked last. He let out his familiar guffaw. "What I am about to teach you, boy, might be a tad *irreligious*," he chortled.

Swinging his legs out, he sat up abruptly and bellowed through the door to Ali-Akbar: "Let the woman in." In walked a woman of indeterminate age. Her carelessly wrapped hair hung in two long, tight braids. Her bare breasts drooped; she had large, dark areolae, and nipples like the tips of pencil erasers. Her stomach was fleshy like a belly dancer's, and her wrapped hips curved in a pleasing, womanly shape. From somewhere unseen, a few curled hairs crept up toward her belly button. I sat up in astonishment and shock: I had not seen a woman's breasts since my childhood visits to the women's part of the bathhouse. She looked us up and down, her hands resting confidently on her hips.

"At your age," the Prince continued talking to me, paying the woman no attention, "I had already had dozens of women and was about to be married to the Shah's daughter."

"Will it be with the boy?" she interrupted.

"Not likely, woman!" The Prince raised an eyebrow. Clearly, she had no idea that a prince of the realm sat in front of her. Bathhouses confer equality on men. "Do you think I would allow a young pup to have his first experience with a woman such as you? You will perform with this man here, while I teach this boy the rudiments of sexual intercourse." She began to protest, and then, no doubt remembering her pay, thought the better of it.

The Prince ordered both man and woman to take off their wraps. She merely lifted hers above her midriff, baring her genitals, and tied an efficient knot with a practiced hand to keep it on her hips. On cue, the man's veiny, placid penis nodded upwards. I had never seen a woman's mound: an upside-down thatched roof with a wisp of hairy smoke leading to her navel. The woman nonchalantly licked the palm of her hand. I lost her hand between her legs as she rubbed her vagina ready. "Don't do anything until I tell you to begin," the Prince warned. He then described in some detail the tumescence of the penis. He told me that a woman needs some lubrication, through manual manipulation of the clitoris and vagina. He did not elaborate on the pleasure aspect—except to inform me that I would enjoy the practice of intercourse immensely.

He then told the man to begin the intercourse with both standing, so that "the boy can see the mechanics clearly." She half-turned and planted one foot on top of the tiled platform where we sat, offering us all her protruding rear end. Her hands were stretched up on the wall like a prisoner about to be searched, her ample ass jiggling, sleek from steam. My throat went dry and my vision watery as I watched the vaporous scene. The man, now intent on entry, grabbed his member. He lowered his hips, hollowing his sternum like a fakir. As he straightened out, his penis slipped inside her in one smooth, hydraulic motion, disappearing into the mound of wet pubic hair. Its swallowing shocked me momentarily; the man calmed my fear immediately by pulling his penis halfway out. He reentered with an expert motion, his loins producing a sharp slap against her buttocks.

Pointing at details, the Prince continued talking calmly and without pause. "Slow down, you two," he admonished. "Just enough friction, my boy; it's nature's way of coaxing your sperm inside her."

By the time you are fifteen, you might know a fair bit about the world. I did not. In school I was a loner, exchanging little more than greetings with my schoolmates. The Prince was right: I had been neglected. I tried dimly to remember some biology, to no avail. But by the time we finished that day, nothing was left to my imagination. You may laugh, my soft bedding, but when you are ignorant, your doubts about the mechanics of sex can paralyze you.

ℒ

Traveling to Europe via the western route, between Luristan and Kurdistan, was a logical choice: the communist revolution in Russia had robbed the northern road of its imperial luster. People now would go by car to Khanaqin—a Kurdish city straddling the Dyala River at the Persiran-Iraq border—to take the train to Baghdad and then on through Turkey. I asked permission to stay in Baghdad for a few weeks before making my way to Europe. In fact, I had no intention of going to Europe: I planned to use those few weeks to go on a thousand-mile journey to the south, to Bushehr, to join my father. I had plenty of money, and no one would notice my absence. Father-and-son adventures would become my school.

The Prince arranged for me to ride with the English consul in the Trans-Desert Mail—a large, mud-splattered Dodge that traveled biweekly from Tehran to Beirut, carrying black mailsacks tied to its mudguards. White lettering painted on the hood announced its official purpose, to deter the casual robber. I sat in the front seat next to the driver, an Irishman called O'Rourke who drove the route often. Everyone—even the two English ladies sitting in the back—called him Arak, after the liquor, though I never saw him take a drink in the four days we traveled together. He spoke Russian and Persiranian fluently, but with a thick accent.

The English ladies appeared to be mother and daughter, both matronly; they had made this trip yearly to allow the daughter to visit her husband at the legation for a few months, her mother serving as *dame d'honneur*. They covered their mouths with handkerchiefs for hours at a time. When they lowered them to speak—to Arak, never to me—it was with the haughty familiarity used for servants. Arak understood his position and did not mind. I minded: I had never encountered a foreigner, least of all a British subject, in the lowly position of a servant. The man spoke *English*. He could rule the rest of humanity! As much as I loathed their superior ways, I accorded the British godlike powers.

We started late in the morning. I had my own provisions for four days, and the Tehran-Hamadan highway was quite carworthy.

As we climbed, zigzagging, toward Aveh Pass, the road began to empty and the air lightened to a lovely breeze. I stretched my hand out of the car and made gliding motions. By late afternoon we had given up the altitude we had gained, descending into Hamadan, one of the oldest cities in world. The ladies stayed at a small, clean hotel. The owner offered us a Persiranian stew made with lamb, chickpeas, white beans, onion, potatoes, tomatoes, turmeric, and dried lime, served in the traditional stone crock. Arak and I slept in the car, he in the front and I in the back. I slept like a child. In the morning the ladies twitched their noses at me as they sniffed the back of the car, but they said not a word.

We drove through white-trunked poplars along a river, until we began once again to zigzag our way up a road cut right into the mountain. The hairpin bends sometimes forced Arak to perform a careful back-and-forth maneuver to clear them, changing gears again and again. The meshing metal screeched appallingly. We reached ten thousand feet. The sky at nine in the morning was cobalt blue, the air fresh; we stopped to take tea at the side of the road. I will never forget that moment, with its sense of possibility, optimism, and adventure. Nothing seemed impossible. An open world lay in front of me as I sipped the hot tea and ate the bread and cheese. I have lived seventy-five years, my springy couch, and I can count on one hand those moments that blend all the emotions in one happy understanding of the future.

We descended once again, 10,000 vertical feet in less than seven miles of road. A dry heat was patiently waiting for us. In order to reach the British consulate by nightfall, we drove all day toward Kermanshah, passing through hills colored red, brown, and copper. We stopped twice to change the tube in the driver's-side front wheel. People on the road were dressed in the Kurdish style: the men wearing baggy trousers with a twisted sash big enough to hide a samovar; the women dressed in colorful layers. The children, tied to their mothers' backs, peeked naughtily over their mothers' shoulders.

Under time pressure, Arak accelerated the car; the heat began cutting our faces. Without speaking, the gray-haired lady offered me a scarf to wrap around my face. I thanked her, also mutely. We stopped to rest in one of the caravanserai that appeared every twenty miles—the distance a camel walks in a day. We ate quickly and prepared to drive on, but the proprietor came running out to warn us not to drive at night. I sensed that his warning about marauders did not simply reflect his commercial interests. But Arak assured him (and us) that he understood the dangers. "As long as you are prepared to plow them down with the car, you are not in any danger."

We saw Arak in action a number of times that night. A silhouette of a rider or two came into view, and Arak immediately plunged his foot on the accelerator. The car surged. At the last possible moment, the rider would give a violent tug at the reins. No pony ever stared down the challenge. The rider's frozen, startled face stared for a moment, before darkness swallowed him, as Arak guffawed and slapped his thigh. I pondered one question: What if the car broke down?

Well after midnight, we drove at last through a wrought iron gate into the British consulate, welcomed by a tall, sleepy Englishman. Ignoring me, he escorted the ladies up the steps; the two disappeared with him into the house without ever acknowledging their traveling companion of the past three days. Arak laughed softly. "It looks like you and I have another sleep in the car." Stung by the insult, I fumed all night.

We arrived in Khanaqin late the following afternoon. I bade Arak a fond goodbye as I boarded the train to Baghdad, in the wake of my two mute companions. We took more than ten hours to cover the hundred miles to Baghdad. Our adieus then were brief: a head nod, as the English ladies scrambled down to the platform.

Had I not been distracted, I should have been agog at this metropolitan city that made Tehran look like a village. Some details seeped in unconsciously, not so much through the eyes as through the nose and ears. My ears seem to have recorded the asthmatic breathing of the steaming locomotive in the station. But did locomotives sound so steamy in 1930? And were there gramophones in the cafés, playing Mounira El Mahdeya? I heard the shouts of boys running after me, reading my blond hair and blue eyes as a sign of money. I remember clearly only my fixed purpose: to board a steamer heading down the Tigris. I stayed at the Claridge Hotel on Rashid Street, parallel to the Tigris—the first luxury hotel I experienced.

I boarded the *Pioneer*, the very steamer that my father, Wassmuss, had traveled on in 1915 as a consul for the German government—marking the beginning of his operations against the British in Persiran. I felt the coincidence as an omen that promised kinship. The

Pioneer had served both the Turks and the Royal Navy in the war; it had seen better days. Under the management of its Turkish owner—a remnant of the vast Ottoman bureaucracy—a first-class berth was now merely an allotted share in a formerly elegant stateroom, stuffy to the point of suffocation. The tenants divided the shared sitting room with a curtain, for privacy. My companions, tourists, were mostly educated Baghdadi Jews who worked for various British banks. They all spoke three or four languages. We spent our days lounging in deck chairs on the covered walkway beside the captain's high pilothouse.

Below us, the lower deck resembled a bazaar: people lolled on squares of carpet or leaned on portable beds, or they brandished clattering cooking utensils. Skimpy tentlike structures on fragile sticks shielded them from the scorching sun. The Turkish captain's dirty military uniform was adorned with unimpressive tin medals; his Ottoman tarbush perched comically on his big head. A large man with a propeller-like, upward-turning mustache, he treated us with the utmost courtesy and the passengers below with the utmost contempt.

The pilot, a tall, ascetic-looking Arab called Al Hamdi, guided us skillfully out of the port. Small islands stood out of the low summer river. People were swimming in the then-clean Tigris, crossing the river in groups, singing and talking as they relaxed on those small carpets of land. Gramophones blared the hearty bird-music of Arabian singers. Passengers, hanging out over the railings, chatted with their friends and family sitting on the islets. Al Hamdi skillfully negotiated the shallow waters, amid the small circular reed boats called *gufas* that revolved around the steamer like the moons of a planet—and we left Baghdad.

Within a mile, all signs of color and life ended abruptly; the landscape became dull. Not a tree in sight, just reeds and bushes and the unchanging, thin-lined horizon. The distant purple mountains behind us—the same ones I had driven through—diminished at such a slow pace that, despite the engine's muttering, I would have sworn we were at anchor, or merely drifting. In those four days, we covered four hundred miles.

Upon reaching Al Faw, at the mouth of the Persiranian Gulf, my excitement surged: a vision of seeing the land of my mother and meeting my swashbuckling father gripped my imagination.

Did he still live in Bushehr? At the palace, I had read the daily papers diligently, finding snippets here and there of Wassmuss's whereabouts. He had developed an almost mythical reputation even among the English, dazzled by his successes. I knew that he had been imprisoned by the British and released in 1920. He lived in Berlin; but in 1926, the *Times* reported that Herr Wilhelm Wassmuss, the famous German spy, had returned to Bushehr and had purchased a farm. "I want to live in peace and quiet among the people I love," he had announced. "I am now a retiree from the German government. My life's adventures are behind me." Would I recognize him when I saw him? Would he embrace me as his son?

In Al Faw, I found a medium-size dhow with a crew of twenty, about to depart from a nearby fishing village to transport dates to India. That afternoon, dressed properly in my suit, I was boarding the topsy-turvy vessel, greeted by the derisive, red-gummed grins of the African crew. We sailed with a spectacular sunset behind us, shades of red I had seen only on posters for Hollywood movies. With a strong tailwind, we reached Bushehr in two days, keeping the northern coast always in sight. The merciless sun had flayed my skin, now hanging off me like potato peelings. The crew urged me to go below deck—but I could bear at most an hour in the dark, suffocating belly of the ship. The overpowering smell of overripe dates numbed my senses, but the boat's rolling sway had me throwing up in gut-wrenching fits, to general amusement. By the time we reached port, I was feverish, seminaked, the color of beetroot from crown to toes. Blinded by the sun, I saw only sudden, starlike fireworks, with an afterglow fading to darkness.

I found—somehow—the only decent hotel in town. In my transformed state, I wrote a note, in German, to my unsuspecting would-be father. I paid the bellboy (who had heard of Herr Wassmuss) to deliver it right away.

> Dear Herr Wassmuss:
>
> I am the ward of Prince Saleh Mirza. Through a letter left to me by my now-deceased mother, Zoleikha of Tangestan, I have been made aware of your relationship to her during the Great War and hence your connection to me. With no expectations on my part [I lied] and no responsibility on yours [I lied again], I would like to meet you at the Semiramis Hotel tomorrow at around six o'clock in the afternoon.
>
> Your son,
> Dal Wassmuss

I retired to my darkened room, exhausted and newly nauseated by the sun's glare in the lobby. A dream mixed with all other dreams: *someone's knocking on your hotel door.* The knocking did not stop. It lifted me from my dreams into a sitting position. I heard someone shout to the bellboy, in a local variation of Farsi, "Open this door or I will kick you downstairs!" In an instant, a heavy man with grizzled hair stood silhouetted in my doorway.

He strode into the room, all bluster and rage, to throw open the window shutters—the better to see his foe?—shoving them with both hands as if releasing the sun's energy, babbling at me all the while. And I now could see him: a heavy, angry, middle-aged man of no distinction. He stopped dead, moving his head from side to side like a dog listening to its owner, shocked perhaps at my blue eyes and blond hair, or by my feverish, confused gaze. The silence lasted only moments. When he screamed again it could be heard throughout the hotel.

"Do you think that I would consort with a peasant woman from Tangestan? The British had a £500,000 reward on my head. Do you think I trusted a mere *peasant* to run my operations? You Persiranians are scum of the earth, with your complicated conspiracies and theories. No wonder you have a miserable country." He made a German gesture, spitting out the word *theories* with a German accent.

"Do you know why I am here?" he continued. I sat mute; it was a rhetorical question. "I am here because I felt responsible for the tribal people. My own government has no honor. They refused to help. Did I abandon your people? I bought this farm to make some money for them. All they do is try to cheat me. I am sick of all of you."

He came closer to the bed. "And now they send me some parentless"—the Persiranian insult denotes a nobody—"kid from some village near the border" (a reference to the fair, blue-eyed Persiranians of the far north). "Are you the best they could do? You don't even look German, boy. Answer me!" He paused only a split-second. "Did the English send you? I know they don't believe me, these shit Anglos. They think I am here to sow rebellion. I am done, I tell you. I am returning to Germany once I get rid of this shit-hole farm. What do these people want from me?"

He turned on me. His left hand tried to grab my shirtless torso and slipped up to find my throat. He pushed me against the headboard. I could smell his sweat that made a ship-shaped outline under each armpit. His eyes were mean, capable of harm. "You signed my name in the book downstairs. You dare use my name as your own? *My name?*" He was screaming now. "You are not fit to wear such an honorable name!" With his right hand he slapped me hard. I began to faint. He lapsed into enraged German, still fixated on his precious name: "*Es steht Ihnen nicht zu, meinen Namen als Ihren eigenen zu gebrauchen. Wie können sie es nur wagen, einen solch ehrenvollen Namen zu benutzen?*" He slapped me once more before the hotel manager and two waiters came into the room and seized him from behind. They dragged him out, still screaming his dire threats.

They called for a doctor to attend to me. I had traveled a thousand miles to see him—and had not uttered a word.

To this day the taste of dates is unbearable, and I cannot stand to hear anyone call me by my last name—*his* name. All my life I have been wandering between that shit-covered letter and that sweaty brawl in a hotel room. Where was the truth? I understood that he knew my mother: he denied giving her a role in his "operations"—something my note had not mentioned. It didn't matter. I wanted nothing to do with this filthy man, so unworthy of my fixation.

He went back to Berlin in April of 1931. In November 1931, a small paragraph on his death, in the *Vossische Zeitung*, indicated that he had died a broken man, forgotten and in poverty. I did not shed a tear.

In the Bushehr hotel, an Egyptian doctor of extreme kindness bathed me in cool water. He put a thick layer of tropical lotion all over my body to relieve the sunburn. He asked that I be kept cool with wet towels and ordered one of the hotel orderlies to guard my room. He of course could do nothing for my mental anguish. I met him years later, at a medical convention in Vienna after the war, when I had already developed some reputation as a surgeon. I introduced myself by thanking him for his kindness to a teenager. Sitting in a

1001

stateroom after dinner, we shared a few *marillenschnaps*. Every five minutes, he'd slap his forehead in wonder, trying to associate the famous surgeon with that boy burned to a crisp, outside and inside, back in Bushehr— "the hellhole of the Gulf," as he called it.

I asked the hotel manager to find me a dhow back to Al Faw. I returned to Baghdad, there to board the train to Istanbul and to the Orient Express, destined for Germany. I had decided to get on with my studies.

My train pulled into Berlin in late summer, on schedule. To my utter surprise, Harold Nicolson was waiting for me on the platform. I seem to remember— probably borrowed from some movie—steam enveloping him, with parts of him coming into view and disappearing. He smiled warmly. "Hadjit has come to pick you up." He looked older and stouter. Having resigned from the foreign office, he would leave Berlin only a few days later.

The short distance from the railway to the center of Mitte overwhelmed my senses. Berlin, proclaimed the third-largest city in the world, was a city at war with its own identity: all structure vanished, the monarchy collapsed, and hyperinflation was on the rise; revolutions were sprouting, amid ruthless political assassinations.

We stopped to look at my school, a Gothic abbey on the site of a medieval monastery: the Berlinisches Gymnasium zum Grauen Kloster, the oldest and most prestigious secondary school in Berlin. In the Gothic arches I saw the shape of a vaulted caravanserai, making Harold Nicolson laugh. He dropped me off at the Persiranian Embassy, where I would stay on and off for the next three years.

As we stood next to the car, outside the embassy, Nicolson grabbed my shoulders with both hands and looked gravely into my face. "I know you admire the Germans, my boy. There is much to admire in this antics. Do not fall for them!" He dropped his hands. "I have promised my good friend Saleh Mirza to keep an eye on you. Call me if you need anything." Extracting from his breast pocket a large, pearly visiting card, embossed with the royal crest, he swiveled me around to use my lean back to write his details. He handed me the card, slid into his car, and drove away without looking back. His hand shot out of the window to wave a vague adieu.

I lived in Berlin for three years with the ambassador and his kindly aristocratic wife, who was a Qajar princess a few cousins removed from Saleh Mirza. She became my surrogate mother. A thoroughly modern young woman who resembled a Rossetti painting, she worked tirelessly with her husband, a quiet man with the dignity of a seasoned diplomat.

At school, there could not have been a more oddball creature than I: my looks pegged me as German, but I spoke with an atrocious accent. Nevertheless, my Persiranian background fit well with the new Aryan philosophy. I make no excuses: I fell headlong for the triumphalism of the Nazis.

Despite it all, these were happy years, spent conjugating Latin and Greek verbs and translating Horace and Virgil. I was not half-bad at my studies. I had arrived for the last gasp of the frenzied, lurid Berlin of the 1920s. Now, in the early thirties, the Nazis had already started to cross the fateful line from erotic to violent. They well understood the overlap between sex and violence in the Venn diagram. Violence would soon engulf the whole, and war was the apotheosis of that principle.

When I arrived, the scrubbing-out of the city's nightlife had only just begun. On Friday and Saturday nights we visited the cabarets to have fun with the expensive girls, but most of us got our pleasures in the dimly lit Tiergarten, where our favorite *Kontroll* girls knew us by name. Perhaps understandably, I developed a fetish that lasted through my student days: I liked to have sex standing up against a tree, with the older whores.

I passed the Abitur with honors, passed the entrance examination for the Humboldt University, and began my ten-year association with Herr Doktor Ernst Ferdinand Sauerbruch, at the Universitätsmedizin Berlin. How proud I was, to work for a man whose skills as a surgeon were recognized by all Europe!

ℒ

The small window in the cell turned dark grey, reminding Professor Dal of approaching daylight. He now fell discreetly silent.

The Fourth Night
0100

The Narrator Does His Fork-Swallowing Trick

"Fork: An instrument used chiefly for the purpose of putting dead animals into the mouth."

—Ambrose Bierce

Dear Ms. Vakil,

I can hardly concentrate on the contents of your email, amid the suffocating smell of garlic, ginger, peanuts, and chili peppers from my Szechwan neighbors. The woman (probably an import wife from mainland China) yaps incessantly, as if constantly negotiating the price of produce in the market. Nevertheless, in this small but comfortable one-bedroom apartment, in a building that has seen better days, I have reached economic equilibrium: I am where I belong.

Do I detect a subtly personal question in your last email? You send your regards to Mrs. Poonaki: an indirect way of asking whether there is a Mrs. Poonaki—so many layers to such a question. I should ask you in turn, with my not-so-straight face, "What are your intentions, young lady?" Forgive my small joke. No, there is no Mrs. Poonaki.

I misunderstood your questioning the documents. Thank you for your trust in their authenticity. Your interest lies with my fictional storyteller, Mr. Hekaiatchi. I confess to you that, beside my incorporeal version, a more solid Mr. Hekaiatchi does exist. I have never met the man. In the eighties, after the Persiran-Iraq War ended, I received a number of messages from him, claiming to have been a cellmate to my uncle Dal. He wanted some compensation in exchange for some "important critical information" about my family.

Please understand that, since my forced exile, I have received a number of, shall we say, "petitions" from family members of the former serving staff. One woman claimed to be the third wife of old Nemat, my grandfather's and father's life-long manservant, and asked for a monthly stipend. I wasn't aware that old Nemat had even a first wife, let alone a third; with us, he lived as a bachelor all his life. Jenia, the daughter of our Armenian driver, whom I remember as a reedy little girl, wrote me a polite letter in labored English asking me to get her a US entry visa, an impossibility of course.

Mr. Hekaiatchi continued his correspondence doggedly for some while, but I have not heard from him in years. The idea of using him as my storyteller came from the details of some of those letters. I confess I am disturbed that you apparently know the man. May I ask the circumstances of your acquaintance? However innocently, you have entered headlong into my story, Ms. Vakil. My storyteller—should I now say *our* storyteller?—must play himself, as accurately as you can describe him to me. Our connection takes on a more personal touch, does it not?

I know well which generation of twins interests you. But your interest in the older, *historical* twins will involve multiple yarns, twined and twisted, threads with a noose at both ends. A quirky symmetry, in the history of my grandfathers and their twin grandchildren—Arya and me—reached into my prison cell and nearly choked the life out of me.

Dear one-woman jury, I intend to prove beyond a reasonable doubt, and beyond mere circumstantial evidence, that my brother and I had the fixed intent to hurt one another. In our snapshots, we looked like funhouse mirror distortions of each other: he was the square version of me, and I the linear version of him. Given the difference in size and strength, he enjoyed the crude, physical thrust, whereas I preferred the deflective psychological parry.

To prove my case, I will need to stretch, politely, our professional frontier. I adhere strictly to the subtleties of Persiranian *taarof,* verbal volleys that do the work, but more gently, of verbal assault. (We Persiranians similarly dance a long dance before moving from *vous* to *tu.* I know of elderly couples who have not used the intimate pronoun throughout their marital life. Silent lovemaking must be their lot: in what circumstance might one use the plural *you* in bed?)

Indulge me: I need to cross a few layers of *taarof* to describe my parents' own lovemaking. The story will persuade you that my brother and I, even as children, did not play around.

During our thirteenth summer, our father, Nima Poonaki, felt obliged to give us a book describing the facts of life. This was the modern, "American" way: total openness with children. Adorning the cover of the book was the figure of a young girl in a frilly dress, holding a Japanese parasol in one hand and a straw basket in the other. Bending one leg pertly behind her, she leaned forward to kiss the cheek of a scruffy boy wearing *lederhosen.* Above the two, small hearts bubbled up and off the edge of the blue cardboard cover.

The pages within, however, were filled with outlines of men and women, x-rayed by the artist's hand, revealing the anatomy of the bladder, uterus, urethra, and fallopian tubes. The male was portrayed in profile, his penis placidly resting on his scrotum; the female was shown from the front, her palms outward, with a dark triangle for genitals and two dotted semicircles for breasts: a clinical depiction of the organs responsible for reproduction. By the end of the second chapter, the outline figures were superseded by color images of the stages of fetal development.

Scientific exactness did not manage to extinguish the aura of mystery around the words *enter* and *penetration.* Soon we were asking our father irritating questions about whether he practiced "entering" our mother. His gruff answer: concentrate on the other chapters; and yes, the act was practiced on occasion, how else did we imagine we got here?

To us, the series of photographs looked incomplete: one more image was needed to complete the development of the fetus. We inhabited, together, an imaginary chorionic sack that enclosed our consciousness, expanding just enough to include the other. And within this sack we struggled—for dominance? For survival? Other people existed on the outside, seen as if pressed against a window, their noses and pale lips distorted flat.

However incomplete, the book opened a door that could not be shut again. In collusion with us were our glands—represented in the book by a squiggly blotch—whispering to us: *not* to pay attention to the book (for glands are not photogenic), *not* to listen to the author (for he had been tampering with the evidence), and not even to listen to our father (whose brusqueness confirmed the existence of an important mystery). Our glands urged us to seek proof, to satisfy curiosity, to remove doubt.

I made the first attempt. I had associated nighttime with the time for penetration—a correct generalization, but one to which my parents happened to be the exception. Night after night, I waited to hear their footsteps coming up the stairs as they gave the servants the final orders of the day: for the hundredth time, a review of the procedure for locking the house, or perhaps the last items for tomorrow's shopping list. Then came the shutting of doors, the sound of locks falling into place. In the distance was the sound of traffic; and closer, very close, was the rhythmic breathing of my sleeping brother, Arya. I'd then tiptoe out of the room, run across the hall, and peek through the primitive but generous keyhole, considerately provided by the Persiranian locksmith. There in the dark, night after night, I could see the outlines of my parents, asleep and unmoving. My curiosity soon abated, and so did the nightly outings. Had it not been for Arya's own exploration, our sexual education would have taken the normal course.

One summer afternoon, I awoke with a start from our mandated siesta. Everyone slept in the summer afternoons; there were no exceptions. But my brother's bed was empty. I jumped out of bed and opened the bedroom door a crack, to see Arya peering through the primitive but generous keyhole. I wouldn't have connected Arya's actions with my own nocturnal adventures, were it not for the figure he portrayed. He wore gray shorts, the English kind, and one of his gray socks had fallen down to the ankle—a picture for which my mind recalled a complement: the girl with the Japanese parasol. I watched, fascinated by my brother's intentness: bent over, hands clasped between his thighs and close to the body, hand rubbing hand. All of a sudden, Arya straightened up and ran back to our room, giving me a mere instant to recover and jump into bed. I wondered why he cried and whimpered so, long after he was back in bed.

I had to find out. A few days later, I waited for everyone to retire for their nap. I listened patiently for my brother's breathing to fall into the rhythm of sleep. Then I transported my own eye to that keyhole, shaped almost like a question mark. As my eye adapted to the lighting, my mind flooded: my first look at hard-core pornography. The wooden shutters of the windows striated a rectangular space, peopled with shiny motes of summer dust. On the bed was a couple, no longer young, making efficient love. The man changed the woman's posture mechanically, marking nearly equal divisions of time. The performance nicely complemented the lessons of the book. The phone rang: the characters, still unrecognizable, now took their bows.

The man reached out to pick up the phone—still on his knees, torso upright, and still inside the woman, perched on all fours. His paunch was distorted from the pressure of her backside.

"Hello. Poonaki." No tremble in that voice. This was the first transformation: my father, in full glory, speaking on the telephone as if he were sitting behind a desk rather than fully inside a woman. "I will call you back." He replaced the receiver on the cradle.

More mechanics, and then the woman sobbed and cried—and now she, too, stepped out for her bow. This was my *mother*, crying from pleasure—definitely from pleasure. I instantly understood the difference, though Arya clearly had not. It did not diminish the shock. No child should witness the means of his own procreation; and no parent should be made aware of what the child has witnessed. How an eleven-year-old might make use of such information is hard to fathom. But I did; and I didn't wait too long.

On a dusty Sunday, the two of us sat in the playroom having lunch at the square table that often served as a bridge table. Lunch was ratatouille, a favorite of the cook when the parents were absent. Prepared *à la niçoise*, it looked revolting. We picked at our food, both of us bored.

Today, I began the needling: "What were you watching last week?" I played innocent, my fork resting on my tongue that tapped it lightly on my upper teeth. One leg was under me, the other swinging.

"Last week?"

"You know, in the afternoon, when you were watching mummy's bedroom."

Arya, obviously uncomfortable, had to think fast. As far as he could tell, I had only voyeured his voyeurism. We both looked up and saw the maid listening attentively.

"Pas devant les domestiques, Dari, tu es devenu fou?" *Not in front of the servants, are you mad?* Clearly, he needed some time to think up a plausible story.

"Not in front of Fatemeh, your favorite maid?" I reverted to Farsi.

"I wanted to see if they were asleep so I could go out and play." He pretended to part with this information reluctantly.

"Is that why mommy was crying?" I imitated him in mock innocence.

Arya tried to recuperate. His face was confused; he was speechless.

I pressed on. "Pourquoi Maman pleurait?" *Why was Mommy crying?* "Do you know Daddy does that to her every afternoon? Do you know why she cries so loudly?" The last question popped out of my mouth. Though it was not premeditated, it inspired its own answer. Arya waited naively to hear an explanation for his weeks of confusion. "Because"—my pirouette was delivered sing-song, as if reciting a nursery rhyme— "because she doesn't want to have any more children like us."

It was like telling a friar in the Middle Ages that the world was round: a brilliant theory. The vectors of rationality fought for equilibrium. Arya's love for our mother, the recent sex manual, and the scene of the room through the keyhole: all adjusted to fit this new worldview. His intellect had no choice but to resolve the inconsistencies—even at the expense of our mother. With the regularity of a metronome, I tapped the back of my fork on the ratatouille, making flat sounds. My swinging leg slowed down to keep time as I watched him. Arya got up and looked at me incredulously but with dignity, his cheeks wet from tears. He walked past me and out of the room without a word.

"Is Master Arya all right?" Fatemeh asked, worried.

"Oh, yes," I assured her, with a pang of disappointment that I must have missed the mark. But I was wrong. Just as I brought the fork up for a mouthful of food, I glimpsed a conspiratorial smile broadening on Fatemeh's face. Arya had tiptoed back and was apparently signaling to her from behind my chair that he was about to make his brother jump. The peasant girl well understood such childish pranks, having bothers of her own.

From behind my chair, Arya threw his arms around me and clasped my relaxed hand—still holding the fork in my mouth—and, with a violent thrust, embedded the four prongs deep into the soft tissue at the back of my throat. The fork also ripped the top of my tongue, broke a molar, and damaged much of my lower gingiva. Fatemeh stared in confusion, her strained eyes registering the full extent of the horror while her mouth, frozen, maintained a frozen grin. As the blood rushed down my throat, Arya held on to the fork while he conjugated into my ear: "I hate you, I've always hated you, and I will always hate you. I hope you die." At that moment, he had the first seizure of his childhood: he collapsed behind the chair, while I began to choke on my own blood.

Dr. Ghasem diagnosed Arya's condition as temporary amnesia. At first, he indeed remembered nothing of the past, but in time—apart from the fork-swallowing incident—his memory returned.

I had become a collector of physical handicaps, having now acquired a permanent speech defect. The English language would suffer the least: the hard *g*, as in the word *garlic*, is replaced by a *k*, giving my speech a more mechanical edge, the sound of horse hooves trotting on cobblestones instead of earth. But the effects on Farsi, my native tongue, were disastrous. All the language's natural guttural sounds, pronounced at the back of the throat, were replaced by softer sounds made further up, giving my speech a foreign tinge. Any attempt at reproducing these sounds simply twirled the spittle within the new recesses, producing gurgling sounds mixed with a possible spray. People were always skeptical of my nationality; they accorded me the respect accorded to those foreigners who have mastered the language.

Ms. Vakil, I can feel you turning your head aside with revulsion at my recollections. More importantly, I can feel your interest waning. Let me shake my poor Hekaiatchi awake. Though he sleeps deeply during the day, he forgets nothing recounted to him by my poor uncle, Professor Dal, who has suffered a great deal.

I can see your eyebrows lifting in disbelief, Ms. Vakil. How do I know that my uncle Dal had been mistreated? Would they not have treated him as a respected political prisoner—at least by feeding and taking care of him humanely? The fact is, Ms. Vakil, that on the first day of our stay, as unwilling guests in my own house, we met. And even to my bludgeoned eyes, he looked a sorrier sight than I.

Let me set the scene. The house had yet to be refashioned into a prison: it had only been seized the day before. During my grandfather's time, the basement served as refuge from the heat and as a storage area for food. My grandmother kept an army's worth of food supplies in that basement; hundreds of glass jars, each labeled in a trembling hand. As modernity arrived, my father had constructed a maze of rooms around the basement—bedrooms for the servants, who previously had simply found some corner of the house to spread their bedding. Every pair of rooms shared a half-window that peeked out at the ankles of people walking outside. The windowless rooms in the center continued to serve as storage, until the revolutionary guards moved in; they used them as "administration offices."

After a long day with the persuasive interrogators, I returned to my cell, dragged by the armpits by two young revolutionary guards. My legs had given up early in the evening, after they beat the soles of my feet; they trailed behind me like two pens trembling back and forth on a seismometer. In another corridor I glimpsed two men coming toward us, dragging poor uncle Dal. As in some diabolical conveyor belt or marching formation, they joined my party side by side, in a smooth turn. For about twenty yards we were dragged in parallel while the guards chitchatted. Naked from head to toe, uncle Dal with some difficulty turned his head towards me. His face was black and blue, with one eye shut. He flashed his large, toothy smile.

"Drag race?"

A large hand slapped the top of his bald head, hard, making it fall backwards. We parted company in silence. I cannot fathom how he survived ten years.

The Fat Storyteller Scribbles Away from His Hideout

"Your tale, sir, would cure deafness."
— William Shakespeare, *The Tempest*

I wake with a sudden start. My Baba sings in my ear like a cuckoo clock. It is cold, yet sweat has glued my scant body hair to my ample flesh. I crick my neck. I assume that I am still in the loony bin. Then, thank God, I see that light is pouring into the room from the wrong angle: from right to left. Shards of light reveal the neatly arranged sacks of rice and turmeric of Mammad-Ali's store. The light makes propeller-like shadows from my head to my toes. My little room above the store holds all I need: a roll of bedding, a small table, pencil, and paper—all, courtesy of Mammad-Ali.

I have been thinking about my predicament. Scribbling away in this safe, aromatic upstairs cave, I have not considered my long-term safety. Even in this benighted country, writing leaves a trace. Professor Dal gave me the name of a publisher by the name of Vakil, a woman who teaches history at Tehran University. I cannot imagine how she could help me. I would not want this story to be public: no question of contacting her until people have forgotten about me. I don't dare even leave my hideout.

Zahra brings me my breakfast with her eyes lowered and her face flushed like a peasant woman working in the rice fields. She wears her chador, too, in the manner of those who do physical work. The matte, body-length black cloth crosses the crown of her head and falls back in a semicircle, like a cape. She takes two ends of the chador, wraps them snugly around her waist from behind, and ties the knot above her belly. It leaves her hands and upper body free to work—and a nice upper body it is, too. Ample breasts under a red sweater stand out with significant jiggle as she climbs the stairs. As

183

she heads down, I steal a look at her more-than-ample bottom, which no chador can hide. I notice her crossed eyes less and less.

∅

On my fourth day in the loony house, I woke at midday, refreshed. I must have missed the oil-well act. Professor Dal had left. The noon sun fell on me relentlessly from the top window, from left to right, imprinting a prison-bar pattern on my clothes. The midday call to prayer always makes me hungry; food arrived within five minutes.

This isn't such a bad place after all, I thought, reflecting on the last few nights. I had listened to a man talking of kings and princes as if they were people of flesh and blood; I had only ever read about such personages. How would the young princes get along in life? And Professor Dal himself: *was* he the son of the German spy? Did he indeed eat and sleep among princes and Englishmen?

At that moment, Professor Dal walked into the cell wearing a strange smile, and without any of the usual pushing and shoving from the guards. He lay down on his thin mattress without uttering a word. As I began to talk, his eyelids did a slow, hydraulic shutdown. He fell asleep, leaving all my questions unanswered.

But as I too fell asleep for the night, I felt him again climb on top of me. "Get off my back!" I squealed, startled out of my wits.

"No choice, my boy; we don't want the guards coming in."

"I just want a warning," I pouted. "Can't you let me know before you climb on top of me? My heart skipped a beat."

"Maybe I should knock, or ring the doorbell?" He laughed quietly, his shaking body causing mine to shake in harmony. "Listen to me, my boy. We don't have time for your petty sensitivities. Tonight I am going to skip ahead sixty years, to tell you about the *other* pair of twins."

I protested that this went against all forms of good storytelling and the rules of plot. I adhered to my Baba's teachings: "Don't confuse the listener by hurrying or by skipping. You must let him follow you, one bread crumb at a time."

The Professor continued as if I had not interrupted.

"Listen well, boy, because the first time you see her, she will be giving birth. Not the most flattering position for a woman you have just met. I will do her justice. I want to introduce her to you as the remarkable child that she was—a Poonaki both by birth and by marriage. You will see her beauty, her loveliness. Through our nights you will love and cherish her. You will cry for her. You will see why we were all in love with her."

I turned over reluctantly, as he positioned himself on my back, his head inches from my ear. The long white hair encircling his bald dome hung over my face and made me want to sneeze.

♌

See her (he began) in her twelfth hour of labor, on the tenth of January, 1954. See her cocooned in a world desperate to straighten itself. In the waiting room, her husband—her cousin, Nima Poonaki—has paced for those twelve hours. She labors mightily. Sometimes she raises herself on her elbows, bares her gums, and then falls back, exhausted and scared. She watches in increasing dismay as, from between her knees, she sees a large puddle of black muck oozing out. She imagines giving birth to rotten, dead flesh, nurtured inside her for nine months.

Not so! Twins emerge, covered by a thin film—not translucent, but shiny black. They are the color of a bruise, with purple limbs like dough; one has a shock of clammy hair. And now she produces copious amounts of the black substance. The bed is soaked black, the fluid dripping on the carpet. It will darken her milk like the swirls of darkness in a pearl. Now it covers the latex gloves of the horrified surgeon, uncomprehending behind his cotton mask. The surgeon watches the woman he secretly loves, as she produces two boys— along with half a gallon of crude oil.

The surgeon removes the mask and, with a *pthew*, spits out a cotton thread. Its sense persists on his tongue like a phantom limb. *Pthew, pthew:* he tries again. The elusive filament at last falls gently on the soaked sheets. The oil seeps into the strand like tea into sugar and it soon disappears.

ℒ

"How could you have known that?" I blurted. "Elusive filament? *You weren't even in the delivery room.*" I objected also to his belabored motif: "And will you stop with all that *oil?* My father used to say that if you get stuck to an allegory, you may forget about telling your story. It gets boring."

"You sack of gelatinous human flesh, do you deign to judge the truth of what I'm telling you? I have no time for silly allegories. The truth of my story is all around you. You, young imbecile, with your unobservant, beady little eyes, you see millions of tiny facts, which you attempt to apprehend with your petty peabrain. Don't you know that truth merely masquerades as facts? You must twist, distort, and wrestle with facts to win even an inkling of what *truth* is!"

Baba, is that you playing tricks? I thought. No, it was Professor Dal speaking the way my Baba used to speak to me when I raised even the slightest eyebrow hinting of doubt. But the doctor had also a more pragmatic argument:

"I was the surgeon in the delivery room. I was helping a woman who was the love of my life give birth to my best friend's children."

I apologized to Professor Dal in humility. I called him my *arbab*, my boss, my teacher, my revered mentor. I begged him not to stop but to continue. The months of frustration and fear gushed out of me in tears, like oil out of a tanker with a ruptured hull.

"Calm down, my soft, fluffy friend. Everything will turn out for the best." He repeated these words over and over while patting and caressing the nape of my neck. "You'll see, the Hamids of this world will not last. Their evil world is doomed. Your Baba's tearoom is more alive than ever. Imagine, there are thousands of people walking past your Baba's tearoom every day and remembering the scalding, bitter tea, the mouthwatering hookahs, his beckoning stories. It is contrast such as this that will serve as the final arbiter of scoundrels. Now, if you will calm down, I'll show you lives that will make your own seem the picture of serenity."

He had arrived at the crux of his story. "Son," my Baba would declaim after afternoon prayer, "the crux of all stories is women, love, and nothing else."

The Professor, however, would say that all stories are about children, cruelty, and nothing else. The stories tell how cruelty creates grown adults whose misshapen character has formed itself around some granule of thoughtlessness, the way a mollusk develops its sharp, chalky spicules.

Stuck together like an oxpecker on his hippopotamus, the Professor and I launched together into the night.

The Professor Dissects His Love for the Lovers

*"There is love of course. And then there's
life, its enemy."*

— Jean Anouilh

It was five o'clock in the morning, and no one slept in the Poonaki house. The French windows exuded comfort; square sheets of lamplight filtered through lace curtains. Every light in the magnificent house seemed to be on. Outside, drops of fat rain fell from the bare cedars; the house, a heap of quicksilver shining in the licorice-black puddles, dissolved under each drop, to reemerge with a quiver in the January wind. The swimming pool sounded like hundreds of hurried, dutiful kisses.

A small door opened in the main entrance. A man, silhouetted, looked up at the sky and made a quick decision. He hurried across the garden toward the gate—a short trot that lapsed into smaller steps, like the older man he was. He jumped over the puddles on tiptoe; with each step across the lawn, his feet sank into a thin covering of melting snow. He held a brown bag at arm's length—as if it smelled, though this was more for balance.

Nemat, the oldest manservant in the Poonaki household, was out of breath when he stopped at the small room next to the gate. His Turkoman features registered a thousand years of living. The cracks and wrinkles on his face joined and parted like estuaries: the ideal *National Geographic* face. He was seventy-three years old, or so he reckoned. He wore a white, starched uniform of the type the English had introduced for their colonial servants.

Nemat didn't bother to knock. The gatekeeper Ghorbun-Ali was famously hard of hearing. He simply walked into the room and flicked the light switch twice.

The large man on the bed sat up, looking at him expectantly. Ghorbun-Ali's shaved head reflected the naked bulb, hanging an inch above him. Nearly Nemat's age, his face had no wrinkles.

Nemat spoke loudly. "Two boys! The master has two boys." The giant looked puzzled. Nemat repeated, this time holding up fingers for the number two, then a fist with a protruding thumb to indicate the male progeny. Ghorbun-Ali's face fell.

"Again?" he asked.

Nemat nodded. "The hand of Ali be with them. Only one"—now using his deaf man's shout—"only one will live to old age."

Ghorbun-Ali got out of bed and hopped on his one leg, smoothly as a hydraulic piston, to prepare for ablutions. His single foot propelled him around the room like a huge windup toy. Nemat left the bag of sweets and hurried back to organize breakfast.

♋

At this point the Professor stopped and remained silent for a long time. "Arbab, master, are you asleep?" I asked.

"No, my boy. I mourn my family. How everything changed after the twins' birth. It drained the love out of the family. How inconsequential our plans are. I think about the dreams we all had for the two of them. But nature had her own ideas."

♋

With all scientific confidence I had assured Mrs. Poonaki of her condition. "You will have your puppies on the tenth of January," I pronounced—and, sure enough, she obliged. I can't exaggerate the effect those children had, on all our lives. Their existence drenched us in unhappiness.

1001

Nature provides a breathless aquacade for our billions of animate sperm. Sometimes she twists the ending, by supplying two winners in the race to the ovum, a photo-finish. These two, however, were not joint winners but a pair of finalists, still competing for a single crown. Had either of them been conscious during the nine months they spent together in the womb, he would, without doubt, have wrapped the umbilical cord around the other's neck and strangled him to death. No witnesses: it would have been the perfect crime.

Dari entered the world first, thrashing like a mackerel on the deck of a trawler. He emerged into the sterilized world of the operating room with an oversized epiglottis obstructing his breathing. I shoved a tube into his gaping, purple face as we deposited him in an incubator, where I surgically corrected the problem.

Behind him, Arya made his way as a healthy, rosy seven-pounder. They were aware of each other, these two, from early on—as neon tubes flickering into consciousness.

This lifelong race of theirs did not begin evenly. As with many babies of that time, a moment of neglect produced dire consequences. One twin got gnawed by a rodent. It disfigured Dari for most of his childhood; what it did to him inside God only knows. The twins still resembled one another, but Dari looked sickly, with a crumpled profile. I could have improved it with surgery, and I showed him before-and-after pictures of fire victims. He always refused, as if determined to bear the burden.

Arya grew into a good, sturdy boy—almost parading his health, good looks, and cheerfulness. We tried everything to bring the two closer. We held elaborate birthday parties, every detail choreographed to avoid any hint of favoritism. We learned never to organize games with the boys competing on opposite sides; it would always end up in a ferocious fight with Arya

191

emerging on top, beating Dari mercilessly. Dari never surrendered, no matter how long the beating went on. By the age of six, their antagonism had infected the household. Constant arguments and fights broke out among us—"It was *his* fault this time," or, "He deserved it, because he's sneaky." I bought my own apartment and moved out, though they kept my room ready for me. We—Lili, Nima, and I—had never before quarreled the way we did during those years.

Wait: First I want to tell you about our happier times—though at the time, it didn't look like happiness. The three of us met properly, as adults, in Paris before the war. Although I did know Nima as a child, I had left Persiran when he was four or five years old.

Born during my eleventh year, Nima was immediately adored by all. I, too, loved him from the moment I set eyes on him, despite being displaced by him. The sole child of a forty-one-year-old prince of the realm, he arrived very much wanted—indeed, celebrated. Imagine: I could tell even then that he brought with him (for a lack of a better description) God's grace. But I am a doctor and not superstitious. Let me say rather: a lucky genetic makeup. I can see I am losing you, my soft sofa. People of all stripes liked him instantly, for he understood little of class subtleties, and cared less. He required little education to make the right moral decision for most of his life, until he at last made the wrong one. Popular with teachers and friends, he broke school athletic records. He played volleyball, he played football—he could play *anything*ball.

The Prince's letters to me, in Germany, were full of Nima, but so laden with disappointment in everything he did that you would think the boy would be beaten every day; the Prince was not averse to corporal punishment. But even so, his letters showed the boy in a good light. He would address me:

Dear boy:

I am in receipt of your grades and the headmaster's report. I am told you have been accepted to the most prestigious medical school in Europe—I dare say, in the world. Your dedication does me proud. Your success is my success. I have also received the second-grade grades for my Nima. The only common theme between the two reports is the effusive description by the ass who calls himself a teacher, explaining away my son's ineptitude: "Nothing too serious, Your Highness," he writes. "We are discussing the second grade here." I asked Nima to bring his books to me. He hadn't even bought them yet. School started two months ago.

Right there and then I made up my mind that a good bastinado would remind the whippersnapper of his duties. Would you believe, none of the servants would mete out the punishment? It gets worse. The boy lay on his back with legs pointing up to the sky, whispering to each servant to go ahead and use the stick, "or my father will get angry with you." One servant, Behruz— you know him, the fellow who could lift a donkey on his back—broke down, kneeling beneath the second-story window where I was watching, crying and asking forgiveness for my own son. I gave up.

Your loving guardian,
Saleh Poonaki

By this time, he signed his name without the customary honorifics. The reign of Reza Shah was in full swing and his reforms endangered all the aristocracy, it was now clear. But I was deeply absorbed in my internship, cut off from the intrigues back home. Then, in 1938, out of the blue, I received the following telegram from the Prince.

Sardar Mirza gravely ill with consumption. Arrive Berlin 2nd of May. Arrange trip to Paris for four. Nima, Nemat, and you will accompany us. Saleh Poonaki.

Once in a while, he still slipped into the royal plural.

In Paris, his brother Sardar Mirza had caught tuberculosis. The disease killed thousands. I knew that the medical world did not have an answer; we understood the cause, but we did not have the cure. Selman Waksman purified Streptomycin from *Streptomyces griseus* in 1943. In 1938, I did not hold out much hope for Sardar Mirza's recovery. So began the month that changed my life.

I first glimpsed the twelve year-old Nima when the party disembarked at the Lehrter Bahnhof, the railway station built in the French Neo-Renaissance style—the envy of all Europe. I was waiting by the west tracks, under the barrel vault roof. Brown shirts and uniformed soldiers made up a considerable proportion of the passengers; the gradual increase in their number did not strike me as anything remarkable.

A thin, straight-backed boy, with a hint of lankiness, walked straight at me, far ahead of his party, smiling widely as if he remembered me well. Without the slightest uneasiness, he walked into my arms, calling me his brother. He kissed my cheeks three times, as I looked up to see the Prince proudly watching our reunion. The Prince then walked toward me, teary-eyed, so unlike himself. "You have grown to a remarkable looking young man," he told me. He himself had aged shockingly. He walked with a thick, plain wooden cane; at fifty-three, his hair was snow white, his face drawn, gray, and tired, his eyes behind the round glasses lusterless. He had seen five Shahs over two dynasties; he had arranged exile for two of them.

"This country is ready for war," he pronounced, looking around the Berlin station. Nemat now kissed both my hands.

I was immensely touched by their warm embraces, after the absence of five years. I understood now that, despite the Prince's special love for Nima, I, too, shared in his fatherly love; in his eyes, I was family. Standing in the train station, I accepted the Poonakis as my only family, the way a born-again Christian accepts Christ. It was to be for life.

We settled at the Hotel Adlon on Pariser Platz, on the same square as the British, French, and American Embassies, and just a few blocks from the Chancellery and other government ministries. The cream of the foreign delegations, as well as celebrities and journalists, would gather for drinks and dinner at the Adlon. The Prince and I dined alone at the restaurant; Nima had been ordered to bed. It was the Prince's first trip to Europe. For all the books and papers he had read, nothing prepared him for the *thickness* of the wealth in Europe: "The doors of ordinary buildings," he marveled, "could be the doors of palaces."

It was during dessert that the Prince tabled the astonishing proposal to adopt me. He would be more than happy, he assured me, if I assumed the Poonaki name; the adoption entailed no monetary inheritance, though it came with some property.

"Your Highness—"

"You can call me 'Father,' the way you used to," he interrupted. "I don't know why you stopped during your teenage years. It hurt my feelings, you know." I was almost too staggered by this to respond.

"Your Highness, I mean, Father, I thought that, with the birth of Nima, you made it clear you had one son." He looked at me as if I had grown horns, but I persisted. "And now, with Nima all grown up, shouldn't *he* have a say in this adoption?" The Prince guffawed like his old self.

"That boy is a strange boy. He came up with the idea of adoption, not me. Well after you left, he still thought you were his blood brother. When I explained to him that I had adopted you, he asked why you had a different name. Before the start of our travel, he came to me to ask if I would give you my name permanently. I told him that I had intended to do so a few years back, but that you had now taken a great interest in your roots."

Now I recounted my adventure of searching for my genetic father, all the way to the South of the country. I told him of Wassmuss' flat denial. "He died a few years back. I did not go to his funeral." I dropped my head in shame.

The Prince had known about my long detour. His agent in Baghdad had telegraphed him the information, in response to his worried queries.

"I guessed you might have gone to find him. I read reports that he had returned; the English were concerned. I cannot tell whether he was your father or not. We will never know. Wassmuss was an extraordinary man. No shame being that man's son."

We talked of my studies, and he listened with great interest. He told me of Reza Shah's autocratic rule. "Much has changed for the good. You won't recognize the city anymore. I fear we have, as usual, put our leader on one of our ornate pedestals. He listens to no one anymore. Only his son can sway him; he loves the boy. The Crown Prince Mohammad Reza has returned from Switzerland and enrolled in the military academy."

"Are you in danger, Father?"

"I can't tell," he shrugged. "Years ago, when I was governor and Reza Shah was only a lowly officer in the Cossack division, they assigned him to me. He and a few of his Cossacks rode with me as protection. I treated him well. I invited him to sit in my tent at dinner. We talked. I think he cherishes those uncomplicated times. He now uses me for some diplomatic chores. In point of fact, I have an appointment to see Chancellor Hitler, along with your host, the Ambassador. The Shah wants me to give him a few rather difficult messages."

I was entranced at the thought that the Prince would actually talk to the Führer: I had swallowed Nazi ideology hook, line, and sinker. The Prince went on. "Now I am concerned—maybe more than concerned: afraid. I have seen the inside of prison a couple of times in my life without too much worry. I understood it as a flexing of muscles by that stupid low-life Tabatabai, who sits at the Shah's right hand. But lately there have been more ominous signs. Three of his closest allies and cabinet members have died: one of them committed suicide; another died in prison."

Eventually we turned to talk of happier times. I introduced him to a few exotic after-dinner drinks, which he much appreciated.

The next day, we received a telegram from Qodrat, his brother's personal servant, begging us to hurry, as Sardar Mirza's health had deteriorated. The Prince stayed one extra day, to meet the Chancellor. The train to Paris covered the 600 miles overnight, to arrive at the Gare du Nord on the fifth of May, 1938. The Prince—who had been irritable throughout the journey—hurried along the platform; the rest of us tried to keep up with him at a half-run without crashing into anyone.

We had never met Sardar Mirza's family; none of us had ever seen the Countess or her daughter Lili. The Prince instantly recognized Qodrat, who, at six-foot-four, towered above the throng of greeters. By now he was no longer a beefy peasant but a well-dressed manservant à l'anglaise—a dignified, tall, white-haired gentleman waiting to greet his grandchildren. (Sardar Mirza, a dandy all his life, would expect no less.) "There he is!" the Prince cried, pointing his cane toward Qodrat's head, as if leading his troops into battle.

At that moment, Qodrat glimpsed the Prince among the onrush of passengers and pushed his way past a protesting guard. Rushing into the throng, he reached the Prince in seconds, followed by the angrily panting guard. Instantly, that impressively tall figure fell to the ground, actually to kiss the Prince's feet. The Prince bent down to raise Qodrat upright, to the stares of the crowd of passengers, no doubt curious about the Prince's importance.

Nima and I spotted the Countess and Lili at the same time. As in a Sargent painting, the daughter stood clasping her arms around her mother's waist, smiling and watching us sideways, as light and elegant as if airborne. Lili wore a white summer dress with a light sweater over her shoulders. Her cloche hat almost covered a fashionable boyish haircut.

Lili's mother, the Countess Anaïs de Grandpierre, was the daughter of the Comte de Grandpierre; she had adopted the title during the looser times of the Third Republic, although she was not strictly entitled to it. She looked older than her age. Ramrod straight, she watched us with despondent eyes, her hand resting lightly on her daughter's shoulders as she watched Qodrat's embarrassing oriental charade. She wore her hair in a swept-up coiffure, by the famous Antoine, topped by one of the simpler Suzanne Talbot hats— worn askew, with a veil covering the left side of her face. In a cream-colored Schiaparelli two-piece outfit: an almost undiscernible image of a woman's face was sewn on the shoulder of the blouse, with an intricate gold filigree of the embroidered woman's hair trailing riotously down the left arm of the blouse to the cuff of the sleeve. The Countess might have stepped out of Vogue magazine.

We approached them. Nima was suddenly as shy as a beaten puppy, with none of the lively enthusiasm he had shown in Berlin. Despite years of French tutors, he spoke the language haltingly at best; now he was tongue-tied. I had to step ahead to introduce myself to the Countess. I spoke French fluently (with an atrocious

German accent). She acknowledged me with a sideways nod and the sweetest smile I have seen on a grown woman. Meanwhile, the Prince extricated himself from Qodrat's attentions and moved to greet his sister-in-law. Qodrat now caught sight of Nemat, after twenty years' separation, hurrying down the platform with his hands full of luggage. The giant Qodrat pounced, almost overturning the old man and kissing him like a long-lost lover.

"How is my brother?" the Prince asked in place of a greeting—so distraught that he forgot his manners.

"Not good, Your Highness," the Countess replied, understanding that his directness arose from deep concern for his twin. "You will see for yourself. We are not hopeful. Mirza is at peace with it." (All of Paris called him simply "Mirza.")

Lili stepped forward and made a soft curtsey, her hands holding the sides of her skirt in a girlish gesture. In a loud, stilted voice she pronounced, "*Cher oncle et cousin, permettez-moi de saisir cette occasion pour vous souhaiter la bienvenue dans notre beau pays.*" A few awkward seconds passed as we all considered how to respond to this formal welcome to France. She then flashed an exact replica of her mother's sweet smile and broke into lively, fluent Farsi—made all the more appealing by the charming French "r". "Really, family, you didn't buy that boring speech, did you?" Everyone laughed, astonished at her fluency. "Baba would have loved to have seen your faces!" She even slipped Nima a wink.

"*Lili, vous êtes vraiment fatiguante.*" The Countess played the exasperated mother: "You are truly tiresome." Lili, turning serious once more, slipped sweetly into the arms of the uncle she had never met. "You smell just like him," she confided. The Prince could only be charmed.

The tension broken, the party moved outside into the soft Paris May morning, to be driven to their apartment in the 16th Arrondissement. Nemat and Qodrat stayed back to take care of the luggage. Nima, the happiest of anyone, chatted with Lili all the way. There was no denying the palpable warmth emanating from the two cousins. Charm—more than intelligence, more than wisdom—would rule their world. Pindar captured it: "These enchanting creatures were created to fill the world with pleasant moments and goodwill." The same could not be said of their issue.

I cannot tell you whether my fascination for Lili started then; my tastes certainly do not lean to prepubescent girls. Yet there was offered a promise of the woman she would become. I observed her candid blue eyes, full of marvel at meeting—for the first time—the oriental side of the family. And, as sad as those days were, that month nevertheless had for me a brightness that I could only credit to Lili's natural exuberance. Walking in through the door, she charged the house with energy. Even the Prince, consumed with worry, was taken by her charm. Who waits for a twelve-year-old to grow up? I did.

We all squeezed into the narrow French elevator, with its zigzag of accordion metal—thoracic, Proust calls it—with Lili and Nima giggling all the way up. The doors to the apartment stood open, as white-haired mademoiselle Marte, the Countess's old governess, welcomed us. A nurse in starched white walked toward us, her forefinger next to her nose as a signal to hush. "His Highness is resting. He had a difficult night," she whispered. The large apartment covered the entire fourth floor. Our shoes squeaked on the polished wooden parquet. The large floor-to-ceiling windows, overlooking George Mandel Avenue, tinkled gently, shivering at our arrival. Nima, all animation, pointed out the Eiffel tower, half hidden behind Le Trocadéro.

Impatient to see his brother, the Prince begged the Countess's permission to stay in his brother's room. "Certainly," she responded generously. "My apartment is on the other side, if you need anything." With heartfelt thanks, the Prince walked into Sardar Mirza's room and remained there, during four nights and five days, until Sardar Mirza had let out his final breath.

A few hours after our arrival, Nima and I were introduced to Sardar Mirza, accompanied by Lili. We wore white surgical masks, though the Prince did not wear any protection. Sardar Mirza was leaning against dozens of pillows on a large bed. He wore a black silk dressing gown, the collar points of his ironed pajamas spread neatly over the lapels. Above his head, a large Monet landscape of Giverny brightened the room with dappled violets. Lili ran in and sat next to her papa on the bed. He stroked her hair. He asked us to come nearer, for he was medically blind. He used a large magnifying glass to inspect us, with unfeigned delight.

As a budding medical student, I well understood his condition. The classic chronic cough. The discarded handkerchiefs, piled in the small cloth-lined laundry basket next to his bed, drenched with bright blood-tinged sputum. His eyes looked feverish; his brow had a sheen of sweat, which the Prince wiped away for him. I could tell he had lost a great deal of weight: the Prince looked twice as heavy.

Yet Sardar Mirza was by far the more voluble of the two, more prone to laughter, keeping up a cheerful banter. He could not keep from caressing his daughter. Each time the coughing wracked his body, we all quieted down. The Prince would caress his brother's head, bending over the side of the bed, while Lili rubbed her father's back from the other side.

I regret not visiting him earlier. He was full of stories of his exploits during the Constitutional Revolution. He knew every important artist of the twentieth century by name, from his years living in Paris. He had met Sargent; he *tutoyed* Maurice Ravel. He had taken tea at the Hôtel de Crillon while gossiping with Proust. He had joined wild parties with Jean Cocteau. He would reminisce with Diaghilev about their self-imposed exiles, after their so-different revolutions. Picasso had done a pencil caricature of him, right after the Great War, showing Sardar Mirza bending with his magnifying glass over a painting—a scholarly harlequin. He and Roger Fry, both strong supporters of the early Impressionists, had collaborated on a few monographs. Through Fry he came to know the Bells, whom he much liked; he preferred the faux modesty of the English to the opinionated panache of the Parisians. He especially disliked Gertrude Stein and her crowd for their firm pronouncements on everything. Such declarations, he protested, presented opinions as facts— an affectation that could only hold them back. Sardar Mirza himself was astonishingly free of aesthetic pretensions.

After the failure of the first Constitutional Revolution and the bombardment of the Persiranian parliament, Sardar Mirza had returned to Paris for good. He rented a suite in the 6th Arrondissement, on the Left Bank. For fourteen years he lived an engaged life, full of parties, museums, and trips to London. That was when the Countess found him once again.

She saw Sardar Mirza, for the first time after twenty-six years, on the tenth of January, 1922, at the opening of a new restaurant. He was thirty-six years old. She recognized him immediately. He was unaware of her presence, just two tables down; indeed, he couldn't see the cutlery on the table without his magnifying glass, which he never used in public. The next time she sought him out was at a party given by André Gide at Rue Vavin. She heard someone asking for "Prince Mirza": a redundance of titles; no one could find him. Cocteau bitched sweetly that Mirza would usually hide in libraries or else "gallantly" aid his hostesses in the bedrooms. (Sardar Mirza used the pen name "Gallant" for his art criticism; there was perhaps some truth to Cocteau's remark.) The Countess found him—not in a bedroom but in the library—in the same pose that Picasso had drawn, examining a pointillist portrait. His method was to internalize a painting by examining it, patch by patch, with his magnifying glass, until his brain had assembled the pieces. Edwardian in his dress, he cut a figure to the Countess's satisfaction.

"And how has Monsieur Le Prince been keeping, all these years?"

Sardar Mirza straightened upright, suddenly alert as if hearing his master's whistle.

"Is that *you*, Anaïs?"

"It is I," she said. They eloped two days later.

In the last days of his life, I attended him (like the physician I was not), trying to make him comfortable in any way I could. His own physician, Doctor Murat—a caricature of a French doctor, with pointed goatee and pince-nez—visited him once a day, more or less out of courtesy. After each visit, he shook his head in despair, tears in his eyes; they had been good friends.

The Prince concerned me. When I would tiptoe into the room late at night to check on Sardar Mirza, I would find that the Prince had crawled into the bed to hold his brother in his arms. They slept face to face. We well understood the contagiousness of the mycobacterium tuberculosis. But the Prince, heedless, handled soiled handkerchiefs and washcloths as he fed and cared for his brother daily. I tried to warn him. I asked him at least to wear a mask. "By putting on a mask," he instructed me, "I would communicate to him that life means something to me—when it doesn't."

"But you have Nima to think about!"

His reply astonished me. "Nima lives in a world that I cannot reach. He doesn't need me. I am not sure he needs anyone." He hesitated. "Maybe he will need *her*. Exceptional, isn't she?" He pointed across the room, where Lili sat talking excitedly with her father, as if oblivious to the fact that she would have him for only a little time longer.

Fifty years later, I still remember being surprised at my anger at the Prince's presumption. So you see, my floating balloon, I had *expectations*. I swear that I did not have any carnal intention toward a twelve-year-old. I had come to envision her, in my mind's eye, as the grown-up woman she would become—a suitable object of my life-long devotion. Indeed, when I saw her five years later, she had grown into the woman I had imagined.

What did I hope for? Her hand in marriage? I was a good-looking man then: I tell you, boy (though you may scoff at this), many women threw themselves at me. I don't mind saying that I had my fill. I vowed never to let Lili see me accompanied by any other woman. She never did. I believe she expected it of me.

People comment that the marriage of these two cousins had been written in the heavens. That may be true. But, surprisingly soon, it was an event on Earth that would seal their troth and steal Lili's heart from me.

Sardar Mirza died on the morning of May 15, 1938, a sunny day. The servants closed all the curtains and began readying the apartment for a week of mourning and for the visits of friends and relatives of the Countess. The Prince stayed in his brother's bedroom, suffering what I can only call a breakdown. Every few minutes, we would hear a cry like an animal's howl that echoed around the apartment and, I am sure, through the building and into the street. The two children sat white-faced, scared out of their wits, among the collection of paintings piled higgledy-piggledy in the overstuffed living room. (These paintings, by the greatest masters of the twentieth century, would prove the kernel of the Poonaki family's wealth over the next thirty years.) The Countess sat with the Prince all afternoon.

Nemat and I took the two cousins for a walk in the Bois de Boulogne, to spare them the Prince's violent grief. We walked aimlessly around a man-made lake. I walked slowly, staying well behind them, and Nemat walked a few steps behind me. The world shimmered in our reddened eyes like a pointillist painting. Families picnicked; children played; dogs ran around. With each ringing of a bicycle bell or clomping of horses' hooves, I shouted unheard warnings to the young cousins, far ahead.

Nima, a spirited boy of thirteen, would veer off to inspect something and run back to report to Lili. I could see him bringing her flowers, a polished stone, a ladybug. Approaching nearer, I heard her say, marveling, *"C'est une coccinelle."* Examining the insect's black spots, they bent their heads toward each other, as the *coccinelle* walked across their hands. By quickly covering one hand with another, they created a giant, endless staircase, which the ladybug climbed or descended at the whim of these two deities. Perhaps in exasperation, the insect now crawled up Lili's bare arm, making her squeal in delight: clearly, Nima had made some headway in cheering her up. The ladybug suddenly remembered her powers and flew away. As the two looked up in unison, their hands shielding their brows against the sun, my brain snapped a shot of them: a brother and sister that God had washed in different dyes—their downy skin milk or chocolate, their eyes dark blue or hazel brown. The childish jawlines, upturned toward the sun, traced a delicate cut-out against the blue sky. My heart melted for the two of them. I envied their naturalness, their beauty and innocence, but I also loved them for it. I promised myself that I would do anything in my power to protect them from harm. Almost immediately, my powers would be shown inadequate.

We had walked past the lake; there was an opening of grass and a soft embankment. Nima ran up and disappeared from view. In the distance, a black boxer ran around his owner, who held a toy bone just out of his reach. The boxer jumped again and again, his compact body doing comical pirouettes. Suddenly, the dog lost interest in the unattainable bone. He turned, one leg still in the air, and looked toward us as we walked—his gaze steady, tongue hanging out, mouth gaping like an anglerfish. The owner tried in vain to get his attention. Licking his face all over, he held his head to one side, his clipped ears erect. As we approached, his tongue did another face-lick—and he came toward us like a shot. Nemat shouted a warning; Muslims, I well knew, are not dog lovers, and I reassured him. Indeed, the dog had little interest in us. Behind me was a Doberman, chafing on his leash as if trying to drag its owner forward.

Now the boxer was running directly toward Lili, who—having grown up with dogs all her life—watched him nonchalantly. I saw her bending to encourage him. I shouted at her to stay still, to let the dog pass and get to the Doberman. Scared by my shout, Lili stood stiff as a stick, as the dog came at a run. My shout brought Nima to the top of the embankment. He broke into an impressive run to intercept the dog—which he did spectacularly. Ten feet away from Lily, the surprised dog crashed into him. Dog and boy rolled over and over in complicated twists, the dog growling and barking. Old Nemat reached them first, but in those few seconds the boxer had bitten Nima four or five times.

Back on its feet, the boxer looked confused: it had no recollection of charging a human. Remembering its intended target, it now ran past us toward the Doberman, though with a bit less fervor. The owner of the Doberman produced a short thick whip, and, stepping in front of his dog, meted out two hard lashes. The boxer yelped and leapt sideways.

We all ran to Nima. He got up, then sat back down in shock. He seemed uncertain which part of himself to hold, hugging his knees and twisting his neck from pain. Lili got to him first, hugging him and crying. His face had begun to bleed. I borrowed handkerchiefs from some concerned bystanders, to apply pressure on the cuts. He had a nasty bite on his lip and nose. Another bite had caught him on the eyebrow and inner corner of his left eye, tearing the flesh near his tear duct: for the rest of his life, he would use drops to moisten his left eye. I told Lily to calm herself. "Take this handkerchief and press it on his eyebrow." She knelt uncomfortably, bare knees on dirt, holding the handkerchief to his face and holding his head with her other hand, as if cradling it against her still undeveloped chest. His right arm had a bad bite and scratches from falling in the dirt; I used lake water to clean the wound and tied a handkerchief around the arm. I left untreated a shallow bite near his bellybutton, where his clothing had provided some protection. I asked him if he had other bites. He shook his head. He made a few hissing and blowing sounds at the pain but did not utter a word.

The owner of the boxer, a blond, fortyish man in tweeds and moleskin, apologized *mille fois* ("a thousand times," making a good try to reach that number). He offered to take us to the American Hospital. Nima finally spoke. He asked, would the dog be coming too? The grown-ups laughed. The owner promised that his wife would walk the dog home.

The laughter brought a smile even to Lili's teary eyes. Still kneeling, she whispered something in Nima's ear. Still cleaning his scratched right arm, I lifted my head in time to see his face take on a shocked look—and then a smile that spread through the cut on his upper lip, a smile that could not be wiped away, even at the hospital, during the stitches and the tetanus shot. It must have been a thousand years later, over a drink, after none of us had anything to lose, that Nima repeated to me her words.

"Mother chose father as her husband when she was twelve, in Russia," she had said to him. "*I* will choose my husband in Paris."

You will understand, my puffy foundation: *I was never even in the garden* (as the Persiranian proverb puts it). How could I have comprehended how far ahead of me these two were?

Rays of yellow sunlight had managed to crawl up the wall and enter our filthy window, high above my head. Succumbing to nostalgia, Professor Dal fell silent.

The Fifth Night
0101

The Narrator's Discourse on Politics, Soccer, and Love

"If God had wanted me otherwise,
He would have created me otherwise."

— Goethe

Dear Ms. Vakil:

It is 0545. I sit in my small apartment overlooking the early traffic on the elevated Route 93. Trucks rudely shake the building foundations. The cowardly yellow sun, like a smear of Vaseline, makes tentative contact with my fourth-floor living room window. It has yet to gather the necessary strength to reflect light from one object to another. On the floor sit piles of books on the early twentieth-century constitutional history of Persiran. Piles of stacked papers are neatly tied with weathered black ribbons. Circles of cracked red wax, mooshed by my grandfather's strong hand, give the papers—forgive the cliché—a literal seal of legitimacy. Limou, my wire fox terrier, sits and looks at me dejectedly. I have just educated her by issuing a bark of my own, to stop her pulling at the ribbons that keep the manuscript rolls in their cylindrical shapes.

I am astounded by your revelations regarding Mr. Hekaiatchi, my fictional storyteller. You must understand the strange predicament this creates for me. Have I created a Golem of my own? Has a fictional character come to life? In his letters to me, some twenty years ago, Mr. Hekaiatchi—not my storyteller, but the man who claimed to be the cellmate of my uncle Dal—wrote about that time with my uncle. I have leavened his narrative with the historical documents in my possession. Mr. Hekaiatchi's pecuniary demands were not exorbitant—but I have not had the means to assess the truth of any of his claims. I say this, though: if the claims of this corpulent man have any validity, he and I must have bracketed the first and the last days of my uncle Dal's ten-year stay in prison. I can hardly know the exact number of nights this man shared a cell with my uncle. It serves my purpose well enough to say nine nights and days, poaching from my own experience. In any case, I date my storyteller's imprisonment with my uncle Dal at about ten years after the revolution, just after the end of the Persiran-Iraq War.

Frankly, I at first thought Mr. Hekaiatchi must be crazy. He made wild claims about his father living in his ear—a theme I have used to lighten my own story. Yet, Ms. Vakil, at times Mr. Hekaiatchi's letters ushered my uncle right into my Boston apartment, with all his quirks and eccentricities. I did not know the details of my uncle's youthful trip to Germany. I had learned already of his wild detour to the gulf, from a letter written by Saleh Mirza to his agent in Baghdad. Mr. Hekaiatchi sounded authentic—but who could tell? Then his letters stopped abruptly. I regret not paying him for his troubles. So many years later, your confidence in his authenticity presents a challenge. Maybe I can reestablish contact with him? Have you kept in touch? Today (unlike twenty years ago) I am in fair financial shape. I could pay a fair price for the rest of his story.

For the past several weeks, each morning before work, I have labored to put together a picture of what happened during those crucial days of our Constitutional Revolution. Your profession is not easy; it requires a judicious mind, something that might not be my strong suit. "Let the professional historians deal with it, Mr. Poonaki!" Well enough: I am not attempting to write a magisterial history of the Constitutional Revolution. But I do have an inquisitive streak. I mean to ferret out my grandfathers' contributions—lost amid the mountains of doodles promulgated by new dynasties as official historical record.

I am puzzled about a chess-move by the reactionary Premier Ain Dowleh (a royal himself, a cousin to the old Shah). It was just three weeks before his Shah's total capitulation to the constitutionalists. He chose to send my grandfather, Saleh Mirza—then a 21-year-old Qajar prince and a budding constitutionalist—to negotiate with a powerful and renowned cleric with a Sharia fixation!

I have surrounded myself with books up to my ears— or at least up to Limou's ears, even pricked up as they are now, alert to some new input beyond human hearing. Now comes the growling, deep in his vocal cords, and then the pointless triple barks that set all the neighbors against me (especially my Chinese next-door neighbors). Deep in my reading, I pronounce "Leeee" in a bass warning voice—and then "mou" in a high-pitched panic, as he begins to bark. Lifting him onto my lap, I continue reading: reading, and rereading, my grandfathers' diaries. Never mind tears: it is worth peeling back a few layers of the fine Persiranian onion.

Court machinations in 1906, during the weeks before ratification of the constitution, centered on the health of the old Shah, Mozaffar al-Din Shah. The overbearing Dr. Schneider had diagnosed him with gout, and then its successor, Bright's disease. Overproduction of uric acid causes renal failure leading to congestive heart failure. Everyone in court knew that the Shah was tiptoeing around his own deathbed.

The proposed constitution had three formidable opponents: the Crown Prince, Mohammad Ali; Premier Ain Dowleh, an old man of sclerotic beliefs; and the cleric Sheikh Fazlollah Nouri. The three of them adopted different tactics to deal with the constitutionalists' demands.

Trained (so to speak) by his Russian tutor, the Crown Prince had grown up illiterate. You remember, Ms. Vakil, that the Crown Prince had his uncles (my two grandfathers) flogged raw in Tabriz. His third-rate tutor, Shapshal Khan, had inculcated in the Crown Prince a deep sense of his God-given right to rule, equal to that of Nicholas II. In response to the initial modest demands for an independent judiciary, the Crown Prince retorted, without any trace of irony: "A House of Justice? *I am the House of Justice.*"

Eight months later, alarmed at the insistent demands of the constitutionalists, the Crown Prince had changed his tune. He had no desire to inherit an explosive situation. If any concessions were to be made, let the old fool, the reigning Shah, make them! Watching as his ailing father weakened, Mohammad Ali sought merely to stanch the bleeding of his God-given powers. Let them have their independent judiciary—even a national assembly. Later, as Shah, Mohammad Ali would retract those concessions: he was made of sterner stuff than his capitulating father.

The constitutionalists' forces had been immeasurably strengthened by an altogether surprising intervention by the British. The acting *chargé d'affaires*, Evelyn Grant Duff, allowed a large legation of petitioning merchants to use the British Embassy as a sanctuary— probably the most selfless act by the English during all the diplomatic history of our two countries. (I know that historians don't like grand generalizations, but can you think of one other decision by the English that did not give with one hand and take away with the other?) By the time this news reached the Home Office, it was too late to undo the damage: the proverbial barn doors were wide open, and all manner of horses were charging in. The three reactionaries—the Premier, the Crown Prince, and the Sheikh—now pretended to support the Constitutional Revolution, while placing their cynical bets against its long-term success.

The old Premier came to power twice more but faded quickly in the annals of history: only someone with your expertise could roll out his name without effort. The Crown Prince ascended the throne on the nineteenth of January, 1907. Two years later, he was deposed, leaving a small ripple in our history. It was rather the ideologue Sheikh, Fazlollah Nouri, who left an indelible mark on Persiranian politics. His *fatwa* against the cinema ended movies in Persiran until his death, and he became a model for Imam Khomeini to emulate. Ms. Vakil, let us stay laser-focused on this man, whose name I hadn't heard until my arrest thirty-five years ago. Now, as in a criminal investigation, I have pinned his photo on my board, with lines connecting him to other historical figures. His strategy shines with the clarity of the self-righteous: to introduce personally, here on earth, the laws God designed for heaven.

As you can see, I am telling the story from both ends: a strong first generation advances the nation's history, and a decadent third generation fritters away those gains. True, the gains the Prince achieved proved modest. And as to the frittering—all good family stories are about frittering.

My early memories are in chiaroscuro. Driving to our country house in Poonak, the paved road gives way to a stone-strewn dirt road, heading straight north for about ten miles across scraggly, flat country with here and there a few clusters of mud dwellings edging the extensive gardens of absentee landowners. The pale lemon-green Vauxhall would take two sharp turns along the mud-and-straw walls of Poonak, passing a group of filthy boys—Hamid among them—playing soccer with a deflated plastic ball. The car would finally come to a stop in front of the large green wooden door (later to become an automated green metal door).

Our driver, Hovanes, was a Russo-Armenian émigré nicknamed Moosio—a bastardization of the French *monsieur*, though not meant as an honorific. For driving, he spread a large white handkerchief over his large stomach to protect his white shirt from the dusty steering wheel. At the gate, Moosio honked the horn: two short bursts, and then a long blast, all with no result. The gardener might be occupied in the far corners of the garden, maybe half a mile away.

Moosio swore under his breath in Armenian and Russian. A sophisticated man and a consummate mechanic, he spoke several languages. Now he levered his bulk down from the car to perform a feat that always impressed my brother and me. By pushing against both doors of the gate, the rudimentary latch gaped just enough for a slender person to pass through the opening. Moosio, far from slender, managed the trick nonetheless. Houdini-like, he'd bend his knees, lowering his body enough to put his face sideways into the opening—no doubt getting a close shave from the edge of the gate. Now, with his left hand braced outside the gate, he would cajole his belly through. From the backseat, we'd unpeel our thighs from the vinyl seats to watch in wonder.

In a letter, my mother compared those double green doors to the pearly gates of heaven. Leaving the dusty road, desiccated under an unrelenting sun, we entered into the dappled shade of a fruit garden replete with cherry and sour cherry, fig and pomegranate, walnut and mulberry and white berry trees. Rows of straw-berries, and cherry tomatoes shaped like pacifiers, peeked red from under dusty green leaves.

We turned into a graveled avenue darkened by a solemn conference of lofty sycamores, and the car at last came to a stop at the bottom of some wide, thin stone stairs. As we climbed the staircase, the trees parted, welcoming us to a platform of daylight.

The view was breathtaking. We could see Tehran, far across the valley to the southwest, and Shemiran, its neighboring enclave, where the aristocracy and foreign delegations relocated for the summer. The mountains to the east extended as far as the eye could see. In the immediate foreground, a low stone wall, matching the stairs, kept us from falling into the green valley of terraced gardens and the river below: a ten-meter fall. Our earliest wall-climbing exploits were in pursuit of our balls, shuttlecocks, and kites.

Here we spent all our summers, from the day the school closed to the night before it opened. I cannot remember how and when we began to mix with the boys from the village, in rough-and-ready competition that defied elitist snobbery. Yet privilege asserts itself: we brought the leather ball that replaced the misshapen plastic ball.

Do I remember the first time I met Hamid? I cannot say I do. We were all thirteen years old when we met, though we must have seen him much earlier. The other boys in the village—poorer, dirtier—fade into dustiness in my memory. I remember Hamid as deferential and defiant at the same time, and covered in dirt from head to toe. Already taller than we were, his head was shaved, showing a number of scars from cracks against sticks and stones. His overdelicate, cocoa-colored face was wild and wily, but also open, with black eyes that reflected light. His voice had already cracked low. His plastic sandals showed splintered toenails. He wore pajama-like trousers that flapped around his delicate but filthy ankles when he ran after the ball. Later, of course, he'd wear our hand-me-downs.

I don't remember ever seeing him laugh; people felt privileged when he bestowed on them his tight smile. I do remember when we became pals. He had a mighty fight with my brother, Arya, resulting in broken bones that sealed a long-lasting friendship between the two of them. It was something entirely different that would stitch him to me.

Our soccer games took place in the private dirt road that led to our gate. The outside of our gate served as one goal; at the other end, where the private road met the dirt-packed country lane, we had fashioned two short wooden posts. The field was a stone-strewn rectangle of dirt, bounded on each side with low mud-and-straw walls that we used as a twelfth player who returned the ball reliably. Strangely enough, we always had spectators—a few stolid peasants, standing next to the walls, watching without much apparent interest.

I attended the games but did not play: I possessed a melamine will; but for most of my life, I remained physically delicate. My brother, strong as a bull, played hard. He had a winsome smile and a genial bonhomie (that seemed patronizing only to me). Several boys wanted to be on his team; others remained loyal to Hamid—less strong, but more skilled. I served as a kind of manager. At my suggestion, one afternoon, we cleared all the rocks from the field and used them to construct a spectator area. I began to come up with new rules for every contingency. What if the ball fell into the gutter? What if the ball crossed the markings representing the goal? And what if Moosio kicked the ball spastically, as he watched from the gate? I began to play the referee. Incredibly, the boys were happy with the new system. Arguments no longer flared, and when issues arose, they looked to me to settle the dispute.

My brother despised my new role. He challenged me in front of the boys. Whenever the argument erupted into a physical fight, back at our house, I got the worst of it. Even more dramatic than our own competition, however, was the crisis of leadership brewing between Arya and Hamid.

Ms. Vakil, today is a Sunday, the kind of bright autumn day that only New England offers. Coming from a long walk near the ocean, I crossed the high school athletic fields. The baseball field, in geometrical patches of diamond and grass, screamed of devoted, expensive upkeep. Behind it were half a dozen immaculately lime-lined soccer fields; more than a hundred little girls, wearing team uniforms, were running around under the autumn sun. And, in this field of dreams, without exaggeration, there were *hundreds* of shiny blue-and-white leather balls stockpiled on the sidelines. When did we get so wealthy? Yet the dusty games we played forty years ago were played with greater seriousness, played for keeps. Our games resembled those YouTube clips where two wild bucks butt horns with that tremendous echoing clash, until one of them gives way.

Ms. Vakil, I acted the impartial referee—but I confess that my calls imperceptibly favored Hamid. My brother, infuriated, saw through me. To him, it was part of our larger, lifelong game. But for once he had it wrong. At thirteen years of age, I had fallen for this peasant boy. I had fallen for his elegance and beauty. What about birth? What of upbringing? How could a boy caked head-to-toe in mud walk through a dusty village with such grace? It makes one believe in a deity.

I might be making this up, but I remember a Friday when a larger-than-usual crowd ranged behind me at my stone fence; it was dusk, and people were back from the fields. I remember some women, or maybe young girls—some with chadors, others open-faced, with dirty, tangled hair and snotty noses. I remember a ferocious, competitive game, sweaty and short-tempered. A contentious goal by my brother: the ball had crossed over the short stump of a post at the other end of the field. He and Hamid were instantly at my doorstep. The crowd peered over my shoulders as the rivals argued heatedly. I disallowed the goal. The crowd murmured approval; Hamid was one of their own. My incensed brother stared at me for a few long seconds, and then, without warning, he slapped me, hard. Hamid grabbed Arya's hand to prevent him from hitting me again. "*Bebakhshesh, agha,*" he said to me. "Forgive him, sir."

As a cloud passes over the sun, a shadow crossed my brother's face as his jaw tightened. "You impertinent peasant!" he spat at Hamid.

And the fight broke out. My brother—shorter, heavier, with a lower center of gravity—dived at Hamid's midriff like a wild animal. They rolled in the dust like two rabid dogs; class distinctions forgotten, they wrestled with boyish grunts. The other boys circled around, screaming. In seconds, my brother's strength overwhelmed Hamid's quickness; Arya was sitting on the hero's chest and pounding him furiously with his fists—unusual, in a country used to wrestling.

Then all movement froze—all sounds, even breathing stopped. The punching had ceased: Hamid had gotten hold of Arya's index finger and was twisting it back with all his strength. The spectators' faces wore an apprehensive grimace. When the crack came, everyone heard it. "Aach!" my brother cried. Getting off Hamid's chest, he shook his hand, as he cursed and circled around like a dog chasing his tail. Hamid shot to his feet like a spring and bent double, panting. His nose was broken, his face bloodied. Then my brother, as he always could, turned everything upside down. Laughing loudly through his pain, he threw his good hand around Hamid's shoulder. "You have guts, you lucky bastard!"

Hamid, still dazed, glanced once toward me, as if asking permission to make peace. He then offered one of his tight smiles. Everyone clapped except me. How much more girlish could I feel? *A boy had fought over me.* I even had an exasperating erection. Moosio drove both of them to the hospital where Professor Dal practiced surgery, and the noses and fingers were fixed.

No need to blush, Ms. Vakil. Boys will be boys—and sometimes girls. The fight did in fact erase the humiliation of my slap. People remembered the fight, but not its cause.

But now, let me transport you back to the era you love. It will take a few shakes to wake the flabby hulk who now slumbers uncomfortably in our shared experience.

The Fat Storyteller Sticks His Covered Head Out

"He will run into any mould, but he won't keep shape."

— George Eliot, *Middlemarch*

Scribble, scribble, Baba. Using this poor excuse of a pencil, I have filled three thin, wobbly-ruled exercise books. As with all local products, the pencil leaves only a blond trace of my handwriting and I must wet the tip to accentuate the darkness of the lead; my lower lip has a permanent mark resembling a tattoo. Still, Mammad-Ali's generosity cannot be faulted. We live in difficult times. War profiteers, charlatans, politicians, and mullahs, all are in collusion. They petition the government to set up factories. They obtain preferential exchange rates. They substitute cheaper raw materials. They pocket the savings, and they resell the leftover dollars.

My manuscript sits, dangerously, on my desk. I have written a number of letters to the sole surviving member of the Poonaki family, Mr. Dari Poonaki. I promised Professor Dal I would contact him on my release from the loony bin. I asked Mammad-Ali to mail those letters with extreme care: you wouldn't want people in the neighborhood to find out that you correspond with the United States. Mr. Poonaki never answered. Did he receive the letters? I did not dare put a return address on the envelope.

I have made up my mind to visit the offices of Vakil Khanum, the publisher of Qajar history. A great risk: my heart races, and my mouth dries up at the thought. What if she reports me to the officials? What if she does not believe me? But I am told that the editor is a remnant of the Shah's regime and has connections to foreign publishing houses. I have sent Zahra to make enquiries—to *smell* the place, so to speak. Not afraid of much, my Zahra climbed four flights of stairs and knocked on the gilt-inscribed publisher's door. She walked in without waiting for a reply, as if it were a government office. She found seven or eight neatly kerchiefed young women working behind computer screens set on small tables. The senior raised her head and asked if she could be of help. Zahra, quick on her feet, asked if they could use a charwoman. Undeterred at being told "no," she asked to see the boss. On Tuesdays and Thursdays, Ms. Vakil Khanum taught at Tehran University; she would be back at the office in the morning.

What impressed my clever Zahra was neither the office full of computers nor the staff's more-than-polite tone to a *chadori* (a covered woman). What impressed Zahra was that all the women in that office *continued to work diligently* in the absence of their boss.

"You don't get that commitment from any dirty-assed official!" she chortled.

I thanked Zahra profusely. I noticed that, forsaking her dark chador, she had donned a handsome kerchief. For my benefit perhaps? A spray of hair fell accidently-on-purpose across her face, veiling her strabismic eyes. Her dark brown skirt outlined and molded an abandon of lovely flesh, like a Persiranian vase. She stepped down the stairs on her strong, stockinged calves, leaving me to my fantasies (which I now share uncomfortably with you, Baba).

To distract myself from unholy thoughts, I wetted my depleted pencil on my lower lip, holding it awkwardly in my fat hand, and began to set down—*the fifth day and night.*

𝒮

I woke that morning to—what else?—the Professor's shrieks. I kept my distance. He asked his question. I answered correctly. Nonetheless, he carried on with his ritual. I noticed that his toes had been tipped with glossy red nail polish. The guards, too, repeated their lines and carried him out. Where they hauled him I could not say. But I was sure of this: I shared my cell with two quite different people. The person who kept me company at night was not the same person who screamed like a lunatic in the mornings.

On the fifth night, he approached me and asked politely if I could accommodate him on my back. I signaled my concurrence by turning onto my stomach. He climbed over me like someone mounting a horse, like a small child riding his dad. He then lay on his stomach and came close to my ear. Sometimes he rolled on his back, one leg crossed over the other bent knee, making it difficult to hear him properly. But that night his voice carried.

"I will recount tonight the most glorious time in our history," he said. "You may think I exaggerate, but it took bravery, luck, and the crazy logic of a few singular individuals to make it happen."

The Professor Has the Twin Princes Pay Dearly for the Right Bill

*"There ought to be a system of manners in
every nation, which a well-formed mind
would be disposed to relish. To make us
love our country, our country ought to be
lovely."*

— Edmund Burke, *Reflections on
the Revolution in France*

On the eve of the Constitutional Revolution, in 1906, Sardar Mirza arrived back in Tehran as a foreigner; his ten years' absence might have been a century. His travels through Russia had been miserable. The 1905 Russian Revolution, as well as the harsh winter, had put a chill on all the fun-loving Russian aristos he had met in Paris. His hair, curly and almost disheveled, recalled the artistic Montparnasse crowd. Otherwise, he was all elegance: the toothbrush mustache, the suit by Creed of Paris, the beautiful silk Charvet tie, the fedora. He spoke a rusty Farsi, rolling his *"r"*s in the manner of the French; he laughed aloud, as if gossiping at Les Deux Magots.

Sardar Mirza arrived in early July, when the court had already moved for the summer to Shemiran, its retreat at the foothills of the Alborz. A car would pick him up the next morning to drive him to court, and his brother would meet him there, to welcome him. He spent a difficult night, acclimating to Tehran.

The morning brought a pleasant surprise, as a Rolls Royce drove up to the front of the house (though a little on the early side). The driver, a tall, muscle-bound, mustachioed peasant, wore a soiled uniform and a cap too small for his large head, which was shaven to brilliance. This was Ghorbun-Ali, the Poonaki doorman, in his youth—before a bout of influenza rendered him deaf and a bullet rendered his leg amputated, producing the distinctive smooth hop of his later years. The young Ghorbun-Ali looked at Sardar Mirza sideways. Could this indeed be a Qajar prince, the brother of Saleh Mirza? No, it was clearly a dirty, Christian foreigner: the upholstery would need a thorough cleaning.

In the back of the car, the dandy Qajar prince—a month shy of his twenty-first birthday—lit his first cigarette and sat back to enjoy the ride, along with the prospect of seeing his brother. They soon arrived at the palace gardens; the Rolls followed the curved road and drew to a stop in front of a crowd.

Sardar Mirza, eager to embrace his brother, stepped quickly out of the Rolls. With *"Mon cher frère!"* still on his lips, he heard the sharp crack of a slap. As he connected the sound to his own prostrate position on the pebbly ground, he heard a loud voice bark: "Bow to the Shadow of God, the Shah of Shahs, you miserable princeling!"

His first thought was, *"Merde.* Did someone slap me on the back of my neck?" His second thought was to wonder whether the fall had torn his bespoke trousers.

He heard the Turkish-accented voice of the Shah: "Don't be so rough on our French brother." The Shah stepped forward. He bent down and gently lifted Sardar Mirza by the shoulders. "My young brother, it might be difficult to recall in these modern times, but we are still your sovereign." The Shah stepped back to inspect Sardar Mirza with some interest. "But let me look at you, little brother."

He held Sardar Mirza by the shoulders, turning him side to side as if examining an intricate rug, when the sound of a car coming through the gates distracted him. The young Prince could now examine the Shah in his turn: the past ten years had done efficient damage. At only fifty-three years old, Mozaffar ad-Din Shah looked quite decrepit, his eyes scared and sick-looking—

rheumy and glazed, with deep purple bags beneath them—above the cartoon-like mustache. He had the gait of a man twenty years older; in fact, he had only five months left to live. Losing interest in Sardar Mirza, the Shah dismissed him. "Welcome back to the court, brother. Now go and greet your twin. He has been a pain to us in these last few weeks, waiting for you."

Only later did Sardar Mirza learn that, by an unfortunate chance, his car had arrived only a moment before the arrival of the English *chargé d'affaires*—hence the large welcoming crowd at the door, including the Shah himself.

His brother, Saleh Mirza—a conservative young man in dress and manner, though not in thought—wore the Abbä, complete with the traditional lacquered penholder of a court official thrust into his cummerbund. The traditional black lambskin headgear stood straight on his head. A thick black mustache extended his face horizontally, undercutting the brothers' physical resemblance. Saleh Mirza stepped forward, and the brothers melted into a close embrace.

"I see that the Shah is still friendly to us," Sardar Mirza whispered, smarting from his recent humiliation.

"Yes," his twin laughed, "he practices the friendliness of *Auntie Bear*." The well-known fable of an improbable friendship between a man and a bear ends in disaster when, one afternoon, Auntie Bear notices a fly land on her friend's face as he sleeps. With the intention of shooing the fly, she picks up a large rock—and smashes the man's skull, along with the fly.

"You're lucky you didn't get a foot whipping this time!" They both remembered vividly that the last time they had been together, they were lying flat on their backs, gazing helplessly at one another. They hugged again.

Nothing had changed between them. They kept each other company through the hot July days and conversed late into the nights. Saleh described the heady political atmosphere, with demands for political freedom echoing on every street corner, and about his involvement with the Society of Lockht O'ur, the secret (but supposedly transparent) "Society of the Naked." Ostensibly a Sufi organization, its mission was political and its goal was a liberal constitutional monarchy.

Sardar Mirza waxed lyrical about the artistic revolution in Europe, and his unfettered life in Paris. He talked about the writers, artists, and composers of the Left Bank, especially Montparnasse. He revered Prime Minister Aristide Briand and the French principle of *laïcité*. "Can you believe it, brother? Briand wrote that the Third Republic neither recognizes, nor subsidizes, *any religion*. Aristide Briand got that law passed by the French parliament, against all odds. Anything is possible!"

Saleh Mirza spoke no less passionately of the recent strikes in the Bazaar and in Qom, and the courage of the clergy and the merchants. The leaders had sought sanctuary for a month in the Shah-Abdol-Azim Shrine—the place where their own father had been assassinated, ten years earlier. "Brother, two thousand people joined Sheikhs Tabatabai and Behbehani in asking for a House of Justice. Our brother the Shah and his Premier finally gave in. *They gave in!*" He shook his head. "Now they are going back on all their promises, and the clergy are back again in the sanctuary and all the Friday mosques. Even Sheikh Nouri is prepared to join the opposition!" He shook his head again, in awe at this prospect.

A week later, the two brothers sat at an open lunch at the Shah's summer palace. This modest palace, built by their father, successfully combined French and Persiranian architecture, with its tall balconies and unobtrusive pillars; scattered around the palace were the houses of the Shah's favorite wives.

Dozens of courtiers arranged themselves on the multilayered carpets. Premier Ain Dowleh, the princes' cousin, was feeling better than he had in months; as host, he cajoled his guests to eat and enjoy. In the middle of the long room, a beautiful cashmere carpet held dishes of colored rice, stews, lamb kebabs; feta cheese cubes were tucked into mounds of parsley, basil, tarragon, radishes and scallions, with soaked walnuts and almonds scattered around as garnish. Dozens of large, steaming oval nans, fresh from the royal baker, were piled in the center, each showing a faint matrix of char from the oven's hot stones.

The sixty-one-year-old Premier was distinguished by an impressive white walrus mustache and contrasting thick, black eyebrows. In his bemedaled uniform, with its wide, gold-leaf epaulets, he was more the stern German Junker than the Eastern potentate. He practiced a divide-and-conquer policy learned from the English—but he was better able to divide than conquer.

A congratulatory, festive air prevailed at the lunch. His Excellency had scored a victory over the sit-in by sending his Cossacks to blockade the mosque. There had been an exchange of a few stray bullets, but little violence; the opposition had blinked first. The two religious leaders, Tabatabai and Behbehani, had agreed to go back to Qom.

"Your Grace, have we seen the end of this matter?" This was a setup rather than a question, posed by the son of the foreign minister. A friend of Saleh Mirza, he was a Russian-trained political scientist, beginning to make his name in the political arena. His father had wide support among the clergy and merchants for his constitutional sympathies, and was even talked about as a future premier.

"Maybe not, but the Bazaar spoke—or, should I say, *remained silent*—last Sunday." The Premier scooped beef stew with a piece of bread. "I can handle the mullahs, and I can handle the merchants, but together they can make trouble."

"Your Grace, then, has not heard?" asked the Prince.

"Heard what?" The Premier looked intently at the younger man.

"Evelyn Grant Duff, the acting *chargé d'affaires,* has been asked to provide them political asylum." Since the British staff had moved to the summer residence in the north, their large compound in Tehran was deserted. Fifty merchants had applied for sanctuary there, under the age-old Persiranian custom of *bast.*

The Premier relaxed. "Oh, I know about Sheikh Behbehani's letter to the *chargé.* I have been assured by Foreign Minister Lord Grey that their gates will remain closed."

"Sir, I am not referring to the letter last week," the Prince said. "My sources tell me that fifty merchants, as well as a number of religious students, have already taken refuge on the grounds. Mr. Grant Duff assured the group that, in a country with a strong tradition of asylum, he could not in all conscience deny that right."

"Did our Mr. Grant Duff indeed use the phrase 'in all conscience'? Conscience! If we had granted Britain rather than Russia a portion of the custom excise tax, we might perhaps have seen a different outcome," he sniffed. "They will not get rid of me without a fight. Now for practical matters." He glanced at Saleh Mirza. "Cousin, I have a small assignment for you, one that requires the utmost delicacy."

ꙅ

Saleh Mirza traveled by car to Qom with two escorts; he was to meet with Sheikh Nouri, the reactionary religious leader. By now, the crowd sheltering at the

British Legation had reached one thousand, and was growing hour by hour. A mile outside the city, Saleh Mirza abandoned the car to approach the house in traditional fashion, by horse—as resolved by lengthy debate in his secret society, Lockht O'ur.

It was late in the afternoon, and the sun had already made its tactical retreat, when Saleh Mirza and his two companions arrived at the house where Sheikh Nouri was staying. The Sheikh lived in Sangelaj, one of the oldest parts of Tehran, amid other prominent Shi'i jurists. His acolyte's house in Qom was of traditional mud-and-straw, with a large, rough-hewn wooden door, as if designed for a donkey stable. Two roguish characters stood guard, outfitted, incongruously, as seminary students. Set into the large door was a smaller door, through which one entered in almost a crouch: a clerical gesture of ostentatious humility that seemed to equate moral goodness with physical discomfort.

In front of the door milled dozens of people, mostly bedraggled, waiting for a free meal. Others were passing petitions or seeking legal clarification for some humdrum activity. Indeed, all legal matters were handled by the religious establishment—and Sheikh Nouri had won the lucrative business of the royal court.

There was no question of making the Prince wait: he had sent word ahead. The two guards bowed. Saleh Mirza removed his shoes. At five feet five, even he had to bow to pass through the small door.

He entered a small, square, flagstone yard, with a pentagonal pool that was used for the five daily ablutions before prayer. The modest turn-of-the-century house featured a wide veranda—a simple tiled platform resembling a stage, where the Sheikh held court. Four doors led off the veranda to the private rooms.

Sitting on a worn carpet and leaning on a large cushion, the Sheikh appeared comfortable in his pulpit, legs crossed, propping an elbow on one knee to support his head on the open palm. His large, round, salt-and-pepper beard met the round white turban hugging his head. He wore the traditional thin, dark brown cloak over a not-so-clean white shirt. His unblinking stare at this visitor communicated pure hatred.

The Sheikh uttered a loud *"Ya-Allah"* to express his great pleasure, and made a show of rising to welcome the young Prince. Saleh Mirza, as expected, made his own show of hurrying up the veranda stairs while loudly begging the Sheikh to remain seated. This nuanced minuet, calibrated to push the other to even greater homage, ended in a tie, as the Prince arrived in time to help the Sheikh, halfway erect, to sit back on the Kashan carpet. The two sat down, each murmuring dozens of greetings "under the lip": intricate linguistic artistry designed on solid Baroque principles. A rough-looking seminarian brought tea.

The Sheikh spoke first. "Your Highness has come a long way to our humble abode just to be served by your willing servant. We hear of much turmoil in the capital." (This was not the "royal" we, but rather a style common among the lower classes, and thus for the Sheikh a studied emphasis on humbleness. The new generation of mullahs has lost this talent.)

The Premier had instructed Saleh Mirza to remind the Sheikh how recently—just a few years ago—he had won the lucrative business of the court's legal affairs away from the radical Sheikh Behbehani, his religious adversary. The Premier's munificence could once again be reassigned. Saleh Mirza had argued against using such a blunt threat, which seemed especially unwise in view of the Premier's physical and political weakness. "Your Highness, such a crude threat will only insult the Sheikh."

"These mullahs only understand the flow of money," the Premier had insisted. "You make the Sheikh understand that if he joins the opposition, he will not receive a penny as long as I am the Premier."

Saleh Mirza now assured the Sheikh: "I am here only to send His Highness Prince Ain Dowleh's best wishes." He opened a line of conversation. "He inquires after your health and asks whether Your Grace has ruled on the matter of the Shah's request for a loan from the Russians. His Majesty's health necessitates a visit to Europe. Does Your Grace deem the loan *halal*?"

"In the name of God the Almighty, I have thought hard on the matter of a loan from the infidels. They have committed untold atrocities to our Muslim brothers in the north, once our own children. God has taken revenge. Like locusts in a field, he has let the yellow race loose to wreak havoc on these barbarians. Now the Russian infidels plan to bleed us dry." The Sheikh had given his answer.

"Your Grace's wisdom is infinite and irrefutable." The young Prince now attacked with all guns blazing: "May I inquire whether Sheikh Behbehani concurs with Your Grace's profound analysis of religious doctrine?" The Sheikh could hardly miss the implied threat of lost revenue, within the barb of consulting his callow rival for doctrinal clarification.

The Sheikh's voice retained its monotone—a practiced skill, as if explicating a point of religious dogma. But his murmured words, spilling over one another, drew a line in the sand.

"To answer your question regarding my most revered brother, I can only say that he has given up his only vice—that of smoking. This has made him the figure of perfection that he is today. Even though my humble presence at the Friday mosque makes little difference—as you can see"—he pointed to a bundle of bedding parked at the door—"as you see, I am a simple itinerant, God's nomad, I am to join my more learned friends momentarily." He smiled at his own dexterity.

Sheikh Behbehani's long habit of smoking had been itself a political statement. Under the reign of the old Shah, Saleh Mirza's father, the country had been placed under a religious fatwa to abandon all use of tobacco products, in protest against the Shah's concessions to Baron Reuter. Even the Shah's concubines obeyed this new restriction—but Sheikh Behbehani had refused, continuing to smoke in public as a gesture of support for the Shah. But by now, Sheikh Behbehani's position had hardened: he would never again cooperate with the crown, let alone handle royal litigation. Thus, Sheikh Nouri dismissed the Prince's bluff of cutting off funds. More surprising was the roll of bedding placed by the door. Clearly, the Sheikh intended to throw his lot with the constitutionalists by joining them at the Friday mosque. A more incongruent misalliance was difficult to imagine.

"I know your sentiments, young Prince. I suspect that your newly arrived foreign brother has brought with him the talk of the common man voting for laws. *Let me warn you.*" The Sheikh paused for effect. "This goes against all precepts of Islam. Islamic law is perfection, handed down by the Koran, and exists in us, like a spirit. We, the clergy, might clarify some points to the ignorant, but we do not question the law. We do not vote on God's law in a plebiscite. Do you not see the blasphemy you are perpetrating with this democracy?"

"Your Grace, the talk is only of a House of Justice, under Shi'ite precepts," said the Prince.

"Ah, you are not keeping up with the latest developments," replied the Sheikh. "We just heard in the last hour that the demands have escalated to a house of *assembly.*" He pronounced it, derisively, as *parleman.* "The British have now allowed three thousand people to sit in the gardens of their legation. I am told that my good friend's son, Mushir Molk, and your own brother, are even now holding classes in the grounds of the infidels." Saleh Mirza managed to conceal his surprise from the Sheikh's piercing gaze, but he was unprepared for the next insult. "You yourself are still a Muslim, Your Highness—are you not?"

"Your Grace knows of my absolute devotion to the Prophet and to Ali and his followers. May I ask, then, why Your Grace is joining in a sit-in at the Friday mosque with all the seminaries?"

"Your Highness, how often does a humble servant of God have the chance to build an Islamic kingdom to the glory of God? Glory be to God, he has deemed it wise to give the two of us the same set of tools, to use for our very different goals." The Sheikh's eyes showed a cat's malice. "Your Highness, if I may be permitted an observation, your visit in Qom raises further interesting possibilities. I would imagine that the public bastinado of an official—for example, of a young prince—might be enough just now to bring down the government."

"I doubt that a few slaps on my feet would have such a grand effect, Your Grace." And now my clever grandfather introduced a gambit of his own. "Still, should a young prince die in your house from poisoned tea"—he opened his mouth just enough to reveal a small bag tucked between gum and cheek—"quite an opposite goal might be achieved. Wouldn't Your Grace agree?"

"Of course, we speak hypothetically, Your Highness," answered the Sheikh, "always careful to consider all angles. Nevertheless, I wouldn't have considered Your Highness the martyr type. To be a martyr to God has its compensations; it is written. What compensation can one expect for dying to achieve the rule of the mob?"

"Your Grace misunderstands my intentions. I am a loyal subject to my royal brother." The Prince paused meaningfully. "Your Grace asked me if I were a Muslim. May I in turn ask whether Your Grace is still a loyal subject?"

1001

"Do not try my patience, young pup." The Sheikh coughed loudly, to prevent the servants' detecting the anger in his voice.

"I must have tired Your Grace." The Prince rose to take his leave. His mission was complete. "If Your Grace will permit me, I will remove my shadow from your presence."

Saleh Mirza hurried back to the capital, certain that events would accelerate. He was particularly concerned at the news of his twin's indiscretion. What could have induced a Qajar prince to enter the gardens of a foreign embassy without his government's permission?

By the time he returned to the capital, the number of people occupying the British Legation in Tehran had swollen to five thousand. By early August it would reach a peak of fourteen thousand people. The throng came from all walks of life, but most came from the Bazaar.

Instead of returning to the court in the north, Saleh Mirza chose to go to his own house in town, a modest dwelling but strategically located. My bed of feathers, you must know the area: with a good arm, you could throw a rock from the Prince's house, and the British Embassy guard would see it land. Back then, there was only an ordinary, traditional house on a good-sized piece of land; neither the large house (where we presently reside as guests, in its basement) nor the gazebos had been built.

In search of the capable manservant, Nemat, the Prince paid a brief visit to his grandfather's workshop. Prince Saleh Mirza's grandfather, despite his illustrious connection, still worked as a bootmaker; his grandson had built him a small workshop at the end of the garden. (It would later house Ghorbun-Ali, the one-legged doorman.) There indeed was Nemat, helping the old man stretch leather hides. The smell, as always, made the Prince gag. He reminded himself that allowing his grandfather to practice his profession was a personal act of humility—and he wondered, in the same instant, whether he had milked that vein sufficiently at court.

Nemat, squatting on his haunches, was pulling with all his strength to secure a cowhide in the vice.

"Nemat, leave that!" he shouted. "I need you here, right away."

Nemat looked up. He was then a fresh-faced, bullet-headed Turkoman horseman of 23. He sprang to his feet and trotted at double pace toward Saleh Mirza.

"Your Highness, how can I be of service?" He had the confidence of his tribal people, unawed by royalty but fiercely loyal. "Anything wrong, Your Highness?"

"I need you to take a message to my brother at the British Legation."

"Your Highness, His Highness instructed me to tell you not to worry. He will be back shortly." At that moment, they heard a commotion at the front of the house. In the next minute his brother approached, clearly full of excitement.

Saleh Mirza held up his hand, stopping his brother in mid-sentence. "I will not ask you if you have lost your senses, for obviously you have. Do you realize that you will bring the wrath of the Shah and the court on us with your visible support? May I remind you that you are the Shah's *brother*? Nouri will use you like a foreigner gone amok; I have just come from him."

"But, brother, you need to see what is happening!"

"I intend to," replied Saleh Mirza. "I need to understand the ebb and flow of this revolution of yours. But I need to get into the compound without attracting attention."

He turned to tell Nemat to fetch the barber. Sardar Mirza's eyes narrowed in suspicion. "You are up to something, brother! Your grin is positively evil."

"Not at all," the Prince smiled. "I have only ordered the barber to give me a good shave."

"You, *shave?* And at this time of the day?" Unimaginable, that his brother would take up western ways!

"I will ask for more than a trim, brother. Do you not agree that, if he is to make a deliberate judgment, a man must hear and see the information firsthand? How else would one advise the court?"

"Oh, no, you don't! Are we perhaps pulling a *Le Boeuf?*"

"Yes, indeed, we did this enough times when we were children." The Prince's smile broadened. "I imagine I might wear your European suit—and, impossible though it might be, I can try to emulate your own buoyant style."

The Prince would never wear a beard again. Under the close direction of Sardar Mirza, the barber gave the most nuanced haircut of his career, almost transforming the Prince into one of the Left Bank crowd. By noon, the brothers—perhaps channeling their mother's teenage enthusiasms—were adding a subtle wave to the new haircut with a heated iron rod. By the time he put on the gray Creed suit, Saleh Mirza looked enough like his twin to fool even the closest of their friends.

To avoid too much attention, they waited for the approach of dusk. The Prince begged Sardar Mirza to stay home. "Please act with gravitas, if any visitor arrives unannounced. Make sure you wear my entire Persiranian garb. I know you don't like my plain black hat; wear it, please!" That traditional astrakhan hat would effectively hide the hair—even though Sardar Mirza loved to mock it. "And if a visitor comes, send Nemat to get me from the legation."

Sardar Mirza replied with a warning of his own, half-joking: "Stay away from foreigners. They will surely know from your atrocious French accent that you are *not* the original."

The entrance to the compound had a festive air. People milled around or lingered outside, as if at the entrance to a fairground. The sun, no longer visible, bestowed a blue tint on the dusty ground. Walking in, the Prince could see that the once-beautiful garden was no more. Near the wall on the left, large vats were simmering on coal fires that threw off showers of sparks. The smell of cooking rice—tons of it—pervaded the air. Dark, mustachioed men vigorously fanned coal fires where kebabs were grilling, on skewers cut from the pomegranate trees. Everything had been paid for by the *Bazaaris*, the merchants in Tehran's Grand Bazaar.

Speechmaking could be heard in every corner of the compound. Saleh Mirza wanted to hear what was being said. He needn't have worried so much about being discovered; the place was full of courtiers. Their mission was to proselytize the masses—or to educate them, depending on one's point of view. Hundreds of tents had been erected by the guilds; the most important had the largest tents. In one tent, muscular men—the butchers, tanners, chicken and lamb sellers—stood listening, unsmiling, to a thin man in European clothes standing on top of a wooden box. In another tent, Saleh Mirza heard the leader of the grocers' guild—sellers of cereals, legumes, forage, and rice—speaking to his followers with surprising directness. He was a man known for his probity: on his word alone, he could raise credit equal to that of all the other merchants put together. (In time, he would become a steadfast member of the *Majlis*, the parliament.) The Prince lingered to hear the words of this uneducated man. Not for the first time, he wondered how a simple grocer could acquire such clarity of thought, while he, a graduate of Dar ul-Funun, struggled in endless disputes with courtiers who had long ago sold the soggy firewood of their souls to the devil.

Standing in the entrance of another tent was a man dressed in fine traditional clothes, obviously eyeing the Prince: no doubt, an acquaintance of Sardar Mirza. Warily he tried to bypass the man, preparing to disappear into the festive crowd at the back of the tent. But the man approached and cut him off.

"Your Highness," the man said, "have you forgotten your servant, Ibrahim Khayatbashi?" This was the leader of the guild of tailors, a rich man who would become a stalwart parliamentarian in the first *Majlis*.

"Not at all, Ibrahim Khan. I am simply savoring hearing the different points of view!" He tried to sound jovial like his brother.

"Then you must come tomorrow. The meeting of the Central Society of Guilds will be convened by the chairman, promptly at ten in the morning. Your Highness won't forget your promise of yesterday, when this is all over?"

What, indeed, had Sardar Mirza promised the man?

"Refresh my memory, Ibrahim Khan," he said.

The man whooped, enjoying his small victory. "I hope Your Highness does not forget our petitions as easily as my simple request! I seek merely to have your elegant suit copied for our clients."

Relieved, the Prince promised he would lend his suit for measuring. In the distance, he spotted his old friend Valiullah Khan Nasr, the master of the guild of medical doctors. Forgetting for a moment his new persona, he approached him for a companionable chat. Valiullah Khan watched in some confusion the comfortable mannerisms of his friend emanating from the shape of man he had met only yesterday. Too embarrassed to keep up the farce, Saleh Mirza confessed to the doctor, swearing him to secrecy.

In his adopted persona, he listened to leaders of the sugar and tea sellers' guild and of the booksellers, who were lobbying for an independent judiciary. The merchant class had clearly been inspired by liberalism—an ideology he resisted. Without adequate preparation, constitutionalism would be a difficult carriage to control. And how to square the religious laws of the Sharia with the secular laws so warmly championed by all the grandees, including his own brother?

From afar, he could see some British officials expounding to packed crowds on democracy and the parliamentary tradition. Even the calculating British had lost their heads amid the general enthusiasm. He would keep his distance from them.

His brother was right: he could not miss the next meeting of the Central Society, if his voice was to be heard. It dawned on him that, this night, he had begun—though reluctantly—to practice the art of democratic politics. He liked it; indeed, it suited his talents. But his meddling, he well knew, could have capricious consequences, in a country such as this.

The black velvet pincushion of the sky was dotted with thousands of twinkling silver pins. The moon swathed in purplish blue the escarpments of the Northern Mountains. With small campfires burning here and there, the compound looked like an army on the march—which in fact it was.

ॐ

I had to interrupt Professor Dal, shaking him like a dog shakes a bone. "Arbab! I heard all about this encampment, when I was ten years old! Every tent had its storyteller, each lamenting in harrowing detail the murder of Imam Hossein—the Shi'ite Karbala tragedy—and squeezing unshed tears from their hearers. My Baba told me that his Baba, the finest *rozeh khan* in the country, joined the tent of the goldsmiths' guild, and he gathered the biggest crowds."

"I am not finished, oh my rubbery padding," Professor Dal chided me. "Are you losing weight? I can't make myself comfortable on top of you."

"Arbab, I haven't eaten a proper meal in four days. I am wasting away," I complained. "Can you talk to the guards when you are out in the morning?"

"Are we going to start with your cheekiness, my boy? You know I haven't left this cell in years. Now quiet down, and I will tell you how the charade unfolds."

𝓈

The following day, Saleh Mirza, once again disguised as his brother, walked the short distance from his house to the compound. Ghorbun-Ali followed carrying his lunch, wrapped in cloth to present a more humble picture. People, he well knew, liked the easygoing ways of Sardar Mirza—and, as the brother of the Shah, his presence lent added importance to their cause. He might even manage to shift the position of the influential Prince—who was himself now influencing these unfolding events, just by becoming a bird in a tree.

The place where we lie in this prison, my boy, is now derided by the rich as the "old" downtown, but it was the poshest part of the city in those days. Ferdowsi Avenue was unpaved, but the British Legation walls, stretching along its length, lent gravitas to the dirt-packed street. A short French balustrade topped the wall, contrasting oddly with its Gothic rib vaults.

The crowd milled about, even larger than the night before. More: thousands of women, in their black chadors or white burial shrouds, had gathered outside the legation, asking permission to enter. To the Prince's vast relief, they were politely turned away.

The legation entrance was blocked by an unruly mob. Ghorbun-Ali now took the lead to push through the crowd, holding the precious picnic bundle above his head and shouting to make way for His Highness,

Prince Sardar Mirza!—which defeated the desired effect of humility, but successfully cleared a passage. The throng propelled the Prince forward into the arched, tunnel-like entrance to the legation garden. Sweat ran down every crevice of his body; his brother's suit, so unlike the traditional robe, seemed designed to trap the heat.

Emerging from the archway, they were accosted by a man wearing Western-style coat and tie, mustache and goatee. He shouted at the Prince, "Take that, you dirty foreigner!" and raised one hand to his forehead, perhaps to shield his eyes from the sun. Saleh Mirza was used to receiving military salutes, though the gesture was belied by the man's hostile words. And then the man fired a shot, almost point-blank—somehow missing both the Prince and Ghorbun-Ali, who instantly aimed a blow with his bundle at the man's shooting hand, just as he fired a second shot. That bullet hit Ghorbun-Ali on the inside of his leg, splintering the thighbone; blood quickly began to spread. The crowd rushed toward the man, engulfing him amid a thicket of legs. He would not survive the beating.

The Prince dropped to one knee beside Ghorbun-Ali. Deferring to his status, the curious crowd kept a respectful distance as they clustered around the fallen man, apparently unconcerned with the fate of the would-be assassin. The Prince pushed the fingers of his left hand into Ghorbun-Ali's wound. With the other hand, he jerked loose the linen cloth from the lunch parcel; the silverware made a racket spilling onto the stone floor. He fashioned a tourniquet on the upper part of Ghorbun-Ali's thigh. Acting in his own persona, he shot orders like a machine gun. "Call Valiullah Khan Nasr from inside, *now!*" he told one man. "You, hold this tourniquet and twist hard!" he commanded another. "Don't worry if he screams." And then, shouting at the crowd behind him: "*In the name of the Shah*, stop beating that man!" Ghorbun-Ali, though close to fainting, marveled to see this foppish, foreign prince turn into a military leader, much like his own revered master. "Well, they *are* twins," was his last thought before he passed out.

୫

The Prince did not miss the ten o'clock meeting, which enacted a *tableau vivant* in a large tent; oil paintings of similar revolutions can be seen in museums around the world. A few men, dressed in the Western style, sit behind the high table, while the bearded speaker stands, right arm raised, and makes a rousing speech. Next to them might be a turbaned mullah, sitting on a square carpet and giving his radical sermon with a hand resting on the holy Koran. The commercial class, sitting enraptured, wear an assortment of garments, from colorful pastoralist wraps to the simple white *dishdasha* of Khuzestan (to underscore the unity of the diverse gathering). The painter might throw in a few snot-nosed boys, playing in the foreground and ignorant of history in the making. The speaker's left hand, with a relaxed open palm, points to them as if to say, 'We do all this for the next generation.' The painter might frame the historic image by conjuring a couple of black slaves on opposite ends, their muscular bodies twisted impossibly, their white eyeballs red marbled and staring in wonder toward the heavens.

In all revolutions there comes a magical time when the most disparate groups come together to move heaven and earth. These magical three weeks had no precedent in the two-and-a-half-thousand-year history of Persiran. The numbers gathered at the legation grew daily: merchants met with princes and guildsmen. Supporting them, the clergy sat in sanctuary at the Friday mosque in Qom. All were of one mind—even if (like the conservative Sheikh Nouri and the progressive Sheikh Behbehani) they could barely speak to one another.

The alliance's first, unanimous demand was merely tactical: remove Premier Ain Dowleh. (Indeed, he lasted in office just ten more days.)

As for the Shah, he spent most of the time resting. Waste was accumulating in his blood: the invention of dialysis arrived twenty years too late to save his kidneys. The Prince, when he was not hobnobbing at the legation, sat cooling his heels at the Shah's summer palace, impatient for a strategy meeting.

The Prince was in Tehran when he received word to meet with the Shah. As the stalwart Ghorbun-Ali had had his leg amputated, a driver was borrowed from the Turkish Embassy for the ride to Shemiran. The Prince mounted the red-carpeted stairs and entered the Shah's office, now virtually a pharmacy. Heavy brown bottles on a silver tray occupied the top of the desk; the room was stuffy and hot and smelled of chemicals. The Shah's chaise longue had been placed next to the desk. He sat, dressed but semi-recumbent, draped in an intricately embroidered brown cashmere shawl, his skin a shade or two lighter than egg yolk.

Like a trapped animal, he watched apprehensively as Saleh Mirza approached. Since childhood, the Prince had recognized his elder brother as a shy, scared human being, utterly unfit for his weighty responsibilities. A thin veneer of bombast was inadequate to sustain the illusion of power. Perhaps to demonstrate that he was still alive and in office, the Shah once gave an order that he be photographed every half-hour.

Saleh Mirza made a deep bow. He began the customary extolling of the Shah's many glories. "May God make luminous your proof—"

The Shah waved him silent. "What news of town?" he asked wearily, in his thick Turkish accent.

"Your Highness, our brother reports—"

"Not *our* brother, *your* brother," the Shah whined. "A traitor, like the rest of those princes who have joined our enemies." Then he recalled the assassination attempt. "You know, I did not have anything to do with the—" he trailed off. "I hate blood. I can't even bear the sacrifice of a camel at Eid al-Fitr; I hire someone to impersonate me, to drive the fatal spear."

The Prince did not doubt him. Not that the Shah would not order an assassination—he would never have to witness the blood himself—but there were others in the movement much more worth killing than his twin. Nouri was the more likely instigator of the assassination attempt. This Shah had never liked confrontation. Hints, insinuations, and tips were more his style—a strategy that had the court second- and third-guessing his every utterance.

"You, at least, have more gumption than the others," the Shah wheedled.

"Your Highness, the committees are discussing constitutional monarchy." The Prince came immediately to the point. "Right now, their demands can be met with the removal of the Premier. If we agree to set up a committee to study the independence of the judiciary, we can put off any drastic changes. We can then shape the mission of the committee, once we secure the support of the clergy. They will never agree to a secular judiciary."

"They want me to remove my beloved cousin, Ain Dowleh. 'To what purpose?' we ask."

The Shah turned his rheumy eyes toward the young man. "Look at us. What do you see? You see a dying man. The choice of a premier is my prerogative. If we bow to pressure and remove him, those cannibals will eat us alive."

"Your Highness, I beg you to reconsider."

The bored Shah, without moving his arm from his lap, waved the outstretched fingers of his right hand a few times toward the door. The Prince would never see him again.

Exiting the office, he was immediately approached by the Shah's chamberlain, who invited him in a whisper to attend the Crown Prince. The Prince reflected that he had never heard the chamberlain's speaking voice—his every utterance was a whisper. He followed the chamberlain into the War Room, a large, wood-paneled hall boasting two newly-installed electric chandeliers.

His elder brother, the Crown Prince, stood frowning at one end of the sleek, oversized mahogany table. He spoke standing up, thus keeping the Prince standing as well, awkwardly backed up against the door. "I hope you are well, uncle?" he greeted him cursorily. "I want you to know that no one knows I am here." He prided himself on his cleverness: a puppet master in a world of intrigue. "Did your meeting with our father go well?"

The Prince again presented his view. To his astonishment, the Crown Prince seemed to understand the gravity of the situation. He was well known to dislike the Premier in any case; he disliked everyone attached to his father's court. It was even rumored that he had provided financial support for the clergy sit-in, just to get rid of the Premier.

"Give them anything they ask, but we will not have our father abdicate in favor of a republic. Our father cannot give our rights away," he pronounced. "Give them their precious *parleman*! I will convince my father to consent. Remember these words: I will not go down the same road that Tsar Nicholas chose last year. Once I am the Shah, I will not let a morsel of my Allah-given powers slide down their greedy throats. To think that walnut sellers want to make decisions on my behalf! As long as I live, I will not consent to a constitutional monarchy."

"As Your Highness knows well, they will demand that His Majesty as well as Your Highness swear on the Holy Koran to maintain the constitution." The Crown Prince stared stonily at the Prince, as if a schoolchild had just asked to be given a stable of horses. The Premier was dismissed within days.

♆

One hot afternoon, about a month after Sardar Mirza's arrival, the two brothers sat side by side on a silk carpet on the veranda of the Prince's house, drinking tea. A fountain splayed in a small pool. Their heads almost touching, they pored over the wording of the newly-issued Proclamation of August 7.

"And what is this phrase: the Majlis will pass laws according to the 'sacred Sharia'?" Sardar Mirza was appalled. "Nouri's handwriting is all over this. I thought the Crown Prince promised you?"

"I would not be surprised if the Crown Prince himself had a hand in the wording. He is happy to sow division," the Prince shrugged. Turning more serious, he switched to French, to keep their small treasons from the servants' ears: *"Il tuerait le demimonde avant de céder le moindre de ses privilèges."* The Crown Prince, he felt, would kill half the world before yielding a single privilege—but why was his brother bursting into laughter?

"*Demimonde*, dear brother, does not mean 'half the world.' It refers to the hidden world of the notorious French courtesans!"

A timid knock sounded on the garden gate. Nemat hastened to open it, straining to keep the sagging door from dragging on the dirt. He returned on the double to whisper in Saleh Mirza's ear. The Prince looked at his brother questioningly. "His Excellency Evelyn Grant Duff, Her Majesty's representative, is here to see me?"

Sardar Mirza held his brother's gaze. "Yes, I have invited him to help us mediate with the Shah on the wording."

"Are you *mad?*" the Prince sputtered. "You have invited, into my house, Her Majesty's representative to resolve an internal matter *without informing the government?* We have now indeed joined the *demimonde!*" To Nemat, he remarked calmly, "When Ghorbun-Ali recovers from his wound, make him the doorman. That door needs a stronger man than you. Show his excellency in."

In walked Sir Cecil, British Minister at Tehran, accompanied by another young man.

"I don't know if you know Mr. Scott, who has recently joined the mission," said Sir Cecil.

"I know Mr. Scott very well." A wide smile began to spread across Sardar Mirza's face.

"Your Highness as always shows me much kindness," Mr. Scott beamed, his stutter much improved. "It is a pleasure to meet your brother, His Highness, after all these years." The Prince and Sir Cecil held the vague diplomatic smiles designed to cover ignorance.

"Brother, Mr. Scott accompanied me on my journey through the Caucasus," Sardar Mirza explained. "I mentioned him in my letters. He also helped us in the British compound a few weeks back. Mr. Scott, you must visit us more often."

"How clever of Sir Cecil," thought the Prince. Mr. Scott provided the perfect cover for their visit—though such subtleties, he knew, were no buttress against the inevitable torrent of gossip and lies.

"I would be delighted," Mr. Scott replied. "Did Your Highness ever reconnect with the charming Grandpierre family?" As Sardar Mirza and Mr. Scott fell into animated recollections, Sir Cecil and the Prince began to hammer out a path to a proper proclamation agreement.

On the eighth of August, 1906, the Shah did indeed sign that third draft of the proclamation—but backdated it to the fifth, to connect it forever to his own birthday. Except for the fact that this wording would be modified, two months later, by Article 2 of the supplementary Constitutional Laws, Sardar Mirza might well be hailed as a founder of a secular Persiran. Following the usual encomiums, the document read:

Therefore on this occasion, our Royal and Imperial judgment has decided, for the peace and tranquility of all the people of Persiran and for the strengthening and consolidation of the foundations of the State, that such reforms as are this day required in the different departments of the State and of the Empire shall be effected; and we do enact that an Assembly of delegates elected by the Princes, the Mujahids, the Qajar family, the nobles and notables, the landowners, the merchants and the guilds shall be . . .

ॐ

"Wake up, my tiny whale pond. Have you fallen asleep during the most optimistic time of our two-and-a-half-thousand-year history?"

"No, Arbab, just resting my eyes," I said.

But, as darkness would soon lose the battle to light, Professor Dal fell discreetly silent.

The Sixth Night
0110

The Narrator Fleshes Out the Already Fat Storyteller

"There should always be some foundation to the most airy fabric."

— Lord Byron

Dear Ms. Vakil:

There should be an emoticon for a crimson face. You tell me that you have been aware of the existence of the Poonaki papers for the past twenty years!?

Of course, the real Mr. Hekaiatchi would have learned about the papers from my uncle, Professor Dal. Are you suggesting that you would have expected those papers to be delivered to *you* instead of to me, twenty years ago? I must insist that, despite your hard work and your persistent sleuthing, I am their rightful heir. Indeed, Mr. Hekaiatchi—the real one, not my storyteller—sent me these papers, *gratis*.

The plot positively congeals: Mr. Hekaiatchi, you tell me, visited you in order to confess to *someone* the story of his stay in prison, having failed to interest me with his rambling letters. Commendable persistence, don't you agree? He believed in the precept—pronounced by the famous eleventh century storyteller, Blackeyes— not to take an untold tale to the grave, for fear of being condemned on judgment day as the murderer of some fictional person.

I, of course, god-like, have done the opposite: I have apparently brought a fictional character to earthly life. As I write this, I continue to modify him to resemble the real Hekaiatchi, the living human being who told us a story that (as reporters say) "checks out." I find I am experiencing guilt. I regret treating him shabbily. Please persist in seeking him; I am not averse to proffering a small sum as a token of our appreciation.

Thank you for the corrections. I have taken note of all your concerns. I may indeed have taken a few liberties in conferring a few extra IQ points on both the outgoing Premier and the Crown Prince. The unintelligent, uneducated Mohammad-Ali—the new Shah—will play his role unerringly and stupidly. I am familiar with the historians' debates about placing words in the mouths of history makers. Who said exactly what, to whom? But I claim the privilege of the raconteur. I grew up sitting at a dinner table where the protagonists, or first-hand witnesses to the pro-tagonists, sat discussing the events recounted in our insipid history books. Unlike my brother, who sat rolling his eyes in boredom, I would listen with a focused fascination. To be sure, I am working to pin down the inaccuracies of memory, using letters and historical sources. But few people wrote candidly in those times; self-preservation argued against creating a critical record. In your precise commentary, do I detect a scholar humoring me? For all I know, you have already discarded the mutterings of a pathetically nostalgic middle-aged man.

I have been browsing through the *1001 Nights*—no question of reading the whole. Did you know that Scheherazade missed out *twenty nights*? She stopped discreetly in the middle of her story, as the 679th morning arrived, and resumed her story after twenty days—perhaps hoping the hearer or the reader would not notice transposing a seven for a nine to get to 699. In the last pages of the fourth volume, we are given the explanation: during those twenty days, she gave birth to twins. And on the last night, she introduces to the not-so-quick King a two-and-a-half year old boy that she claims, proud as a peacock, to have birthed without missing even a night. (Please don't take offence, Ms. Vakil: they don't make women like they used to.)

My paternal grandmother, Choti, was fearless, like her son Nima, my father. Though devoid of affection for any individual, she espoused a universal love for the down-trodden. Fortunately, she left a large trove of written words. I will also throw in a few other letters, from brother to brother, that enhance her claim as a completely modern Persiranian woman. (I will destroy the more salacious letters between my grandfathers, as best left private among the dead strewn about in this account.)

I rate my French maternal grandmother, Anaïs (the "Countess"), as a tough cookie in her own right. She had total contempt for anything natural: the greater the sophistication of the human hand to fashion, distort, and manipulate the environment to our own design, the greater her liking. She saw the act of giving birth the same way. "An inhuman process for making humans. Why couldn't we just pluck humans out of the earth like tomatoes?" she asked. "After all, we shove them back into the earth when they die."

Sardar Mirza was buried in 1938 in a Montparnasse grave. He had bought three vertical plots: the other two were for the Countess and Lili, my mother. They both would make good use of them.

My bereaved maternal grandmother, the Countess, and my paternal grandfather, the Prince, grieved together. They grew close to each other in the weeks the Prince remained in Paris. He shared with her his concerns: about Nima, my father, and his lack of care in his studies; and about Reza Shah's autocratic and erratic behavior, then reaching its apogee. The Prince saw himself as a potential target—like other notables who had gone missing, or died mysteriously in prison, or committed suicide. And, if something of the sort should happen to him, Nima's future looked bleak. The Countess offered both of them an indefinite stay—a kind of self-exile—at her home in Paris, but the Prince could not imagine living outside of Persiran. The solution was to place Nima at boarding school: Le Rosey, in

Switzerland, where the Crown Prince, Mohammad Reza, had gone to school. "You know," the Countess observed sagaciously, "we are in no less danger in Europe. *Tout cela finira mal*—it will all end badly. But the Swiss know how to take care of themselves."

That is how Nima stayed back in Europe while the Prince traveled back to Tehran. The Countess took Nima to his school, Le Rosey. Though Crown Prince Mohammad Reza Shah had proved both a fair scholar and an avid athlete, my father became a legend only as an athlete. He broke every record in goals scored by a soccer player. He excelled at the 110-meter hurdle, where his national record held for ten years: his long legs ate up those hurdles with such grace that people criticized him for not trying his best.

Then the war came. As the Countess had predicted, the Swiss stayed neutral; Nima continued at Rosey. On June 5, the Germans started Operation Fall Rot, and seventeen days later France was conquered. The Countess detested the Pétain government. "This is what you get," she sniffed, "when a peasant becomes a general."

By 1943, life had become unbearable. My grandmother helped the French Underground with money, even providing refuge in her ancestral home for a few of its endangered members. The Germans had questioned her once: teutonically, with polite thoroughness. My father graduated that same year. (*À peine*—"barely," as my grandmother commented dryly.)

She decided to move them all back to Persiran. Two years earlier, Reza Shah had abdicated in favor of his son, the former Crown Prince, now titled Mohammad Reza Shah Pahlavi. The Allied forces now occupied the entire country: the British in the oil fields of the South, and the Russians—with a force of 60,000 men—in the North. A puppet Soviet government ruled in Azerbaijan, sympathetic to the communists and utterly disregarding the central Persiranian government. One imagined Stalin licking his chops, waiting to inherit the rice basket in the North with the Caspian and the oil fields into the bargain.

From the day she set foot in the Prince's house to the day she left at war's end, two years later, the Countess deeply regretted her move. *"Sales gens, sale pays, sale culture,"* she said of our beloved nation: "Dirty people, dirty country, dirty culture." The Prince's wives, and Nima's mother in particular, were (to say the least) inhospitable toward the Countess. The three were united also in rejecting Reza Shah's prohibition against wearing a veil or the traditional chador in public: they committed never to emerge from their oversized gazebos, so long as the law remained in force.

None of this bothered Nima and Lili. They had entered their own sphere of bliss, into which no worldly misery could intrude.

My parents wore their invisible glitter lightly. When the question arose of my father's pursuing higher education at the polytechnic institute, he promptly enrolled in the Officers' Cadet School instead—a rare act for an aristocrat. Most of the cadets came from the newly risen middle class. And, once again, my father would follow the new Shah's academic path: he had himself graduated from the Officers' Cadet School after attending Le Rosey. My father managed to get permission (through some well-placed favors) to come home a few nights a week, sparing him the boredom of the dormitory.

Whatever time my parents had, they spent together. They traveled to the farthest parts of the country. They trekked on camels on a fifteen-day crossing of the great desert. They climbed Damavand, at 5674 meters the highest dead volcano in the Persiranian plateau. They took long, sweaty treks in the lush jungles of the Caspian. They did not, however, face the wilderness as lonely hippies: they traveled with servants; and, wherever they traveled, the local grandees received the Prince's son with respect. They both loved hunting. My mother had hunted all her life, on the family grounds outside Paris. She shot well, but she preferred to watch my father. His accuracy in bringing down a moving gazelle had even the guides in wonder.

A few months after the war, our uncle Dal arrived from Germany—close to death, skeleton-thin, hollow-eyed, with thinning hair. The Countess devoted a few months to help bring him back to health, and then she planned to return to France—and she asked Lili to accompany her. The canny Countess no doubt understood the effectiveness of pressure; and when the young couple announced their plan to get married, she smiled and hugged Nima as affectionately as if he were her own son.

They married with little fanfare. Uncle Dal and the long-serving Nemat acted as witnesses; a few of the officers from the Cadet School, along with the Prince's three wives, attended the ceremony. The Countess left the country alone—and older: as the poet says, "One shade the more, one ray the less, / Had half impair'd the nameless grace."

Nima graduated that same year, in June of 1945. The school placed a premium on physical courage and sportsmanship, so at graduation he was awarded a number of prizes, to be presented by the young Shah. The war years had considerably diminished the pomp and circumstance; the small band, more wind than music, made a brave attempt at a few crescendos. The Shah brusquely signaled the band to cease and began to walk toward the cadets.

That summer, the young monarch faced one of the greatest challenges of his reign. The Soviets were refusing to remove their forces from Azerbaijan. Stalin's puppet Tudeh party was flourishing in the Northern

Province. The English had no forces left in the country; the only remaining hope was the U.N.—and the Americans, who (at last) distrusted the Soviet Union's ambitions. Standing on a playing field to dispense ribbons could not be considered the best use of the Shah's time.

As the Shah approached my father to confer on him the rank of Second Lieutenant, his military commander formally announced, "Second Lieutenant Poonaki." My father saluted at attention.

The Shah raised an eyebrow, "*The* Poonaki?"

My father answered in the affirmative. For an awkward moment, the strange circumstance of the Prince's "natural" death hung in the air. Then the Shah addressed the General in French: "We have to watch this young man." An ambiguous comment. Did he mean: We have to watch this young man—after all, my father killed his father? Or did he simply mean, let us watch the progress of this promising young man?

"I am at His Majesty's Service," Nima answered—in his perfectly accented French.

The Shah, amused, asked him where he had learned his French.

"Your Majesty, I have followed your footsteps here from Le Rosey." The Shah, delighted, asked for the latest gossip at the Swiss school, and they spoke for a moment before the Shah moved on. I need to underscore, Ms. Vakil, that my father was not an ambitious man. But he fell for the young Shah—and the Shah, in return, fell for his Lancelot. My father was soon invited for a Friday volleyball game, where he impressed players and onlookers alike. His young wife, Lili, created a sensation in her own right.

My father's entrée into court brought him into day-to-day decision-making. He attended all operational meetings. The Shah perhaps needed someone he could trust, a friend. He understood that he was caught in a complicated political web, surrounded by remnants of the Qajar court, who had connections to every foreign legation in Tehran—including some collusions that suggested out-and-out treason. He considered my father a discovery of his own, conveniently disregarding my father's own illustrious Qajar pedigree.

My father, for his part, had deeply held ideals regarding the role of aristocracy in a monarchy, seeing himself as a vassal to the king. He gradually took on the role of secret envoy from the Shah to General Razmara, the commander responsible for Azerbaijan, who had been tasked by the Shah to assess the strengths and weaknesses of the Northern Province—the next likely target of the separatists.

General Razmara, in turn, sent my father on several secret trips to the mountainous Azerbaijan region to report on activities of the pro-Soviet communist separatists. As dangerous as these missions were, my father loved the physical challenge. With his innate understanding of geography, he quickly learned the paths and byways. He spent weeks with the local villagers, passing as a small landowner. He would come back home unshaven and dirty but energized. He remembered these months as the happiest of his life.

He and the General spent hours discussing tactics. They agreed that the communists had lost standing with the locals. In a clever move, the Shah ordered countrywide elections. The constitution provided for the Imperial troops to protect the impartiality of elections—including in northern Tabriz. Once the Soviet troops withdrew to the border, the Tabriz separatists would have to face the Imperial Army on their own.

As you know, Ms. Vakil, our textbooks grossly exaggerate the scale of our little provincial war at the end of World War II. Skirmishes, in fact. Yet credit must be given where it is due. In a time of complete paralysis and in an atmosphere of massive distrust among politicians, the country faced the threat of losing the north—its most fertile province. Indeed, Stalin would use similar puppet governments to ensnare all of Eastern Europe. The Shah's bold moves, though small in scale, saved the country.

The Imperial forces, under the command of General Razmara, moved in three columns; the Shah surveyed the troops from his airplane. The western column, guided by my father, advanced toward the highlands dominating the town of Mianeh—the third most important town in Azerbaijan, dating to the Median Empire. There they faced a stiff resistance mounted by General Daneshian, a thorough Soviet stooge; his forces were dug in, and he warned that they would resist to the death.

The Imperial troops had much to prove: only five years earlier, Reza Shah's newly trained army had melted away at the first indication of Russian aggression. In the north, the mountainous terrain and a cold winter did not make progress easy. A few soldiers broke or injured their ankles on rock-strewn marches and were treated in medical tents. The detailed planning was paying off.

The western column challenged the Soviet forces installed in the highlands above Mianeh, the area my father had reconnoitered. The sole bridge had been destroyed on the orders of General Daneshian, but with the help of his local contacts, my father was able to bypass the bridge, crossing further down the river.

They fought for a day, supported by planes and artillery working with precision. When a stray bullet grazed his lip, my father had already witnessed the communists break ranks and disappear along the porous frontier with the Soviet Union. (Later, Mohammad Reza Shah would survive an assassination that shattered his front teeth; he later joked with my father, "Who is following in whose footsteps now?") General Daneshian, too—disregarding his orders to shoot deserters and stand and fight—disappeared behind the Iron Curtain, taking with him all the cash deposits of the local bank. The victory was complete.

Ms. Vakil, I can swear to the authenticity of these stories; they were repeated to me often by my father. Those were happy times.

The celebratory mood was soon dashed, however. My father was well aware of Choti's anti-Shah activities. (He always referred to her by her nickname, never as "mother.") She was in hiding; he had not seen her in eleven years. One month after the victory, he received a morning visit at the house from General Razmara himself. The General, in full uniform, stayed in the car; he was anxious to get back to the court. My father joined him in the back seat of the roomy Hudson sedan.

"Lieutenant," the General began, formally, but immediately softened his tone. "Son, we have just arrested your mother, Jaleh Darbandi, on a tip from one of her collaborators. There was some shooting around their safe house. No one was hurt—but your mother and four accomplices have been summarily court-martialed. They will be shot at dawn." He paused. "I wanted you to know first."

My father sat in silence. Then, following his instinctive navigational sense, he asked the General if he could accompany him to court. "His Majesty does know," was the response. "He has given his approval." My father repeated the request. The General gave a sad smile. "But, lieutenant, you can't go to court in *pajamas*."

The interview with the young Shah, late that evening, was a breeze. Always kind with him, he listened to my father's plea for mercy. "Why do you care—she left you when you were a kid!"

"Your Majesty, I am asking this more to honor the memory of my father. He loved her till his last breath." Mentioning the Prince's last breath was probably not a calculated comment, for Nima was the least calculating of men; but it must have stirred a smidgen of guilt in the Shah. It was common knowledge that his father had murdered the Prince—as Choti would remind her son a few hours later, when he saw her in prison.

"Very well. But she needs to leave the country and never return. Send her back to her spiritual father, Stalin. Let's see how she likes living in Moscow! I hear the food lines go on for miles." It was later rumored that the Shah had spared her only because Stalin warned him not to execute the leaders of the Tudeh communists (in fact, a number were executed). In the following years, Nima and Dal would intercede successfully with the Shah to spare several political prisoners on death row.

Choti was being held in a dormitory at Doshan Tappeh Air Base, east of Tehran. Nima arrived there after midnight, directly following his meeting with the Shah. He remembered little of her from his childhood, except her breezy, distracted acquiescence to anything he asked of her. She sat erect on a tidy cot among dozens of other bare cots.

Her looks took his breath away. At thirty-eight, she had matured impressively: her face thin, almost manly, with its light spider wrinkles; shoulders back, small breasts provocative under a short-sleeved shirt. Her short hair was glamorously disheveled. She was dressed in men's military slacks, given her after her capture.

She looked at him, just as he remembered, in an inspecting kind of way. Nothing surprised this woman. "Have you come to commit matricide, son?"

"*Choti,*" he emphasized the name, "I am not sure you can call me your son. And, no, I am not a murderer. I am here to prevent your execution."

"After killing all my comrades in Azerbaijan in the name of that bloodthirsty Shah of yours, I can classify you as murderer, don't you think—*son?*"

"You sold your country to a foreign government!" His temper momentarily got the better of him. "Not to mention your husband and child." He knew he was pleading for some explanation.

She looked at him with genuine pity. In her labyrinths of dialectics, he appeared as a misguided man in need of enlightenment. "Don't you see—you, your father, all of you, me," (she pointed to herself) "we are unimportant, as long as so many millions suffer. What matters it, that you spent a few years without me at your side?"

Nima shook his head, defeated. You might as well put a horse and a wolf in a room together and expect them to get along. He told her that she would be flown to Moscow, never to return. There was a glint of happiness in her eyes, like a saint's exaltation on his deathbed. But her final words were chilling.

"You tell that Shah of yours that tonight he made a mistake to spare me. I will work for the rest of my life to bring him down! Don't think for a moment that I will show you mercy, if you get in the way."

ॐ

I find it difficult to keep an accurate memory of my parents, Nima and Lili, whose preoccupation with each other effectively excluded us. That my severe-looking father had a playful, adventurous side, I can report only from hearsay. And my mother's aloofness —distancing herself from all Persiranians, including her children— developed only later in life, I am told. They both felt guilt-ridden at betraying their class, their heritage, and most importantly our patrimony.

My brother and I grew up in a Tehran on the make, very different from the sleepy town my parents knew.

We experienced the first burger joint, called Hotshop, an American creation that arrived in the sixties, with its vast, uninterrupted windows. We frequented the first skating rink, the Ice Palace, and the bowling center, designed to appeal to a child's garish taste. New movie houses multiplied in the capital, with massive Cinerama projectors bringing to life *How the West Was Won*, forgotten were those silk- and velvet-curtained screens, of quaint dimensions, that had opened a few years before with great fanfare to the Pahlavi national anthem.

All this we enjoyed, accompanied by a driver and our tawdry French or Spanish governesses, whose enthusiasm for these activities only emphasized their unfitness for their role as educators. These flashy improvements bolstered a general crazed optimism, an unfounded confidence in the continued improvement of our lot as a nation.

An upsetting incident marked, for me, the end of childhood, and maybe even of optimism. In our 14th year, on a sunny spring afternoon, Arya and I sat in our lemony Vauxhall at an intersection, waiting for the light to turn green. I lounged in the front seat, my elbow hanging half out of the window. From nowhere, there appeared at my window the crazy smiling face of Ali-Shisheh, the deaf and dumb beggar who pranced through traffic wanting to clean the windshields of the cars waiting at the lights. His sudden appearance startled me, but soon his garrulous humming had us laughing. I began to fumble in my pockets for coins as the light turned green. Ali-Shisheh loped along next to the car window, as Moosio, the driver, began accelerating into the intersection. The next sound I heard was the screech of brakes: Moosio had stopped for a motorcyclist racing through the red light, across our path. But Ali-Shisheh, oblivious, pranced ahead of our car. The motorbike hit him instantly—as smoothly as if every driver had rehearsed the accident. I cannot remember the impact. I saw him for an instant, a marionette-like figure in the air. His arms and legs were splayed, as if continuing his usual cartoonish frolic. The motorcycle leaned to one side—then actually speeded up in a shower of silver sparks, as it hit the underside of an approaching car.

We later learned that both the motorcyclist and Ali-Shisheh had died instantly. From that day on, I don't remember seeing regular beggars in the streets— probably due to a citywide policy of banning them.

Ms. Vakil, let me thank you again for your candor. After your last email about Mr. Hekaiatchi, I have updated "our storyteller"—allowing him to tell his story with greater moral authority. I hope that I have accurately paraphrased your encounters with him. He has a few complimentary lines concerning the character of Vakil Khanum, who matches you in every detail. Your tireless involvement needs to be acknowledged. You are indeed a lady—a *Khanum*, in its most lady-like meaning.

The Fat Storyteller Swaps Pencil for Microphone

"It even tempts him to blurt out stories better never told."

— Homer, *Odyssey*

Baba, I can feel your pride in me. With the help of the good Zahra, I actually visited the editor, Vakil Khanum.

We played at being James Bond. Zahra called for a taxi around two in the afternoon, when the traffic in Tehran pretends to flow; these new phone-taxis are taking over. No, Baba, I am not a profligate. They use inconspicuous cars, not the ghastly, orange-painted, matchbox-size Peykans which, beside packing the passengers in, Baba, always charge me double the rate, if they even deign to stop, that is. We quickly snuck into the car and headed uptown. I wore a chador; no harm in being careful, Baba. Zahra was holding my hand underneath the chador; I couldn't tell if this was for support or . . . well, no matter. The pitter-patter of my heart, like aftershocks of an earthquake, must have conveyed my sentiments through the tips of my fingers.

Doctor Vakil sat behind her desk, surrounded by half a dozen typing *houris*. A handsome woman, though underfed—she doesn't hold a candle to my Zahra. Did I say *my* Zahra? I promise you, Baba, nothing untoward has occurred between us. Not even last night. Last night! You can't believe how she frightened me!

I was sleeping happily in my dreams. As a matter of fact, you were there, in our modest garden in Karaj. The sun shone, and I lay on the steps, warming my bones like a crocodile in an African river. I awoke with a start, frightened for my life, at the sound of creaking on the stairs. The creaks were minutes apart, as if someone stood immobile before taking the next step.

I whispered an aggressive, *"Who goes there!"*

Zahra's head appeared, quietly laughing. "Quiet down! You will wake *agha-joun*, my dear father."

She crept into my bed—she was clothed, Baba, I promise—and snuggled her backside in my folds. I felt as grand as any man has the right to feel. I am sure I held the smile through the night. I awoke this morning to an empty bed.

I wasn't always an obese man, Baba, as you well know—overweight, maybe. Like any normal boy, I reached the age of puberty with a confused anticipation of future conquests. Dreams of riding greedy thighs, licking light salt sweat, sinking into a yielding breast (if you can pardon my vividness)—until the day my autonomous glands went into the overdrive that no doctor could arrest. My present weight of 320 pounds is just part of it: my voice kept something of the purity of boyhood, my manliness never reached its full potential, and my beard remains light fuzz on my crumpled chin. So, feeling *grand* was a new experience for me.

I myself doubted the reality of Zahra's presence in my bed last night—until I felt her hand reach for mine, under our feminine disguise in the taxi.

Let me get back to Doctor Vakil. She received us politely enough, though I could detect a fuzz of irritation beneath her genteel courtesy. She wore a simple scarf, embroidered becomingly with white, placed lightly on coiffed black hair. Feeling confident in my material, I suggested that we could talk in more private surroundings. She closed two milky glass doors to create a small private office, safe from prying eyes. The incessant clicking of the houris on their keyboards instantly faded.

She offered us the two chairs in front of her desk. No doubt Ms. Vakil came from the old society—familiar to me, though not to Zahra—with none of the superciliousness of the rich. Zahra nevertheless took on the role of a subservient serf, refusing to sit. She cowered in the corner whispering inanities, until Ms. Vakil curtly said, "*Beshin,* Zahra." The direct order to sit seemed to assure Zahra's sense of her own place. Now she sat on the edge of the wooden chair, holding her chador closed with her teeth and staring at her feet.

I hate chairs with arms. I sat self-conscious, feeling my flesh spread beneath them. The next moment would be still more awkward: I removed my chador.

Ms. Vakil, taken aback, shook her head. "What is the meaning of all this?" She had a way of lifting one arched eyebrow that reminded me of my school principal questioning our existence. I mumbled an apology and asked for patience as I launched my introduction. "Vakil Khanum, my name is Hekaiatchi. A few months back, I spent some time in prison with a Professor Dal." Immediately the eyebrow shot up again. "I know, I know," I hurried on. "Everyone thinks he died right after our revolution. In truth, he died only a few months back." The eyebrows found an equilibrium. "He lived in a lunatic asylum—I mean, a mental institution. What I mean is—it was a *prison,* parading as a mental institution." I was uncomfortably aware of the impression created by showing up in a woman's disguise and immediately disclosing one's recent sojourn in a madhouse.

"Mr. Hekaiatchi," Doctor Vakil interrupted, "I am sorry for your incarceration. Please understand that I do not doubt what you say. We live in farcical times." She gave a glance at my chador. "*All* becomes possible—when fear propels us to camouflage all human expression." The ground beneath me began to feel more solid. "Let me say at the outset," she continued, "that I knew Professor Dal well. Years ago, before the revolution, I met him a number of times. I was in my twenties. I had just returned to take a position at the University of Tehran, teaching Qajar history." She hesitated, as if debating whether to share her own experience, and evidently decided against it. "You will also be pleased to know that I have been to the famous Hekaiatchi tea house in the Bazaar—in better times, of course. I presume you are the son of the famous storyteller, Abol-Hassan Hekaiatchi?" Ach, Baba, *she knew you!* I melted with pleasure, making the chair creak. After all these years there still existed people who appreciated the art of storytelling. "Mr. Hekaiatchi," she continued, "what I fail to see is how your experience in this 'institution' might affect an ostracized professor of history."

I began to tell her how I had ended up in that institution. I told her about my shock at Professor Dal's antics and how he lived his double life—by night, recounting soberly the history of the Poonakis—indeed, the twentieth-century history of Persiran—and by day, ranting like a madman who believed that he was the source of all the oil produced by the world. I briefly related Professor Dal's history: his difficult childhood, his sense of belonging, once in Germany—and his Nazification; finally, his accepting the last ten years as punishment for his acquiescing in German war crimes. I recounted for her Tala's artfully conceiving the twin princes and the boys' travel to Tabriz, including the attack by wolves, the bastinado meted out by the Crown Prince, and the sweet encounter of Sardar Mirza with the French count's daughter—in a czar's palace, no less. But it was when I began to recount the activities of the twin brothers during the Constitutional Revolution that she began to write notes—discreetly, so as not to distract me.

My well-practiced ability to remember details impressed her. She interrupted only a few times, for some point of clarification; otherwise, she let me talk. She seemed surprised that a relatively unschooled bumpkin could discriminate the subtleties of character of ayatollahs and prime ministers of a century ago.

Unconscious of my surroundings, I must have talked for hours. When she finally interrupted me, the room had darkened; the clatter of typewriters had stopped long ago. Zahra was asleep on the chair; her mouth, in the shape of an *O*, made the sweetest of snores. I brought myself back to the present.

"Dr. Vakil, I have written down most of this history. I have told you only half of it; there is much more."

"And I want to hear more."

"Vakil Khanum, will you want to publish this history?"

She said nothing for a long time.

"Khanum," I began.

"I heard your question, Mr. Hekaiatchi," she said. "I want to answer you in a way that will not sound insulting." She took a breath.

"You come from a long oral tradition. History told from generation to generation; stories repeated again and again, to leave the next generation with a moral sense of what has come before them. Details get distorted, but the gist of what you convey stays strong. Unfortunately, in our times the *detail* has taken on an inordinate importance. Not a sentence can be proposed without three scholars ripping each other to shreds over the connotations of a word." Painful experience no doubt informed these words. "From my studies and readings, what you recounted this afternoon rings true—but ringing true, unfortunately, does not satisfy today's scientific methods. I would like to see what you have written. Better still, I would prefer to tape your narrative: you have a gift for telling your story. That way, for future generations"—she pointed vaguely to the darkened room outside her office, where her houris did their work—"for future scholars, doing research in a more amenable environment, your tapes can provide a kind of signpost to guide their hunches. Do you understand me, Mr. Hekaiatchi?"

I slumped back into my chair, which creaked and squealed. I was tired and disappointed. But I was also intrigued at the idea of using my God-given talents of storytelling, instead of scribbling with a short stump of a pencil to make ghostly gray markings.

Dr. Vakil began clearing her desk into her brown leather satchel.

"Wait." I had remembered something important. She looked up from the open satchel. "On the fifth morning, when Professor Dal came back to the cell, he acted strangely."

"How do you mean—strangely?" she said.

"That morning, when the guard brought him in, he looked agitated. He sat on his bed like a fakir and stared at me disconcertingly, for a long time. But I had learned not to engage him in conversation during the daytime. He finally said to me, as if to a stranger, "I don't know who you are, but I have watched you all day, *and I don't think you are one of them.*"

✑

"*Arbab*, it's me, Hekaiatchi," I protested.

"We have just a few days left," he continued in the same tone. "Do you know where you are? This house belonged once to a great man—a great man." I knew that the great man was the Prince. "You have to promise me that you will let his grandson know," he demanded, now in his normal voice.

"*Arbab*," I hastened to assure him, "you have told me a great deal. I will not forget. I have a great memory trained for exactly this sort of story." Now he looked at me derisively.

"What stories are you talking about, you foolish peasant?" he said, once again in his daytime character.

"Here I sit, underground, the fount of all this country's riches. All I have to do is tighten my asshole and the next day the price of oil will jump two basis points." He positively jeered. "Who'd believe anything you, a servant's child, would say?"

My anger at this abuse must have blinded me to what he then told me. A *servant's* boy!

"You see that wall outside?" he demanded, pointing at the obstructed view out of the half window. "That was one of the houses that the Prince built for each of his wives. That one he built for his first wife, the daughter of his brother Mozaffar al-Din Shah. He became brother-in-law as well as uncle to the next Shah. *All the Poonaki papers survive in that house.*"

My eyes must have conveyed my doubt. Professor Dal bristled. "I put them there myself, just days before my arrest—ten years ago."

He lay back on his bed and fell immediately asleep. He never mentioned those papers again.

ℒ

Vakil Khanum was now all attention. "Of course, you must get those papers!"

Seeing the joke, I smiled. "Of course, I will have them for you tomorrow. I will simply go back to my captors, my good friends, and get them to help me load a truck with the suitcases."

"I am not joking, Mr. Hekaiatchi. If you get the papers, I will first authenticate them. We will then release your oral history. And, at the same time, some prominent university in the United States or the United Kingdom will receive a generous cache of historical papers from an anonymous source."

"We have to get them," chimed in Zahra, now wide-awake.

"I will do what? How?" I was almost pleading. "And what will become of me, when they figure out the connection?"

"From what I have heard today, it seems clear that you are done in this country already, Mr. Hekaiatchi," Doctor Vakil said, not unsympathetically. "You and your wife could go to live in Turkey, or even the United States." Zahra and I glanced at each other, embarrassed at the word "wife." And now I worried that a sheath of historical papers could cause our separation. Zahra, I later learned, saw differently.

"In any case, I want to begin taping your oral history, Mr. Hekaiatchi," Ms. Vakil continued. "Not here. In my apartment, Mr. Hekaiatchi."

That is how I came to swap my little pencil for a sturdy microphone. Now I got up to leave, but she motioned for me to sit back down. And then I received the biggest compliment of my life: "You can't leave without telling me about the sixth night!"

My smile almost split my face into a crescent.

☙

On the sixth night, the Professor was clearly weakened beyond measure. He walked haltingly to my place. I had to help him climb up by supporting one leg, as he mounted me like a peasant mounting a donkey. He then fell forward with a thud, the sound of meat falling on meat in a butcher shop. The long, dirty, puke-scented white hair fell on my shoulders next to my nostrils: they had not cleaned him up properly that day. For a few minutes, I thought he had passed out. I called his name a few times. I began to speculate whether I had a dead man on my back.

All of a sudden he came to, with a chortle. "Did you think me dead, my boy? I doubt you can pull off a repeat of the Count's escape!" I had to ask what he meant. He was genuinely shocked. "You mean you have not read

The Count of Monte Cristo? What storyteller does not know the story of the Count? Have you read *The Three Musketeers*? No! What about *Robinson Crusoe*?" I have since bought a translated copy of *The Count of Monte Cristo*—and I now get the joke, though I could hardly swap myself for the body of an emaciated dead man in a body bag.

That sixth night, he talked in earnest.

The Professor Proves that All Is Unfair in Love and War

"Post Lux Tenebras: After the Light, the Dark."

— Job 17:11-13

I can't tell you exactly the date when Nima and Lili became lovers. But, soon after the misadventure with the confused dog in the park, they began a teasing game that anticipated (perhaps by years) any physical lovemaking.

I was puzzled, one afternoon, to hear Lili make a cooing sound I could not decode. It was just a few weeks after the dog incident. She seemed to be imitating a French owl: "*Ooù, ooù.*" Then I realized that she was asking, in French, "Where? Where?"

"Where the dogs met," Nima answered her.

"That won't do." Smiling, she shook her head.

The next time I heard this exchange was a year later, in Gstaad, Switzerland. We were once more in deep mourning. Back in Tehran, I had received the telegram announcing the death of the Prince at around the same time the news arrived at the apartment in Paris.

The Countess and I agreed that we would meet in Gstaad, where Nima's school wintered each year to escape the dense fog that settles on Lake Geneva. By the time I had traveled the 500 miles, the Countess and Lili (with half that distance to travel) had already checked in at the Hotel Palace.

Vacation places rarely match the photos on their tourist postcards: Gstaad is an exception. No artist could capture the consistent blueness of the sky, the vibrant whiteness of the snow, the complicated transparency of the icicles. The air is so fresh that doctors once thought (understandably) that it could cure all lung diseases.

I arrived on a cold, sunny day, around lunchtime, and walked through the town to the hotel. Built on a promontory above the station, the aptly named Palace Hotel hovered like a white fairy castle. Visitors dressed (in those days) in tones of dark brown sat on the balconies having lunch. Others walked stiffly on their heels, carrying their wooden skis. A man dragged a huge wooden luge full of shrieking kids. It was my first visit to a ski resort.

I met the Countess in the lobby of the hotel. She offered me lunch. I declined, eager to meet Nima. I have always disliked giving bad news (though my profession required it) and I wanted to get it done. The Countess understood. We walked out to the hotel skating rink to pick up Lili. She had grown as tall as her mother. New to the sport, she skated awkwardly, her arms bent forward like the legs of a beautiful insect. She looked breakable, in black pants and a black turtleneck. She skated toward us, panting, her cheeks red. She put her arms around my neck to greet me—and pulled me wobbling onto the ice. She laughed loudly, like a man— like her uncle's guffaws. Her laugh was so sudden, so authentic, it made me laugh with her, embarrassing the Countess, who operated under more severe rules of propriety.

We walked to the school chalets, just outside town. Two large chalets sat next to one another; traditional gabled roofs and wide eaves sheltered long balconies that stretched the length of each building. A few smaller chalets completed the winter campus. It was certainly the rarest of schools, even for those times.

A sharp wind hurried us in our winter coats. The Countess had alerted the headmaster to our arrival. The school hallway was a chaotic mishmash of adolescent boys, shouting to each other with their pubescent voices in half a dozen languages as they returned from the afternoon sports. Every one found a way of stealing a glance at Lili. I asked one of the boys, in German, if he knew the whereabouts of Nima. He answered in French: "I saw him in his room not five minutes ago." Without looking at me, he stared directly at Lili, and then shrugged. "Follow me."

I heard Lili say to her mother, "I can't wait to touch him." Not an iota of sexuality in the remark: it was simply her natural gift for communicating warmth.

In the corridor on the third floor we saw even more boys, all in their socks, slipping and sliding toward their rooms. Our guide motioned us toward the last room in the corridor. The Countess knocked on the door softly. "May we come in, Nima?"

Nima was standing in the middle of the room; he was in white long johns and thick ski socks, with his torso bare. By now he stood six feet, a man-child: above the toned stomach and chest, his face kept the innocence of a twelve-year-old. He looked at us in confusion. His face lit up—and immediately darkened.

"Is it father?" We could scarcely look at him.

"Heart attack." I shared the only information we had been given. We were all aware of the possibility of foul play by Reza Shah; he had a reputation for interfering in the Lord's timing for us.

Tears crazed his cheeks. Lili went up to him. He placed his face on her shoulders, hiding his face in her hair, and we heard his quiet sobs. The Countess and I left them together in the room.

I wish the Prince could have seen the love this boy bore him. For the Prince, the only way of showing love was to do one's duty, making the loved one proud. Any outward display, he thought, descended into sentimentality. But what of his love for his own twin? The pain of that love came from somewhere he could not control. Once, talking to me, he thanked God that his brother lived far away—to spare him, I wondered, an ungovernable demonstration of love?

We had Nima pack a bag and return with us to the Palace Hotel. There, once again, we spent a week together with a backdrop of death and mourning. And once again, as I recall those days, they shine with the brightness of happiness. Not one of us begrudged another's laughter; not one of us felt that we were disrespecting the Prince's memory.

We rolled down snow banks. We enjoyed dinners: the young cousins got tipsy on a few glasses of wine and laughed. Their *fou rires*—mad laughter—would infect the Countess and me, and our laughter sent them off on a new round of hilarity. The Countess and I argued interminably about Mr. Hitler's actions, always saluting our positions with a glass of grog. She tried to tell me of her experiences during the First World War. "I lost cousins and friends the same age as you are today. I sit here enjoying your company, and theirs," she pointed to Nima and Lili, playing checkers in front of the fire. "Those poor boys are dead. No one remembers *why* they died. They missed out on this." She gestured around the beautiful sitting room of the Palace Hotel. "And all the time, people drank and laughed, without a care." I would answer her with some Nazi propaganda pap. She'd shake her head and drink to my *santé*.

Days of foolery followed one another. Nima and Lili might be sitting, some sunny afternoon, on the balcony full of skiers, munching on a Grand Marnier-soaked crêpe—and then, without a sign, they'd rise with one accord to race up the mountain until, thoroughly spent, they both fell on the snow. Exhausted, a new bout of *fou rires* would come over them, bringing smiles to the faces of everyone looking on, envious, from the balcony. Who couldn't tell that these two puppies, the same age as Romeo and Juliet, would end up as lovers? The answer of course was *me*. I saw only children playing.

How could I forget? Walking out of a restaurant, in gently falling snow, the Countess suddenly pushed a handful of snow down my collar. We all four broke into a take-no-prisoners snow fight under the street lights. Then the Countess smiled at me her sweet smile, that mother and daughter shared. Dazed, complimented, I understood her needs. When she came over to my room that night, I tried making love to her standing up—the only way I had learned from the Prince, and practiced on the whores of Berlin. She stopped me gently. Over the next few nights, she patiently extricated me from that strange perversion.

The night before I left, I walked over to Nima and Lili, sitting with their heads close together over a bowl of cheese fondu. They had pieces of bread on skewers that they dipped into the bowl, then stretched high, the cheese elastic. Their heads stayed close together, and I heard Lili again ask, "Where? Where?" Nima smiled at her indulgently.

"Where it snows and the wolves gather," was his response.

She gave his response serious consideration, gazing thoughtfully out the large picture window. Then she shook her head. "No, it won't do." He shook his head in agreement. They both looked up at that moment, not startled but happy to see me. She waved her silver spear, offering me the cheese-covered morsel. The gooey cheese almost scalded my mouth as I took my seat. When I could talk clearly, I asked what game they had been playing.

"Game?" Nima asked.

"Oh, it's not a *game!*" Lili corrected my misunderstanding. "We are planning the place for our first lovemaking."

I almost spat out the cheese.

They both laughed at my reaction. "Not right away!" she protested, punching me in the arm.

We then talked casually of other subjects—but I had a new and unwelcome understanding of my world. I was doomed to live a hankering, incomplete life. More than that: I saw clearly, in that instant, that this couple— whom I loved, whom I envied, whom I considered my only family—would parade their love, their happiness, and even their unhappiness in front of me, oblivious, innocent of any intent to torture.

I don't recall any sadness at our parting. Living within a few hours of one another, this was not a final farewell. We could not have envisioned the coming catastrophe, the open-fanged monster that lurked just a few months in the future.

My cushy cushion, it is difficult to identify happiness. You can be drowning in a sea of happiness and not recognize it. After the glorious week, we parted. Except a few hours during the war, I would not see them for six years. Before I talk more of love, I need to talk of war.

My heart broken, I nevertheless returned to Germany full of piss and vinegar, anxious to get on with my medical studies and convinced that Europe was headed towards a new dawn. My airy pouf, I insist that I *delight* in this imprisonment, for I have come to comprehend my great guilt. Half of Europe had a premonition of the evil lying in wait. I did not.

I can never escape the shame of those six years of war. An apology followed by an explanation is no apology at all. I do have an explanation, but it only sharpens my guilt. Behind the fact of my youth and the slippery slope of gradual indoctrination—behind those circumstances, there was a streak in my character that I can only consider corrupt.

But I swear to you today that I never saw any of the experiments attributed to Herr Doktor Sauerbruch. I saw him as a surgeon only. In surgery, he dominated the operating room. He shouted, he ordered, he bullied. He once cut an intern with a scalpel, snarling at him to remember the scar as a lesson. He operated sometimes on three people at once; after pushing us all to prepare the patients, open them up, and put in place the Sauerbruch pressure chamber (a bellows of his own invention), he would rush in to make the crucial cut on the open thorax. So as not to impair his sense of touch, he operated without gloves.

You have to understand, my boy, that in those days no one dared question a surgeon, let alone a German surgeon. The patient had no rights. Herr Doktor spoke to patients and their families with a directness bordering on cruelty. "No, madam, your boy will not survive the night. Please pay the cashier on your way out. No, sir, your wife will surely die under the knife, but she will teach my students a thing or two." Today, this seems inconceivable. His absolute confidence in his own powers frightened us all, I can assure you. Yet it empowered us to emulate him. We gambled, we experimented, we ventured into untried techniques— and medicine made great strides. Did some of the experiments verge on reckless negligence? I don't know. But I promise you that we did not practice pulling the wings off flies.

When Herr Doktor Sauerbruch became a member of the Research Council, we could not have known the nature of the research. By 1942, he was the Surgeon General for the army; I hardly ever saw him thereafter. But I cannot swear to being unaware of his work on mustard gas. The neatly recorded statistical tables lying around on desks were clearly visible; the nurses' whispered gossip about a place called Natzweiler-Struthof was often audible. I chose to ignore all of this. I saw myself as a pure surgeon—a higher species, born to cut into human parts and put them back together. During the war years at Charité hospital, I performed thousands of surgeries on returning soldiers, first coming from the far-off Russian front, then coming from just across the river, and finally from Berlin, from places within earshot, just down the street. I aided and abetted.

How can I explain to you those final months, the Battle of Berlin? We were bombed daily. When we took direct hits, we simply moved to a different section of the hospital. Soon we were operating with the open sky visible above us. We continued to wade through muscle and bone. Imagine operating on a human when you are thirsty and haven't eaten for days. For our cigarette breaks, we walked out to a landscape resembling Hell. The Berlin of my student days had been erased. We saw a newly-bombed bakery amid trees decorated with human flesh. We saw Nazis execute elderly people—recruits into Goebbels's *Volkssturm*—for lacking the strength to lift an antitank weapon. In the final month, SS officers would drag their "volunteers" into the hospital, incoherent with fever; and at the smallest resistance, the mere twitch of an unwilling muscle, the officer would execute the patient with a bullet to the head. We saw hundreds of these conscripts hung from lampposts, wearing signs proclaiming their cowardice. People talked of suicide parties as the most rational solution to the problems they faced every day. Wild animals from the zoo roamed the city; no one seemed surprised to see monkeys peering down from the vantage point of a tree. Rampant dysentery, typhoid, and diphtheria killed half of all newborns.

When Marshal Georgy Zhukov's occupying army arrived at the doors of the hospital, luck (I learned) was on our side. He appointed old Sauerbruch as Berlin's chief of public health. Unlike other Russian commanders, he prided himself on his army's discipline. In other parts of Berlin, Marshal Malinovsky's army ran amok. Indiscriminate rape was the right of each Russian soldier. Our nurses were spared only while they were in the hospital. Anyone attempting to look for their family members went missing.

Though I was living in the basement of Charité, I ceased working there when the surgeons became butchers. One surgeon used a meat cleaver to amputate limbs, insisting that, in the absence of anesthesia, his technique was more humane. That deranged man killed dozens before he was stopped from performing surgery. Little remained of my Germanic pride or my juvenile, capricious dislike of the English. Each spring morning, I rode out on the bare metal rims of my bicycle; I had painted a red cross on a sheet and wore my tattered white uniform with a stethoscope around my neck, to advertise my profession as boldly as possible. I carried my most treasured belongings in a black medical bag: my stainless steel surgical tools.

The noisy, lively Berlin of my youth had become a city of aimless ghosts. My most striking recollection during those weeks was the silence. On some streets, not a single building stood; on others, only facades, apparently waiting for some phantom director to shout, "*Action!*" The Russians ransacked on an inconceivable scale. They broke factories down bolt by bolt with the forced help of the Berliners, who worked as if in a trance. Special trains transported the loot to far-off places, often to be simply abandoned at the tracks. They stole the art stolen by the Nazis. I am told the basement of the Hermitage museum is crammed with Old Masters, never seen since the war.

On my daily treks, I used my medical skills to eke out a living. I mostly performed abortions, in unsanitary conditions, on women raped, multiple times, by Russian soldiers. I would attempt to dissuade them from undergoing the procedure: I explained the risks of the unsanitary conditions, the lack of medicine and of wood to boil hot water. I guaranteed that there would be complications—fever, bleeding, even death. Nothing would deter the women from wanting the foreign body torn out of them. They displayed an unsettling but rational intensity, a vehemence that contrasted shockingly with their expressionless daily search for food and water.

At night we—whoever was around—listened to the BBC on a wireless in the basement of the hospital, where most of us slept. Everyone listened for news of the advancing Americans. None of us could understand why we were abandoned. A trickle of Allied officers visited the Russian generals, but there was little sign of the Allied forces. The race for Berlin was a myth; it never happened. We came to learn how Uncle Joe Stalin had hoodwinked Roosevelt in Yalta, to Churchill's frustration.

It was on one of those nights, in the timeslot when BBC broadcasted cryptic messages for hopefuls, that I heard a message I knew was meant for me. Correspondent Lewis John Wynford of the BBC repeated the message on three succeeding nights. In his so-English accent, he said, "Hadjit will pick you up at the same place that he left you, if you will let a bear hug you." I knew that my protector, Harold Nicolson, ran the BBC. Only later did I learn that Nima and Lili had been working tirelessly to find me. Nima had contacted Harold—a name he had heard from the Prince—to find out whether I still lived.

I knocked for the first time at the remains of the Persiranian Embassy, "the place where Hadjit had left me"—well aware of the absurdity. The Russian army had set up their camps in the middle of the major streets, with several tents pitched right in front of the embassy. I felt foolish exposing myself to the mercies of five Russian soldiers who took exception to my presence. A tall, bearded, young soldier with round spectacles, probably the Communist Party enforcer, asked me in halting German what I thought I was doing there.

Pointing to the red cross on my bicycle and then to the embassy building, I introduced myself as a Persiranian doctor stranded in the middle of the war. The tall young boy translated my explanation to the group, to peals of conspiratorial laughter. My life was in the balance. These men, mostly Russian peasants, were hard, stupid, kind, cruel, malicious, and country-smart all at once. I had seen them kill without compunction, as if stepping on an ant, in the doorway of a random home. A large, beefy, red-faced soldier poked me with his finger and, with a crafty look, pointed to my head.

"Otkuda u tebya zheltye volosy?"

To my absolute astonishment, a small, dark Tajik man translated into Farsi: "He says, 'Where you got the yellow hair?'"

I lied, in my most bookish Farsi: "Tell him that I come from the Caspian region. I wouldn't be surprised if the yellow hair didn't come from across the border, from one of you."

The small man raised an eyebrow, surprised at my fluency, and translated. At this the men again burst out laughing, in the open way Russians have.

I hung around the area for several days. I helped their injured. I bound their broken bones, extracted their teeth, and punctured their pus-filled boils. They, in turn, fed me. On the afternoon of the fifth day, as had become my habit, I made my rounds of the soldiers camped on the grounds of the embassy. The soldiers sat around a campfire in the street, talking loudly. A Russian man, out of uniform, walked toward me. He smiled with arms outstretched. *"Davno ne videlis' tovarishch,"* he said, and bear-hugged me. Then he whispered in my ear, "I am Alexander Werth, a BBC correspondent. Harold, my boss, asked me to help you find your way back to England." He then stepped back and, in exaggerated Russian, said, *"Tovarishch, vy smotrite gorazdo ton'she, chem v proshlyi raz my vstretilis'.*" I did not react. He then switched back to English. "Don't fret, old boy, I just said that you had thinned out since we last met. An Allied truck will be leaving Berlin tonight. I can get you on it. Are you game?"

I nodded stupidly, tears welling in my eyes.

"Why don't you come with me now?" he said, *sotto voce.* "Leave your bike and walk with me." I picked up my bag of instruments and followed him while he chattered loudly in Russian to me. I felt that God had ordered the Archangel Michael, in the form of Alexander Werth, to reach down into Hell.

♋

Professor Dal fell silent for a long time. A thin smear from the cell window, like a low wattage fluorescent light, told me that we had little time left.

"*Arbab,*" I whispered. "What happened to Nima and Lili?"

"You have a voyeuristic streak in you," he teased. "You want to ask me, 'Where? Where?' Where flowers carpet the earth and the butterflies gather," the Professor replied, sing-song.

♋

The war years made it difficult for the cousins to see each other. They wrote each other only on rare occasions; neither of them possessed the knack of putting something interesting down on paper, as if they existed for one another only in person. Often during their lives they would live apart, in a variation of "out of sight, out of mind"—more or less the way siblings take each other's existence for granted. I never saw them pine for each other. But when they were together, the rest of the world (with the exception of me) dropped away.

It was the middle of the war when the cousins met again. I had received a note from the Countess, via a military dispatch, asking for help to ease their passage back to Persiran. My warm relationship with the Persiranian Ambassador to Germany resulted in two passports, for the Countess and Lili. Nima would travel separately, from Switzerland; all three traveled as Persiranian citizens. The Countess must have felt the claws of the Gestapo closing on her: she had given a significant part of her fortune to help the French underground. Despite my (still-intact) Nazi sympathies, it never occurred to me to act anything but honorably where she was concerned. They broke their trip in Berlin for a couple of days. As the battle of Stalingrad wound through its gruesome conclusion, I could spare only a few hours for them, away from the grim work at the hospital.

We met for lunch at a miserable small restaurant. Berlin's great suffering was still in store. All three wore sensible wartime clothes. The Countess had aged visibly; her face began to show the network of fine wrinkles that would resemble the surface of the sea on a mildly windy day. Gone were the stylish dresses; she wore a matronly tweed suit that was large on her fragile body. The two cousins had lost their facial resemblance. Lili had filled into woman of head-turning beauty. Her hair short, she wore gray skirts with sensible shoes and always the same military-style cap, I suspect to hide her beauty. Nima wore a white shirt, gray sweater vest, and brown corduroy trousers, looking more the Spanish partisan than the Persiranian aristocrat. But the shared *air de famille* persisted in their lanky gait: the two walked in long strides ahead of the Countess, who called them her gazelles. The Countess tried hard to convince me to accompany them to Tehran. I now wish I had— but I felt I could not leave when so many injured needed help. I had come to believe that I was needed in Berlin more than anywhere else.

Lunch over, the Countess and Nima waited outside the small restaurant. It was snowing lightly. Looking through the window, I could see small patches of snow accumulating on the shoulders of their coats, as I waited for Lili to emerge from the bathroom. As I held her coat, she slipped into it like a boy: two arms at once, shrugging it on carelessly. Suddenly I could not resist throwing her the line they both used: "Where? Where?" My shy grin gave the game away.

She looked straight at me, as if experiencing a revelation. Shaking her head with a sad smile, she came closer and caressed my face with a cool stroke of her hand, at the same time kissing my other cheek. "It's no use, darling Dal. Find yourself a better woman than me. He and I are connected in ways far more complicated than just love."

Thirty years later—upstairs, in the room just above this cell—when she no longer lived with us, I asked Nima the same question. An old man asking a middle-aged man: "Where? Where?" He looked at me with the same revelation Lili had experienced that night in the Berlin restaurant. By that time, I did not care who knew; I was merely surprised that he didn't. A woman is the first to know of a rival; a man is the last. "You also loved her?" he blurted, stupefied.

"You were never a perceptive man."

He generously agreed. Then he answered: "Where flowers carpet the earth and the butterflies gather."

Nima's tone was contemplative. "Lili and I were never in a hurry, you know. Back in 1943, Tehran was a sleepy town, and no one bothered us much. Politics no longer mattered, as the country had been taken over by the Allied forces. I arrived to inherit a large household. But from the time the Countess arrived, she became a grumbling concierge. She regretted leaving her countrymen. She regretted having set foot in our dirty, godforsaken country. By the way—" he suddenly looked up at me. "Did you sleep with my mother-in-law?"

"Yes," I confessed. It was difficult for me to imagine the Countess as an old woman. I reflected how the acid of age wipes away layer after layer of one's personality, until nothing remains of the vigorous original. The woman who in youth was all generosity now counts each penny. The old man who faced artillery in war now fears getting into an elevator. Worse still, the young will forever remember us the way we are now. What happened to that adventurous young girl who proposed marriage to a Prince in a Russian Palace? Or the mature, lovely woman who guided me inside her with such patience, cooing into my ear a woman's requirements, without a hint of emasculation?

"Gstaad, right?" I nodded.

"Lili was always much more perceptive than I."

"She knew?" I don't know if I was more embarrassed or pleased.

"She guessed."

"When we came here, the Countess was so angry at everything she saw that she even turned on Lili. Partly to escape her, and partly to be with each other, we began traveling around the country. But the 'where' eluded us. Nowhere looked right. Until one weekday in early spring, we decided to climb Tochaal alone, a day trip." Seeing my astonishment, he smiled. "That's right—the same place that half of Tehran climbs every weekend.

"Lili saw adventure in everything. She liked to push further. The day was windy but warm; we walked forever. Once we realized we could not get back the same day, we pushed up into the mountains. Around 2:00 in the afternoon, sweaty and covered in a layer of fine dust, we arrived at a small yellow valley, covered with hardy sunflowers, daisies, and the odd wild orchid. We sat there, well protected from the wind, with rocks on one side forming a high, smooth, striated wall. The field gave a sense of privacy. A sheen of water covered the rocks from the melting snow; you could hear the burbling of water higher up. Lili went to the rock and stripped her top off." Nima again saw the surprise on my face. "Now who is being dense? By that time, she and I had nothing to hide from each other.

"She put her palms against the wet rock and then pressed them against her face, making a hand-print on each dust-covered cheek. She squealed in delight as she applied her cold palms to her body. She shouted for me to come over. I stripped and joined her. We began applying our freezing palms to different parts of each other's body, almost like children drawing on a steamy mirror. Then our passion overwhelmed our curiosity. We began to use our hands more caressingly." Nima smiled at the memory. "Then the miracle occurred. I saw Lili's eyes grow large as she looked at something over my shoulder. I turned to see thousands of butterflies of different colors, skimming over the field of flowers. Who could have guessed that that area was known for its appeal to butterflies? Lili ran into the middle of the field, hands waving wildly among the sunflowers, daisies, and wild tulips. Half naked, with her boyish haircut, her face wet, her breasts free, and butterflies scattered all over her—I cannot remember seeing anything more beautiful in my life." He paused, and his voice became almost a whisper. "We didn't need to ask the question. *There* was where."

⚮

Morning had come. Professor Dal fell silent, but very indiscreetly. For the old man had an erection pressing against my back, while his tears ran down my neck like snowmelt on the rocks in the mountains.

The Seventh Night
0111

The Narrator Helps with a Piece of the Puzzle

To die before being painted by Sargent is
to go to heaven prematurely.

— H. H. Munro,
The Complete Short Stories of Saki

Dear Ms. Vakil,

Thank you for sending me the four digital recordings of Mr. Hekaiatchi's oral history. I never imagined his reedy voice to have such a high pitch, like an old recording of Alessandro Moreschi.

I am overwhelmed by your generosity of spirit and your trust. I will pay you back in kind. I have hired Digiscribe, a local scanning company, to begin the digitization of all the documents in my possession. I will put the originals at your disposal. I know from your letters that you visit the Boston-area universities with some regularity.

I understand your concern about destroying any letters concerning my paternal grandmother. And I agree that she has her own place in history, as one of the most active women members of the Tudeh party—the now completely discredited offshoot communist party, organized by Lenin himself. My concern lies in disclosing my grandfather's prurient attraction to a sixteen-year-old, which few readers could place in its historical context: that is, in a time that only superficially coincides with the West's twentieth century.

The Prince wrote to his brother in Paris, describing Choti, as he called her, like an old man entranced by a heavenly houri. It was 1924, and he was thirty-nine years old.

> My darling brother, the light of my eyes, the beat of my heart,

297

The kind of love you lugged in your heart since the age of twelve for your dear wife has finally arrived not a day too late, in my old age, in the guise of a sixteen-year-old girl, woman, angel, devil. She has plaited a vine around my heart that she can squeeze at will and rob me of that very will. That she loves me not a jot, troubles me not a jot. I have written to you of her as the daughter of Darbandi, my Secretary. You never met him: a clean, careful man with unusual probity for our times. Choti, his daughter, has been a good companion for Dal these last years. A fiery girl that I am afraid someday will get us all into trouble. None of the womanly concerns for her: she reads, she argues and next she'd be climbing the pomegranate tree because she fancies a piece of fruit. Her father screams at her for walking on top of the walls. He warns her that she will lose her virginity if she were to fall off the wall. She laughs her abrupt laugh. She orders the servants as if they were her own. They act as her slaves. She walks about the house uncovered. She has no concept of shame or embarrassment. On our first night, she undressed from head to toe. Brother, I don't believe I have ever seen my other wives so completely naked. She stood there staring at me like the daughter of Eve, curious and yet not curious. I very nearly lost my masculine abilities. God forgive me, I even doubted her virginity. Thanks to God she bled profusely.

I will write you at length at the end of the month. These are difficult times. Our dynasty rules no more. I have organized yet another exile for our grandnephew. He lives quite near to you. Reza Khan, now Reza Shah, has shown me kindness, but when all is said I am a Qajar. I am content to retire with my darling Choti at my side. Stay well, brother, and be of service to our grandnephew.

Your imperfect half, Saleh Mirza.

You note, Ms. Vakil, the incriminating modifier "profusely": the idea of a sixteen-year-old made to bleed by a forty-year-old makes for speedy judgment.

I have returned from a yoga class and am full of ideas. The yoga building sits in a narrow strip mall dwarfed by a gigantic Toys "Я" Us whose black corrugated wall rises to the blue sky, a two-dimensional Hollywood cutout building. The yoga studio, on the second floor, sits above a Build-A-Bear Workshop that also sells tinseled artificial Christmas trees. The birthday parties, held inexorably each hour, enjoy a full minute of silence while the kids ensconce a plastic red heart within the bear's cotton stuffing. They then suture the teddy bear with deep reverence—and instantly, the sound of whooping children penetrates our meditation practice. Today, while in the contemplative yoga mode, they gave me a "madeleine" moment: those faux-tinsel decorated trees took me back to a childhood Christmas.

Each year, my mother put up a gigantic tree with the most exquisite trimmings. The tree sat in the corner of our grand entrance, visible to all visitors for a month. Hung from the tree were hens made of blown glass, clasping miniature enameled eggs with their feet. Tied among the pine needles were tiny Waterford crystal bells, silvery yet translucent, chiming delicately every time the outer door swung open or shut. Small glass clown faces, in Christmas red and green, were suspended in a basket. There were ornamental antique watches, angels kneeling on scrap snow, Dresden paper medallions, Swarovski edelweiss blossoms, and scores of hand-painted, blown-glass globes adorned with glittering crystal in red, green, gold, and silver. At the top of the tree, instead of the usual crowning star, rode Papa Noël, Lone Ranger-like, mounted on a goose with a lemon-colored beak. Goose and rider were affixed to a globe announcing *Joyeux Noël* in jubilant italics.

All this my mother administered deftly, with her managerial, take-control skills. First the servants brought up the hundreds of leather boxes. A treat in itself, our job was to unclasp the boxes to reveal each object, ensconced in its bed of cut velvet. Some boxes had small fleur-de-lis clasps, others had hooks-and-eyes made of bone. Our special favorite was a magnetic stainless steel bead sewn into an alligator leather strap, that fell into place each time with a confident and satisfying click.

Decrepit ladders were brought out from every corner of the garden to surround the tree like ancient scaffolding. My mother ordered the household staff around with complete confidence. As they hung onto the ladders in awkward, yogic postures, she would abruptly change her mind; with even more confidence, she would demand that the object be moved to the other side of the tree. Then, frustrated at the slowness of the *domestiques*, she would dash to seize a ladder to do the job herself—and now mayhem would break loose. Everyone in the room rushed to stop her, as if her life would be at risk if, God forbid, she climbed two rungs of a ladder. Our God-fearing Muslim household treated this woman as an ornithologist might treat an endangered hummingbird: a rainbow-plumed rarity to be protected at any cost. The tree trimming completed, packages began to fill the space under the gigantic tree and, eventually, half the parquet floor.

The year 1963 stands out in my memory. The Countess, our Parisian grandmother, came to Tehran that year, under protest—her only visit since the war years. It is the only time I remember seeing her; we were nine years old. She refused to leave her bed during the day. She never set foot on the streets. But she treated us with affection, gazing at us with deep, woeful eyes from a thin, ravaged face, her skin hanging from cheeks to neck with parallel creases. The gift she brought us made that Christmas memorable.

Christmas in Tehran: to us it seemed normal. A glittering, mountain-like tree amid mounds of colored packages; the redolent smells of pine and parquet polish.

Today, I am struck by the tolerance of the ruling class toward these emphatically non-Moslem festivities— something that would be unthinkable today. Persiran indeed enjoyed the most tolerant years of our modern history during my brother Arya's short lifetime: 1956– 1972, RIP.

Only one other period of our history can compete in tolerance: the glorious twenty months—1907 to 1908 —of the first Constitutional Majlis.

෴

In 1907, Sardar Mirza (the fun-loving twin), stood for election to represent the "estate of nobles and landowners" in the Majlis, the parliament. Once elected, he immediately joined his natural allies, the liberal radical faction. In its twenty months of existence, the parliament achieved much, and pissed off many. It reduced (as it thought) the powers of the Shah, and it put limits on religious authority. All his life, Sardar Mirza would take pride in those twenty months.

But no one understood better than the Prince the grand failure that loomed. He stayed deliberately aloof from his brother's democracy set.

The big debate of the first parliament revolved around the supplementary 125 articles of the Constitution—four of them in particular.

Article 2, written by the reactionary Sheikh Nouri, would establish a council made up of five of the highest-ranking religious leaders, to sit as judges *above* the senate—a kind of Shi'ite supreme court, designed to filter out any gaseous utterings of parliament that lay outside the laws of Sharia. This was sold as "clerical constitutionalism." This outrageous proposal launched a series of mass demonstrations that forced Sheikh Nouri once again to take sanctuary in a mosque.

Articles 8, 19, and 20—copied from the Belgian constitution—would enshrine the protection of minorities, compulsory public education, and freedom of the press. The liberal wing finally managed to enact these three basic rights. But in exchange, they conceded on Article 2, creating Nouri's religious supra-parliament. (Ms. Vakil, you may recall that the devil offered a similar pact to my adopted country: all those beautiful amendments, the Bill of Rights, were paid for with the slavery compromise.)

When our fathers agreed to enact Article 2, it was considered a dead letter: they felt certain that the other religious leaders would not share power with the hated Sheikh Nouri. Indeed, for over seventy years, Article 2 sat inert—a viral time bomb, ignored by successive governments. In 1979, the Frankenstein monster woke with a start, because one old man remembered.

I would like to shout from rooftops to enlighten my American friends, who seem to think of their Constitutional Convention as some kind of natural evolution. No: the American republic was quite simply a miracle, the greatest fluke of Western civilization. How did it happen that this country, at the moment of its nation-building, had at its disposal half a dozen civic geniuses—who were also reasonable people?

𝒮

The present brought by our grandmother, the Countess, hung for years afterward in the petit salon. It was a large wooden jigsaw puzzle, showing the picture of a young woman in a large white hat, circa 1910. The hat's gauzy scarf, knotted under the chin, formed a perfect isosceles triangle, a fabric frame for my grandmother's twenty-year-old face, looking out at us with sarcastic, arching eyebrows. The eyes created deep pools, reflecting an unseen chandelier.

According to custom, the gifts were opened with ceremony among a party of invited guests. The Countess was perched on an armchair in the middle of the hallway, wearing a Chanel ensemble; a tear-shaped sapphire locket rested on her cashmere orange sweater. Although it was midnight, she held her Hermès bag, as if prepared to step out onto the Rue Saint-Honoré. Everyone else oohed and aahed as presents were unwrapped.

We unwrapped the heavy wooden puzzle, with the picture on top of the box (the mark of an easy puzzle). The Countess, Anaïs de Grandpierre, looked at her daughter and proclaimed, in practiced tones: "*Mais voici ma jeunesse, imaginée par Belleroche.*" It was indeed a picture of her youth, as imagined by the famous artist Albert de Belleroche. My brother and I were less impressed by this brush with a luminary of the Belle Époque than by the jigsaw puzzle's smooth, wooden whimsies—its pieces in the shapes of birds, rabbits, swords, angels, and snowflakes.

My grandmother's youthful portrait had one unique characteristic that captured the imagination of a nine-year-old. The artist had centered the painting on a tear-shaped, sapphire locket that rested between her young breasts, which were properly covered by her white muslin dress. The bright azure stone formed a single puzzle piece, the central piece of the puzzle—much as my grandmother became the center of attention that night, the object of general admiration.

The next day, Christmas day, my brother and I delighted everyone by solving the puzzle in less than half an hour, working in my grandmother's bedroom, where both our parents had joined her for tea. With dramatic effect, I picked up the last, central piece. I placed the jewel, cut in precisely the shape and size of her own locket, between my grandmother's painted breasts. The ensuing hoopla was memorable. It was occasioned not by our puzzle-solving skills but because—perhaps for the first time—my brother and I had cooperated without an ugly incident. My mother, a born optimist, saw in this rapprochement a model for future gifts. For the next three years, she gave us complex jigsaw puzzles with themes like 101 Dalmatians, or ones with irregular shapes that looked like the chalk outlines of murder victims. One year, my grandmother sent us the world's most difficult jigsaw, of a Jackson Pollock painting.

Whether as testimony to our achievement or to flatter the Countess, the completed puzzle was placed on display on a mahogany table in the petit salon. A few days later, I slipped unnoticed into the petit salon. Using the tip of a silver letter opener, I gently pried out, with some difficulty, the centerpiece of the puzzle, its jewel—the locket.

With my grandmother still in residence, the staff immediately went into a panic. My mother, cool as a cucumber, summoned the local carpenter, Master Reza. He was no master: filthy and half-shaven, with sockless feet in plastic sandals, he stands as an early prototype of today's Islamic bureaucrat. He was ordered to fill the empty space with glued wood shavings. There was no question of having him create a new piece; he didn't have the skill. My mother then used her thin paintbrushes, used only for the New Year's egg painting, to complete the illusion. She then ordered Master Reza to glue the puzzle to a frame; she then had it hung high on a sidewall, where her mother's weak eyes would not detect the missing locket.

The impetus behind my theft remains unclear to me. Why do boys keep their prized assortments of shoelaces, coins, or stones? I hid the piece in an unused chimney hole that was covered with a tin top when the heater was not in use. Some nights, I removed the piece from its hiding place and slept holding it tight in my fist. I must have thought it the most perfect, most magical object in the universe.

Years later, I made a pretense of finding it. By then, my grandmother was dead, the sixties were at an end, and the jigsaw had been stored away in some suitcase in a basement. My "discovery" created momentary excitement at lunch, though my brother looked suspicious. But there was no move to restore it to its place. It became my personal lucky charm. I drilled a hole in the wooden piece—which by then barely resembled a locket, its paint worn off like a bad decal. I used a leather string to wear it around my neck. It fit a teenager's look. My mother saw it as a sentimental homage to her mother.

A year later, I gave the charm to Hamid, during the holy month of Muharram. The memory of the soccer game had faded, as had the purple welts around his eyes. The small bump that remained in the middle of his nose transformed his boyish look. The village, along with the rest of the country, spent the month mourning the martyrdom of Hossein, the grandson of the Prophet—memorializing the tragic events of Ashura, the tenth day of Muharram. Like villages throughout Persiran, the Poonak villagers had organized *ta'ziyeh* plays, based on the last days of Hossein. The performance would be mounted on a special stage commissioned by my father, who had of course donated the land.

We arrived at the village in early afternoon, well before "curtain time." Word came that one of the villagers, caught up in the frenzy of sanctified grief, had seriously injured himself by repeatedly slashing his forehead with a straight poniard. Immediately my father and Hamid's father (who was the village head) issued a joint order to warn of the serious consequences awaiting those who allowed or participated in the self-mutilating nonsense. Ms. Vakil, let me not riff on the absurd practices encouraged by our religious leaders. Self-flagellation exists in many religions; but our soft-skinned mullahs act only as cheerleaders for the populace to beat their backs raw. I don't remember seeing a mullah use a scourge on any part of his body.

My father then listened to villagers' complaints about water rights in the valley. An agitated group of farmers from the lower valley shouted their concerns. Peasants always acted confrontational, arguing loudly to authority. I think they sensed they didn't speak the same language as the landlords, so they needed to speak *loudly*—much like immigration officers in the United States. But in any dispute over water rights, the loudness was not mere form; it expressed desperation. That year, severe drought had changed the green of much of the eastern valley into shades of dry yellow. The river had dried up. The petitioners, leaning on their wooden shovels or shouldering their ancient, two-sided pickaxes, looked angry, suspicious, crafty, dusty, tired, and, more than anything, miserable.

My father relished dealing with concrete local problems. No detail was unimportant to him. A streak of common sense mixed with his populist candor would usually dispose of problems; he was in a class by himself. He somehow managed to reason with men whose emotions had moved them far beyond reason—a seigniorial man out of step with his era.

After an afternoon's discussion, the peasants, though not beaming, left with a more thoughtful manner. The rest of us retired to the schoolhouse to eat supper as we waited for the play. Later in the evening, we walked out through the dusty alleys of the village, between the low house walls of clay and straw.

The stage, or *takieh*, stood a hundred yards beyond the last walls of the village. It was a simple, square, cement structure. Behind the platform, gigantic vats sat on small stacks of loose brick, where crackling fires cooked the white rice. Our cook, old Nemat's nephew (with an even flatter Mongolian face, if that were possible), dished out the rice by burying the plate into the mound. Retrieving the pyramid of rice, with a twist of his wrist he'd display the plate on top of his bunched fingers. This he offered with a magician's smile, to the delight of the peasants who stood by, transfixed and gaping.

Piled to the height of a child stood stacks of fresh *sangak*, the delicious bread that bears, like a martyr, the marks of the stones in the oven, in little burned semicircles. Sheets of it were offered freely to everyone. Behind the fire and the vats, the hard desert rose in the north into gentle purple hills. Much farther still, though appearing deceptively close, was the magnificent Alborz mountain chain, slicing the land out of the sky; it guarded, and still guards, the city of Tehran, the shimmering carpet of light a good ten miles away.

By the time we arrived at the *takieh*, the villagers were already gathered. The women sat along one side of the stage on *kilim* carpets. All wore the long, black veil. The men stood at the corners. My father sat on the only chair; I stood a few feet behind him, among the villagers. We faced the stage, with the mountains as backdrop. A warm, westerly wind blew from the desert and made the gaslights around the stage whistle. Jackals and wolves howled incessantly beyond the valley.

A quick, nervous beat of the drum was followed by silence. Another burst, its sound hanging in the night. The professional storyteller, speaking in a clear voice, approached the stage. He would stay on the stage throughout, following the pulse of the audience. He was narrating the tragedy in lightly rhyming verse, leading up to the point where the caliph's army would encircle Hossein and his seventy-two followers.

Listening to the narrator, I felt someone close in front of me. I looked down and saw a dark, smiling boy of ten with large brown eyes: the schoolkeeper's son, no doubt seeking a better view of the stage. Placing my hand on the boy's shoulder, I turned my attention back to the play. I felt the boy against my crotch. What seemed quite innocent at first soon transformed into a slow, circular, sexual grind. Feigning inattention, I steadied him. The boy moved a step away.

Glancing to my left, I saw the yellow smile of an old man a few feet away, elbowing his neighbor into the joke. I moved quickly: with my open hand, I threw a hard blow to the back of the boy's head. The boy stumbled and fell on one knee under the gas lamp. He got up and disappeared into the crowd. My father, one eyebrow raised, turned in his seat; the phalanx of men interpreted his look as admonishing silence. The old man had wiped away any trace of his leer.

"The boy is smitten by the perverse tickle." I looked behind me and saw Hamid smiling.

I smiled back. "I had heard he had the disease, but I am surprised by his impudence."

"Is it a disease between two grown friends?"

"It is certainly not *impudence* between friends," I answered, not meeting his eyes.

A cacophony of noise now enveloped the *takieh*. In one part of the stage, the marriage of one of Hossein's nephews was being celebrated. On the other side, the other nephew was being mutilated by the caliph's army. The women sobbed, as if on cue. One of the characters sang:

> What ails thee, black-hearted friend of mine?
> Why such haste to murder the House of Ali?

I withdrew from the crowd. Walking down into the valley through a portal, I descended, sideways, the giant set of stone stairs, made of flat rocks from the riverbed. I sat down under a large mulberry tree that even in the weak moonlight cast a shadow darker than the night. I could hear the *ta'ziyeh* winding inexorably toward its tragic end. There was a quiet rustle in the silence, just a few feet away. "Who is it?" I demanded, standing up.

"It's me, sir," said Hamid, silhouetted a mere six feet away. I saw no shadow of the future, no reflection of the past—purely the present moment.

"You have come to apologize for the boy," I said—unconvincing even to myself. Head down and silent, Hamid stepped forward, two confident steps. The gaslights above were dragons breathing fire through their noisy copper vocal cords: too much noise, too much light. I retreated a few steps deeper into the shadow of the tree, stepping awkwardly over protruding roots. He walked forward again, head down, eyes downward, seeming less confident, until I felt his hand on my belt. Only then did he look up. I felt his sweet breath. My palm felt the bristle of his shaved head. Accompanied by the sobbing of the humans above and the screaming of the jackals below, I shed all rules and taboos.

Now we heard the procession begin above us, parading down all the alleys of the village, marching to the hard slaps of hands against bare chests and the clinks of chains against flesh. Still we lay curled up together. I experienced with astonishing clarity—*myself*: what I liked.

That is when I gave him the centerpiece of the puzzle. He wore it under his shirt.

Ms. Vakil, I have said more than I should. A love story, when it is a first love, can make us believe in a soul. Forty years later, the memories of it are part of the building blocks that make up my existing soul. I trust your discretion.

You will ask me whether I chose Hamid for the damage this could wreak on my brother's psyche. It was a side benefit, I don't doubt: Hamid's presence among us changed the calculation. But love conquered hate. I knew that I could devastate my brother with the revelation. He loved Hamid like a true brother; every daring adventure, they did together. But, like a woman,

I understood instinctively that Hamid belonged to me,
if I kept my silence. I was not prepared to lose Hamid in
order to inflict pain on my brother. It never crossed my
mind.

The Fat Storyteller Experiences War Through His Future Father-in-Law

"I have spent more than half a lifetime
trying to express the tragic moment."

— Marcel Marceau

Baba, my outing to Vakil Khanum did me much good I have cautiously come out of my shell. I expect any day to get my head chopped off—but I rejoice in my newfound freedom. Of course, the last thing I want is to attract attention from two blocks down the street. I wear a raggedy American baseball cap all the time, and I keep my head down as I go about the shop. I work behind the counter when Mammad-Ali's hands are full—full of boxes and packets of stuff. He is a tiny man who wears pajama-like pants and an untucked dark-blue shirt; his small wrists, ankles, hands, and feet stick out like a sparrow's claws, but he lifts weights like a porter at the shipping docks. He throws a fifty-pound gunny of rice on his shoulder and climbs up a ladder with it as casually as a construction worker. Thank God he sees me as your son. He treats me with the respect accorded in your generation—non-existent today. He never asks me to perform manual labor. I would be humiliated if I had to take a heavy load up a ladder.

With the war at an end, Mammad-Ali's small shop has filled to the brim. They had difficult years, Zahra tells me, when the shelves stood empty. "We sold old batteries, scrap metal," she told me, her hand balled into a fist. Now business is brisk. Zahra works in the back filling orders and watches the accounts like a hawk. I have come to love this little shop, with its smells and overstuffed shelves. I like to take the broom and clean the wooden floors; I clean up the shelves with a sense of belonging and owning. Once in a while, I throw a stick of chewing gum or a chocolate gold medallion to one of the neighborhood kids, with the casual flick of the wrist that Mammad-Ali used when we were young. Pretending busyness, he never lifted his head to look at us; he didn't want to be embarrassed with a "thank you."

The other evening, Zahra went out with her friend Khadijeh to walk in the Bazaar, leaving me to close the shop. Hearing a strange murmuring coming from the back room, I walked cautiously to investigate. I thought it was mice. I found Mammad-Ali, sitting on the rough-wood tabouret next to the bench, lost among boxes of soap and detergents. Resting his head on the palm of his hand, he was crying piteously, but ever so discreetly. I rushed to enquire what the matter was, but he straightened his head and forced a smile. But too much had been revealed.

"I lost two boys in the war with Iraq," he breathed. "Fifteen and sixteen, angels walking on earth. I wanted to hide them. I wish they had inherited my crossed eyes, like my Zahra has. But they ran away to register with the militia; they both signed Passports to Paradise. They were down there early in the war, about the time Saddam had agreed to keep the old frontier. Mr. Hekaiatchi," he looked up at me. "The old man," he meant Khomeini, "he rejected that offer after only twenty-four hours. We fought for six more years because of his decision, without gaining a single pebble of land. He took a single day to decide the fate of thousands, who died in the most horrific ways. You tell me, Mr. Hekaiatchi, who does that? I lost my younger son Mohsen a month after they ran away, during Operation Ramadan to capture Basra. He volunteered to run through the minefields. His brother, Ali, wrote me in ecstasy that Mohsen had disappeared to Heaven. He could not find any part of his body. When I heard he had died, I closed the shop. I left my thirteen-year-old Zahra with the neighbors. I boarded the bus south, to try to save my Ali.

"Mr. Hekaiatchi, I arrived in Khorramshahr. God had created hell on earth in that place. The city had been

destroyed and recaptured by our forces. I thought I had
arrived in a place of Djinns and unformed animals, with
frog eyes and square plastic muzzles. Men walked half
naked, caked in mud from head to toe, training for some
unknown mission. Children ran around playing, as if
back in the neighborhood, except that their heads,
torsos, and remaining limbs were covered in bandages.
Then I noticed people carrying pieces of carpets, sheets
of vinyl, sheets of cardboard, to transport bodies, limbs
dangling. In this chaos no one would know where my
son had been sent. No one knew where anyone was. I
volunteered as a water carrier just to get fed; I carried
two buckets on each end of a long rod balanced on my
shoulders. I spent a month behind the front lines. Mr.
Hekaiatchi, I cannot tell you the horrors I saw.

"In search of my son, I stumbled into the areas where
they kept the Iraqi prisoners. Wretched people, half
naked, they wallowed in the dust on the ground. No
shade to protect them. To me, they looked no different
from us.

"One morning, I came across a mud and straw stable.
Two guards in front signaled to me to take a detour.
Mr. Hekaiatchi: don't have any children. Their dangers
make you forget your own safety. I had made up my
mind that I had to search for my boy everywhere,
regardless of the risks. I threw my head down and
approached them. They screamed at me, pointing their
rifles at me. I just pretended deafness. When I got close,
I brought my head up offering them water. They looked
angry but calmed down once they saw my eyes, my
small stature and old age. My looks are not always a
disadvantage, you see: people look at me and judge me
soft in the head. As they drank, I peered behind them.
In the stable, four gorgeous white horses blew fluttery
air through their nostrils. I had never seen horses like
this. I had imagined them when your father described
Rostam's horse, in the old tearoom. I wish I had never
found out the reason for this stable and the guards.

"As days passed, I got closer to the fighting trenches. Mere boys sat glumly, waiting for orders to sacrifice themselves. Bored, praying for time to pass quicker so that they could die sooner. Nine or ten-year-olds, what is the logic in that? Then, during one of their human wave attacks, I saw them using one of the white horses. There sat on one of these horses, in the dust storm, an older man dressed in white like Imam Hossein, with a green turban on his head and a green wrap around his midriff. The soldiers watched him without comment, but the boys looked at each other with excitement of seeing an apparition. When the bugle to attack sounded, the man raised his hand and—would you believe it—he had a sword with the same shape as the one your father used, to bring his stories to life in the tearoom. He marched the horse parallel to the trenches and then turned directly toward the enemy lines. He galloped forward, disappearing in the dust as if leading the charge. No doubt he veered off toward the stables, to spare any danger to the horse. I watched from afar as the boys ran out after him, fearless, with no weapons. From afar I saw only gentle puffs of smoke. I could not hear the mines blowing them into nothingness, like my son. Groups of men carried the injured back quickly, shielding them from view of the next wave of volunteers. Those boys cleared a path for the soldiers, who then followed in their exact footsteps. The men, no less brave, met withering fire from the well-entrenched Iraqis. I cannot tell you how many people died during those attacks. It must have been tens of thousands.

"I arrived about the time they wanted to capture Basra. Mr. Hekaiatchi, I could no longer pray. Watching these boys and men die senselessly, I lost faith in the Almighty. For one month I looked for my Ali. When I finally saw him, my heart wanted to fly out of my chest. He wore an oversized soldier's uniform, with a regular army helmet covering most of his face. I could recognize my boy's posture even among ten thousand soldiers. He looked like a boy playing at war. I ran to him. To my surprise he tried to ignore me. 'Ali, my son,' I cried, 'don't you recognize your own father?'"

Here Mammad-Ali broke down again; he cried for a while before he resumed his story. "My son told me that he had seen me more than three weeks before. He had been hiding from me, because he knew I had come to take him back. He being my only son, and I being more than sixty years old, I could claim him from the war. He told me that he wanted to follow the path of martyrdom, like his brother. He then told me, with all the intensity of the young, that he had seen Imam Hossein with his own eyes. When he said that, I immediately regained my faith, Mr. Hekaiatchi. Like a miracle, I understood: I could distinguish the work of God from the work of man. What was in front of me, what these Mullahs preached, our holy revolution—this was the work of man. I had seen the horses. I saw no difference between your father's stories and what these religious men had fed my boys. I am a simple man, Mr. Hekaiatchi. Had I not seen that day the stable full of white horses, I also would have believed my eyes. I will regret all my life my loss of faith for those few weeks. God will punish me for doubting him—but now I understood the power of knowledge. Didn't he put us on this earth to do the best we can? For the first time in my life, I regretted not having an education or giving my boys a good education. Education is about *seeing the horses*. That is why, when I returned, I did everything to educate Zahra, as a school-age girl. You are my witness, she is a demon with numbers, isn't she?" He smiled through his tears, as proud as a peacock.

"You couldn't convince your Ali?" I asked.

"I couldn't tell if it did any good. He told me that his life now belonged to protecting his friends there. No way for him to come back while this war continued. I threatened to claim him through legal means. He looked at me with a look of someone three times his age.

"'*Agha Joun*—Darling Sir,' he said. 'It does no good. The day after you get me back, I will escape again. You can see the chaos here. No one here will report me. There are ten-year-olds here whose parents don't know where they are.'

"I had to accept his logic. I returned on the next bus, bidding him a careful war. Miraculously, he survived two more years in that chaos. I got letters from him from time to time. His last letter came in late February. He told me proudly how hard they had fought through the marshes of southern Iraq. They captured the Island of Majnun, only forty miles north of Basra. I never heard from him again. He died during Operation Kheibar, at age eighteen. They sent me his body on the first day of spring, New Year's Day. They told me to rejoice at my son's martyrdom and forbade me to cry for him. I could only thank God that their mother never had to witness the death of two sons. No one should go through what I have."

Baba, I cried from the depth of my heart for Mammad-Ali. Worse still: in all the time I had been a guest in his house, I had never asked this generous man about his children. I remembered his two sons, younger than me by quite a few years; how could I have forgotten? Neither he nor Zahra ever volunteered the information, always solicitous of my feelings. For the first time in my life I began to cry for someone other than myself. Mammad-Ali, touched by my distress, slipped into my arms like a small baby. He tried to pat me somewhere appropriate, but his hands could not reach my back. He opted to rub my stomach instead. He kept calling me his son. We stayed that way for a while.

෧

A few days later, Zahra and I set out to launch my oral history. On this visit, I did not use the chador to hide myself. The previous day's snowfall had settled the pollution. We saw the garbage collectors going out on trucks, armed with long sticks to shake the snow off the tree branches. I gave the taxi driver the address of the Saman apartment block—one of the first luxury apartment blocks of the city. Despite their age, the twin apartment towers could still impress my poor Zahra. We walked through the plaza to enter the second tower; we crossed the shiny stone lobby to the desk, where a man looked at us suspiciously. Zahra's chador looked out of place. The man at the desk called upstairs.

"A Mr. Hekaiatchi here to see you," he said. I could hear the mosquito buzz of the phone's earpiece. Without looking up, he told us to push the elevator button for the top floor.

My sweet Zahra had never been inside an elevator. She walked in suspiciously, even scared. I pressed the button for the top floor. The elevator started with a jolt, and Zahra grabbed my arm. "God protect us," she murmured, distracted the next moment by the sequence of lights next to each floor number. The elevator door opened into an apartment that impressed me and knocked Zahra's breath away. A white-haired woman dressed in modern clothes showed us into the living room and asked, whispering, if we wanted tea. Evidently the maid, she looked richer than anyone Zahra had ever known. She brought the tea and told us that Khanum would be down soon. *Down?* I thought. Zahra missed the significance of the statement. "A *house* inside an apartment block," I whispered to her. On the table in the living room, a cassette recorder sat ready to take in every word I would say. I liked that, Baba. I could practice the art you taught me for so many years.

Vakil Khanum walked in, without a headdress, and greeted us in the friendliest way. She looked beautiful. Her thick black hair—each strand straight yet in harmony with the rest—swayed like the hair of a princess. Her dress ended just below her knees. Zahra actually gasped. "Zahra, you can take your chador off," said Ms. Vakil. "No man will come in. I assume you are comfortable with Mr. Hekaiatchi." Zahra dropped her chador reluctantly as far as her waist, but kept it on, always conscious that a man might walk in.

Vakil Khanum walked to the tape recorder. Next to it lay a heavy microphone, like a metal ice cream cone. She picked it up and showed me a small switch on its stem. By pulling the switch back and forth, I could stop the tape reel from advancing, or restart it when I was ready to speak again. This calmed my nerves. With this device, I could stop for a sip of tea or a bite of the delicious cream-filled cones set out on their filigreed silver tray.

"If you are ready, Mr. Hekaiatchi, Zahra and I have little else to do but to listen to your fascinating story."

ℒ

I had suffered a night of gas-filled stomach problems. I had not slept well at all. That morning, Professor Dal did his usual oil-producing act, throwing his head back with his arms outstretched like a man on a cross. And this time, each fingernail had been lacquered with glossy red polish, applied with the meticulousness reserved for women's nails. His toenails still showed the remnants of the red polish from a few nights ago, cracked like a teenager's. Why would they take a prisoner and do his nails? Could this be some modern therapy to cure this madman? Yet he was not mad at night. I had two different cellmates. At first, I had feared the daytime Professor Dal for his madness; and later I dreaded the discipline of the nighttime Professor Dal. By now, I did not fear either one. I had accepted them both. I had even come to look forward to the nighttime Professor, not just from boredom but from curiosity. What man in prison doesn't like a good story?

That night, he again climbed on top of me.

The Professor Evokes the Revolutionary Grandfathers

"Then went the jury out whose names were
Mr. Blindman, Mr. No-good, Mr. Malice,
Mr. Love-lust, Mr. Live-loose, Mr. Heady,
Mr. High-mind, Mr. Enmity, Mr. Liar, Mr.
Cruelty, Mr. Hat-light, Mr. Implacable,
who every one gave in his private verdict
against him among themselves, and
afterwards unanimously concluded to
bring him before the judge."

—Pilgrim's Progress

After a brief eighteen months, the first constitutional period ended abruptly with the clatter of cannons. As the Prince was wont to say: *I told you so.* Mozaffar al-Din Shah, having signed the Constitution, died within the week, leaving the throne to the petulant thirty-eight-year-old Crown Prince Mohammad Ali (the Prince's supercilious nephew). With the new Shah, of course, came the ever-present Shapshal—his uneducated, self-indulgent Russian tutor—wearing his prim smile. Shapshal's investment had paid off handsomely, and he bathed in the glow of success.

But a far more serious Russian waited in the wings, about to step into the limelight: Colonel Liakhov—in full Cossack uniform, complete with Russian-style epaulets and the perfectly groomed mustache and beard favored by his master, Czar Nicholas. Chin held high, with one arm behind his back and the other hand resting on his sword, he presented the tableau of a man certain of his own superiority. He headed the so-called Persiranian Cossacks, a regiment formed by the Prince's father in 1882 and paid for by the Persiranian government; it was meant to be an extension of the Shah's will.

The coronation was held on the nineteenth of January, 1907, just two weeks after the old Shah had gone to the Almighty. The Prince had advised Crown Prince Mohammad Ali to delay his coronation for a few weeks, to no avail. As his first act of statesmanship, the incoming Shah snubbed the Majlis—again against the Prince's advice—by refusing to invite any of its members to the coronation. The courtiers of the new Shah spurned the Prince; Shapshal had become the Shah's closest confidante. The Prince persevered nevertheless, out of loyalty to the tradition of monarchy, in an almost desperate search for a new, workable version of constitutional monarchy. "Which one of us cockroaches is prepared to interrupt 2,500 years of our tradition?" he asked himself.

Toward the end of June, in the heat of summer, the Prince drove to the Shah-Abdol-Azim Shrine, a few miles south of Tehran, where his father had been assassinated ten years earlier. This was not, however, his yearly pilgrimage to the impressive marble tombstone of Naser al-Din Shah. For the second time, he was visiting Sheikh Nouri: once again, the old Sheikh had launched a sit-in, filling the courtyards of the mosque with a thousand of his followers.

This sit-in was the Sheikh's greatest success. Eighteen members of the *ulama* and thirty members of the mid-level clergy had joined him; together, they presented a unified clerical front to the parliament. As the Prince had predicted, the Great Atabak was once again Premier—almost his only ally in the new regime. The Great Atabak was the quick-witted and loyal Premier at the time of his father's assassination.

The growing three-way struggle between the Shah, the parliament, and the Sheikh provided Atabak ample room for maneuver, and the Prince's visit was his opening gambit. The Prince brought with him a special gift from the new Premier: several large trays of sweets, whose hollow bases concealed wads of tightly packed bills to help the Sheikh feed his followers.

"A *second* visit from Your Highness?" Sheikh Nouri's voice echoed through the vaulted ceilings. "Much water has gone under the bridge since the last time Your Highness and I talked." Sheikh Nouri looked in excellent fettle. The mosque was cool and dark, after the hot trip in the official car.

The Prince had come to discuss a joint communiqué by all parties, to agree to the new extension to the articles of supplementary laws. No one had predicted this compromising approach. The Shah had imagined the Great Atabak his ally; the parliament, too, expected a reactionary—as Premier to three Shahs. The Prince's father had died in his arms outside this very mosque.

But Atabak had arrived in Tehran after three-and-a-half years of traveling in Europe, which had given him a more liberal perspective. The wily Premier managed to get the monarchy and the parliament to compromise on the supplementary laws, using the clergy on each side to push toward an agreement. His arrival had been a blessing for the Prince, who found his natural place alongside the pragmatic Premier.

"Sheikh, you have made yourself quite comfortable here," he began. The white-turbaned Sheikh sat cross-legged, as a group of five senior clergy, kneeling behind him, wrote letters. A group of young seminary students stood behind him, staring at the ground until summoned.

The main activity centered on the fight with the Majlis. Since no newspaper in the capital would publish the Sheikh's fiery articles, an aggressive propaganda effort had been launched inside the mosque, accompanied by the clatter and rasping of the printing machine. The *Rulings of Sheikh Fazlollah Nouri* would pound the opposition, who had been denouncing him and his followers as godless heathens. The entire bureaucracy of Qom had been transferred to the mosque, and the Shah had quietly allowed the Sheikh to use the country's telegraph lines.

The atmosphere of this meeting was less tense; no doubt the Sheikh saw the Prince as a representative of the new Shah, whose support he enjoyed. For the moment, the political powers were at equilibrium. Each faction had made a move and was waiting for the reaction. Nouri had the most leverage; but the Majlis was now working, in fits and starts, like a real parliament, pushed along by guilds and societies that were popping up like wild grass. The Great Atabak danced among these factions with a sure footing that reflected his experience and age. The Prince played acolyte, learning the art of governance from this master artist.

"We make do with what we have; God provides the rest." The Sheikh smiled—playing the modest mendicant—and pointed to the trays of sweets the Prince had brought. He beckoned the Prince to sit, and a sherbet of sour cherries appeared on a silver tray.

"Your Highness has matured in the last year. Your brother, unfortunately, continues to be a thorn in our side. But then, a father cannot expect all sons to be a comfort in his old age." One of the Sheikh's own sons had indeed publicly opposed him, in favor of the parliamentary radicals; this allusion was thus in the nature of a peace offering, sharing a more or less private concern. The Prince ignored the bait.

"Sheikh, the Great Atabak sends his greatest respect. He bids to tell you that the Majlis has agreed to your conditions with regard to Article 2; it will be the law, as written by you. They want your assurances that henceforth you will not congregate but will allow the Majlis to do its work." The Sheikh, enthroned in that damp mosque, was at the zenith of his power. Using the parliament he abhorred, he had succeeded in institutionalizing the Sharia council as a filter for all laws coming out of the Majlis, including the supplementary laws to amend the constitution. But he had further demands, and now he jumped on his high horse.

"Your Highness, be my witness: for the past year, we have been insulted—accused of theft and of bearing witness to false documents, and falsely accused of hiring brigands to beat and murder ordinary people." His voice began to rise. "Our religion has been mocked by Babis and Baha'is who have taken over the souls of our brother Muslims in the Majlis. Praise be to God, we have on the throne a Muslim who understands the dangers to our revered country. He has seen it wise to bring back from exile an excellent leader of men, His Excellency Amin Soltan, the Great Atabak."

The Prince could easily put a name and a face to each of the felonies that the Sheikh now flatly denied, with such flowing effrontery. Sheikh Nouri had indeed helped create riots in Tabriz, Anzali, and Rasht, among other cities, working hand in glove with the Shah. Only a week ago, some of his roughs had beaten an employee of the French Legation. This was a ruthless man, an intriguer as well as a believer; he could have given Machiavelli a few new chapters.

"Great Sheikh," the Prince replied, "the Atabak you have praised so wisely bids you farewell. He asks you to leave the sanctuary of the Mosque of Shah-Abdol-Azim in safety. Your place is in Qom, taking care of the spiritual needs of your followers." The Sheikh's residence had always been in Tehran, of course. "Your work here is complete."

"Complete, you say?" Outrage flashed in the Sheikh's eyes. "My work has just begun. Have you not read Article 1 of the constitution? It says: 'The religion of Persiran is Islam, according to the orthodoxy of Twelver Shi'ism, which faith the Shah of Persia must confess and promote.' Do you see anywhere in that

Article the words *Bab* or *Azali?* His majesty has asked me to help him promote our faith. I will do so to my dying day."

"Sheikh, Article 2 guarantees Article 1." This would have been a good place to rest his case. "Their Reverences Sheikh Tabatabai and Sheikh Behbehani have both agreed with you. They convinced the Majlis to include your exact text. You have also given your word to protect the constitution."

The mention of Sheikh Nouri's rivals was a serious mistake. In a fury, the Sheikh grabbed a piece of paper from the pile next to him.

"*They* dare to guarantee my behavior—in writing!" he shouted, waving the document. "They have pledged to those infidels, sitting in that chamber of evil, that they will expel me from the capital if I pitch a tent?" Spittle sprayed the paper clenched in his trembling hand. "Those ignoramuses dare to question my learning?" He began to fire off a string of theological examples, evoking murmurs of support and blessing from the group of clergy sitting behind him.

By now the entire mosque was hushed, awed by this full-bore attack on two of the most revered clerics in the Shi'ite world. The Sheikh concluded with a direct challenge. "Your Highness may throw my own words into my face until Judgment Day. Your Highness should remember that I will swear to a lie, a hundred times a day, with my hand on the Koran, if it furthers the kingdom of God on Earth."

With that, Sheikh Nouri unclenched his fists and exhaled, switching easily to the pedantic, repetitive, lecturing tone of mullahs the world over. "Each time we meet"—his smile was angelic—"Your Highness seems to have an excitable effect on his servant. Still, please let the Great Atabak know that all will end well. We cannot give the same guarantees that our revered colleagues give *on behalf of others*, but we shall help defuse the situation as much as is within our power." Having ceded the main point, he returned to the attack. "I wonder: where would Your Highness come down, in the choice between building God's kingdom on Earth and building a kingdom of man?"

"Your Reverence knows I am but a lost child when faced with theological conundrums," replied the Prince. "I am a pious Muslim." The Prince chose his words with care; he did not want to anger the Sheikh, now that he had agreed to disband, but he could not accept his premise. "It seems to me, Your Reverence, that a man who takes charge of building the kingdom of God on Earth will inevitably build a kingdom for himself."

The Sheikh laughed discreetly into his beard and then gestured with his hand, palm upward, toward the Prince, like a conductor introducing a virtuoso violinist. "His Highness puts us all to shame with his wisdom, and so young, too."

§

"Do you pray, boy?" Professor Dal asked.

(What is it with all the questions?) "Arbab, I have forgotten the words," I replied. "I used to pray when my father was alive. We used to pray together when I was a kid. After he died, I fell out of the habit. I have been a bad Muslim."

"A bad Muslim, you say. You are not even close to being a bad Muslim. You, my pile of leaves, are only a *naughty* Muslim. If you see a flock of sheep, can you tell which one is the worst sheep?"

More questions? He thankfully did not wait for an answer.

"It is the wolf!" Professor Dal laughed at his own joke. "Let me tell you who is a bad Muslim. No, let me tell you who is the *worst* Muslim: those among us who prey on people's belief in order to further their own glory. We are now in the age of wolf in wolf's clothing."

He laughed at that too, with an extended cough that sprinkled my neck with spittle and dug his ribs into my skin. After a few minutes he calmed down and went on with his story.

Fast forward nine years. Sardar Mirza sits, miserable, in an open carriage drawn by two equally miserable, thin-flanked horses, their faces hidden in bags of hay. Mounds of steamy dung mushroom from underneath their rising tails. The carriage sways widely, its wheels squeaking. On this early October morning, the sun's rays have lost any ability to warm the air; the dark blue of the sky wears the shadow of the mountain range like an emerging beard.

He was traveling to attend the traditional graveside observance marking the fortieth day following the death of a man he had never met—and could only revile: that of Abbas Agha, assassin of the Great Atabak. It would be a strange gathering. Sardar Mirza would attend the ceremony as a gesture of support for his radical and liberal friends in the Majlis; he had even agreed to say a few words at the gravesite. This was the first time that he and his brother, the Prince, disagreed passionately. They had not talked to one another for a full week—something he could not recall happening previously, for even a single day.

The assassin was now to be known as "Mujahid" Abbas Agha: the Liberal party had designated him a martyr to the revolution.

The last day of August was a day no one would soon forget. Sardar Mirza ran into the house, filled with ominous news that would, in the next instant, appear irrelevant. He was eager to inform his brother of a traitorous Anglo-Russian deal to partition the country into "zones of influence." His English friend, Mr. Scott, the *chargé d'affaires* in Tehran, had sworn him to secrecy. The rumor at the foreign office was that in St.

Petersburg, the Russians and the English had signed an agreement to divide Persiran into zones of influence. But as he entered the house, shock replaced outrage: his brother sat in the hallway, soaked in blood and crying inconsolably. The servants stood by, helpless.

Sardar Mirza rushed to take his brother in his arms, to console him, to ask if he was hurt. "They have killed him," his brother moaned.

"Who?" asked Sardar Mirza, softly. "Who has been killed?"

"The Great Atabak. I was with him. I traveled with the Great Atabak, to present the letter from the Shah to the Majlis." He sobbed like a child and struggled to recover his breath. "You know that Atabak had persuaded the Shah to sign the supplementary laws. I tell you, brother, he felt triumphant. We walked out of the Majlis with Sheikh Behbehani. We were blinded by the bright sunshine. I never saw the assassin. When I heard the crack of the revolver, I thought some carriage wheel must have broken. The Great Atabak collapsed in a heap. I wrapped him in his cloak. I laid him flat on the floor of our carriage to stanch the bleeding. I sent a servant with a message to fetch a physician. Within half an hour of reaching home, he was no more. I have lost a father all over again—*and in the same manner.*"

The newspapers the next day were full of the story. A soldier had attempted to stop the assassin and been stabbed. The gunman finally turned the revolver on himself, thus becoming the favorite martyr of the liberal establishment. In his pocket they found four capsules of strychnine, along with a piece of silver nitrate; a scrap of paper bore the inscription, "Abbas Agha, banker of Azerbaijan, member of Society, National Martyr No. 41." That there were apparently forty martyrs ahead of him posed a puzzle: did all the others have a previous engagement?

As Sardar Mirza's carriage neared the cemetery, more and more carriages joined his, jamming the road. The men walking easily outpaced them. A strangely festive mood prevailed. Sardar Mirza was astonished at the size of the crowd. This, he felt, was almost a moral validation of his decision to attend the funeral; his brother, he knew, was unimpressed with throngs of people—a rabble celebrating the assassination of a devoted servant of the state. The crowd thickened so much that the carriages simply stopped.

Sardar Mirza got out and walked along with the crowd toward the gravesite. He fell in step with Jahangir Khan—at thirty years old, perhaps the most famous editor in Persiranian history. He was slight but manly, with a handsome face and a ready smile. Clean-shaven except for a thick, groomed mustache, he wore Western suits, shirts, and ties. His satirical paper, *Trumpet of Esrafil,* was the first to abandon the florid formal style for the vernacular. (Esrafil, God's favorite angel, will announce the Day of Judgment by sounding his trumpet.)

His journal's cutting articles shredded the opponents of the constitution, and even on occasion insulted the Shah. Nevertheless, Sardar Mirza considered Jahangir Khan his closest friend, and an ally in helping to frame the constitution. Both men had an eccentric and unpredictable brand of humor. After working long nights on the supplementary laws, they would play tricks on their colleagues, or recount humorous stories until people exhausted themselves laughing.

"I looked for you in the heavens, and now I find you still here on Earth," was Jahangir Khan's greeting. "Has His Highness perhaps lost his teeth? Or perhaps it is just that smiling on this occasion would be misplaced; but surely it is not as gloomy as that. I know you have some doubts about attending. At least you will hear Malek Mutakallimin compete with you in the oration?"

Jahangir Khan referred to an ally of his, a heretical preacher.

"Your friendship with these Azali Babis will get you in trouble!" Sardar Mirza rallied. "You are accused of converting: is it true?"

"It isn't wrong to admire Malek Mutakallimin. We are not so different, he and I. He preaches in simple language so that people can see clearly the liberal side of Islam. I write in the vernacular to make people understand democracy."

"Flirting with the Babis is dangerous," Sardar Mirza counseled. "You will be looked on as an apostate. Even the liberal clergy will not support you. And we don't want to have you weakened." The Babis and Azalis, a relatively recent Muslim sect, infamously denied that Mohammad was the last Prophet.

As he got closer to the gravesite, the smell of flowers became ever more cloying. The guilds had set up tents and were giving out refreshments. Schoolchildren had the day off, and were either singing patriotic songs or just running around. Trays of sweetmeats were stacked high, to be distributed after the ceremonies. A group of men beat their chests, likening the death of the assassin to that of Imam Hossein. A large portrait of the martyr had been set on a wooden easel: the clean-cut youth, with a modern, shaved face and thin mustache, looked unseemingly sophisticated.

The crowd felt suffocating. Shouts now filled the air: "Clear the way for His Highness Jalalu-Dawlah." So: the Shah's powerful cousin—a leading reactionary—was gracing the funeral of the assassin of the Shah's handpicked Premier? Did *everyone* want to take credit for the killing of the Great Atabak, a man who, with all his warts, embodied the art of compromise and diplomacy? The world had turned upside-down.

Four strong men pushed them aside, bearing a large flower arrangement. The Prince, Jalalu-Dawlah, followed proudly, wearing a near-smirk. Recognizing Sardar Mirza, he looked the other way. The smirk left his lips.

Now someone began to recite a flowery poem in praise of the young martyr:

> O Abbas, o courage incarnate, who guided by honor,
> Saw thy country sore wounded, and laid healing
> ointments upon her.

Sardar Mirza could not bear to stay any longer, let alone offer a tribute to the memory of an assassin—no matter what the politics required. He whispered an apology to his companion and hurried away.

♫

"Are you awake, my bed of feathers?" Professor Dal misunderstood my reverie. I could see the revolution keeling leftward; I wanted to tell them all somehow to work it out. Maybe, if they showed reasonableness, maybe I could awake from this nightmare, safe in my tearoom.

"I am awake, Arbab. How did it end?"

He laughed. "Are you not paying attention? I recounted that part last night. It ends like it will end for you and me: we all die."

"I meant with the revolution."

And the Professor continued his story.

♫

Life sometimes imposes a rare, abrupt turn that can redefine our path. Sardar Mirza's course correction began with that funeral. His political life lasted just nine months, ending with a shattering cannonade.

Those nine months were packed with activity. The Shah paid a historic state visit to the Majlis and, for the fourth time, swore to be faithful to the constitution. Sheikh Nouri was less accommodating: he set up tents in the public square in front of the Majlis, under the protection of the Russians, and denounced the "takeover" of the government by the Babi and Azali infidels. This sparked a crisis. The Shah ordered a cannon attack on the Majlis—but his Premier, the leader of the (pro-constitutionalist) cabinet, refused the order. That recalcitrant aristocrat was swiftly imprisoned; the chains around his neck would lower his head in a permanent bow. A British attaché rushed in to rescue the chained Premier from certain execution; he had been an Oxford classmate of Foreign Minister Sir Edward Gray. The Premier left for London the next day.

Meanwhile, four thousand men from all the different guilds and societies had armed themselves and taken up positions on every roof in the district, overlooking both the Majlis and the nearby Sepahsalar Mosque. The radicalized Northern provinces sent violent telegrams threatening the forcible removal of Mohammad Ali Shah. Even the more radical representatives became alarmed at seeing the entire populace swing toward anarchy. And at this point, the Shah capitulated on all demands.

But this was merely a play within a play.

The Shah hosted a meeting with six of the most important nobles and notables of the realm. None were radicals; all had worked within the framework of the constitution. He received them with unusual kindness. They spoke of their fears for Persiran's independence and warned that Russia was planning a land grab in the North. They begged the Shah to free himself from the Russian Shapshal—even accusing Shapshal of trying to pawn the queen's jewels. (This was true, but they might have reflected that Shapshal acted only under the Shah's orders.)

The Shah agreed to consider their suggestions. He then got up abruptly, dismissed his six guests, and retired to the women's quarters. The notables, beginning to descend the stairs down to the elaborate palace gardens, suddenly heard a bugle sound. In an onrush, the Shah's private guard surrounded and arrested the more outspoken of the group.

The Shah's betrayal of the nobles disgraced him forever in the Prince's eyes. He now swore to help depose his nephew, by whatever means; and, indeed, his power and knowledge could significantly help the opposition.

The larger drama played out in front of the parliament building, where a thousand Cossacks stood and waited. An hour after sunrise, a carriage rolled into the square carrying Colonel Liakhov with six other Russian officers. The Shah had appointed him Governor General of Tehran. "A *Russian* Governor General? Impossible!" The Shah's loyalties would that day become clear.

Sardar Mirza watched the unfolding events from a window in the Majlis, in dread mixed with fascination. As a member of parliament, he knew that his name was on the Shah's expulsion list. And now, along with a dozen other distinguished representatives, he was trapped inside the building. It must be another of the Shah's bluffs.

The morning sun, ready for first prayer, had just cleared the buildings to the east, capturing the brass metalwork of the carriage and turning windows on the west of the square to pure copper. The dome of the Sepahsalar Mosque shone like a planet, half lit and half obscured. The Shah's troops, under the command of Liakhov, ranged in a three-quarter circle a few layers deep; the troops extended into each of the narrow streets, blocking all routes into the square. Parliamentarians were permitted to pass through the ranks of Cossacks to join their colleagues inside the Majlis, but no one was allowed to leave the square. Sheikh Behbehani and Sheikh Tabatabai, the religious liberals (and Sheikh Nouri's enemies), had been ushered through with utmost respect. The president of the assembly and the editor of the Majlis newspaper were the last two people allowed to enter.

Colonel Liakhov, his nose seemingly skyward in a constant snub to the world, stepped out of the carriage ahead of his fellow officers. "It is a miracle he can walk, with his head so high," parliamentarians joked. The colonel walked toward a white, caparisoned horse. The soldier holding the horse's bridle brought his hand toward his ear, fingers splayed—a peasant version of a military salute. Liakhov mounted the horse to ride in front of the troops, ordering soldiers to left and right. Pointing at the six cannons that occupied the center of the square, he indicated six strategic locations around the square. With great effort, groups of soldiers rolled the cannons to their new positions.

Inside the parliament building, a perspiring young nationalist in a Western shirt hurried down from the roof, to offer the representatives a desperate proposal. "I can take him down, I know I can!" he said in Turkish to Sheikh Tabatabai. But no one had the authority—or the daring—to give such an order. To be sure, the Russian government had washed its hands of Liakhov; but even so, to kill a Russian colonel could have swift reper- cussions—especially in light of the Russian ultimatum to the government not to let the English meddle in their zone.

"I can pick off Shapshal instead," the young sniper proposed, as a more practical alternative. The hated Shapshal, with no military rank, was at that moment swaggering in and out of the Cossack formations. "We can call it an accident."

"You are a brave young man," Sheikh Tabatabai replied. "But there will be no shooting today from either side. Trust me."

As if to support that claim, someone announced, "Liakhov is getting back into the carriage; he is leaving the square!"

Sardar Mirza returned to the window. His interest was, as always, aesthetic: the scene looked festive, colorful, like the painting of a Napoleonic victory. He was feeling hopeful—until the first cannonball hit the windowframe, splintering the wood and shattering the glass into thousands of thin shards.

At the sound of the blast, they all bent over as if by instinct. Crouching, Jahangir Khan saw his friend, Sardar Mirza, turn his face slowly toward him, inhabiting his own surprised universe.

He looked like a hedgehog: his face and torso were covered with small splinters. Nothing above his waist was spared: eyelids, nose, ears, face, neck, chest. His friends laid him down under the table beneath the window, for protection from the continuing barrage of cannon fire. Splinters embedded in his stiff shirt stood at attention and bowed with every breath. Other slivers created dozens of white marks on his skin, with a rivulet of blood, tiny at first, seeping out of each wound. His face became a sheet of blood. He would later swear that the last clear image his eyes registered was that of the cannonball itself. This was unlikely, but he could never be dissuaded.

The Shah's betrayal was complete. Only the previous evening, he had sent reassuring messages authorizing a mixed committee of nationalists and royalists. Three of his cabinet ministers had immediately met with the President of the Assembly; dispersing at midnight, they had agreed to complete their work in the morning. Sometime after midnight, the Premier sent a message to the President of the Assembly announcing that the Shah had agreed to all their demands—a complete about-face from his earlier position, when he demanded powers equal to those of the Kaiser. It seemed to be a replay of six months before, when the Shah blinked first.

During the past three weeks, ever since the arrest of the notables in the imperial gardens, the Prince had kept his brother informed of the palace's decisions. In every letter, he warned Sardar Mirza about the Shah's real intentions. "Here is a rule of thumb. Always believe his outrageous demands; never believe his conciliatory statements."

Lying helpless under a table, Sardar Mirza listened to eight hours of bombardment and fusillade, while Jahangir Khan and two Azali preachers painstakingly extracted each splinter from his body. To avoid vibrations, they waited for a lull in the bombardment before pressing the sharp end of a steel pen nib (cleaned of ink) at the root of each splinter, while pulling it out with a pair of small tongs—making sure that no remnant remained in the wound. They waited until the last for the most painful and danger-filled task: extracting the splinters from Sardar Mirza's eyelids. The sharp splinters had gone through the eyelids and damaged the cornea beyond repair. The art enthusiast would be virtually blind for the rest of his life.

He continued to lie under the table, groggy from pain and with his eyes wrapped in a piece of sooty cloth, hearing the cannonade and the panicked voices of people running in and out. From the roofs above them came the sound of vigorous resistance. Early in the day, an excited voice announced that fifty of the Russian foot soldiers had dropped their guns and joined the defenders. Sardar Mirza wondered why they had dropped their guns. The same man soon returned to tell of some Persiranian Cossacks who had tried to ride away from the fight; after a Russian officer shot three of them, the rest had fallen back in line.

His lips felt like balloons, his face huge; it was covered in blood and dust like a dish of rice with elderberries. He brought his arm up to touch the wounds, but the gentle hand of the Azali preacher, Malek Mutakallimin, placed it back down. The dust in his mouth and throat made him unbearably thirsty. Half asleep, he was roused three times by rousing cheers. Each time, someone explained that another of the cannons had stopped working. By the afternoon, only the cannons to the right were still delivering their barrage.

"Nothing is left of the Sepahsalar Mosque," someone said. "All is lost."

"All is lost, Your Highness," Malek Mutakallimin repeated in Sardar Mirza's ear. "This level of resolve by the Shah bodes badly for us. You might want to make your peace with the Almighty." The men in the room could see that the end was closing in. The resisting force had been killed or captured. Amid sporadic gunfire, they waited for the final, ferocious Cossack attack. In the group were the two renowned Sheikhs as well as two popular Azali preachers, joined by two cheeky newspaper editors, two committed representatives, two Majlis presidents, and a high court judge. All had been listed as enemies of the Shah.

Then, someone discovered that the cannonade had created a large hole in the back wall. Jahangir Khan crouched next to Sardar Mirza beneath the table. "Your Highness, we need to move you. Do you think you can move?"

Jahangir Khan and Malek Mutakallimin helped Sardar Mirza to stand, bringing back to life dozens of little rivulets of blood. His chest burned where the largest splinter had lodged. His legs worked well enough; he needed only a hand from Jahangir Khan— more comfortable than being held up under the armpits. Emerging from their doomed shelter, they walked out behind the parliament building into a park they knew well. Dazed and covered in dust, after surviving eight hours of shelling, could they now simply walk out into this peaceful park?

The smells of trees and climbing honeysuckle filled the air. They walked through the gate, and an elderly servant, bent in a permanent bow, opened the door to the residence. Lifting his head with difficulty, he was clearly shocked at their appearance and tried to shut the door again, thinking these were beggars looking for their evening meal. They persuaded him to call for his master.

The owner of this refuge was none other than the Shah's brother-in-law, Mohsen Khan. He had heard the day's cannonade; the last thing he wanted was to get involved with the enemies of the Shah—but these were no ordinary refugees. Sheikh Behbehani now asked for asylum in traditional formal language, a formality respected by authorities that would allow even the Shah's brother-in-law to declare his house a refuge. On the point of assenting, their host recognized the two Azali preachers and Jahangir Khan, and he refused entry to the three of them, as apostates. The two Sheikhs concurred with that decision. Sardar Mirza, cocking his head to hear better, pleaded with the Sheikhs to remember how, just a few hours ago, they all had acted as comrades in arms. How could they leave any of these representatives of the people to the whims of a man with blood on his hands? They must know that the Shah would mete out the harshest of sentences, especially to his greatest nemesis, Malek Mutakallimin. In the end, no amount of arguing could convince Mohsen Khan to open up his house to the three friends.

Sardar Mirza had no choice but to refuse the hospitality of the house. He accompanied his three friends outside, against their loud protestations. They were joined by two senior statesmen, Hakim Molk and

Momtaz Dowleh, as well as Haji Ibrahim Aqa, the representative from Tabriz; they refused to enter the house on principle. All the others went inside quietly, their deep shame evident in their faces.

"Will you refuse us water?" the apostate preacher asked.

"I would refuse you life," Mohsen Khan said with venom, "but I am no Yazid." This was a reference to the hated caliph who refused Imam Hossein water before slaughtering him. The master of the house shouted for water to be brought out to the front; he then shut the door on the seven of them.

They collapsed on the ground near a large tree in the graying dusk, some of them barely able to hold up their heads as they discussed their options. Aware that the British had played a divisive role in the last few weeks, they decided to approach either the Ottoman or the French Legation, in groups of two or three. The sudden appearance of the Shah's soldiers on the scene rendered this discussion moot. Sardar Mirza wandered away from the group in blind confusion until one pitiless soldier grabbed him by the collar, knocking him to the ground and pulling him toward the street like a bag of onions. Sardar kicked helplessly, trying to stand up, and pulled at his shirt to avoid strangulation. The soldiers now tied five of them together with a long chain that had enough neck and hand clamps to hold dozens of people. In a near faint, Sardar Mirza had the strength to reflect on life's ironies: just a few hours before, the man who dragged him with such contempt would have fallen on the ground and kissed his feet. He heard the crack of a rifle butt; a man groaned, "They have killed me." They had indeed killed the brave Haji Ibrahim Aqa, deputy from Tabriz.

The two senior statesmen, Hakim Molk and Momtaz Dowleh, had managed somehow to hide among the trees in the park. The head gardener was a friend of Hakim

Molk's manservant; without hesitation despite the danger, the gardener brought the two men to his own room in a corner of the park—acting with more honor than his master. At midnight they moved to the house of Hakim Molk's manservant, and the next day they asked for sanctuary at the French Embassy.

Sardar Mirza and the three remaining men were stuffed into a cage made of broad, rusted pig-iron bars, balanced on top of a rickety wagon. A soldier kicked at the cage door four or five times to get it shut. They were then transported to the imperial gardens, past small crowds watching the procession. "We are to be made an example of," Malek Mutakallimin predicted. "The Shah no longer feels the need to keep up appearances."

Saleh Mirza arrived at the imperial gardens after dusk. Azudul Molk, the head of the Qajar family, was able to inform him that his brother still lived. Mohsen Khan, the Shah's brother-in-law, had reported that five "Azalis" had asked for asylum, including the Prince's brother (now tarred as an apostate). The brother-in-law and loyal subject of the Shah could not in all conscience grant the filthy, apostate sons of dogs a morsel of food, let alone his house. A second call informed them that the prisoners had been caught trying to escape. Chained by the brave soldiers of the Shah, the prisoners would arrive at the palace in an hour or two.

The Prince began his first round of begging, addressing the head of the Qajar family. "I cannot predict the Shah's intentions yet," was the answer. "I will do what I can, but I have to warn you, he is not in a forgiving mood."

The vile cart carrying the prisoners at last creaked into the garden of the Shah. Nothing could have prepared the Prince for the state of these men, as they stepped onto solid ground—covered in dust, haggard, in chains. And what was wrong with his brother's face, below the handkerchief that covered his eyes? And why did he turn his head back and forth, not watching where he stepped? No force could have stopped the Prince from running to embrace his brother, in full view of all the courtiers and guards—except for the steely grip Azudul Molk held on his wrist.

"Do not make a fool of yourself, son, or we will lose your brother as surely as the sun will rise in the morning. The Shah has signed the death warrant of four of the prisoners." The Prince lost color at those words. "Consider them dead: the two Azalis, Jahangir Khan, and Malik Mutakallimin. There are others on the execution list as well, including a cousin of His Majesty. *And your brother;* we will need to plead for him separately."

The prisoners were taken behind the stables, to join more than two dozen other men from all walks of life, chained together like themselves.

All that night, the Prince sought an audience to beg for his brother's life; but the Shah had retired to his private quarters, to his harem. The Prince pleaded with anyone he could find, to persuade the Shah to spare his brother's life. Many courtiers listened with sympathetic faces, but few could offer any hope. Around midnight, the Prince bribed the guard to let him visit his brother at the back of the stables. Walking into the pitch-black stable, he heard the clomping of the horses' hooves and their soft snorting. He walked to the back of the stables. The prisoners sat leaning against the wall of mud and straw, under a bright moon.

Sardar Mirza sat, awake, at the end of the chain link: the pulsing sting of hundreds of wounds prevented sleep. The Prince sat gingerly next to him and softly called his name.

"Is that you, brother?" They hugged and kissed each other as in childhood, oblivious to the chained men watching them—who, indeed, despite their own misery, shed some tears at the two brothers' devotion. Talking late into the night, the Prince gave Sardar Mirza more hope than he could muster himself. He left before sunrise, to begin his rounds of diplomacy before the first prayer.

The next morning, the guards came to take Sardar Mirza, Jahangir Khan, and Malik Mutakallimin out of the chains. Two guards attended each prisoner, placing two rough ropes, with rudimentary hanging knots, around each neck. Their feet still wet from prayer, the guards dragged the prisoners into a circle of dirt, surrounded by trees; the ropes scraped their necks red. On one side, the Shah, gimlet-eyed, sat on a straight-backed chair, fists on knees. Behind him stood Shapshal, along with Azudul Molk, a courtier named Amir Bahadur Jang, and a few spectators. There was no ceremony. There were no speeches about their guilt or ill deeds, nor any account of the process of judgment by which the Shah had passed their death sentences. The Shah, confident in his ultimate power to grant or take life, sat silently as the three prisoners faced him.

Behind him stood a bull of a man whose hairy shoulders stuck out like mounds on either side of his neck. His short, black beard, dense as a carpet, reached almost to his eyes, which were lusterless and black. He wore a leather apron.

"Do a merciful job," said the Shah.

The thick-set man, a former butcher of sheep and cattle, approached Jahangir Khan. He had a slow gait; his hips sashayed and his hands hung apart from his body, like those of a gunfighter. He faced Jahangir Khan squarely. By his side, in his right hand, he held a small, slender dagger pointing, strangely, up toward his own wrist.

"Make peace with your maker, you miserable traitor," he shouted, looking around at the audience as if in a show. At the sound of his voice, birds flew out of the trees; silence followed.

"Long live the constitutional government!" Jahangir Khan pointed to the ground as he uttered these words: "O, Land, we are killed for the sake of your preservation." The last two words were muffled: the two guards next to him had begun pulling the two ropes in opposite directions. As they pulled harder, Jahangir Khan's face turned purplish red. Parts of his face domed, like a tin can of spoiled food. His tongue fattened, protruding from his mouth. A small rivulet of blood dribbled from the corner of his mouth down the right side of his chin. A jerk of his head threw a large clot of blood from his mouth onto the leather apron of the executioner nearby. Instead of moving back to avoid the splatter, the executioner stepped in closer. Eye to eye with the dying man, he slipped the thin poniard between two ribs; he rested his left hand on the right shoulder as leverage, gave a forceful thrust, and the poniard dug its slow, viscous journey to the center of Jahangir Khan's heart.

The executioner stepped back as the editor of the most famous paper in the history of our benighted country exhaled a last, impossibly long breath, before folding, lifeless, onto the ground. "Here dies a traitor," the man shouted, pointing with both palms. Malek Mutakallimin, standing inches away, was frantically reciting verses of the Koran under his breath. Sardar Mirza, unable to see, understood only that his friend had died horribly.

Now the executioner looked sideways at the preacher. Thinning his eyes, he brought his finger next to his own temple like the horn of a bull, then pointed the finger at the preacher to designate the next victim. "Prepare to die, you apostate vermin," he shouted in his theatrical style.

"I am at peace," Malik Mutakallimin said. The guards immediately began to pull the ropes, flattening his dusty, bushy beard around his neck. He soon suffered the same fate as his friend. Turning from the two bodies lying in a heap, the executioner moved toward Sardar Mirza, who was rotating his head this way and that, trying to discern by sound what had happened to his friends. His air of innocence broke the hearts of the assembled grandees.

Sardar Mirza heard a sudden cry of anguish from his brother. The Prince appeared from nowhere and threw himself in the dust in front of the Shah's chair.

"Your Majesty, take my life; spare his," the Prince sobbed. The company gasped at this humiliating prostration: all the gravitas, confidence, and solemnity of a genuine prince of the realm had disappeared. Before them, in the dust, lay a desperate man.

"Your Majesty, his death is my death. Kill me now— or, if he dies, kill me later."

The Prince looked up from the Shah's feet with wild eyes. Azudul Molk and Amir Bahadur Jang simultaneously bent down to whisper counsels of moderation into each ear of the Shah. They urged a stay of execution. Azudul Molk advised against spilling the blood of a relative, a young uncle. Amir Bahadur Jang exhorted that the young man had suffered enough. Besides, this young man was a lightweight; why lose, in the process, the Prince, a young man of promise? For no one could doubt that they would surely lose the Prince.

The Shah's jaw was clamped so tightly that the muscles of his neck protruded. Grudgingly he stayed the execution, with a discreet motion for the executioner of unclenching his fist a few times. It was all the same to the former butcher, who departed with the same nonchalant gait. The two dusty bodies lay crumpled like heaps of clothing. Their bodies were later thrown out like garbage, into the moat outside the gardens.

For the second time in his life, Mohammad Ali Shah had tried to kill his uncle, Sardar Mirza. And once again, like that childhood beating, though his wounds might have taken him, he recovered. Exiled by order of the Shah, he left without regrets, never to return. This time he did not forget or forgive: to forget would have been an insult to his fallen friends.

Professor Dal ended the chapter. "Say goodbye to Sardar Mirza, my boy, for you already know his end: it will come in a comfortable bed, surrounded by his loved ones in Paris." He exhaled. "Now we must both sleep. I am dead tired. I need you to help me over to my side. I don't seem to have command of my limbs."

I lifted this collection of connected bones that weighed next to nothing, and by the time I crossed the room he had fallen into a deep sleep.

The Eighth Night
1000

The Narrator Remembers the Night of the Cornflakeses

"Some facts should be suppressed, or, at least, a just sense of proportion should be observed in treating them."
— Sir Arthur Conan Doyle, *The Sign of the Four*

Dear Ms. Vakil,

I again take note of your semi-hysterical concern about any destruction of letters. You say you see the letters between the brothers as the quintessential story of the awakening of the Persiranian women. Yet at the same time, you doubt their authenticity; you are certain that men did not write salaciously about their wives. Ms. Vakil, these brothers did. These more private letters have better claim to authenticity. They are in the Prince's hand. He never would have tasked his secretary-cum-father-in-law with copying letters that referenced Choti, his wife. In our times, of course, such peccadillos are amplified until they blot out all aspects of a grand personality.

I hope the development of Mr. Hekaiatchi's character meets with your approval. I listen to his recordings again and again, with a fascination bordering on obsession. I am astonished at his feats of memory. I dare say, had he possessed a more commanding voice, he might have satisfied his father's stringent storytelling standards. An innocent, he sits in that uncomfortable social position where a wrong marriage will push him down to the lowest rungs of society. You can hear him express these qualms clearly, as he contemplates meeting with you and reflects on his living quarters at Mammad-Ali's shop. But who am I to speak? No need to marry low to descend one's own ladder.

Here in the heart of puritanical Massachusetts, I lead a strictly moral life: moderate drink, a judicious number of acquaintances, mild exercise, and limited use of pornography. If I were to admit to any excess, it would be my love of film.

Middle age has brought with it a number of mild ailments, requiring me to follow a high-fiber, low-calorie diet. I walk over to my apartment window holding my bowl of granola, adorned with banana slices and pink yogurt. I eat the tasteless granola, using the yogurt to dampen the crunching sound I hate. In my inner eye I see myself as a thin, well-maintained, fifty-something man, with hair more white than black. I am grateful to have hair. Barefoot, bathed in early northern light, looking far out beyond the traffic on I-93, I believe I look like someone in a cereal commercial.

I report small details of my life this late in our correspondence to assure you of my normalcy. A hard-to-relinquish habit practiced by us Persiranians in the U.S.: to pander, as an acclimatizing exercise. I have educated myself in the finer points of American football, for which I care not a hoot. This tells my interlocutor: "I am not *that* kind of Persiranian, but *your* kind of Persiranian." What makes us so compliant? Why do we seek the good opinion of Western man? I want to say it is because I have good reason to be ashamed of the current behavior of our government. I am. But the case is far worse: for the past hundred years, we practiced a shameful, fawning foreign policy, all the way up to the last days of the last Shah of Persiran, who consulted with the British and U.S. ambassadors about each of his bowel movements.

Ms. Vakil, as I get closer to current history, the history I witnessed as a child, my narrative begins to resemble a gossip column. The excessive name-dropping—my mother called it social chin-ups—can be forgiven in my case, for I am no longer in that social setting; and no one, except perhaps historians, cares about these pusillanimous people long gone.

I realize that I have bullied you into reading about my own clan by interspersing the more strategic material that interests you. I promised to tie neatly my own final days in prison into events that occurred seventy years before. I am about to offer you some interesting details regarding the rise and fall of my father, Nima, during the self-deluding years of the last Shah of Persiran.

The year 1953 represents a political black hole. As if we'd hit an event horizon, we emerged from that year amnesiacs: the slate was wiped blank of political expectations and understanding. It was the year of the CIA-aided coup. Afterward, we developed a Stepford society, loyal to our newly-wedded American partner.

The Americans themselves lost their virginity that year, by engineering the return of the young Mohammed Reza Shah from Italy, at the expense of Premier Mossadegh, a fiery, aristocratic, brave, and popular statesman (and, incidentally, a cousin of my grandfathers). The Americans acted on their own, without even consulting the British, whose oil problem they had stepped in to resolve. CIA chief Allen Dulles approved the expenditure of one million dollars to bring down the Premier.

Prior to the coup, Mossadegh had on a number of occasions asked for my father's support, cousin to cousin. Nima refused every time: loyalty to royalty. "How could I support you against a man I grew up with, who is my sovereign?"

Mossadegh invoked the memory of the Prince and especially of Sardar Mirza, who had defied his own aristocratic heritage. "Times have changed, my son," he argued. "Your loyalty is misplaced. His father, Reza Shah, killed your father. You of all people, so beloved by the villagers, must be able to see the people's misery. If we don't do something for them, the Tudeh communists will."

Nima remained a steadfast royalist. He instructed my mother Lili, in Paris, to send the Shah money, in his Italian exile; the son, he felt, need not pay for the father's sins—even for his suspected role in the Prince's death. After the coup that brought down Mossadegh, my father welcomed back the Shah and his beautiful wife Soraya, greeting them as they descended from the plane. His cousin never forgave him.

The coup was a terrible precedent in American foreign policy, because it worked so well. Kermit Roosevelt acted as puppet master, handing out cash to the mob, masterminding a crude but lucky operation to restore an autocratic monarchy. Its success built false confidence at the CIA. Years of bizarre operations followed around the world, creating disastrous "blowback" (a word introduced in the Persiranian context), but the many failures counted less than this single success. Here, Ms. Vakil, we can observe the soft underbelly of democracy, its structural amnesia. Every four years, all is forgiven and forgotten: a kind of mass confessional. It works well for those inside. But what of us, the non-voting victims of a capricious foreign policy, who live with its consequences?

Am I getting plaintive in my old age? I do not wish to expound upon the cluelessness of American foreign policy, Ms. Vakil, but rather to underline the political complacency of the post-Mossadegh period in our country. As for us, our Stepford period was the most pleasant and economically uplifting period of our history. I don't remember discussing any issues remotely connected to civil society. Reading the spirited letters exchanged by my grandfathers, I almost envy their era, in spite of the ever-present sense of violence. Their debates *mattered.* After 1953, political talk was a pointless gargle of gossip, rumors, and innuendoes. These Poonakis were celebrities, not leaders. The aristocracy abandoned its age-old responsibility to balance the monarch. Contrary to the theory that a family fortune degenerates in the third generation, in our case it was the *second* generation that dropped the ball.

For five years after the coup, Nima and Lili were fixtures of the Pahlavi court. They accompanied the Shah and Queen Soraya everywhere on their official travels. My mother and the Queen, both children of European mothers, became fast friends. I remember the silver daguerreotypes displayed on tables and framed photos hung on walls, showing my parents posed with celebrities, politicians, and royals: Audrey Hepburn and Tony Curtis; Nixon, Khrushchev, and Eisenhower; Queen Juliana of the Netherlands, and Gustaf VI Adolf of Sweden. For years, Gary Cooper would insist on having dinner with my mother when he visited Paris. (His religious rants would bring the dinner to an end, with my mother declaring herself "dead of boredom.")

The goodies began to flow from the limitless American spigot, becoming by 1979 a veritable gush. Ms. Vakil, I confess myself an unapologetic materialist. Ask any man who has lost it all: having is better than not having.

After the 1953 coup, my father fell in love with Americans. He replaced his favorite German pen with a sleek Parker 51. The Mercedes was exchanged for a sky blue Oldsmobile; Grundig for Westinghouse; Wagner for Gershwin. With the zeal of a convert, he attended to every detail: he bought a grill for hamburgers (used mainly to fire up the coals for hookahs); the rectangular swimming pool became kidney-shaped (later restored to a rectangle); he built an outdoor bowling lane (open to the elements, it became a carpet of splinters). We chewed bubble gum and read comics. Large-bodied, important Americans frequented the house. Young Americans with shiny braces on their teeth displayed their smooth swim strokes, making us look like paddlers. The wives accompanied them unannounced, irritating my mother.

These chattering American wives had access to heaven. They could walk forth at any time of day, in their bobbed blond hair, pencil-sharp high heels, and polka-dot tank tops, and enter paradise. The local land of plenty was the air-conditioned American Armed Forces Supermarket in Tehran, a place of shiny floors and shinier metal carts, wheeled along aisles lined with shiny stacks of canned food. Even my mother briefly lost her bearings. You could mail-order *anything*. A large wooden counter was attended by a polite young private who wrote down my mother's endless requests for cigarettes, chocolates, scotch, and hula-hoops, which the American taxpayers' money would locate somewhere in the world.

For us, the American Armed Forces Supermarket was also the place where "cornflakes" became the generic name for all cereals. There were, of course, Kellogg's Corn Flakes, but also the crepitating cornflakes now known to me as Rice Krispies. There were the Aleph-ba (Alphabet) cornflakes and the brick cornflakes, better known as shredded wheat. The culmination of our supermarket romance was the Night of the Cornflakeses, which launched my father's short career in government: overnight, he was transformed from an aristocratic friend to the Shah to a sensation embraced by the Americans.

Once a year, my father invited the resident foreign diplomats, ambassadors, consuls, attachés, and young career men to a sumptuous dinner party. The house was scrubbed from top to bottom for the occasion. Huge carpets were brought out of the bank vaults. Extra cooks were borrowed, and the large kitchen in the basement reopened. The servants starched their white uniforms as stiff as a calling card. The food preparation began days in advance—soups with dried fruits like pomegranate and sour cherries; *dolmas* expertly rolled and stuffed with meat; rows of skewered kebabs and meatballs. There were various *polos*: sweet saffron rice fragrant with cinnamon, adorned with apricots and lima bean sauce, or chicken and lamb. For dessert there would be baklava sprinkled with rosewater, grated fresh fruit topped with crushed ice, rice pudding, and baskets of fresh fruit, all served on silver and gold trays.

My mother's absence on one of her long sojourns in Paris meant that my father would plan that year's formal dinner, in late July of 1959. My father decided to add a gastronomic surprise. The guest list, as in the past, included a who's who of Tehran's diplomatic circle: the U.S. ambassador and his wife accepted the invitation; the Soviet ambassador came without his wife, but with his panoply of medals; the virile Turkish attaché wore elegant lemon-colored gloves; the sophisticated Indian consul stepped carefully, to avoid harming any microscopic life beneath his feet; and the Spanish diplomat gleamed in his velour dinner jacket. The guests circled one another, wearing permanent smiles that looked like birth defects.

No less impressive was the guest list from the home front: the ineffective Premier brought his French wife; his cabinet—composed of three future prime ministers, all just as ineffective—revolved around him. The diminutive court minister appeared and quickly disappeared into the crowd. The handsome founder of the newly formed intelligence and security service, SAVAK, mingled with the crowd: twenty years hence, he would be assassinated by his own organization. The minister of finance, a military man through and through, disliked everyone—including my father. An industrialist, said to own eighty-three percent of the nation's heavy industry, walked in with his heavy wife. The prince-merchant of rugs, the only man representing the Bazaar, presented his hosts with Turkoman rugs.

Stiff khaki army uniforms moved among the black ties. The ladies were dressed to the nines, none adorned by any Islamic garment. There were no turbans to be seen: one grows nostalgic for those days.

The evening began with a cocktail party in the garden, with white-gloved servants serving whisky and sodas. Dinner was announced at 9:00. The guests, tipsy with drink on their empty stomachs, made their way to dozens of round tables laid out in the salon and the connecting dining room. At my father's table sat the most respected guests: the American and Soviet ambassadors, the Premier, the court minister, and their wives.

Before dinner was served, my father, full of spirit and energy, made a short speech in praise of the American ambassador. Each fulsome adjective made the eyelids of the Soviet ambassador flutter like the wings of a mosquito. Father closed the speech graciously: "And finally, ladies and gentlemen," he said, "in honor of this great American, we will begin our dinner with a typical American dish."

A polite round of applause. The lights dimmed. The chirping of crickets could be heard outside. A few seconds ticked by in anticipation, and then the doors of the dining room were flung open for a line of waiters holding aloft large silver bowls. They moved as efficiently as a precision dance troupe to begin serving the guests: bowl after bowl made the rounds, filled with various brands of cereal—an array of cornflakeses. Soon, Honey Smacks, Sugar Puffs, Life, and Special K made tidy mounds on the large plates designed for rice and kebabs. The ladies looked left and right, their mouths turned down, at the approach of these delicacies: Cocoa Puffs—those bland orbs of corn, oats, and rice, flavored dimly with cocoa; Trix—orangey orange, lemony yellow, and raspberry red, looking like a dessert; dry Weetabix to sponge the saliva. The guests were speechless.

At this prodigious offering of cereal, the American ambassador half rose from his chair only to fall back again, silent. The guests fell into two groups. Those who were familiar with cornflakes protocol valiantly ate the dry servings sans milk, not wanting to offend my father. Those unfamiliar with the food, dismayed at the insipid taste, ate them in silent curiosity so as not to offend the American ambassador. A fat Italian man-boy with fuzzy sideburns exchanged a look of conspiratorial delight with the velvety Spanish attaché; this event would nicely augment their repertoire of foreign horror stories, to be retailed in more civilized surroundings. The English consul and his wife were perfect sports. The vegetarian Indian, oblivious, munched happily. That night, bottles of expensive wine washed down unusual quantities of dry Rice Krispies and Shredded Wheat.

While the dining room crunched and crackled, the American ambassador undertook diplomatic efforts to inform my father of cereal etiquette and to extricate him from the embarrassing situation. "You know, sir, in our country, children also indulge in a bowl of cornflakes for breakfast," he said. "Sometimes they mix it with sugar and milk." (The "also" and the "sometimes" represented the diplomatic effort.)

The Soviet ambassador, also ignorant of cereal protocol, misunderstood this delicate explanation as mere exaggerated national pride. "Yes," he thought, "and we serve caviar to our donkeys!"

"An expensive breakfast," my father thought, in agreement for once with the Soviet ambassador. He had just paid an arm and a leg for the imported stuff at the American Armed Forces Supermarket.

"With what utensils do you eat these cereals?" the court minister asked. "It seems to me that a fork is out of question, and it is too slippery for a spoon. Are fingers permitted? You know, Her Majesty, the Queen of England, uses her fingers to eat chicken."

The Soviet ambassador remained silent, seething.

"Do you eat this in the Soviet Union?" the Premier asked, examining the flakes dispassionately like a scientist.

"No, Your Excellency," bluffed the Soviet ambassador. "We experimented with the form a few years back, but our people were not impressed with its nutritional content."

"Not impressed?" the American asked. "For Christ's sake, we are talking about *cereal*. What's the big deal?"

"Precisely. No big deal," the Soviet replied.

The American rose to the challenge. "We would not expect to impress the Soviet people with only taste," he said. "Please observe around the room the variety of the offering, Your Excellency. To us Americans, *diversity*, the right to choose, is the spice of life."

"Spice? You call the taste of these cereals the spice of life?" A number of people, at this point, were prepared to agree with the Soviet. "It's an illusion of choice that you Americans suffer from. As far as I can see there is no difference between *this* and *this*." He pointed to the silver bowl of Raisin Bran, being whisked away, and a bowl of Uncle Sam cereal that appeared at his elbow.

The Soviet continued. "It is certainly not like the difference between a *pechenochnyi tort* and a *pirozhok*, with onion, mushroom, meat, and rice stuffing—or, better still, the difference between a chicken Kiev and a blini with caviar and cream. Don't you think?" The clever Soviet by now had the guests on the verge of tears, at the thought of the Russian delicacies. Then, to reinforce his credentials as an ardent communist, he announced, "All our cuisine, I might add, emanates from peasant food."

"Caviar comes from peasant food?" inquired my father, underlining the diplomatic *faux pas* that had escaped the others at the table. "Maybe your red caviar is served on your peasants' tables, sir. On our side of the Caspian, we produce the finest caviar, fit for royalty the world over."

"I did not mean to insult Persiranian caviar," apologized the Russian. "We all know the quality of the sturgeon growing on your sweeter side of the Caspian."

The American ambassador, now on his hind legs, began his offensive. "Our cereals were not made to titillate the taste buds, Your Excellency, but to improve the health of our people. The point for us is that free citizens manufacture a variety of cereals, without needing a decision by any governmental bureaucracy. Yessir!" He spoke in one breath, as if a french fry were burning his mouth. "Our trust in our system of enterprise and in our people allows private business to bid for all our military contracts. *We trust our fellow countrymen.*"

The Russian began his next windup. "You are a good lawyer, Your Excellency," he said. (Indeed, the American had a degree from Columbia Law.) "Me, I am only the fat peasant son of an even fatter peasant." He alone laughed at this witticism. "But, Your Excellency, as we Russians say: 'We don't swat flies with our noses.' You would agree, I think, that we have surpassed you with our rocket technology, all of it directed by our Central Committee."

My father's passion for technology had little to do with armaments, and now he took the opportunity to expound cheerfully on all the wonderful American devices he had gathered in his house, even offering to show the Soviet ambassador one of the earliest televisions to be seen in our country.

Nima's encomium to consumer goods gave the American ambassador a perfect opening. "You must not be afraid of new ideas," he lectured—grinding the Russian's rockets as if stepping on a handful of Rice Krispies.

"We are afraid of nothing," replied the Soviet.

An evening that had begun in culinary disaster ended with the American ambassador's undying gratitude for my father's—quite oblivious—debating assistance. Within a few weeks, the American ambassador's detailed report to Washington precipitated Nima's rise in the government; thanks to the Freedom of Information Act, I have that report in front of me. The Russian's report to the Kremlin lay dormant for eight years, when it caused his downfall.

The famous Nixon-Khrushchev Kitchen Debate occurred in Moscow just a few days later, on July 24, 1959, and it matched the debate at my father's dinner, metaphor for metaphor. Few might have noticed the significant precedent of the night of the cornflakeses, but the American ambassador did. His report, written following the Kitchen Debate, stakes his ground like an inventor with a priority patent claim.

꼬

A few weeks later, at the imperial court, the Shah sat playing Belote with three close friends: Professor Dal, my father, and a Mr. Hajebi. Mr. Hajebi, an elegant man of little talent, was famous for one affectation. Claiming to have a quad in poker, he would throw down just three kings: "You, Sire, are my missing king of spades."

Professor Dal and Hajebi played with cigarettes dangling from their mouths, an eye shut against the curling smoke; the Shah smoked using an onyx holder. My father held his cigarette between his curled index and middle fingers, a Bogart affectation.

"The American ambassador tells us that you are a brilliant man," the Shah said to my father. "We know you from our youth. We remember guts—but not brilliance. Cut."

Professor Dal cut the deck. The Shah picked up the cards and began dealing in quick impatient flicks: three cards to each player, then an additional two.

"I wouldn't take notice of the ambassador's comments, Your Majesty."

"The ambassador advises us to give you a position in the government." The Shah placed the remaining cards in the middle of the table, face down. He flipped over the top card, the ten of hearts.

"I would not take his advice, Your Majesty, or we'll be short a hand," said Professor Dal, with either a wry smile or a grimace from the smoke curling toward his right eye.

"*Atout*," my Father announced.

"Do you want to have a position?"

"I am getting bored, Your Majesty," my father replied. In those days, they were simply friends; there was little of the ceremonial pomp that reigned in the late sixties.

"Why didn't you tell me? We could have arranged something earlier."

"Pass," Hajebi said.

"Pass," Professor Dal said.

"Still, we can kill two birds with one stone. We satisfy the ambassador, and we get to do a favor for our friend. Not a bad deal." The Shah examined his hand. "*Sans Atout.* But what should we give you? You are not exactly the academic type."

"Your Majesty doesn't have to give me anything."

"We think we do," the Shah said. He picked up the ten of hearts and held it midair, ostentatiously pondering. Then, as if an idea had just struck him, he slipped it among his own bouquet of cards. "We have the ideal position for you."

The men looked up from the table. Smoke whorled from four cigarettes; the noise of the party in the large hall intruded into their alcove. "You can have the *sports portfolio*," the Shah pronounced. He deftly spread his cards, face down, on the green felt, and picked up the remaining cards. He began to flick, almost joyously, three more to each of his loving subjects, dealing himself two.

My father looked up, also pleased, for he loved sports of any type. He saw Professor Dal's head dip, ever so slightly, in warning. Unsure what to do, he plunged forward, as with any challenge. "Your Majesty does me great honor." The other two saluted my father with their tumblers, smiling.

"We are not sure that we are doing you an honor," the Shah answered. "This decision is wrought with politics, you know. You will be the first non-military man to head the Federation of Sports. That is why your relative, there, was trying to warn you with his headshake."

They all laughed. Five years after the American coup, a certain purity of spirit still existed among them. "As long as you don't pull a Thomas Becket on us, we can keep playing cards." The Shah, unknowing, foretold Nima's fall from grace. He smiled warmly, as a father might. The Shah did not, however, mix business and pleasure. He saw the world in three groups: people who worked for him and had to obey him blindly; friends; and everyone else. My father now straddled the first two categories, a no-man's-land.

Ms. Vakil, I know you will recall our national folk hero—a wrestler, who was, without exaggeration, the most popular Persiranian figure of the twentieth century. Even my brother and I, who disagreed about all topics, would rehash every detail of his matches.

Every man, woman, and child in the country loved him—except one person with great power.

The Shah could not abide the Wrestler's popularity. He constantly asked friends to compare the two of them. I remember one night, after a few drinks, Professor Dal recited to us from The Brothers Grimm's "Snow White"—in German, so the servants would not understand:

> Mirror, mirror, on the wall,
> Who is the fairest of them all?

The answer was left unspoken: "Your Majesty is popular, 'tis true, but there is one more popular than you."

Indeed, the Wrestler perfectly fit our ideal vision of our people, as the salt of the earth, with strict chivalric ethics. Growing up in the south of Tehran, the poorest part of the city, he frequented the traditional gymnasiums, where local champions compete in games of strength. Our Wrestler was a round-cornered rectangle, densely filled. He had soft, vulnerable, brown eyes. I can see him sitting on a mat after his match, leaning on an elbow, his broad smile transforming his face like sun coming from behind a cloud. No shopkeeper in his neighborhood ever accepted money from him.

Though the Wrestler won a number of medals, by no means did he dominate his sport. In one interview, he confessed that, early in his career, his back smelled of the mat because of the many times he had been pinned. He won a gold medal at the Olympics and two other golds at world cup events. Early in his career, he said he envied the extra half-meter that the gold medalist stooped in receiving his medal. Second place, he said, is as far from first as a servant is from a minister. Then, when he did win the gold, he wondered why so little had changed for him. "I was the same circus animal going to the mat—only more people salaam me."

A certain vulnerability comes through in his interviews. At the world championship, he wrestled his early Swedish nemesis, Palem, first losing to him and then defeating him. His feelings were hurt when, after each match, Palem withheld the traditional kiss. "I had dried my face," he reflected, puzzled. It did not occur to him that the icy Palem had probably never kissed his mother good-bye.

At thirty-three, preparing to go to Tokyo for his fourth Olympics, the Wrestler had no illusions. He knew that he was no match for the young Russian Medved, who would become the greatest freestyle wrestler ever. Our hero came in only fourth— unmedaled, with deep scars.

Like Mohammed Ali, his political stance also gave him trouble. In the tradition of dedicating his efforts to a higher authority, in Tokyo, he honored Mossadegh and the Persiranian National Front—and not the Shah. In a last-minute change, another Persiranian athlete was substituted to carry the national flag in the Olympic procession. The Wrestler was forced to take a two-year hiatus. My father persuaded the Shah to let him wrestle at the world championships in Ohio, at the advanced age of thirty-five.

The Wrestler's suicide two years later, in Room 23 of the Atlantic Hotel in downtown Tehran, came as a shock to the nation. He had taken poison. A nation of conspiracy theorists dissected the details. The lack of foam in his mouth was proof that the poison had been administered after his death; the SAVAK was accused of injecting air into his veins. My father was horrified when I, as a ten-year-old, asked him whether "they" had killed our Wrestler.

The day after his death, the daily newspaper sold 1.5 million copies instead of the usual 300,000. Pictures of our hero's body ran in every paper and magazine in the nation. Clearly visible on his chest was the long, ugly, zipper-like scar from the speedy autopsy.

Concerned that the public reaction could be explosive, my father—as minister of sports—hastened the burial. Indeed, the Wrestler's friends had to wrestle his body away from a mob to set up an orderly viewing. The line immediately grew a mile long. The following day, with much difficulty, the body was transferred to an ambulance, on a carpet covered with cashmere cloth. The ambulance drove off at top speed, followed by hundreds of mopeds and motorcycles. At four in the afternoon, they arrived at his birthplace and buried him. On the traditional seventh day, a million people attended his grave. My father, afflicted with "diplomatic flu," stayed home: no official could have attended without suffering some consequence—either from the crowd, or from the Shah.

All the evidence pointed to premeditated suicide. He left a brief note holding no one responsible. A one-line diary entry attests to his preoccupation with death, and suggests domestic problems with his wife of two years. "Please God, bless our ending," he writes. "Why did you create me?" Then, three days before his suicide: "Sport is good. Winning is good. Losing is bad. Marriage resembles sport." Two days before his death: "She threw me out of the house screaming at me to get the hell out" —and this note in the margin: "Suicide is so difficult. You have no idea how bad I feel." He asked a notary friend to witness the transfer of his home to his two sisters, and another notary to witness his will. At thirty-seven, given his political stance, he saw no future. "After our due date," he wrote, "we get thrown into the garbage."

The Fat Storyteller Squirts His Way to Happiness

"Premature for whom?"

— Christopher Hitchens

Baba, tell me: are we born with the mold of our favorite woman in our heads, to compare every woman we see to that mold? Or is it a slower process, in which our ideal woman changes as we see, smell, touch, hear, and taste different women? When I was a child, you recounted to me the stories of the one thousand and one nights. You sketched women with such delicacy and detail that, before I even knew the facts of life, I would stiffen with pleasure. You once described a princess whose "waist was a hair's breadth." Of another princess: "her body bent daintily with the weight of her breasts." You could make a boy's head twirl with your insinuations: "He stretched his hand toward the warm shadows of her thigh." Baba, I lived with that sentence for weeks. When you said, "They confused each other with kisses on the mattress," in some way I understood. You must have amused yourself telling such suggestive stories to an eight-year-old.

Baba, I don't know how to tell you what I am about to tell you. I have wanted to confess to a painful situation that has been going on for a while. I did mention Zahra's visit to my room that night. She has continued to tiptoe into my room, slipping into my bed each night as stealthy as a submarine; she claims that lying ensconced against me allowed her to sleep more comfortably. Hours before breakfast, she leaves my bed, so as not to raise any suspicions. They are a traditional family. Unfortunately, her visits disrupted my sleep. Her ample backside fit perfectly below my belly. You are familiar with my accidental spills; they have gotten me into trouble many times. In my visits to the New-City, before the revolution, the whores would kick me out of bed and follow me onto the veranda, shouting abuses at my manhood. In truth I was the ideal customer to them, no trouble, and for the customers in the courtyard below, a good laugh.

I shock you, Baba. Visiting whorehouses in New-City? Uncle Saiid, your brother (God bless his soul), brought me there for the first time, perhaps prematurely, when I turned sixteen. I hope he is with you, keeping you company. He made me laugh so. He never made mention of my weight or joked about it. That day, he told me to accompany him to collect his shirts from the tailor. Why we had to go so far from the Bazaar to get his shirts soon became clear.

The Hosseini brothers made shirts. One brother was deaf and the other dumb; they lived symbiotically. The front of their house was a legitimate tailor shop. The yard at the back had a door that opened discreetly to the New-City. There, Fatmeh, their sister, conducted the more profitable business, as the madam of a full-fledged whorehouse. After a bout of mildly deviant sex, the customer would come away with one of the brothers' abysmally low-quality shirts—camouflage, so to speak. For years, men recognized one another's indiscretions by their colorful Hosseini shirts.

Like the other working houses in the area, the shop had its own small yard, with metal folding chairs for the waiting customers. The first-floor windows were covered with the same material from which the Hosseinis made their shirts: glued-on curtains of blue or red checks, or gauzy light yellow.

We entered the shop through the front. The two Hosseini brothers—droopy-eyed, kind-faced men of about forty—were sitting on a heavy blue metal desk. One munched on a sandwich; the other bit into a raw onion like an apple. He asked, loudly if somewhat garbled, about our pleasure. Uncle Saiid did the talking. The hearing brother (with the sandwich) quickly transmitted Uncle Saiid's message in a kind of sign language. The deaf brother spoke again, directing us to the yard.

Fatmeh, their sister, a retired whore, greeted us with her deep laugh. She was an enormous woman. Her blue negligee and black fishnet underwear showed her breasts, two fireworks that had exploded sadly on the way down. When she laughed—after almost anything a paying client said—she threw her head back, placed her pudgy hands on her belly, and let out a throaty shriek that lasted a single second.

Uncle Saiid smiled at me. "I planned to give you a present for your sixteenth birthday," he said. "I hope you enjoy it."

I was sent upstairs with great fanfare to lose my virginity. All the customers agreed to let me go first. Although well on my way, I had not yet reached the weight I support these days. The room was dark. A young, hefty peasant girl leaned back against the headboard of the bed. Seeing my diminutive you-know-what, she placed a pillow under her hips to make contact easier for me. A frilly peasant skirt hid the prize. I lowered my trousers and hopped toward her. Unsure of the mechanics, I tried to lie over her as gingerly as possible. Telling me to wait, she brought her skirt up to her waist.

Baba, you must know the rest. The sight of her hair down there, curling up to her belly button, was enough for my own fireworks to go off and quickly expire. She looked at me, pleased with the outcome—easy money, no hassle. But just then, in my post-non-coital slump, I fell onto her heavily.

"Get off me, boy. I can't breathe!" Baba, I tried getting off her, but somehow my watchband had become entangled in her earring.

Uncle Saiid, sitting in the courtyard—along with a dozen or so customers, the door boy, and Fatmeh—

heard her scream. I would later hear his account, too many times to count. *"There's* a man to match your girls," he said to Fatmeh, smiling proudly. Fatmeh issued her laugh and gave a quick, worried glance upstairs. She said to a large, mustachioed Turkish street seller, "Get ready, you're next."

Just then, a louder scream erupted, amid a string of shouted insults. Everyone in the courtyard rushed up the stairs—the door boy first, with Uncle Saiid on his heels and everyone else behind. The boy flung the door open. They saw a young, plump peasant girl sitting on the bed and screaming. There was blood on the pillow and a great deal more on one side of her face. With my trousers around my legs, I tried to explain.

At the back of the crowd at the doorway, another scream joined in: Fatmeh, now making up for the years of forced jollity. She hurled her huge body at me, and we both fell on the bed. The peasant girl, seeing the new danger, lifted her scream an octave. By now free of the entangled watch, she flitted out of the way; the crowd expressed its delight at the sight of her breasts. She gave the onlookers a quick smile of appreciation, just before the leg of the bed gave way. Fatmeh and I rolled off to continue the scuffle on the floor, with me jammed underneath the madam, between bed and wall. Uncle Saiid pulled her off me.

Then the Hosseini bothers arrived. The wrinkles and bags under their eyes had somehow pulled themselves up, and their faces held a hard, murderous expression. The deaf one spoke in an incoherent jumble, his words mixed with the stench of the onion. I began explaining, without myself knowing the explanation. Without warning, the dumb brother slapped me hard across the face and nose. Now everyone jumped in to separate everyone else. It took some time—and some hard cash from Uncle Saiid—to restore calm.

In the next few years, I tried a few times to test my ability to delay gratification. But each time I take a glance at the place we all came from, I lose control.

Now Zahra lay, *uninvited,* in my bed, her heart-shaped backside well ensconced under my belly. Half awake and half asleep, I must have rubbed her the wrong way, and the resulting wetness woke her up. I expected her to be outraged. Instead, she cleaned me with heart-wrenching gentleness. But Baba, would you believe that, in my renewed excitement, I had a recurring incident? Zahra smiled: she felt complimented, she said.

The next night, she took matters into her own hands—you know what I mean—and she did the same the next night. On the third night, after I had been satisfied once, she offered me the taboo entrance: with strict integrity, she insisted on the protection of her virginity. Baba, for the first time in my life, I resided in a woman's body without immediate consequences. After our act, the longest and sweetest five minutes of my life, I told her about all my past troubles with women. She smiled. "There's nothing wrong with you down there. You just need a warm-up before parking the car in the garage!" She laughed a delicious laugh, like silver raining down. Baba, with that laugh she captured me for life.

We had a grand old time for some weeks. I began to sleep better than she did.

On a Saturday morning—the first day of the week, with a day's work ahead—we had fallen asleep after a long, frolicsome night. I woke with a start to see tiny Mammad-Ali looking at us from the head of the bed—if possible, even more cross-eyed than usual. At the sight of his daughter in bed with me, he stuttered and spat Zahra's name like a serpent spitting venom.

"Get out of that bed, you daughter of a whore!"

Zahra, cool as a queen, stepped out of my bed in her nightgown. She picked up her chador from the chair and covered herself, with an elegant whirl of the hand. She did not leave. She did not scream; neither did she say a word. She stood at the head of the stairs and watched her father.

Mammad-Ali had a surprise for me. From behind him, out of nowhere, came a switch. He whipped it a few times in the air: whit, whit. Without warning, he began hitting my exposed legs, as the nearest part of my body. The bloody mark of the stick appeared instantaneously. Recoiling in horror, I struck a womanish pose, now exposing my flank.

"Ay, ay!" I shouted. "Have you lost your senses, old man?"

"I will now demonstrate to you who is the old man in this situation!" Whit, whit—immediately my thighs began burning. Staying exposed in bed would not do. As I scrambled around the room, he shouted at me for hurting his daughter's chance of a good life. "You, sir, need a good beating. I will take care of that for you, sir, right now!"

I again heard the whoosh and felt the sting on my skin.

"Stop beating me," I squealed, crashing into the large sacks of pistachios and rice. Pounds of rice spilled over the floor like waves of white ants.

"I will beat you, sir, for the sake of my daughter and for the love I had for your father. You need a beating, and I am the man to give it to you!"

Whiz, my skin broke into fresh welts. As I retreated, my shoulder caught the shelves full of goods. A bag of walnuts on the top shelf did a slow-motion dance, as if of two minds: to spill or not to spill? We all stopped to watch, as hundreds of nuts fell to the floor with the sound of a thousand horses clomping around the room. The beating resumed.

I began to beg. "Why are you beating me, Mammad-Ali? I love your daughter."

Mammad-Ali stopped again. He looked at me incredulously. "You love my daughter? And that is how you treat a woman you love, by robbing her of her virtue? You should have come to me for her hand."

The thrashing began once again. I felt the burn on the backs of my thighs; he continued to find his target with remarkable accuracy for a man with his poor eyesight. I fell to the floor among bars of soap and a large tin of yellow cooking oil. I put my arms up to defend my face from the relentless whipping.

"For the love of God," I whimpered, "I swear by everything you believe in that I will take your daughter to the notary this hour and marry her."

He raised his hand to recommence. Zahra interrupted.

"That is enough, Agha-joon," she said. "I told you he is an honorable man."

She came over and grabbed the stick from Mammad-Ali, who yielded without protest. He now smiled at me benevolently, with the gaze of a loving father.

"Son, you have to forgive me. I lost two sons in the war. She is all I have left. I couldn't leave her future in the dark. Now I have gained a son." Mammad-Ali's acute-angled eyes glistened with a film of tears. I sat there, stupefied. My hand, finding itself at rest in the can of cooking oil, began unconsciously rubbing the oil on my wounds.

Mammad-Ali approached me as I sat, legs apart, on the floor. He crawled between my legs in an attempt to give me a full hug. When that failed, he opted to pat my stomach, as he had when we first bonded over the loss of his sons. I continued to rub the magic cooking elixir on my welts with some satisfaction.

"Agha-joon, go get some sweets. We can celebrate for breakfast," my practical Zahra instructed. Mammad-Ali went happily downstairs without further debate.

"How did he know?" I asked.

"I told him."

"You *told* him?"

"Yes," she said. "How long do you think I would have let you park in the back garage, for goodness sake?" She laughed her special laugh.

"Why did you let him beat me mercilessly for so long? I feel like a hundred bees have stung me."

"Oh, that. That was his idea. He figures that once he and your Baba are together in the other world, your Baba will appreciate and thank him for being a good father to you."

"My Baba never beat me in my life."

"That was his point."

That evening, welts and all, I went back to see Ms. Vakil. Zahra went out with friends to shop for her wedding. Baba, I wanted to talk to her alone; I had developed a good relationship with Vakil Khanum. No, Baba, I didn't have dishonorable intentions. You can tell she is out of my league. My Zahra fits perfectly that mold that God creates in our brains.

What nags at me, though, is the poverty of Zahra's surroundings. I prefer the smooth-sliding elevator door in Vakil Khanum's apartment building. I like gliding onto her parquet floor; in my socks, I feel a hundred pounds lighter. I like the discreet lighting that falls on her paintings. I like that she has her own library. I like the cream puffs waiting for me.

On that afternoon, I sat in the living room and waited for her to come downstairs. The elderly housekeeper came in with tea and sweets, more quietly than a house cat; I noticed her only when she appeared from behind me with a full tray, and placed it on the glass table without a clink.

Vakil Khanum walked in with the authority of a general and looked at me with mild amusement.

"What today?" she asked. "And what happened to your face?"

"I ran into a branch." She didn't ask for details.

I outlined for her the story of the unnamed wrestler, warning her not to mention his identity in the narrative.

"Why not?"

"I don't know," I shrugged. "Professor Dal asked me not to mention it. He feared it could revive questions better left unanswered." My face pleaded silently for discretion.

"Not to worry," she smiled. "I will respect your—or Professor Dal's—wishes. You do know that everybody will know anyway."

Then she got to the main point. "Have you gotten any further with retrieving the documents?"

I hemmed and hawed.

"You know that all this"—she pointed to the tape recorder—"has little weight without some original documentation." Now she shrugged. "Take the microphone and begin your narrative."

I at once began the story of the Wrestler and the Shah.

The Professor Remembers the King and the Wrestler

"All good drama has two movements, first the making of the mistake, then the discovery that it was a mistake."
— W. H. Auden, *The Dyer's Hand*

I spent my eighth morning in this prison, still with no outside contact. It must have been Friday. I stared at the wall all day: no one on earth cared if I spent the next fifty years in this place, turning into something like my cellmate.

This morning differed from other mornings, lacking any oil production—maybe because it was Friday and a day of rest. He slept well past midday; the guards did not intrude. When he woke up he sat cross-legged, like an Indian fakir, watching me with an unwavering, malevolent stare.

"And who might you be?" he demanded at last.

"*Arbab*, I am Hekaiatchi." I was bored with this act.

"I have seen you before," he remarked. "Have they put you here to discover my deep wells? It's no use, you know." He launched his grandiose persona; I ignored him all day.

That night we regained our normal footing, so to speak. The moon, a thin Islamic crescent, contributed little light. I saw Professor Dal's outline walk toward me with an old man's methodical shuffle. With great difficulty, he crawled from the end of my cot along my legs, like a mountaineer climbing a smooth rock. He used the strings of my pajamas to pull himself up; I held onto them tightly to preserve my remaining modesty. Then he grabbed my shoulders with both hands and heaved himself up to his usual position, his breath coming in quick gasps as if running a long race.

"We're coming close to many endings here, my boy," he whispered. "Give me a moment to catch my breath."

❧

Tonight I will be less than truthful with you. Please understand, my boy, I don't mean to lie to you. But I cannot tell you, with any confidence, that any of this actually happened.

Nima was in the last year of his government career, about to be wrestled to the mat and finished with a karate chop. I had moved back to my upstairs room—here, at the Poonaki house. People now thought me mad; the only people who paid me any attention were Nima and Lili. So, you see, my prison here did not differ so much from my self-imposed exile. Of course, I could walk in the garden at that time, but I did not in fact venture outside. My conversations with Nima were limited to Friday evenings, when we had a standing dinner date. Once in a while, Lili joined us.

She now lived mostly in Paris. The sight of their two boys depressed her: she could not abide their constant fighting. The Shah's divorced second wife, Soraya, had also chosen Paris as her domicile, and those two beautiful, elegant women became friends. The sixties had rolled into Europe. Their pictures, in a Paris nightclub or at a Monte Carlo beach, graced the gossip magazines.

The Shah had remarried. Lili could not transfer her loyalties to the Shah's new queen as easily as Nima did. Nima's allegiance lay only with his Shah, not with any consort.

Nevertheless, a slow change came over everyone's relationship with the Shah. His upsurge of self-confidence in the early sixties at first did the country good. I spent many pleasant evenings playing cards there; we did not interact in the political arena. But when a man comes to power, he is surrounded by whispers—advice and rumors about the disloyalty of rivals, the treachery of officials, the fickleness of friends. Perhaps he starts to develop a messianic vision. Whatever the truth, the foreign press published a piece diagnosing a case of megalomania and paranoia.

Leaving aside the question of megalomania, was the Shah paranoid as charged? Strictly speaking, paranoia means an irrational fear of imaginary threats. The Shah had survived numerous coups. He had managed to avoid one assassin's bullets; another time, the bullets lodged in his face and shoulder. All of his early premiers plotted his downfall, as did the Americans, the English, and the Russians. No, there was nothing imaginary about the threats he faced.

He made a clear distinction between friends *outside* and friends *inside* the political game. The latter served him up plots, seasoned with intrigue and simmered in conspiracy. Any action must be cleared with him; he expected blind obedience. If he gave an important position to a trusted friend, that friend lost his trust.

Nima always saw himself as a friend—but now he was a player, an inside participant. Nima's dilemma was perhaps inevitable: he would be commanded to perform actions that his conscience would not allow.

Persiranian sports, under the banner of wrestling, had a golden era during Nima's years at the helm. Beginning with no medals, in the Olympics or world championships, the Persiranian wrestling team garnered dozens of medals during his stewardship. In those early days, the Shah loved success in sports more than anything. For five years, then, all went well.

The difficulties began with a seemingly innocuous request by a stranger who had been sent to Nima's office by the minister of education, to whom he reported. Small and fit-looking, full of enthusiasm, the stranger presented his proposal: a Federation of Karate, under the aegis of the sports ministry. Nima refused, politely but firmly. He had already banned professional wrestling as a form of entertainment: its fatal incidents, though infrequent, disqualified it as a discipline. He viewed karate similarly. The man politely took his leave.

A few months later, we all accompanied the Shah for a vacation at the Caspian. I sat on the royal deck under the shade, while Nima and the Shah went for a spin on the Riva.

෪

"What is the Riva?"

"Apologies, my not-so-fluffy bed. The Riva is a yacht made of beautiful mahogany. It cannot be described to someone who has no concept of boats."

I said nothing. No point in antagonizing the old man.

෪

They jumped into the boat as two friends, helping each other board—the Shah muscular and broad shouldered, Nima sinewy and lithe. Both of them, in the prime of manhood, were tanned and handsome, in swimming trunks and dark sunglasses, smelling expensively of suntan lotion and sea air. They sped off, the Shah at the wheel.

The combination of gasoline, seawater, wood, and suntan lotion smelled vital, expensive. I remember thinking of them as two princes of the realm. I felt optimistic about the country. It was 1965. The Khomeini altercation seemed to be safely behind us. Kennedy was no longer alive to harass us, and our oil revenue was finally under our own control. Technocrats were returning from studying in Europe and the United States, full of ideas.

Somewhere, far from land, the Shah eased up on the accelerator. The two men talked under the midday sun. In that hour, the balance of our lives changed. Nima came back looking as gray as used asphalt, under his tan, and said nothing that day. That evening, we had dinner on the second floor of the beautiful Hotel Chalus, on the narrow terrace. Who can forget those soups served from silver tureens, or the lightly burnt smell of the succulent chicken kebabs?

𝒮

"*Arbab*, have mercy on me, we are in a prison. I haven't eaten anything worthwhile for eight days."

"Yes," he said soothingly, "you have lost your legendary padding. I will skip the dinner for your sake."

𝒮

Later in the evening, we walked together in the hotel's orange and lemon garden, surrounded by its intoxicating scents. Dressed immaculately in light blue pants and a short-sleeved black shirt, Nima looked like a Hollywood star.

He related to me how the Shah had headed away from the port, out into the open sea. They enjoyed the high speed as the boat crested each wave and landed hard. After ten minutes, the Shah cut the throttle. He wanted to talk; he switched off the engine. The boat floated up and down with the swell of the sea.

The Shah mentioned the visit of the man who wanted to start a karate federation. "Why did you refuse him?" he asked.

Nima reminded him about the wrestling-as-entertainment fiasco.

"Right," the Shah acknowledged. "Nevertheless, we want you to organize and encourage the new federation. We will provide the funds."

The request did not seem outrageous. The king of the realm wanted to introduce karate to his people. What could be the harm? Nima, curious, asked the Shah about this new enthusiasm. The Shah answered with a simplicity that revealed his arrogance, or maybe his naivety about the extent of his power.

"You know, the university students go out on demonstrations as regularly as a woman's period." He smiled at his own quip. "Instead of sending the military, with all that entails," he said, "we want to have a group of young men trained in karate, at our beck and call. They could take care of the lighter work with the students."

"But, Your Majesty, shouldn't these people be trained, under the army's supervision?"

"We just said," he emphasized, "we don't want them to have any connection with the government. We want a group of young men who voluntarily defend our point of view. Lord knows, none of the rest of you will."

Nima began to respond, but the Shah cut him off by slamming on the accelerator, nearly throwing him overboard. The Shah had left his youthful days behind. But despite his promise of funding, the launch of the Federation of Karate was pushed back again and again, due to budgetary constraints. Nima began to hope that the Shah had forgotten about his scheme or had found another way to solve his student problem.

But a more serious rift appeared, intertwined with the conversation on the boat, involving a wrestler whose name I cannot mention. I happened to meet the Wrestler at the height of his career, when he came for a medical consultation.

"You met him?" I said (also avoiding his name).

"I did."

"What was he like?"

Professor Dal merely laughed and continued.

The Wrestler suffered from epididymo-orchitis, a bacterial infection of the scrotum. A deeply shy man, he could hardly meet my eyes as I explained the diagnosis. After much hesitation, he asked me if everything would be all right when he got married someday. I assured him that he needn't worry; a few weeks of antibiotics would cure him.

He had bigger problems than the swelling of his scrotum. He had taken fourth place at the Tokyo Olympics; his lack of a medal had in fact pleased the Shah. But despite his poor showing, large crowds waited to greet him at the airport. It was *this* that the Shah was unhappy with.

Worse still was our hero's public support of Mossadegh and the Persiranian National Front. The Shah issued an ultimatum: unless he recanted, his wrestling days were over.

"The popularity of this man remains to me unexplainable," the Shah once complained to me.

Surprised, I counseled him: "Actors, I have heard, hate to play roles opposite children and dogs. Your Majesty, leaders such as you do not engage in popularity contests with children and dogs." He laughed—but I doubt he heard.

Nima arrived on the sports scene at a time when the unnamed one had passed the peak of his career, by now decorated with medals of all colors. Now the Wrestler, refusing to bow to the Shah's demand, went into retirement, to the great distress of his fans. Thus it was that, during the qualification rounds for the world championship, Nima entered the stadium amid unrelenting chants of the hero's name. The chants had a dangerous pitch. Nima decided to address the crowd with a conciliatory speech; he himself enjoyed a modicum of popularity, though hardly in the league of our Wrestler. Nima promised the crowd that he would do everything in his power to bring the unnamed one out of retirement.

Nima phoned me, in a dither, right after his speech. The next day, true to form, there was a summons to come to the palace and explain that promise.

We sat that evening at our usual card game. It may have been one of my last visits to the palace. Another doctor sat as the fourth hand with Hajebi and me; so, when Nima walked in, there was no place for him to sit. He stood. The Shah did not look up.

"I'd appreciate your explanation of why you would countermand my orders."

"Your Majesty, I only promised them that I would try. I did it to prevent an incident. Your Majesty, he is already thirty-five years old. His effect on the team would be only psychological."

"Are you daft, or just pretending to be?" The Shah threw his cards on the table in disgust. "You have put us in an impossible position, Nima. If we refuse, we look mean and we invite more trouble going forward. If we allow him to come back, we have given in to a mob. God forbid that he wins a *medal*—the country will toast him for the next hundred years. Do you understand our position now?"

"Yes, Your Majesty." Nima looked shocked at the insulting words. "Your Majesty, I think it best for me to give you my resignation forthwith."

The Shah's color changed. He looked incredulous. Looking at the other three, he invoked them as witnesses to the stupidity of the man standing in front of him.

"And what do you think your resignation will signal to the country, except my anger at your meddling? Then what? Do I let the man wrestle after you have resigned?"

I had pondered the matter much of the night. "Your Majesty, may I suggest a possible solution?"

The Shah gave me a wilting look. "Riding to your family's rescue? Say your piece."

"Your Majesty, simply *order* the man to come back to wrestling. Most people know only that he has retired. Tomorrow morning the newspapers will headline, 'His Majesty Orders Wrestler Out of Retirement.'"

"What if he refuses?"

"Nima will go down today to invite him back to the team. He won't refuse Nima."

The Shah picked up his cards with a shade more enthusiasm. "Keep me informed of your progress, Nima." In an icy tone, he added, "This will make *me* the favorite of the mob."

Nima began to take his leave, but the Shah remembered a small point. "You will make sure he does not pick up a medal."

"I am sure he won't."

"Not good enough," snapped the Shah. "Do what you have to do to make sure he doesn't." Nima, uncomprehending, stood still.

"Don't keep playing the innocent. Pay the organizers to give him a difficult draw."

The card game revived, and Nima left.

Nima soon delivered as promised. The unnamed one kissed both Nima's shoulders, a sign of his deep respect.

"Your asking me to rejoin the team means a great deal to me. I will get in shape for the meet."

Now Nima faced a delicate situation that he lacked the tools to handle. At the age of thirty-five, no one could win a medal. What harm could there be if the man wrestled his strongest opponents early in the draws? He would have to face them at some point in the world tournament, he reasoned, so why not earlier rather than later?

In those days, a modicum of corruption infected all the sleepy sports. Backroom deals ensured the strongest possible end in the finals; a weak contender would throw his game, to give a teammate with a stronger chance a more favorable draw. Money passed hands.

So it was that our hero drew, in the first round, the Turk and the Russian, two young and celebrated champions. No one could have foreseen the humiliation inflicted on the unnamed one in the process of being eliminated. In the last bout, the Russian handled him with such ease that his teammates at the side of the mat cried openly. As he walked off the mat, he stripped the straps from his shoulders and told his crying teammates, "I am done. Think about yourselves." He turned to Nima with deep disappointment. "You fed me to the wolves, Mr. Poonaki. Was it necessary? I came here to win a match or two from a Bulgarian or a Canadian. How can I face my countrymen? *How can you?*"

He helped his teammates during the rest of the competition by standing in their corner between rounds, acting as coach and water boy. Nima did not return home from Manchester with the team. Instead, he flew to Paris, where he stayed for a month. He seemed to be recovered when he and Lili returned. The Shah welcomed him warmly. He played cards with us once again.

Lili warned me. "Nima has changed." She shook her head slightly. "He avoided everyone in Paris."

By that time I had developed my own troubles. I had lost a great deal of weight and was feeling fragile—though, despite what you might have read, I was quite sane.

During one of our private dinners, Nima told me that the Shah had again mentioned the Karate Federation. Dejected, he told me that he planned to resign after he returned from a series of four friendly wrestling meets in Moscow. I thought it wise; I had not wanted him to take the job in the first place.

Why go to Moscow? I wondered. Russian relations with the Shah were already strained, due to his pro-American stance, and the Soviets never had liked Nima. I warned him to be careful. These friendly meets represented a rapprochement, he told me, and were much encouraged by the Shah.

Within days of arriving in Moscow, Nima made headlines. During the first of the "friendly" meets, in response to the atrocious refereeing of the Soviets, he pulled out all his wrestlers—a gutsy and (he confessed) impulsive move. The Persiranian ambassador in Moscow phoned Nima to call him a fool. Nevertheless, the referees behaved with a smidgen of fairness for the next three meets, producing an even split, two for two.

Greeting Nima afterward, the Shah whooped with laughter; his pride at Nima's audacity was apparent to all in court. For the next two weeks, Nima rode high on rumors that he might be granted a full ministry. "He is, after all, from the Poonaki seed," was the refrain.

But Nima had broken some other crockery, while in Moscow. On the last night of his stay, out of some misguided sense of duty, he met his mother, Choti, for a drink. They talked for an hour; it seemed to him a promising rapprochement. He even fantasized that he could get the Shah to pardon her. Twenty years in Moscow had taken a toll. Her voice quavered distressingly. Nima only knew of her teaching position, preferring not to believe the rumors of her KGB affiliation.

"You look handsome in middle age." She raked a finger through his sideburns that had turned grey, exercising her prerogative to touch people as she pleased. They sat in the bar reserved for foreigners; she looked around in surprise to see that such luxury existed in Moscow. To Nima, it looked tawdry and cheap.

"How are the twins?"

Nima had his stock answer. "The troubled twins give us four times the trouble."

"Never met my niece, Lili, but she looks ravishing in those French magazines—gallivanting with the former Princess Soraya." Choti hurried to answer, unconvincingly, Nima's unspoken question. "We get special access at the University." She changed the subject. "With the new queen about to give birth, I suspect there must be tension at court for both of you."

Nima was by then a little tipsy, and he let out that he planned to leave office in the next few months. Almost motherly, she pursued her trouble-in-paradise line of questioning.

"He made me humiliate a wrestler I loved," Nima finally blurted out.

"But surely there are other more suitable positions for you."

"Never will I serve him again."

The Soviet military attaché in due course delivered the tape of the conversation to the Shah through General Nematollah Nassiri, head of SAVAK—with the compliments of Yuri Andropov, newly appointed head of the KGB. The ax fell swiftly. The next day, the papers reported the dismissal of Nima for "malfeasance involving government funds." Lili chipped in with her own money and the sale of many works of art. I gave Nima everything I owned, to help replace the monies that had mysteriously gone missing from the coffers of the ministry of education. The furor continued for months, and it seriously depleted our wealth.

Nima could not understand the harsh treatment. The Shah frequently dismissed people, but seldom with malice. Nima contacted old friends, well-connected people, the court chamberlains; few would speak to him, and those who did were unable to explain the anger leveled at him. His own treatment of the unnamed one had shaken him at his core, and now the loss of the Shah's trust broke him.

Some months later, the court minister informed me of Nima's faux pas in the Moscow hotel. The Shah had declared, "So be it; *he will never serve us again.*"

"If it was possible for him to love someone," said the court minister, "it was Nima. Nima broke the Shah's heart."

This Nima understood. He had little use for abstract concepts, for generalities such as nations, organizations, or even a people. But loyalty to flesh and blood, to friends—he well understood. There were no excuses: he had failed his own high standards, twice in a matter of months. He had been disloyal to the Shah and to the Wrestler. But for a mother to set up her own son for destruction: this was unforgivable.

ॐ

Professor Dal was silent for a while. Then he quoted a poem I had heard my Baba repeat many times:

When the unjust judge
Without justice,
Horrible, horrible things are done.
But more horrible things are done
When justice judges
The unjust judge.

The sun had just cleared the window ledge. Professor Dal fell silent. I did not notice him going back to his bed.

The Ninth Night
1001

The Narrator Comes Clean

*In the groves of their academy, at the end
of every vista, you see nothing but their
gallows.*

—Edmund Burke, *Reflections on
the Revolution in France*

Dear Ms. Vakil:

Qui vivra verra. How you sadden me: my now-real
storyteller dead at the age of forty-six, from a heart
attack. Penniless, divorced, and forced out of his *second*
tearoom by his wife and his best friend. It gives my story
a poignancy that I did not anticipate. But I now
understand how I came to receive all the documents.
Ms. Vakil, I will remain grateful for your support, and
for your introduction of Mr. Hekaiatchi, who has
merged by now with my storyteller.

You have inherited these papers deservedly, and in
strangely circuitous fashion. Had you known that they
were in my possession these past twenty years, you
surely would have contacted me.

It was only when I read my Uncle Dal's portrayal of
my grandmother Choti that I learned of her betrayal.
My father never broached that subject. He took complete responsibility for the break with the Shah.

Ms. Vakil, you have convinced me. I will release all
letters, including the more spicy ones. I beg for your
prudence. I attach the scan of the last letter in which the
Prince refers to his Choti.

> My Brother, my missing heart, my completed half:
> Choti has left me and I am powerless to command
> her back. The new laws and my precarious position
> with the all-powerful Reza Shah tie my hands. I know
> her circles: Godless communists, irresponsible writers,
> and irreligious politicians. I have lost face. Everyone
> knows of her escape from my house. The great Prince is
> now officially a cuckold. I have spies on her. I could

damage her. Yet brother, I don't have the heart to be cruel. She is like an animal. Not a morsel of self-consciousness. She does. She acts. She is like the game on the mountains, running to and fro across God's terrain, who knows why a certain direction: the spirit takes them. The moment commands.

When the moment commands, she straddles and rides me, always naked to the toe, like I am an instrument of her pleasure. Her eyes closed, she disappears. I watch her, the line of her pubic hair my absolute horizon. I admire her like one admires a variegated part of nature: her litheness, her boyish flexibility. When she comes back to herself, she cares not a hoot for my pleasures. I see I have fallen in to the present tense. She has left without saying goodbye to Nima. The boy is confused but reticent. He will survive. I had her on loan for eleven years. And here is the worst of it, brother: If she decides to come back, I will take her back.

Brother, keep well. Your burnt half. Saleh Mirza.

I understand, Ms. Vakil. Without the originals, these attachments are worthless. I have arranged for the originals to come under your control by giving the collection to the Boston Public Library (no, *not* to the arrogant Widener at Harvard)—and naming you its executor. After such a long correspondence, close to two years now, you may wonder, "Why the lack of trust?" I simply want to ensure that the original papers will never end up in the hands of the hyenas back home.

I want the record to remain clear between "our" and "their" revolution. Their revolution happened by chance. They point to the distribution of the Imam's cassette tapes in mosques as evidence of a superior organization. Please. Most of the people protesting in the streets didn't know who these people were. The truth, Ms. Vakil: the revolution fell into their laps. With little sacrifice, they rode the ultimate wave better than any surfer. Even today, they look surprised.

More than a hundred years have passed since our constitutional revolution. The religious constitution beat the civil constitution, with a half-Nelson. A series of cynical acts achieved the complete collapse of any democratic instinct in the Persiranian psyche, resulting in a country utterly bankrupt—by any metric you wish to use.

I imagine that, in 1979, this herd of ignoramuses experienced heady emotions: everything was alive with possibility. As Khomeini made his awkward descent from that Air France plane (his bulletproof vest required the help of the French pilot), no doubt high fives and pumping fists—or the clerical equivalents— were exchanged in Qom. For a century they had dreamed of building the kingdom of God on earth.

Thirty years have passed; the protesters soon recognized the failure of the experiment. But do we really need another upheaval? *It can always get worse.* What I want is to blink and, presto, have them disappear from the face of this earth. Let Heaven have them. Let our complex, difficult, wonderful world be managed by non-criminals, with all their shortcomings.

"Our" revolution—the earlier, constitutional one— sprang from a humanist tradition. I want to make outrageous claims for it, to announce that I consider our revolution the purest of them all. In its failure, it never copied the inhuman aftermath of the French Revolution. It petered out after victory, so diffuse, so confusing, that it perhaps represented how we were as a people.

Ms. Vakil, I merely want to put the facts into perspective. Maybe I should reword: I would like to put the Prince's perspective into perspective.

After the bombardment of the parliament, Mohammad Ali Shah's despotic rule was entrenched. The Russians looked unbeatable, with their proxy Colonel Liakhov at the head of the Cossack Brigade. The constitutional forces were in disarray—killed, exiled, in prison, or in hiding. For the next eighteen months, the reactionary forces controlled all institutions; the capital belonged to them.

The resistance—at first defensive—started in Tabriz. The Shah ordered a siege of the city. The Tabrizis knew the Shah only too well, but the Shah, never a quick study, didn't know his Tabrizis. He threw everything at them: not only the army, but also the infamous brigand Rahim Khan and his five hundred mercenaries, empowered to loot and rape the citizens of Tabriz.

The people put up barricades to resist the reactionary forces. An illiterate man named Sattar Khan emerged as strongman on the side of the constitutionalists—a bandit himself, and a former cellmate of Rahim Khan's. He organized a ragtag army of four thousand troops, and, during ten months of street fighting, they captured two of the city's twelve districts. Sattar Khan expelled first the bandits and then the religious Islamiyah Society, hated even more than the brigands. The barricaded city quickly recovered and began to go about its business.

The frustrated Shah appointed the old Premier, the reactionary Ain Dowleh, as governor; he stationed troops outside the city. By February the reactionaries encircled the city and began, in earnest, a starvation siege of Tabriz. Toward the end of April, Russian troops—no doubt with an eye on southern Persiran—crossed the border and occupied Tabriz, ending the siege and disarming the resistance.

A number of other cities, taking their cue from Tabriz, mounted similar resistance to the Shah's autocratic rule and set up their own constitutional governments. Isfahan was the first; other cities followed. In May, a revolutionary army from Rasht moved to Qazvin, just ninety miles north of Tehran. This rebel army from the north joined another from the south, closing on Tehran in a pincer movement, right under the nose of the Great Powers. By early summer, the foreign press was predicting the fall of Tehran. Fall it did. The Shah's forces surrendered; the Shah himself escaped to the Russian mission in Zargang, as Russian troops descended on Tehran to reestablish "peace." It was the beginning of the end of the Qajar dynasty.

I am coming to the end, a number of ends. We have taken a stroll through the terrain of my life—you and I, Ms. Vakil. Taking your lovely hand, like an eager real estate agent, may I now show you around the house itself?

No incident is for me as brightly lit as the hunting trip, the trip when I was born again. The silvery river rises—a thread of saliva—from deep within the violet mountains. Black pebbles along the riverbank, smooth and hard, clatter under the hooves of the mules, whose tails flick unceasingly at flies. Heaps of dung fall to the ground. Four sheared sheep accompany us: the trip's provisions. The guide, broad-shouldered, with a thick mustache and a rifle across his back, has a permanent smile. Behind him is Arya, also broad-shouldered, straddling a mule, relaxed and confident, speaking excitedly to the guide. Our father, Nima Poonaki, with one night's white stubble, wears an American military combat uniform. He speaks to a peasant passing gingerly between the mule and the rock face. Behind them, I ride: delicately ugly, lips chapped into cracked scabs, out of rhythm with the mule, jaw set in determination. Hamid rides half an animal's length behind me. Farther up the mountain, he will be a shield against the precipice.

We arrived at the campsite around half past two, through a narrow passage halfway up a mountain. From a distance, the tarpaulin tents, ready for our arrival, resembled green mold on a stale piece of bread; coming closer, they fluttered like flags before a battle. The camp was set up on a flat piece of ground surrounded by dry mountains the color of metal, as if camping inside a volcano. The tall mountains gave the sun just a precious few hours to cross the sky. By the time our party arrived, the sky was changing into a deeper cobalt blue. The shadows grew longer, jagged like the mountain peaks surrounding us.

Hunting on the south side of the Alborz chain was difficult. We pursued wild ram, antelope, and stag. The objective: go after the longest antlers. All hunters want to set records.

No sooner had we arrived at the campsite than one of the guides spotted a brown bear standing on a small rock plateau, half a mile down a gorge. Trying to not spook it, the guide whispered "bear, bear"—*khers, khers*—the sound soughing around the camp. Indeed, clearly visible through the binoculars, the bear, apparently oblivious to human presence, paced and circled. Its snout, chalky with dust, burrowed furiously at its front left paw. A splinter must have dug deep between the foot pads. He twisted his powerful back into primordial sine waves. The pain no doubt accounted for his disregard of the smell of humans.

My father laid claim. Then my brother begged to take the shot. Disappointed, but proud, my father consented. The humans began circling. We were lying two hundred yards from the animal, against the wind.

Arya lay on his stomach and placed the gun on a flat stone. Hamid, as always on such manly occasions, abandoned me to lie next to Arya: in sports and hunting, they were brothers, I the woman standing back. It was at those times that I hated Arya the most. Hamid whispered some advice to Arya, like a caddy to a golf pro. Everyone quieted down. We heard the wind. We heard the inattentive bear making baritone sounds like a dog's growl. It circled ever more tightly. The first bullet caught it below the chin on the upper chest, a bullet from a big-bore rifle with plenty of stopping power. The impact threw the animal flat against the rock. The second bullet, right through the heart, produced less drama, but this was the one that killed it. Arya's shooting was as good as any that anyone could remember. The two guides immediately ran up the slope toward the dead animal. One of them signaled to us by drawing the side of his hand across his own throat.

By the time we arrived on the scene, the two guides had cut the gut low between the legs to the solar plexus. Sudden yanks of the knife jerked the bear's limp head, rippling the snout back to reveal ugly fangs.

The taller guide reached both hands inside the gut and grabbed for the innards, rolling his eyes as his hands searched. His right hand emerged to seize a knife, and he promptly offered the living-hot liver to the family. Everyone refused except Arya, whose acceptance prompted Hamid also to take a piece. The guide cut two pieces, and they both chewed for a long time. The stockier guide was already making a meal from the kidney. The rest of us watched Arya and Hamid; my father smiled and shook his head in pretend disgust, proud as a Persiranian peacock.

That evening, we sat around the fire in thick sheepskin coats as the temperature dipped from a high of 100 to below freezing, in just a few hours. Spirits were high. We ate tough kebabs, drank lip-searing tea, and smoked soft opium, under a sky so clear you could touch the stars.

This was the night before my second birth. I can't claim to have had premonitions. The memory of that night—its clarity, the primeval violence of the hunt, the mix of humans of all classes celebrating the kill, telling ancient stories—has washed over me so many times that it has the static quality of a marble sculpture; flowing memory, frozen in vivid colors.

Arya went to bed about eleven o'clock. Hamid bid us all goodnight and retired to a tent of his own. He had taken on a middle-class status, and the mountain people treated him with respect—though to my father (who still helped with the cost of his education), Hamid remained the son of a village headman.

I turned on the flashlight. One of the men had prepared the bedding for my brother and me. One corner of the rough, brown blanket was folded back in a neat triangle. It struck me as a dog-eared page, a reminder of where I was that night. We slept like children.

The next morning, everyone was up at 4:30. My father, as was his habit, went off with a guide and a mule toward the western regions of the mountains. He liked hunting alone. We three, with the other guide at the front, made our way toward the south. The servants stayed at the campsite, to await our return in the afternoon.

We rode all morning, climbing high. The mountains were dry, the sun cruel, the paths dangerous from the flat stones everywhere. We found some game: small herds of ram in the opposite mountains, a long way off. The guide, with a naked eye, would point them out to us. We, focusing our binoculars, were still blind. Then some imperceptibly small movement would make the herds on the gray mountain suddenly visible, like bacteria stirring under a microscope.

Around two in the afternoon, disappointed, we decided to head back. Hamid and the guide talked animatedly, riding ahead of us. Arya rode mid-distance, and I came last. From the little nods of his head, I guessed Arya was catching a few moments of sleep on top of his mule; the dullness of riding under a hot sun has that effect. Less confident of my skills, I rode more apprehensively. If the guide had seen Arya nap, he would surely have warned him of the dangers of the slippery path.

The path wasn't particularly narrow, but it was covered with flat, thin stones many layers deep, accumulated from some avalanche. When Arya's mule slipped on the path, just ahead of me, my first reaction was to laugh. Then Arya slipped too—and then he slipped more, and disappeared before my eyes. The guide and Hamid were a hundred yards farther along, already on the trail below us. I jumped off my mule and looked down the mountainside but couldn't see anything. I shouted loudly—but in the thin air, against the soft wind, my voice did not carry. I began to inch down, on my ass, to where Arya had disappeared.

I saw him. First I saw only his hands, holding on to a jagged piece of rock. He must have slid down a chute or animal path, on his stomach. The small promontory he was grasping curved out like a ski jump; it must have slowed him enough to catch hold of its edge as his body slid off sideways. His legs swung into view and disappeared, pendulum-like, as he tried to leverage himself up like a rock climber. I slid down and looked at his blood-pumped fingers, holding on for life. I moved closer.

"Easy, damn it," he said, "you're pouring stones all over me."

Hamid and the guide now looked up; from their vantage point on the path below, they could clearly see him dangling.

"Can you hold on?" I asked. Changing position, I lay down on my stomach with my head toward the edge until I could see the top of Arya's head. Below him was a forty-foot fall. I secured my toes in a dried-up root sticking out of the ground like an old suitcase handle. I slithered on my stomach down toward him and grabbed at Arya's wrist, while he held on to the slippery rocks with the other hand. My rat-scarred cheek was driven into the hard ground. I could see the guide and Hamid running fast up the path to help.

"*Pull,* so I can get my left elbow up." I didn't pull, but just held the weight. The wrist I held was getting badly cut against the rock.

I confess, there was something I wanted from him. "Tell me that you remember stabbing me with the fork."

"Tell you *what?*" Arya's strained voice held no fear. I repeated the question, one word at a time.

"Yes, yes, I remember sticking the fork into your throat. I *lied* about my amnesia."

"Don't patronize me; you aren't in a position to."

"What do you expect me to say? I have told you a thousand times that I don't remember."

"I expect you to tell me what we had for lunch that day."

The guide and Hamid had reached the top of the path. "Hold on, I am here," Hamid shouted to me.

"How could I tell you what I ate years ago?" he hissed.

"It's the only thing that will save your life. It will make it clear between us." The sharp edge of the rocks now cut into my wrists as well, as his weight pulled me down. But for my foot hooked into that rope-like root, we would have both gone down.

"I don't remember, damn you!" Now there was a trace of healthy fear.

"They are getting closer; I won't wait that long. It's only between us, I promise you."

Hamid and the guide were sliding down on their backs. They shouted, but I couldn't hear what they said. I was listening for my brother's admission. I heard him say something, but I couldn't quite make out his words.

"What? I didn't hear you." It was the most ruthless question of my life. I felt the powerful hands of the guide grabbing my ankle, then Hamid's hand holding my knees.

"*Ratatouille!*" Arya shouted. I began pulling him up. Hamid fearlessly slid down on his chest next to me. Arya looked at Hamid with a strange, shocked face.

How our hands slipped out of one another at that instant, Ms. Vakil, I could not say. I intended to pull him up. I knew I had the strength to hold on longer. All this palaver took maybe a minute—maybe less. Maybe it was enough time for our palms to get so sweaty that they slipped past each other, sending Arya toward his death.

It was a quiet fall. Thud. The back of a fork hitting ratatouille. I turned and saw Hamid's pained face as he tried to tuck my silly pendant gift back into his shirt. Coming loose, it would have dangled directly in Arya's line of sight at the moment his hand slipped from my grasp.

Taking the path, we ran down to where he lay between the rocks. No miracle was at hand; he was dying. The right side of his face looked as if a bottle of red ink had been poured on it. His body shook in small quivers from shock. I sat next to him. His eyes opened for an instant. We looked at one another, long and hard. His body shook violently and then stopped. Under the unwatching, godless sky, I had killed my brother.

I felt reborn. His death did not produce a sense of either freedom or remorse; it felt like a natural conclusion, the final stage of a birth orchestrated by nature. The fact that he remembered deliberately forking my tonsils was neither here nor there.

The guide's face was bloodless, gray from fear. He could only imagine my father's reaction. Hamid sat on his haunches next to me, his hand passing over his face as if trying to wash it for afternoon prayers. My memory confuses the order of our conversation.

I said, "His hand slipped."

Hamid said, "You let him go."

Or perhaps—I said, "I let him go."

And he said, "His hand slipped."

Neither of us spoke of that puzzle piece, the pendant.

It makes little difference; the mechanics of the slippage did not constitute my guilt. But the jury would surely find me guilty of delay, of imposing those seconds of interrogation.

Let me give you one more glimpse of the camp: the tents, the campfire, the bear. I can see tears rolling down my father's unshaven face. I see Arya's body, wrapped in a white sheet, thrown over the back of the mule, now blindfolded to keep it on the path—his head and feet swinging in unison at each step. I take my bow before the distorted faces of the spectators; I join them with all the malice in the world.

The next time I see Hamid it is four years later, when he comes to my house to arrest me. I am choked up, Ms. Vakil, as if in pain. How can I be choked up, with so much hate? Can one love a person one dislikes? Or dislike a person one loves?

I will now let my fat avatar, for one last time, close the house for good. He is no longer a fictional artifact, Ms. Vakil, is he? He is the most unlikely of men to have done history a favor. He died at the age of forty-six without taking his secrets to the grave. Let him and his ancestors rest in peace.

The Fat Storyteller Sings

"Everything that goes into my mouth
seems to make me fat, everything that
comes out of my mouth embarrasses me."
— Gabriel Garcia Marquez

Baba, I am to be married. Are you happy for me? I want you to forget all the hanky-panky. She will be Mrs. Hekaiatchi. I want your blessing, Baba.

"What will you do for money?" you ask.

I have enough stashed away now. My work with Vakil Khanum has been lucrative. I finished it without getting myself into trouble. As you will see, we don't have to emigrate to Turkey. I know I disappointed you when I signed over your teahouse, but what could I have done? They kept me for nine nights in the most horrible conditions. I was wasting away in that madhouse.

I have deep-mattressed some money. Mammad-Ali, my father-in-law, will put up his savings to help us start a small teahouse nearby. Baba, I promise you that Zahra and I will work our hearts out to make a success of it. It won't have the beautiful pool and fountain in the middle, or the fenestrations in the upper walls, or the woodwork, or the gold-encrusted cushions. A small teahouse is a beginning. You know the place. You remember Alireza, the small, snot-nosed friend I had. You offered him a handkerchief every time you saw him; he felt at ease wiping his nose with his sleeve. He'd smile that funny, shy, bewildered smile at the offer of a piece of cloth. He never worked out the connection. He was the son of Tavakol Agha, the locksmith in front of Mammad-Ali's shop. We could hear the constant whirl of his grinding machine all day; he worked night and day to feed his family.

Last month, Tavakol Agha died of a heart attack while hammering away at a sheet of metal. He was 48 years old. I ask you, Baba, how could someone so young die from a heart attack while vigorously hammering? God, in his mercy, gives us no warning. I am convinced Tavakol Agha died from the pressures of this new life.

Alireza wants nothing to do with shaping keys to holes. He worked alongside his father all his life. Baba, you have no idea, but he has grown into a good-looking man. Now he wants to be a television actor. Baba, at least you can count on me to try to hold on to the traditions you passed on. I have a surprise for you. I know that Alireza's workshop is just a hole in the wall; it is all grease and oil. But it has a high ceiling, with opaque windows that let in a diffuse light in the main room that reminds me of our—I mean, your—teahouse. This place needs a good cleaning, and a few dishes made by Zahra. Baba, she could cook a crow and make it taste good.

"You could do better," you buzz in my ears. No, Baba, I could do a lot worse. You do not understand the times. One day you wake to see a friend turn into an enemy. The next day the same enemy reverts to being a friend. The effects of the war have produced the Sisters of Zainab, a women's religious order upholding Islamic regulations. I have never seen women with such foul mouths reminding young girls of their religious duty to be pure. The roving bullies in the street make up the rules on the spot.

I have grown, Baba. I have to act with skill. I now have Hamid the Jackal for a friend. Under his plush wings, I will prosper. Please, Baba, don't prejudge my choices. For a long time, I was terrified of seeing him in the street. For months, as I lived in the room above Mammad-Ali's shop, I was scared of stepping out of doors. You called me a coward. Well, I stepped out to meet Vakil Khanum. Everything changed. I am about to become a businessman. I am starting a family. I know Hamid put me in the madhouse—but he also got me out.

I haven't told you about my visitor on the ninth day. That morning, still sleeping, I heard the clanging of the door as they came to take poor wasted Professor Dal away for his ablutions or makeup—he never revealed to me what they wanted from him during the day.

To sleep better, I faced the wall. Another late night with Professor Dal on my back had taken its toll; I needed my sleep. Baba, I could have lived that way for years: waking up around noon; eating the grub, bad as it was; relieving myself at around three, in the privacy of my own cell—with great satisfaction, I might add; waiting for dinner; then having the Professor crawl on top of me to tell me stories well into the night. Maybe they might permit me a walk in the garden? A man could get used to a life without struggle.

Then I felt the presence of someone next to my bunk. Before I could turn around, one of the guards had taken hold of my ear and was pulling it to the point of tearing it off my head. "Ay, ay, ay," I howled as I followed the hand out to the corridor, to the laughter of the two guards. I received my ration of kicks to my backside—now painful, for I had lost some padding during those nine days.

This was my first time to set foot outside my cell. Disoriented, I stumbled behind the hand dragging me by the ear. I stepped into a windowless room that looked blindingly bright. Fluorescent lights shone on the spotless metal sinks around one side of the room, similar to the chemistry lab in my high school. On a blue towel sat a neat row of sparkling, metallic surgery tools. There were a few pieces of electronic equipment, like radios with big dials. White tiles covered the floor, which had a large drain in the middle. A number of people had congregated in the room as if waiting for me. Believe it or not, Baba, I recognized Hamid right away, joking and laughing among them. His audience accorded him a great deal of respect.

Hamid winked at me, smiled, and motioned to the guard to let go of my earlobe. Two other Islamic brothers, ferocious-looking men, immediately stopped their laughing.

Baba, I cannot tell you the effect these two had on me, when my eyes met theirs. You remember when we went to the zoo that time when I was six? I embarrassed you by howling to go home, frightened out of my wits by seeing the yellow eyes of the lions in the cage. I instantly sensed their complete indifference to my being. I understood myself to be a piece of raw meat. Baba, these men had the same gaze—but much, much worse. They weren't indifferent to my being.

From past experience, I lowered my eyes immediately. Such people's first question was always, "What are you looking at?" I could expect a beating, no matter what my answer. Hamid came over and put his hand around my shoulder. "Salman, my brother," he said. "Do you know where you are?"

"Mr. Poonaki's house," I said without hesitation.

One of the men whistled. "Impressive," said Hamid. "Have you been talking to the mad Professor? You know, he never talks to us." He looked accusingly at his goon and stepped closer to me. "What has he told you?"

The other man, too, walked toward me.

What did he mean by "us"? I wondered.

"Are we not in a mental institution?" I asked. I immediately sensed that I might put the Professor in danger. "You have put me inside a cell with a raving lunatic," I complained. "All I hear from him every night are screams and shouts while he sleeps. His nightmares haven't let me get a wink of sleep in the last week," I said.

I was not convincing; both men now started toward me.

"Easy, boys," Hamid said. "Let's not forget why I am here. Give us a second alone, and I am sure I can convince Mr. Hekaiatchi here to cooperate." The two men shrugged and one of them stared at me menacingly before leaving the room.

"We'll be outside if you need us, Hamid *Agha*."

"Salman *Jan*—Salman dear," Hamid crooned. "Do you know where you are?"

"A mental hospital?" I offered. My question contained a world of hesitation.

"I mean, do you know what this room is?" he asked. I looked around. "Let me give you a tour." He threw a chummy arm over my shoulder and moved me around the room. "See this? It looks like a radio, right?" I nodded in agreement. "Well, it isn't a radio. What it does is give you a high-voltage shock that will make you forget who you are. That is not the worst of it. The worst of it is that they connect it to your *balls*. Now, I have never tried it myself, but the two gorillas you just met tell me that your balls get so shocked"—he grinned—"that they suck themselves right up inside your body. They go so far up that they have to punch your bladder hard to get them to pop back out again. Then they zap those fragile, wrinkly little sacks again: punch, zap; punch, zap; again and again." He then walked me a few feet farther, his arm still on my shoulders, pointing with his other hand. "Brother, see these shining tools? Each tool has been designed to hurt you in ways you could not imagine. That one there peels the nails off your hands. There is a special one to de-nail your toes. The cute little hammer is used to break the fragile bones in your foot—one at a time." He said all this without drama, until I was crying in fitful sobs.

Hamid, the solicitous tour guide, his hand still heavily on my shoulder, looked up and pointed to various heavy-duty hooks screwed into the ceiling. "You see those, Salman?" He gestured as if to an exquisitely tiled dome. "They tie your hands behind your back with chain link. Then they hang you on those hooks. By the way," he said, looking me up and down, "you look good. Have you lost some weight? I should tell you that even if you were as thin as I"—gesturing to his own lean body—"dangling from those hooks would pop your shoulders out in under a minute. The agony, I am told, makes you black out, but only for a few seconds, and then you come to—and you black out again, and so on." He waited a moment while I sobbed.

"But the worst is not all this," he went on. "The worst is for me to leave you alone with those two animals for just an hour." He nodded toward the door where they waited outside. "But I can get all this to go away, with one signature."

Uncomprehending, I looked at him. "What signature?"

"I need you to sign your tearoom over to me," he said.

"My tearoom?" I asked. "You already own it."

"Ah," he said, turning slightly red, to my surprise. "You know that, and I know that, but a slight complication has arisen. You remember the local mullah, Haj Rajab?" I nodded. "Well, he has come to me with a letter—obviously forged, mind you—from your father. In it, your father promises to transfer the teahouse to the local Islamic foundation. I have already shown the court that the hand of your father differs markedly from that of the letter." Hamid twisted uncomfortably. "Haj Rajab has given up the claim, but he now has told the Islamic court that I have cheated *you* out of your inheritance!" He laughed indignantly, as if to say, *Who could question the motives of a man such as I?*

"Two things have to happen." His two fingers waved in my face, like a donkey's twitching ears. "First, you need to sign these papers, today." He pulled a sheaf of rolled papers from his inside jacket pocket. "Second, I will fetch you tomorrow morning. We'll pop in to see Haj Agha at the revolutionary court, and you will swear on the Koran that you transferred the property to me."

"Swear on the Koran?" I protested. "I will be doomed to eternal damnation. I can't do that."

Hamid looked at me incredulously. "Do you want me to leave you with those animals?" He made a feint toward the door.

Baba, you'd be proud of me. I stopped crying. I talked to him man to man. I said, "If they kill me, you won't have a teahouse." There was a subtle shift in our relationship. "Hamid *Agha*," I said calmly, "why don't I sign this document outside these walls, where we will have proper witnesses?" He looked at me and laughed.

"You are learning, my brother," he said. "I will pick you up tomorrow morning. If everything goes without a hitch, I will owe you a favor."

Baba, I wanted nothing more from him than to get away from this insane-asylum-cum-torture-house. I wanted to get as far as possible from Hamid, the man responsible for all my misery. The next morning, all went as planned, and I ended up, scared out of my wits, living on top of Mammad-Ali's store.

Darling Baba, please understand: I have welcomed your constant buzzing in my ear all these months. It reminds me of your care, your love for me. I have disappointed you often in life, but losing your teahouse tops it all. Through it all you have stayed by me, angry, judgmental, and demanding, but caring. I had no one else to give me succor during these months of sitting in the attic and writing down someone else's life. I have looked up to you, respected and loved you without reservation. Now I need your blessing. I see a new beginning for us—Zahra and me.

This afternoon, I will be taking the suitcase full of papers to the Spanish Embassy, way uptown. I called

Ms. Vakil. She arranged for the Spanish consul to take the suitcase under diplomatic seal to Boston, to be given to the public library there. Boston is a city in the United States, Baba. The same city where Mr. Dari lives. Can you believe it? Tonight Vakil Khanum will pay us a pretty penny for the papers. We deserve it, Zahra and I. But that is not all. We made a great deal more money than that while we were getting hold of the papers. I must tell you of our daring operation. Baba, you will be proud.

Remember when I went to see Vakil Khanum and she told me that the stories passed to me by the famous Professor Dal were worthless? Don't misunderstand, Baba, I told them with well-modulated voice. She liked it. But she needed *documents* to prove the stories about the twin princes. Imagine, Baba, that every time you told the story of Rostam and Sohrab in your tearoom, someone in the front row, drinking his piping-hot tea, would demand that you show Sohrab's birth certificate. Or that someone would shout from another corner, "I don't believe you, Hekaiatchi, unless you show me Rostam and Tahmineh's marriage license."

You must appreciate the times we are living in now, Baba. It is not like you used to say—that the telling story is in the telling of the story. The world has changed. The telling of the story is in backing it up, with document after document.

Anyway, good Professor Dal also told me about the hidden suitcase of papers in one of the summer gazebo-like houses. All the way back from Vakil Khanum's apartment, Zahra harped on how we might get to that suitcase. Quiet as a mouse, shy as a rabbit, but she perseveres. "Which of the three houses?" she whispered, even before we had settled in the taxi taking us back home. "What floor do you think they have been stored on? Do you remember if they were guarded? How many people worked in the insane asylum? Did they all go to sleep at night? How many guards at night?" I couldn't answer any of these questions. I had entered the main house just once and left it once. And good riddance.

From my room upstairs, in Mammad-Ali's attic, I could see the goings-on of the teahouse. Since my outings to see Vakil Khanum I had become more daring, so, whenever I saw Hamid leave the teahouse, I showed my face around the neighborhood shops. People remembered me and glanced at me with sympathy. They welcomed me in their shops. I began to feel part of the neighborhood once again. Then, with more daring, I started to visit the Bazaar during the day— even without checking Hamid's whereabouts. One day I bumped into him as he hurried into the Bazaar. There was no strange reaction; he just said, "Where have you been? Come and see me, I am in a hurry now." It was my own fears that made me think Hamid had me in his thoughts. A weight lifted from my spirit: I liked hanging around the Bazaar, seeing the people I had grown up with.

Zahra was not one to let go of an opportunity to build our teahouse. One day, she brought Alireza to lunch. He was not too bright but a good egg. He left school in the ninth grade like I did, and we went our separate ways. At first I experienced an intense jealousy. His looks made me self-conscious. I thought Zahra must have brought him for that purpose: to make me jealous.

Alireza ate Zahra's food with a good appetite. Bending toward the tray, he plowed his piece of bread into the heap of rice and swept it upward into his mouth under the full mustache, while straightening his barrel chest in one smooth motion. He thanked Zahra after the morsel went down, before diving again into the round metal tray heaped with rice. The poor man ate as if he never had home-cooked food. As we finished lunch, Zahra brought in the tea, swinging that magnificent backside. Poor Alireza looked starstruck, watching her behind while she fiddled with the samovar. This too made my blood boil.

Sitting down, Zahra told Alireza about a relation of hers who had an abandoned house uptown in Ferdowsi Square. The relation had lost his key. Could Alireza help? Alireza, twirling his mustache in that way, reminded me of a cock ready to mount his hen; he assured her that no door had ever resisted him for more than five minutes. Although this last statement sounded to me like a direct flirtation, I resisted my natural impulse to throw him out. Zahra told him that her relatives worked all hours of the day, and asked if she and I could meet Alireza at the place at 10:00 in the evening to get a key made. Baba, I promise you that my jealous mind was so distracted that I didn't realize that Zahra had just arranged to enter one of the gazebo houses—from the back door on the alley.

Even that night, accompanying Zahra, I still didn't recognize where we were. We arrived a bit late, around quarter past ten in the semi-dark alley. Alireza was already there next to his rolling cart, which was decorated with hundreds of keys, strung on large steel rings hanging from nails, along with tools, rags, pieces of used sandpaper, and a manual cutting wheel. Here was an artisan, helping a husband and wife get back into their house.

Finally, I put two and two together. Aghast at Zahra's audacity, I hoped that Alireza's boast about doors had not been idle chatter. Indeed, he quickly presented Zahra with a grin and a key, which he blew on to remove any remnants of metal shavings. I marveled even more: my Zahra had delayed fifteen minutes to allow Alireza to make the key without us being exposed. Baba, I tell you, she would best any man with her cleverness.

Zahra tried the key in the lock. It buried itself smoothly in the circle of brass and spun effortlessly. The door opened like Ali Baba's cave. Shutting the door again, she thanked Alireza with a promise of another lunch. For some reason, we walked away from him down the alley—though we should have accompanied him; after all, we lived in the same neighborhood.

Once Alireza was gone from view, Zahra retraced our steps back to the door. She looked up and down for passersby, opened the door, grabbed my coat, and pulled me with her into the dark house. She giggled with excitement.

"Have you gone crazy?" I whispered. I gave up and joined her giggling.

Baba, here is what will impress you. She had a *flashlight* in her bag. How she thought everything out remains a wonder to me. We began to inspect the place. The light could not be seen by people in the front house, where I had been imprisoned: all three buildings had been boarded up years ago. I had been able to see part of this building from my cell in the basement.

The interior smelled of mold. The plaster walls, all water damaged, looked bloated. Large wooden crates were strewn on the floor; the furniture must have been securely packed years ago, to be sent overseas. The crates looked impenetrable. Certainly, we did not have the tools to break those thick wooden crisscrossed planks. A sense of childish excitement came over us. We had stumbled on the entire household possessions of a wealthy family.

We did not find the papers mentioned by Professor Dal. We would need help to get inside the crates. That is when I recalled that Hamid owed me a favor.

I discussed it with Zahra, who observed that Hamid could not be trusted.

"True, but we have no choice. We can't walk into the house with a crowbar."

Hamid had enough pull to navigate in and out of the three houses. If he could commit me to an asylum and release me on his say-so, he must have the run of the place. After thinking it over for a while, Zahra announced that she would come with me to see Hamid in the teahouse. I agreed immediately. Zahra, always fearless, could help me pull this off.

We went directly to the teahouse. As we entered, memories flooded my head and disrupted my resolve. Though the teahouse hadn't changed much, the clientele looked much improved. Either Hamid had become much more powerful, or he needed to keep up appearances after his squabble with Haj Rajab.

I knocked at his office door. He sat alone, without his usual sycophants, just where my father had sat. Surprised to see me with a woman, Hamid was courteous. As the new rules required, he did not allow his gaze to rest on my Zahra. The rules were in his favor: my Zahra's squint can make people uncomfortable. I don't even notice it anymore, unless in company.

Hamid repeated his welcome and we sat down. After a few awkward seconds, he asked me how I had been doing. Looking at Zahra, I answered, "Thanks to God, all is well." And then I reminded him of his offer from months ago, in the "resting home," as I called it.

I could see he appreciated my delicacy. He asked me how he could help. I told him that some valuable objects of mine had been confiscated. I knew of their whereabouts, and I would appreciate his help in getting them back for me. He said that he would be glad to help, but was there anything in it for him? That, he explained, would make him much more enthusiastic. I told him that he could take the expensive furniture stored in this place—as long as all the papers we found went to me.

He looked at me appreciatively. "I always take eighty percent of all jobs; before you protest, let me clarify." As was his habit, he brought up three fingers and wiggled them. "You will not get burdened with one black coin of the expense. I will pay for all the people we need." One finger went down. "I will pay for all the equipment." Another finger went down. "And I will pay the rent of all the cars or trucks needed." He put his hand down. "You need only sit back to get your twenty percent."

"Hamid *Agha*," Zahra spoke for the first time. "We are about to get married. Why not give us *thirty* percent, to help us toward starting our life?"

Hamid laughed. "Gutsy lady; I like her," he said to me, his mood lightening. "I will give you twenty-five percent as a wedding present."

"Agreed," Zahra and I said in unison. I insisted again that the papers belonged to me. Then I told him the location. He looked at me as if I had pulled a trick on him.

"You mean—those buildings are not empty?" he asked, incredulous. "I have been going there for more than ten years and never checked those dilapidated buildings. They plan to demolish them in the next few months." He laughed. "This is going to be piece of cake!"

The next day, Hamid brought three trucks and five men with crowbars, *in broad daylight.* Baba, imagine how easy some people have it. We didn't even enter from the back alley. Three trucks rolled in behind the beautiful, palatial building, and each backed up to one of the gazebo-like houses. An army of hired Afghani workers jumped out of the backs of the trucks. A few of the guards from the lunatic asylum came over to help, tearing off the boards to let light inside the abandoned buildings.

The crowbars went to work. Box after box yielded its treasure of magnificent, well-preserved furniture. Dining room tables, crated in sections, could each sit forty people. Side tables emerged, of a delicacy I had never seen, their brass legs depicting animals, claws and all. There were statues of turbaned black slaves carrying food and water, their bodies twisted like the branches of a tree; writing desks, Baba, with soft green leather covering the surface, and you could not tell where the leather ended and the wood began; and beds so large they seemed made for my wedding night, if only I had a room that could accommodate one of them. We found fine leather suitcases filled with women's clothes packed in foul-smelling naphthalene; and kitchen tools, brass pots and pans, leather boxes with silver hairbrushes, large mirrors with frames that looked like golden suns, boxes of objects I could not name.

Hamid and Zahra began laughing. But I had a worry. Through box after box, I could not see any papers. There were boxes of leather-bound books bound tightly in plastic; I looked through many of the books to see if any papers had been placed between pages. Not a piece of paper fell out.

Sometime in the afternoon, I happened on two large boxes in the upstairs room of the middle house—the house that probably belonged to the Prince's first wife, the Shah's daughter. The boxes were filled with photographs of the Poonakis in an assortment of silver frames, all tightly bound in plastic covers. I sat down to begin unwrapping each frame, fascinated by the photographs of the Poonaki family. Thanks to the Professor, I felt I knew them on intimate terms, perhaps better than I knew anyone in the world.

I went through three generations of photographs. The young princes posed in sepia: two peas in a pod, heads shaved, in uniforms with large white collars. Or they stood in the middle of a large group of kids around their father, Naser al-Din Shah—a photograph probably taken during the spelling bee. There were pictures of each prince sitting on the knee of their older brother, Mozaffar, the new Shah, before Sardar Mirza's trip to Paris. There were photos of Sardar Mirza growing up in Paris. There were a few pictures of the young Prince, the more famous brother, as a student at the Dar ul-Funun, the technical school.

There were clearer photos, as the two men began to appear in group pictures with premiers and representatives—official photographs, with the names at the bottom in faded ink. I read the name of every politician involved in the first revolution. The photos left no doubt that these two were in the thick of it. Then Sardar Mirza drops out; he has gone back to Paris, now half-blind. There were many pictures of Saleh Mirza, known everywhere as the Prince, for he was a true prince. A serious man, he never smiled for a photograph. He holds his cane between his legs. His youthful slimness has been replaced by a manly girth. You would not want to cross him.

What struck me in these photos was that these men did not look so wealthy. Even the three Shahs of that dynasty wore shoes that looked worn and shabby. In sharper black-and-white photos, Nima and Lili grew up, looking naughty: Nima swinging from branches; Lili in France, pulling the hair of a classmate. They looked beautiful, they looked rich and happy. Their wedding pictures, much later, made them look like Hollywood stars.

There were happy years traveling with the young Shah Mohammad Reza—our last Shah—with his second wife Soraya. There were, indeed, pictures with queens, presidents, prime ministers, and movie stars. And then some color photos.

Zahra joined me and glanced at the photographs. She looked shocked at the lack of modesty of Mrs. Poonaki: the women wore European clothes. I tried to explain that, in those days, people wore what they wanted. I remembered such people visiting our tearoom. If you wanted to walk with a chador you could; if you wanted to wear a low-cut dress, you could. Zahra was not mollified.

Now there were pictures of the second pair of twins. I couldn't fully see Dari's face, with the rat bite, as he always held his left side facing the camera. Lili and Nima stood apart, unsmiling and gazing downward. Hamid came over in time to comment on a photo of the twins at thirteen or fourteen years old, happy and smiling; a peasant boy stands between them, arms around each other's necks. The peasant boy was beautiful.

Hamid pointed. "That is me," he grinned. "Spoiled rich kids. I am going to be richer than all of them one day." He got up and left.

How could I have been so stupid? Baba you have said that coincidence in storytelling is equivalent to superstition; both are disrespectful to God's reality. But perhaps coincidences in life just show our ignorance. The name is popular—but there were not *two* Hamids. How had I not put two and two together? Everything under his control, everyone at his beck and call: this was a place he knew intimately from boyhood.

Now two Hamids rushed in from two different worlds, two different times, two different histories, and blended into one. No one in the world but me could know these two people as the same ruthless person. Understanding is forgiveness, but I can never reveal my insight.

At five in the afternoon, I slipped out to a pay phone to relay to Vakil Khanum the bad news that we could not find the papers. She asked if we had missed a safe, perhaps. I told her that the workers and crowbars had stripped all the sodden walls, with the ease of dipping a spoon into a bowl of yogurt. The fronts of the houses now had only windows. The workers had even stripped the parquet, to sell to a scrap lumberyard.

I told her about the photographs. She said she would pay a nominal sum for them. They were worth saving for posterity, although photographs of the era were plentiful. The photos did not corroborate the Poonakis' involvement in the constitutional revolution.

My spirits low, I went back into the house. I wanted the story of this family to survive: they had done and suffered and sacrificed so much. Zahra and Hamid were speculating how much the furniture would bring. "I should have driven a harder bargain with Hamid," she whispered to me.

I went upstairs to get the photographs—but the workers must have taken them out. I ran down the stairs, two at a time. One of the lower stairs gave way under my weight and threw me face-down into the foyer, like a cartoon character. Hamid ran to help me up. He did not laugh; there was a genuine concern in his manner that touched me, even in my pain.

"I need the photographs."

"That wasn't the deal," he replied, all business. "Those frames will bring a pretty penny." Zahra, to my chagrin, nodded agreement.

"I don't care about the frames," I almost wailed. "You can keep those. I want the photographs. Under our agreement, they are paper, so they belong to me."

"Yes. A deal is a deal." Hamid dropped back into friendliness. He ordered the two boxes of frames to be brought back in from the trucks. "We clear out in the next hour. You extract all the photos, and we will take the frames to sell to the silversmith."

It wasn't about the money anymore. I sat down on the bottom step as the workers brought back the boxes. There were maybe a hundred and fifty frames of different types: round, square, rectangular; small, medium, large; silver, onyx, gold. Zahra sat next to me to help extract and sort the photographs. We began, carefully, with the smaller, round ones stacked on top.

Then, Baba, came a surprise like Ali Baba's, when he said "Open Sesame" and discovered the cave. When we began on the larger frames, I unhooked the back of the first one—and instead of filler paper against the backing, I found a document, in what I guessed was the Prince's hand. It was beautiful script; the writing continued sideways in the margins, at the angle customary in that era. I opened the next frame: another original document was stuffed behind the photograph. I went outside and found a suitcase of old clothes, which I emptied onto the floor. In the next hour, the suitcase was completely filled with historical documents, going back to Naser al-Din Shah's reign.

That is how I saved for posterity a suitcase full of priceless documents from my country. This will be the best thing I will ever have done in my life, Baba. I hope you are proud of me now!

Hamid, to his credit, did not mind. In the next few weeks he paid us a good sum. Whether it was twenty-five percent of the loot, we will never know—but it was enough to get us started, in our marriage and in the small teahouse we rented from Alireza. He did not become a TV actor; he worked for us as a waiter, occasionally—and infuriatingly—ogling my Zahra's backside.

I went directly to the Spanish Embassy. I did not want those documents to remain in Mammad-Ali's store an hour longer than necessary. I then did what my conscience had been telling me to do. I changed the address: instead of the one given to me by Ms. Vakil, I used the address I had for Mr. Dari.

The embassy doorman received the suitcase from me without a word. Everyone was being careful: the government monitors the entrances of every foreign embassy. You see Baba, I have gained a modicum of courage. Then I went back to Ms. Vakil's apartment, as darkness fell, and reported on my adventure—partially. I did not tell her about finding the papers or about the address. It was not a lie; I just did not volunteer that information. Baba, I am hoping that her contact at the Spanish Embassy would not call her.

I had made a promise to Professor Dal. He asked me to make sure the papers reach the last member of the Poonaki family, and I have done that. Mr. Dari will not know who sent him the papers. Zahra's reaction was not pretty, when I returned empty-handed from visiting Ms. Vakil—but we have made a pretty penny from Hamid anyway.

In Ms. Vakil's house, I picked up the microphone one last time to complete the story of my life. Imagine, my voice on that thin milky brown ribbon might travel to the United States and reach the ears of Americans. Baba, who else could I share this story with, if not with you? Maybe one day I can recount it to my grandchildren; it's too dangerous for now. As for me, Baba, you can rest. You need not hover over me to buzz advice in my ears. I have taken all your counsel to heart, for you are wise, Baba. Now, go and rest where your father is resting. Just know that your son has a good start: a good wife, a generous father-in-law, a small fortune, the respect of the neighbors, and a corrupt and brutal government. What more could a man want?

The Professor Ends All Stories, Including His Own

"Either he is dead, or my watch has stopped."

— Groucho Marx

On that ninth morning, I returned to my cell feeling tip-top, having stood up to Hamid and postponed signing the papers. The promise of leaving the next day even had me whistling. But then I heard Professor Dal, lying in his bunk, also whistling. The sound was most worrisome: gurglings came from deep in his lungs; his labored breathing ended in a puny whistle, like a comical snore. I touched him on the shoulder to make sure he wasn't choking on anything. He started up like a jack-in-the-box.

"Right, ho. Time to go."

"Today was my turn to go," I told him. "You can rest."

"Rest?" he asked. "How can I rest? I need to produce oil, or this country will go down the drain." He laughed at his own pun. "You get it, don't you? Down the drain? By the way, who are you? My new cellmate?" I stayed silent. Even I can learn.

Then he got up, naked, and stood in the middle of the room. He made a pathetic figure, even more so than the first day I saw him. He was a skeleton. His large teeth protruded from a mouth that had receded so terribly, he could have been featured in an anatomy textbook. The eye sockets were deep and hollow, and his blue eyes, protruding, looked like a fish's. His body was without muscle or fat; the two sides of his pelvis resembled kidney-shaped skillets. Now he grunted, making forceful facial gestures to get his bowels and bladder moving, throwing his head back to allow oil to jet through all his orifices. Nothing came out. His eyes widened in surprise, making him look even more skeletal, and he went back into his pose, grunting like a man focused on defecating. Nothing. The effort yielded him only a high-pitched fart. It lasted longer than one would expect, and ended in the pathetic, out-of-tune rumble of a deflating balloon.

Tears ran down his wizened face. Pointing to the tears, he lamented, "*That* is the extent of my production. This country is fucked. What will they do without my oil? I don't know who you are, young man, but you are one of the luckiest men alive."

"How so?"

He tapped his index finger next to his nose. "Because, young man, you are the only one who knows that we have run out. No one else knows this fact," he whispered. "You have a short time to make use of the information."

He headed back to bed and fell into an unhealthy, whistling sleep.

I spent the afternoon mentally luxuriating in the thought of leaving the place. I thought of the different kinds of food I would eat, of going to the public bath, of sleeping on a clean bed. My fantasies soon hit the wall of reality. I had no money. I had no place to stay. I didn't dare go near the places I knew in the Bazaar. Torn between reality and fantasy, I dozed off. I was awakened in the dark by the Professor.

"Boy, are you there?"

"I am, *Arbab*."

"I don't seem to have control of my legs," he said. "Can you come and help me get to you? We have some unfinished business."

I shuffled to his bed and picked him up like a child, with one hand beneath his head and the other supporting his knees. Indeed, he weighed less than a child. I sat on my bed, leaning against the wall and cuddling him in that position: he could not have balanced himself on my back. I pulled my legs up, to cradle him more comfortably. He no longer seemed concerned that the guards would notice our silhouettes. His head lolled against my neck. I felt huge pity for this man, who had loved one woman so utterly, so selflessly, that just sharing the same world with her had been sufficient reward for his devotion. This man who—judging his youthful Nazi sympathies to outweigh all his humane efforts in the operating room—considered his ten years sitting in this prison as his just desserts.

"I don't know what you are thinking about," he barked in my ear, "but I don't like it. If you are feeling sorry for someone, feel sorry for the dogs of the world, not for humans."

"I am not feeling sorry at all. I am overjoyed," I said. "They are letting me out tomorrow."

"I bet that I will leave this place before you ever do." He laughed.

"They promised me."

"What deal did you make?"

"Nothing."

"Liar."

"I am signing over the teahouse," I confessed.

"Good boy, nothing of substance. Your soul is intact."

"It's only everything I own, everything my father and grandfather left me. My patrimony. What am I going to do in the streets tomorrow?"

"Go find yourself another tearoom, but live your life without fear of others. Haven't you learned anything from me, boy? I have told you stories of the most powerful people—kings and grandees, opportunists and religious zealots, down to the wisest men, all eating dirt and being eaten by dirt. Tonight I need to tell you about endings. Just like death that comes to us abruptly, I will make quick work of them; besides, I have exhausted all my beginnings."

♌

The saddest time of my life came a few years before I found myself imprisoned here. I was living in this very house, in my own apartment, quietly, content to be forgotten. This house, so full of life and people for seventy years, had died the slow death of all neglected houses. Arya's death had destroyed the last semblance of family life. Soon after the funeral, Lili left for Paris, resolving never to return to Persiran. Dari went back to his boarding school in England. I lived here with Nima, who spent his time drinking in the other wing of the house, bereft and alone. Servants found new positions, in the lively houses of the nouveau riche. A couple of older servants stayed, moving like ghosts as they brought me my meals. I, of course, was the mad aunt in the attic.

Nima and I seldom talked to each other, not out of anger or even irritation, but because we had both lost interest in life. I watched from my window (two floors up from this cell of ours), as Nima walked in the unkempt garden. Strange how a home could become a prison—even before it was turned into a prison.

One warm May night, I was awoken by a knock from the servant who took care of me. "*Agha, Agha,* Sir, Sir! Please come quickly. *Agha,* Sir looks in a bad way."

I walked down to the first floor. There was no need to hurry. Somehow, I knew what I was about to find, entering the *petit salon* where we had celebrated so many birthdays, so many gatherings, so much laughter. I found Nima's head bent, unmoving, on the beautiful leather-topped desk, lying in a pool of vomit. He had drunk from a bottle of weed killer that lay near his hand. It had burned through his esophagus and stomach lining. He had chosen a most painful death. Yet he had uttered not a sound to alert anyone to what must have been a writhing, harrowing end.

The bloated, greenish face had lost any semblance of its good looks. His bulky frame showed no trace of his athletic prowess. There sat the body of an ordinary middle-aged man. While I sat in my room growing old, I had been unaware of his physical and mental deterioration. Like everyone else, I only saw his kindness, his universal popularity, his complete naturalness in every interaction. *Tout le monde l'aimait, mais personne ne se souciait de lui.* Lili would never tire of repeating: "Everyone loved him, but no one worried about him."

When did Nima lose his young, willowy look? Where did the weight come from, that appeared on his shoulders? The extra weight kept his face tight, shiny, and jolly, like a face-lift. In pictures taken in his youth, the transparent, black pools of his eyes reveal his sensitive nature. Now the eyes were hidden behind puffy slits, making him look mean, though he was the kindest, most generous man I can remember. The puffiness came from excessive drink, and the drink came from depression. What did we know about depression in those days? Lili would have insisted, "He has nothing to be depressed about."

I had cried for him ahead of his death; he had been dead as a man for years. He had borne up under the slow degradation of everything he had believed in, the moral deterioration he had himself experienced, and the embarrassments he had suffered. But the unforgiving stare of Lili, as he told her of the death of their son Arya, could not be borne. All women blame their husbands for the death of their children. They trace back the smallest detail, those times when the father pushed his children to take a risk. When you lose a child, you need to find someone to blame.

Nima didn't leave a note. I called in a favor from a well-known professor I had taught as a medical student. He diagnosed a heart attack as the cause of death. The subterfuge may not have been necessary: there was only a two-line announcement in the daily newspaper. The court said nothing. I called Lili in Paris to give her the news.

"Please take care of him like you always do," was her response. "I will let Dari know in the boarding school. He is now the bearer of our family's name." She was abrupt. I remembered Switzerland: how kind she—and we—had been to young Nima, when his father died. Now a phone call would do, to announce to her son his father's death.

That was the last time I talked to Lili. She died later in an avalanche, a freak accident at Chamonix while skiing. The French press made a buzz; *Paris Match* trotted out her photos with the young Shah in the fifties and sixties. Lili belonged to the French.

With both parents dead, Dari decided to forgo university. He managed what was left of his inheritance with considerable energy. If it hadn't been for the religious invasion of all our lives, I dare say Dari could have become a successful man.

The death of the Prince had more meaning than the suicide of his son—for the Poonakis, for the country. It was 1939, dear boy. Imagine a cell like this one, maybe larger, maybe smaller—I never saw it. I received a telegram from the Prince's secretary:

RETURN IMMEDIATELY STOP PRINCE
ARRESTED BY REZA SHAH STOP SERIOUS
SITUATION STOP CROWN PRINCE CANNOT
HELP STOP

In point of fact, Reza Shah liked the Prince. In his young Cossack days, the Prince had shown him much kindness. Yet he had had him arrested twice before. Those two arrests had been merely symbolic, for the benefit of his political foes; Reza Shah liked to demonstrate his power. There had been no hard feelings on either side.

But Reza Shah had changed. He had already murdered four of his closest allies, people who had helped him gain power and maintain it. The Prince's secretary worried, correctly, that the arrest this time had to do with Reza Shah's increasing paranoia, railing against competitive political forces that didn't exist. Only the Crown Prince was able to soothe his father's sudden tantrums, but in this case (or, by this time) he was powerless.

The Prince was imprisoned at the age of fifty-four—though he felt himself a full twenty years older. He had already seen too much disorder, too much greed, and far too many promises broken. He had presided over the exile of two Shahs: his hated nephew, Mozaffar Shah, and his innocent great-nephew, Mohammed Ali Shah. He had seen, without much regret, the passing of his own Qajar dynasty: their time had come and gone. He had assisted loyally with the new Pahlavi dynasty; a conservative at heart, he could not bear to preside over the end of twenty-five hundred years of monarchy.

The Prince's servant, Nemat, accompanied him even to the prison. "Would Your Highness like some tea?" he would ask, through the opening in the cell door.

"No, thank you. Go to the house and fetch me a blanket. It is getting cold. Winter is upon us earlier than I imagined."

"Yes, Your Highness. I will be back by lunchtime."

Three days earlier, the head of the Tehran police had knocked at the Poonaki door. They had sat down to tea. The man, looking woebegone, had explained his orders with embarrassment.

"Not my first time, is it?" The Prince put on a brave face. He well knew of the recent arrests and the reported deaths. Few had left the prison alive in recent months. He did not hold out much hope.

With a European war looming on the horizon, the Prince disagreed with Reza Shah's tilt toward Germany. He saw no future for Persiran in opposing both Russia and England. He was wise enough not to share his counsel with Reza Shah; this man saw advice as a challenge to his authority. In a word, the Prince had retired. He repaired to his country house in Poonak, where he could tend to his fruit trees.

In prison, he missed his garden. The leaves on the ground would be sticking to the bottoms of people's shoes. Was it already October? As small boys living at court, he and his brother would enter the house, remove their shoes, and then peel the leaves off each other's soles. They had chosen the prettiest ones to press between the pages of the large Larousse dictionary. The Prince had never recovered from the death of Sardar Mirza, the previous year. There was a physical hole in his body, where his brother should be living, under his own body's protection. The Prince longed to join him. He sighed frequently.

He now opened a book to read Oscar Wilde's "The Ballad of Reading Gaol." The book had been translated the previous year by Prince Firouz—in this same cell, before he was strangled in prison by the order of Reza Shah. Prince Firouz had been the last survivor of the four statesmen who had helped Reza Shah capture the crown.

> And all, but Lust, is turned to dust
> In Humanity's machine.

He closed the book. The word "lust" seemed to capture a passion for life, a desire to matter—an impulse that is hard to destroy in people. *Had* he mattered? Had he helped make changes happen? Or had he been just a cog in a machine that grinds everything to dust?

Thirty years before, the country was finding its way back from civil war. The Prince, with the energy of a twenty-five-year-old, had indeed made a difference.

Underneath all the celebrations, the various factions were rearranging themselves. The swift fall of the Shah had caught the Russians and the English by complete surprise. The Shah had lost his title rather than his head: he became Mohammad Ali Mirza, now a mere prince. A man of limited intellect, he had professed no vision. He had overreached, and the forces of change had overwhelmed him.

His swift fall caught the Russians and the English by surprise. The democrats' newly-liberated talk was uncomfortable for the Russian czar, and it set a frightening example for Imperial Britain. The court itself was in complete disarray; only a few men of sense would support the monarchy in earnest. The northern and southern provinces, victors in the struggle, understood little of the life of the capital, let alone of a court in disarray.

After his year of humiliation, the Prince sat at the center of the disparate groups, wooed like a lovely young bride. He quoted to me, with relish: One day you sit on a saddle; the next day you carry the saddle on your back. Letting out that great guffaw of his, he recalled those days. "Suddenly the English would come to my house, like in old times, and the Russians sidled up to me at court without shame. Those proud Bakhtiari peasants required lessons in etiquette. The winning armies from the provinces ran all over the streets, making people's lives difficult—and they needed food."

The Prince recounted to me with particular pleasure his negotiations for the exile of Mohammad Ali Mirza (never referring to him as Shah), who had taken refuge in the Russian Embassy. "We got back the crown jewels. The Russians wanted us to pay his debts with the crown jewels—just imagine! *They were not his to spend!*"

He leaned forward for emphasis. "You know me to be a generous man, but in this case, I enjoyed driving a hard bargain with him." He leaned back, smiling. "Don't misunderstand, he had been given a generous pension—but he forfeited it when he broke his word and tried to reclaim the crown. I split hairs on every demand he made. We questioned his representatives until we almost came to blows." His eyes sparkled at the memory.

"I did it all for my brother, you know," he said, turning serious for a moment. "But you know what? I did it mostly for myself. I could never forgive him our bastinado, that day in Tabriz." He slapped me on the back with another guffaw.

During that tense time, he visited Sheikh Nouri in prison. The Sheikh must have been the same age as the Prince was today, sitting in just such a prison. It was his third meeting with the Sheikh. Their first meeting had been neutral; they comprehended the forces shaping their destinies, as they jockeyed for position. Their second meeting took place—unknowingly—in the eye of the storm. With the civil war over, all the cards had been played. The Prince drove in midsummer to a dingy prison to see the Sheikh.

The Prince had volunteered to visit him, but not out of malice. He believed that informing a man of his death sentence should be done as humanely as possible. The Sheikh had been convicted of responsibility for the death of four people, by a panel of nine judges. Sheikh Nouri indeed had few friends left; the clergy considered him high-handed.

The Prince, too, distrusted the Sheikh, considering him far more dangerous than the ex-Shah. As a "friend of the court" (so to speak), he had argued to the judges, individually, that Sheikh Nouri presented a danger to the stability of the country; he was known to break his word, and caused injury or death to innocent people, in collusion with the former Shah. Indeed, the Sheikh had played the most revolutionary hand of anyone, for the highest stakes. And he had lost.

The Prince, mindful of protocol, sent word ahead. He walked into the Sheikh's cell with a serious face. The Sheikh looked thinner; without his turban, he looked like an ordinary merchant. (As the Prince liked to say, "Don't remove a man's headgear, if you prefer to keep a high opinion of him.")

"Welcome to my humble abode, Prince. Why so glum?" Sheikh Nouri bantered. "Who died?"

The Prince was silent.

"Ah, I see," said the Sheikh. "By what method?"

"Public hanging."

"Public, is it? Do you think I shall serve as an example? My friends tell me you yourself did your utmost."

"For what it is worth," said the Prince, "I did not want it to be *public*."

"Are you prepared to be remembered as the man who executed the first *mujahid* in our country's history? I have that privilege, you know. Are you ready to open your family, your descendants, to the charge of *mullahcide*?"

"Sheikh, I don't know about the privilege. But I know that you caused a great deal of unnecessary harm to this country. The committee was unanimous. Your colleagues in *atabat*, living in Iraq, consented." To mention that the Sheikh's own son had concurred with the sentence would have been unnecessary cruelty.

"You give me too much credit," said the Sheikh. "My colleagues give me too little. If they had given me my due, I might not have been so obstreperous."

At the Prince's mystified expression, the Sheikh began to explain himself. "Your Highness, ever since I was a boy, no one could ever match my religious learning. Yet the Almighty saw fit to make my nature a jealous one. This jealousy"—he waved his hand vaguely—"when it rages, it takes control of me. Every time I heard someone praise Sheikh Behbehani or Tabatabai, it left me enraged. What can I say," he smiled gently, "but God willed it so."

"Sheikh, you are saying that all those sit-ins, the beatings your people meted out, the pain you inflicted on the constitutionalists—all arose from jealousy of your two colleagues?"

The Sheikh almost jumped off the floor with anger. "*God* placed this single crack in my character, to give me the grit, the courage, to carry out his work!"

"And what work would that be?" the Prince asked.

"Go read your constitution. I have planted the seed of Heaven within your godless document; I persevered, propelled by this imperfect, unreasonable emotion that possessed me. And you, too—despite your outward logic, you run on"—he hesitated and rubbed his beard—"I would say, *anger*. Yes. You don't have an ounce of jealousy. Your engine runs on the fuel of anger."

The vein pulsed on the Prince's neck. "That seed of Heaven you claim to have planted has been uprooted. No one paid it heed. Do you see any laws go to the *ulama* for approval? Your own colleagues in parliament killed it."

"You and I do anger each other, don't we?" The Sheikh's tone held no hint of mockery. "Don't be angry with a man you will shortly kill."

"You and I think as differently as a table and a chair. We never could have been friends."

"Remember, Your Highness, that the seed of a tree may take years to root itself. Time is on my side—" he paused, without expression—"whether I live or not. Will I see you tomorrow?"

"Yes."

"If Your Highness would bid me good-bye now, I do need to write my letters. I will not send you in peace nor forgive you. I prefer that we remain enemies. You will be in my thoughts and letters."

"We are judged by the quality of our enemies, Your Grace."

Sheikh Nouri's hanging, it was hoped, might chasten the other clerics. A large crowd gathered the next day at Gun Square—men, women, and children. A group of six- and seven-year-olds, probably from a religious school, bowed their heads and moved their lips in prayer. Only one among them held his head high and looked steadily toward the gallows, with a hateful gaze that today would be instantly recognized.

The Sheikh faced his death bravely. People said he even kissed the rope. The Prince told me that did not happen, and he quoted the Sheikh's final statement: "On the Day of Judgment, *these men* (pointing at the Prince) will have to answer to me for *this* (pointing to the rope)." He continued as if speaking to the Prince. "I was not a reactionary, no more than Sheikh Behbehani and Sheikh Tabatabai were constitutionalists. They wished to beat me, and I wished to beat them, was all."

Throughout our lives together, the Prince would recall that speech and shake his head. "Beneath a noble deed," he would reflect, "flows a sea of misguided intentions."

Sheikh Nouri may have heard his eldest son at the foot of the gallows urging the national volunteers to bring this sad business to a speedy end. He recited these words: 'If we were a heavy burden, we are gone; if we were unkind, we are gone.'

The crowd cheered—for the execution, not for the Sheikh. "Do your work," were his last words, spoken to the executioners. The length of rope tightened, causing the turban to fall from his head. The photo of his body swaying from the rope is thus indistinguishable from any other robber or murderer. The Prince ordered the body brought down within minutes rather than, according to custom, leaving it on display as a warning. A group of seminary students watched the Prince with unadulterated hate.

Sitting in this prison, twenty-eight years later, he had ample time to reflect on that old rivalry, driven on his side by loyalty and on the other side—as the Sheikh had admitted—by vanity.

The prison cell grew chillier. Where was Nemat with the blanket? Or even tea? A clang of keys sounded at the metal door. "Thank God!" the Prince breathed, looking up. A large man stood silently in the doorway. "Who are you?"

The man kept a respectful posture, hands clasped before his crotch, eyes to the ground. "Your Highness, my name is Ahmad the Six-Finger."

Automatically, the Prince looked at the man's hands. Ahmad lifted both his enormous hands to show the extra digit hanging loosely next to each of his pinkies.

"They aren't good for much, Your Highness. They only get in the way of work." The sound of the muezzin calling the midday prayer echoed into the cell.

"Do I have time to pray?" the Prince asked.

"You do, Your Highness," said Ahmad.

As the Prince stood up, Ahmad held the ewer for him to wash his hands. The Prince completed his ablutions, unfolded his silk rug, and handed Ahmad some money. He placed the prayer stone at the head of the rug, to rest his head as he kneeled before God. Outside he could hear Nemat greeting the guard, who stopped him from entering.

The Prince, kneeling, mouthed the last words of the midday prayer. Now he heard Nemat begin to scream, wailing, "What are you doing to my master? Don't kill him, please. Are you not *humans?*" And then, "Master, are you there? Master?"

The Prince could feel the useless sixth fingers drape onto his clavicles. The grip around his neck tightened so fast, it might have been a housewife handling a chicken. One imagines that his last thought must have been, "Where can I find my brother?"

§

Professor Dal brought me out of my teary state. He spoke in a resigned whisper; I could hardly feel his breath on my neck. "I received the official telegram the same day as the one from the Prince's secretary."

PRINCE DIED OF NATURAL CAUSES STOP
HEART ATTACK STOP NO NEED TO
INTERRUPT STUDIES STOP FULL STATE
FUNERAL STOP REZA SHAH PRAISES HIS
SERVICE TO THE NATION STOP

His voice was now so hoarse, I could hardly hear. He nuzzled closer to my ear and I felt his eyelashes brushing my cheeks. "My boy, you have heard much. It will take you a lifetime to understand the dust side of the equation. You will leave this prison in a few hours, to live your life. Keep these stories alive, and you will keep alive the Prince, the Poonakis, and me." His voice gathered some strength. "Stories are not made of stuff that turns into dust. With every repetition they come back to life shining in a slightly different way. *That* is how we thumb our nose at this ruthless nature, so dedicated to destroying us. It must piss her off that, swirling in your head, all of us who are dead and gone are still at play. Piss nature off, my boy."

Before I could get angry with him, for he had once again insulted my ancestors, his eyelashes stopped brushing my neck and his chin fell so heavily on his chest, I thought I heard his neck crack. Under the weight of his upper jaw, his mouth closed in a slow hydraulic motion. His skeletal cheek pressed against my chest. I lifted him into the middle of the cell. Red rays of the early sun had just cleared the top of the cell's half-window. In the middle I stood, a 300 pound piece of lard, cradling the skeleton of an old man like a newborn feeding on my droopy breasts. I wanted to shit, piss, and vomit all at the same time, in his honor. Instead, silent tears ran down my cheeks.

Can a Narrator Die?

*"When my head is off, set it on this plate
and have it press down firm upon the
powder to stop the bleeding. After that
open the book. The least of the secrets
being this: when my head is off, you turn
three pages of the book, then read three
lines upon the left hand page, my severed
head will speak and answer any manner of
question."*

— One Thousand Nights and One Night

Dear Ms. Vakil,

I have delivered all the historical documents as
promised. I am compelled to write these last pages,
though they possess nothing of historical interest that
would require you to read them.

What man can write hundreds of pages about his
family, revealing the most intimate details of his life, and
never revisit the pain he experienced during his two
hundred hours of incarceration, in his own home?

Life should be a smooth gliding stylus on a vinyl
record, producing beautiful music. God, in a surge of
naughtiness, picks up the arm of some poor soul's record
player and scratches the vinyl, back and forth, with the
vehemence of a five-year-old. We then live the rest of
our lives hearing only snatches of repeating music.

The time has come for me to relive those nine nights.
I do not have the mental mechanism to exile these
memories to some cordoned-off part of my brain. Maybe
it is all retribution for that minute of self-indulgence
that meant the end of my brother's life, on the rocks of
the Alborz mountain range. It will not surprise you to
learn that my favorite constitutional protection in my
adopted United States is the Eighth Amendment: *the*

punishment must fit the crime. The ordinary citizen is spared cruel and unusual punishment, regardless of the crime committed.

Try to imagine that first night. The servants' room in the basement was not so different from the one Professor Dal occupied for ten years, on the other side. The room had an ordinary door, with an old-fashioned keyhole that locked from the outside. One gazebo-like house could be seen from the half window, at the top left. I could hear the rooms filling with other "guests" all around the basement.

The room still had some of my childhood bric-a-brac: a broken balsa wood model airplane and a soccer ball, both removed by the next day. The first night passed without incident. I was issued prison garb: a pair of pajamas with vertical stripes, and a pair of plastic sandals. I had a vain aversion to wearing the footwear. Imagine, I was preoccupied with how my naked feet stuck out of some plasticware. A polite voice through the door requested that I leave my own clothes next to the door, to be collected when dinner was served.

"When dinner is served?" Was my jailer a disgruntled butler? An unimportant detail, but it underscores the deliberateness of it all. That first night was the last scene before my enforced transformation, before the forcible stripping away of all privilege.

What do we mean by the word *privileged?* When the structure of life and upbringing for generations is surrounded by privilege, no matter how unstable or violent or pampered, it seeps into the personality. An aristocratic upbringing leaves deep, physical traces of self-assurance—you might call it arrogance—inseparable from the development of one's brain. Why did I resist days of torture, refusing to sign over all my possessions? I did not care for the loss of worldly goods, for I could not comprehend what it meant to be not rich. I promise you it was not bravery. No: it was a lifelong, biological stamp of entitlement. This would require high bursts of stress applied by true experts, to burn off enough synaptic connections to bring me to heel—to trump a lifetime of biological engraving. They needed to transmute who I was, my very selfhood, into another state of being. They were impressive, efficient—perhaps artists. In a matter of days they succeeded in sculpting a different person, one I would remain for the rest of my life.

As two young men escorted me out of my cell the next morning, I had no idea what awaited me. We walked to a familiar corner room in the basement, the one belonging to old Nemat: his seniority had entitled him to the largest room. It had a high ceiling but no windows. The concrete walls bounced sounds back like a tennis ball—no chance of them reaching someone outside. Two bureaucratic-looking men, small but muscular, sat behind a small table. Their mustaches distinguished them: flared or not flared.

I was seated in front of them, on a heavy wooden chair with a strangely high back and two kidney-shaped tables protruding from the armrests. Almost a classroom chair. One man had a broken nose, with a lived-in face under lank black hair; he looked tough but friendlier than the other. The other, much younger, had his black hair cut short, *en brosse,* implying a serious work ethic. No lips defined his mouth, just two lines like dried fig skin.

There was also a third person. Hamid—still exotic-looking, after all—sat against a corner wall. He did not make eye contact with me. The youths who had escorted me disappeared. The two men looked at Hamid and then began the questioning.

For three hours, questions regarding my background and life continued steadily without respite. They listened politely and nodded in encouragement. I sensed that their aim was to link my family as closely as possible to the Shah's regime. It was not a difficult task.

"How many times did your father meet with the Shah?"

I could have given the Woody Allen answer. He was asked how many times he had been beaten by his parents: "Once: it began in 1939 and ended in 1975."

At around noontime, the bureaucrats left the room for a few minutes. Hamid still sat in the corner of the room.

"Do you know what they want from me?" I asked him.

"They are about to tell you."

We sat in silence.

They returned with a sheaf of papers. One of them fanned them out on the table, like a card dealer. "Please sign these—they are all in triplicate, so don't miss any—and you can go back to your room." Room, not cell.

"Can I read the contents?"

"If you must," the lipless younger one replied.

They were mostly legal documents: powers of attorney giving full control of all my affairs to some unfamiliar religious foundations in Qom. They stipulated that the transfer of all my property, to these causes I had never heard of, took place without any undue pressure from any person. "Undue pressure" had an ominous sound, but I refused to sign the documents. I volunteered to pay *khums*—one-fifth of a Muslim's income, as religious tax to the local mosque. I thought I was negotiating.

My noncooperation didn't seem to surprise or disappoint the two men. One of them took four lengths of rope from under the desk and tied my arms and legs closely to the chair. It dawned on me at last that this was a specially designed chair. The rope went in and out of an outer vertical bar as it secured my arms from below the armpits all the way to my hands.

The older-looking man faced me while the other went behind the chair. He rolled his sleeves up his arms in three neat folds, very deliberately, and began to limber up his shoulders like an athlete before a meet, followed by a few neck exercises. He cracked his hands by interlacing the fingers and pushing them outward. He then slapped my face with his right hand: a lazy, meaty slap, a warm-up. It shocked me. Being hit in the face for the first time in your entire life is a significant shock. You may laugh, Ms. Vakil, but here is what I honestly thought: "It hurts, but it's not a big deal." Before I had time to recover, his left hand slapped me unexpectedly and threw my face to the right. Unhurried, he continued slapping me without a pause, for a long time. As I began to black out, I heard the other man ask him, with concern, "Are you tired, Habib *Jan?*"

"I can do with some help," Habib answered. I deciphered the message: they could take turns and go on forever; I could not. Indeed, they now changed places. One had to hold the chair steady from behind. The lipless man mimicked his elder to the smallest detail; he rolled the sleeves back on his thicker, hairy arms. His first slap overwhelmed my senses. The second slap came from (I think) the left. What are the chances—*two* ambidextrous torturers?

I heard myself asking him to stop, right then, for I could not imagine I could take much more. He did not stop. I would discover that this also was part of the script. Once a cycle started, they focused on completing the reps, like bodybuilders in a gym.

How long it went on, I cannot tell. They did not again offer me the choice of signing the documents. They beat my face until I could not feel any part of it. My teeth loosened in my mouth, which bled to the point of choking. When I began to choke on the blood, they stopped, put my head down gently, and let the blood flow. The gentle caress on the back of my head reminded me of my mother's hand, during bouts of childhood sickness requiring me to vomit. At a moment when I was sure my neck would break from being thrown left and right, they would stop and talk about soccer scores. Clinicians, they understood the limits of the human body.

Sometime in the afternoon I passed out. They toppled the chair backwards—no doubt it was so designed; I now lay on my back with my feet upward. They then beat my feet with a doubled-up cable. I could hear myself begging for forgiveness. I told them *it wasn't me*, though I knew not what I repudiated. I promised I would do anything they asked. I would sign the documents. I called to Hamid to stop them, for the love of God.

It was late afternoon when the two youths came in again. They got their arms under my armpits and dragged me back to my cell. I saw Professor Dal being dragged past me in the corridor; I know this was not a hallucination, as it was only the first day. What they wanted of him I had no idea.

The first thing I became conscious of, back in my cell, perhaps hours later—who knows?—was someone massaging (I swear) ointment into the bottoms of my feet. I could hardly talk: my jaw was swollen past my mouth.

Then someone began feeding me broth, through my clenched teeth. Opening my eyes in the semidarkness, I could see enough to recognize Hamid, nursing me. Self-pity overwhelmed me. I held on to his thighs, my head buried against his knees, and begged him not to leave me alone. Hamid obeyed: he climbed into the bunk beside me and held my broken body in a tight embrace. In a soft voice, he told me he loved me; he kissed my ears again and again. He said he would do everything he could to save me. We talked in whispers until I fell asleep, still in pain.

I woke up alone, groggy. My face weighed a ton; my feet must have had thick shoes on them. I moved them slowly over and tried to put them on the ground. Some unconscious part of my mind refused, anticipating the pain.

The same two youths arrived and carried me out. I hung tightly onto their shoulders, trying to keep my feet off the floor. They helped. As on the day before, the two men sat behind the desk. They inquired politely about my health. As before, they glanced at Hamid, sitting in his corner. Was there some signal? They started with the identical questions from the previous day. They wrote the answer to every question with the same attention as before. They went out. Hamid never moved. When they came back, the lipless carried the sheaf of papers, fanning them with relish in exactly the same way. They again offered me the pen.

"I don't believe you need to read them again, do you?"

Today, there was one difference. Hamid still sat on the far side of the room, but his role had changed. His presence gave me warmth, perhaps something like courage. Perhaps I hoped for his intervention. Again, I refused to sign. They looked at each other without registering surprise or satisfaction.

They asked me to strip down. I removed the prison pajamas. "Everything, please," the lipless one said. I stood naked. The older man tied my hands with the rope, tight and neat, like the winding on a motor. They asked me to stand on the chair, which sat in the middle of the room. I did it with difficulty. They both helped. The older man stood on the chair behind me. He got hold of my arms and pushed them up. Only then did I notice a heavy meathook sticking out of the ceiling. He placed the rope around my hand neatly on the hook: a perfect fit. Before I could begin to wonder why Nemat would need a meathook in his room, the man stepped off the chair. He supported my weight while the other pulled the chair out from beneath my feet. His face was near my privates, but he didn't glance at them.

My brain worked on the short-term problem of survival with surprising efficiency. First it celebrated the relief and joy of having my soles dangled in the air, barely brushing the floor, my toes helping to support my weight. Then it tried to ignore the problem of my body weight pulling on my shoulders with increasing intensity.

The bureaucrats began to get ready. My shoulders felt like they were about to pop out. Then I heard the whirl of an object moving fast. A hard, rubbery, thick whip kissed my midriff and wrapped around me. The searing burn came as it unwrapped from my body, so hot that I looked down expecting to see blood everywhere. Again I felt the tight hug of the rubber, in the same nonchalant, unhurried movement they had used slapping me the day before. In two strokes, they communicated the horror of the next few hours. In two strokes, my brain analyzed the information. These two men would not stop even if I tried to sign the documents then and there. I would have to endure my day's quota. My brain understood, in those two strokes, that that would be impossible. It ordered my throat and mouth to begin screaming.

They had waited patiently for me to come to again. How they knew, I cannot tell: I knew better than to advertise consciousness by opening my eyes. The two switched places often, as they lacerated my body from top to bottom with their rubbery whips. I saw my torso produce gray ridges, winding around like highways seen from the air. The lacerations refused to bleed. Hearing my shoulders pop out, one at a time, I again blacked out from the pain.

What happens when one experiences extreme pain? The "I" in the brain runs around searching for a place to hide. The "I" splits into the "I" that desperately needs relief, plus another "I" that begins to observe the miserable "I". That day, my second "I" began to distract the miserable "I" by slipping into a past world, where life had offered sweet comfort. I began to focus on the details of those nights when I sat outside our country house watching the stars, the same stars my grandfather would have watched. The continuity of life, the calmness, the oneness, helped.

At some point, they cut me down. I assume I lay flat on my back on the floor. The lipless one grabbed my hand and brought it up to him, my hand hanging strangely in his grip. As he put his shoe on my shoulder, I began screaming. He told me in a quiet, confident voice that he was not going to hurt me any more that day. He made a sudden twisting movement, and my shoulder popped back into its socket. He repeated the same movement on my other shoulder.

I awoke as before with Hamid at my bedside, applying ointment. "You must sign first thing tomorrow," he said. "You can't resist them. These two are the best of the SAVAK, the Shah's secret police. The Americans trained them for years."

"Help me!" I was whimpering. "Tell them to stop, I didn't do anything."

"I am powerless until you sign. Once you sign I will see what I can do to free you. I will arrange to fly you to Europe or America." I must have looked surprised. "You can't stay here anymore."

He fed me broth, as before. I fell asleep on his lap while he sat on my bunk, smoking furiously. The tip of his cigarette did red pirouettes above my head.

I woke up the third day in a daze. My mouth was caked; I could taste blood. My body felt balloon-like, extended, thick and rubbery: a whale floating in the ocean—like my face felt the previous morning. Such expertise they brought to their craft. Beat the soles of my feet and face one day. Beat everything between the next day. My body inside the pajamas, surprisingly, was as thin as before.

Then I experienced a time-space jump—transported, as in a science-fiction film.

I heard the cell door open. The next moment, I was not in the cell or the corridor; I was sitting in front of the desk. The fanned document lay spread before of me; a pen floated in front of my eyes. I think I shook my head in disbelief; the pen fell with a loud thud on the papers. I felt confused—I had the intention of signing. Why had they not allowed me to sign? My hands and feet were tied now, just like—when? Yesterday? No. The day before. But now a thick leather belt secured my head to the chair. They upended the chair: feet up, back lying on the floor. Now I remembered the beating on the soles of my feet. Two days ago? My brain ordered the screaming to begin. No one was beating the soles of my feet; I stopped screaming. I heard the men discuss their schedule. The older bureaucrat seemed to disagree with the plan. My riotous heart pounded. My eyes darted right and left. I saw there was a large tin ewer, for watering the garden.

The older man, with the broken nose, dragged it over. Hamid handed him a hose that was attached to a brass faucet sticking out of the wall. I had grazed my shin against that faucet years ago, running away from my brother to the sanctuary of Nemat's room. The vessel began to fill; I heard the tinny echo of water hitting the bottom. Then water hit water and the pitch changed, betokening some impending cruelty.

The lipless one pinched my nostrils hard with his thumb and forefinger. I opened my mouth. He stuffed a towel-like material in my mouth, shoving it in until I gagged. He then inserted cotton wool in each of my nostrils, using his pinky to pack more and more cotton in my nasal passages until my eyes teared up from the pain. Doctors, with their patients under anesthesia, do similar packing after a nose job. I could just breathe through the sides of my mouth. Every breath made me panic that I was not getting enough oxygen.

Habib, the older man, brought a chair. He placed it so that my head, still on the floor, was aligned between the chair's front legs. He sat: I could see his legs and crotch above me. He lifted the large ewer and placed it between his legs, balancing the bottom on the chair. He poured a few drops on my face. He adjusted the chair. Poured a few more drops, made more adjustments. He admonished his partner to pay attention. He then began to pour the water continuously over my face. While the ewer was being refilled, the lipless one pinched both my cheeks outward so I could breathe.

Ms. Vakil, you know that waterboarding has been in the news in the past few years. From the Spanish Inquisition to today, variations of the method have been used. The Islamic Republic of Persiran no longer uses this technique—although, as we know, this "water curing" leaves no marks. Many have died at the hands of people less skilled than my handlers. No description can do justice to the suffocating experience I went through that day. The water pours incessantly on the towel and the cotton. The water clogs the material and stops any chance of air getting through, and you cannot breathe. If you are swimming in the depths of the sea and you run out of oxygen, you begin to race to the surface. But there is no surface. You escape the terror only by blacking out. Panic, the most effective psychological torture, grips you. You understand clearly that you are about to die. Then you black out. As soon as you come to, it all begins again.

The surprise is not blunted from the previous half-dozen times. You experience the same sharp horror each time, again and again. I can report that transporting yourself to a separate "I" does not work. For this is not pain, it is panic, a struggle to avoid certain death. The most basic animal instinct is assaulted and tortured. That day, I must have passed out close to a dozen times.

Back in my cell, the physical effects of that day dissipated rather quickly, while I still recuperated from the beatings of the first two days. Hamid again spent the night with me.

The next morning, the process began predictably: dragged, sat, questioned, offered a pen. I refused. *Why?* Stripped, bound, upended, waiting. For a beating, or something more abstract?

I could see the two men's trousers, their backs to me. They busied themselves at the table. I heard metal clanking. Hamid sat against the wall on the floor, on his haunches, watching me.

I could hear the breathing of a gas flame in the basement room. I saw them turn. I saw a gleaming piece of metal in the lipless man's hand. I couldn't determine its use. I felt it bite across my right toenail and burn the skin underneath. Then came a searing pain that went through my leg, thighs, and body and brought me back to full consciousness. A struggle between man and nail ensued while I went back to pointless screaming. He held my ankle with the other hand as support. He twisted the heavy pliers clockwise, then counterclockwise, back and forth, until the nail came off its bed. You could see the effort he put into it, but at the end the nail separated easily, like pulling apart a stick of Wrigley's gum, with a satisfying tchk sound. He exhaled in triumph.

Ms. Vakil, I am told I am a lucky man. For the practice of de-nailing goes back centuries. The European Christians introduced a sharp wedge of wood between flesh and nail. Hammering the wedge with patience separated the nail from its comfortable bed of flesh only after a long time.

They took their time going through all my toes. They wanted me conscious. They asked Hamid—who looked as white as the plastered walls—to hose me down. I was allowed to drink as much water as I wanted.

I tried to push my brain toward remembering the pleasant evenings. Both "I"s still screamed. The pain could not be ignored. And now, there was a third "I" watching the second "I" that was unable to escape from the wretched, screaming "I." You might laugh, Ms. Vakil, if I told you that this third, more peaceful self was eight years old, and he found comfort by resting his head on the chest of my beautiful fourth-grade teacher, Mrs. Doustan.

Fourth grade was in some ways the pinnacle of our education. My father enrolled us in a local Persiranian school, vetoing the French schools preferred by my mother. (In high school, finally, we were sent to the Francophone school.) Our first grade teacher, an Azeri woman, incessantly called us *eşek* ("ass" in Turkish). She might have been teaching quantum mechanics, in her thick Turkish accent, for we could not understand anything she said.

Our second grade teacher was the athletic instructor, whose viciousness was moderated only when my mother threatened to close the school—after he lifted me off the floor by my ears. For the rest of the year he mocked me as a tattletale sissy, unlike my tough brother.

For third grade we had Mr. Dadgar. He'd hover over you and then, with astounding speed, he'd mete out a slap for the most trivial infraction. When I walked into the fourth grade classroom, the expectation of finding an angelic teacher could not have been further from my mind.

1001

Mrs. Doustan was like a busty version of the Russian ballet dancer, Svetlana Zakharova. Her elegance enthralled me; an unbearable crush possessed me. I had her embalmed forever in my memory. Now I asked for her succor, like a religious martyr asking comfort from the Virgin Mary before being burned at the stake.

"Why didn't you sign?" Hamid was clearly exasperated when he came in that night.

I couldn't talk. Physically—I was unable to answer him. I wanted to say: I was going to sign, but my head shook no. I wanted to ask: Why don't they offer me the choice of signing while I am wide awake from the pain in the middle of the day? Why don't they ask me to sign every five minutes, like in the movies? I did not have the ability to form words. I already knew, there was no answer. And I knew that if I refused to cooperate, I was to experience a full day's torture.

Hamid brought mercurochrome to prevent infection, applying it with the soft brush as lightly as possible. I could feel every hair of that brush. He gave up and poured it all over my toes; it colored me with that yellow-orange color so familiar on the scraped knees of children thirty years ago. That night, for the first time, my body went into shock. I trembled so violently that the bed shook. Hamid brought in two more blankets. He tied a piece of cloth around my head and jaw, twisting the knot hard on top of my head, to keep my teeth from chattering uncontrollably. He sat on the bed holding my body between his legs, with the blankets tightly wrapped around me. We stayed that way all night, while I leaned back on his chest, going in out of consciousness—or, maybe, sleep.

I heard the door close at five in the morning of the fifth day, as he left my cell. It felt like waking from the anesthesia after serious surgery, but with a strangely clear head. The question had to be addressed: *What was Hamid's role in my imprisonment and torture?*

The first night he spent with me, he told me that he worked for the most influential people in the newly-born Islamic Republic, someone he could not name— hinting that he had access to the Imam himself. I laughed (weakly) at this pretension. "I haven't seen the twelfth Imam's return," I quipped. "Which of the twelve do you mean?"

He ignored this provocation. He said that when he heard about my imminent arrest, he wanted to take control of the operation for my sake. I now asked myself the obvious question: if Hamid had such access, how could he have allowed me to be tortured for days? And what was his relationship with my two torturers? They could order him to give me water and wash me down. Yet, some detail had given me the impression that *he* was the one giving the orders.

That was it. The two men always looked at him before starting the day. They looked for his approval to begin. He had been playing me for a patsy: if you don't know who the patsy is, *it's you.* How else would he be able to come to my room each night? My weakened state had stopped me from thinking clearly. My dependence on him for that nightly psychological balm had blinded me to the reality of the situation.

This new realization piled on the pain. The injustice of it reduced me to nothingness. Like shutting off an old-fashioned TV, the screen in my head was reduced to a tiny dot of light, ready to be extinguished.

A few hours must have passed, before the sun lit my cell.

The shaft of light, and my self-righteous anger, brought my devastated ego back to life. Anger, I think, keeps people alive. I made up my mind that I would fight until death. Bullshit. What my helpless anger bought me was a day of the most painful torture I had experienced so far.

When they came into the room that morning, I begged them to drag me backward. Each toe supported a rock formation of dry, clotted blood painted with Mercurochrome, ready to break off to start the blood flowing again. As they dragged me backward through the corridors, I noticed some builders constructing smaller, no doubt more secure, cells.

The lipless man once more fanned the documents in front of me. For an instant, I detected the pride he took in this sleight-of-hand maneuver. In that instant, both men saw it too. Maybe they picked up on some change in my demeanor.

"I am sorry, Habib," the card dealer said to his mate. "It won't happen again."

They did not even wait for me to refuse the daily offer of signing. They brought out the rope and started to tie my hands and feet to the chair. I stared daggers at Hamid to communicate my moral outrage. What was there to see? A half-shaved shell of a man with eyes more closed than open, head lolling on his chest and spittle running down his chin.

For my moral outrage, they fell on me with two electrical probes. The all-purpose chair was used to tie my hands above my head. My knees were placed on either side of the arms of the chair, with my legs tied down awkwardly to its sides, like on an obstetrician's table.

The electrical source was the bulb socket above our heads. A twisted pair of wires went to a simple box like an old radio, with a big, black knob. From the box, two thick wires emerged, one with a blunt end like the nipple of an aroused woman, the other with an alligator clip. Ms. Vakil, pardon my mentioning that the lipless one deftly stuffed a wetted steel wool pot-scrubber into my anus. He then wrapped a bare wire around my penis, ending with a few loops around my scrotum. He twisted the two ends of the wires and rested them on my perineum. To complete the wiring on my body, he connected the end of one of the twisted wires by burying it deep into the steel wool scrub.

Finally, he toweled me vigorously to dry any sweat off my body. This prevented the lowering of my body's resistance to electrical shock and thus averted damage to my heart. They worked to inflict pain. Accidental death had to be avoided.

Preparations complete, Habib took over. They worked me all day with those electrical probes. I can hardly remember the details. I do recall the smell of burned skin, and the loss of memory; psychiatrists have assured me this is a typical reaction. People struck by lightning have memory gaps that can span days. But I carry the visual proof of that day on my body—from the painful muscle contractions accompanied by burns from the high current. They worked mostly on my extremities—nipples, penis, anus, testicles, legs, and arms. I can count over a hundred spots on my body: the deep blue-black dots, the color of newly picked, dusty blueberries, cover my legs and arms like measles. To this day, an erection shoots mind-numbing pain into my scrotum and anus. Thankfully, the pain returns me to my flaccid state for days afterward.

I remember the start of the electrical shocks. Then, all of a sudden, I was sitting in front of the two bureaucrats; Hamid was sitting in the corner of the room. A pen was offered to me to sign the fanned documents. Why had they departed from their routine? A second chance in one day? No thoughts floated in my brain, yet I felt distracted by that nothingness.

I looked down. I now wore fresh, clean prison garb. My torturers and Hamid wore different clothes than a minute ago. How had that happened? The wire and the radio-like voltage booster had disappeared. The bulb, back in its socket, irritated my eyes again with its bare, relentless, stare. Strangely, except for a tingling all over my body, I sat half-stunned but free of pain. It was as if anesthesia had been administered while I wasn't looking.

Mercifully, I had lost 24 hours. My brain, respectful of its need for continuity, had sewn together two separate parts of my life without bothering with the hours in between. My rational "me" now focused on explaining the continuity problems I observed.

Since the last twenty-four hours had been erased, my anger of yesterday morning was undiminished. Fed on that anger, I again refused to sign.

In my confused state, I detected a grudging respect from my torturers. It did not change their behavior. They continued with their efficient system, which had no doubt paid off again and again. I was again tied to the dreaded chair, my hands splayed on its two TV-dinner-tables.

I guessed their intention instantaneously. I never saw the tool they had used on my feet, but from a sitting position I could see the pliers clearly: a stainless steel tool, or maybe even titanium, belonging more to an operating room than to a hardware store. Each side of the pliers had a generous roll of accurately machined metal. The two sides met at the lip, not sharply but exactly. This task required a tool that could hold a thin piece of material securely, without the need for undue operator pressure.

Today was the turn of my fingernails.

The thin-lipped one, back in charge for the day, first put a large green bucket underneath each of the kidney-shaped tables protruding from the chair. Then he pulled up a chair and sat facing me. A cigarette dangled from the corner of his mouth; he kept one eye closed to protect it from the upward-curling smoke. He did not disappoint. He chose first to pull the nail from my right index finger. Every fiber in my being tried to curl in the cursed finger. He simply used his other hand to flatten my finger. With the plier held to the tip of the nail, the smallest backward pull kept my finger rigid.

Ms. Vakil, you have heard me scream and beg sufficiently. At this point allow me to hit the mute button. I will simply describe the mechanics of the operation. Here the thin-lipped man expertly twisted his hand clockwise in a screwdriver fashion. I say expertly because his twist went further than one expects from a wrist. I saw the left side of my fingernail curl up and rip from its pedestal. He twisted it the other way, and a similar swelling of the nail occurred before it tore off. It sounded like peeling off two pieces of Scotch tape. For the same reason that it was difficult for me to curl my fingers in (the laws of mechanics prevailed), it must have been difficult to pull the nail out from its roots horizontally. Right away, I found out that he was not confined by the dimensional constraints of my finger. He had little difficulty tearing the nail upward toward the back of the hand while twisting the tool.

The black rivulets of blood started in the thin crevices underneath my now-naked cuticles. Stamped on the white cushion of flesh were neat rectangular striations from the missing nail; they directed the blobs of blood to cover everything and spill on the desk. The blood ran down into the green bucket beneath. All thought out and organized. From the experience with my toes, I knew that it would congeal into an uneven cake of clotted blood.

He used a surgical wipe to press on the finger. The alcohol content caused me to black out. The telescopic "I's" quit on me, one at a time. There was no escaping the pain.

I remember waking in the middle of that night. I was feverish and drenched in sweat. A wet cloth covered my brow. Hamid sat on the bunk next to me with a bowl of water next to him. He'd wet the rag, squeeze the water out of it, and then apply it to my brow. In anger, I threw the rag across the tiny room. The sudden movement of my hand sent five painful jolts through my fingers and nails, making me scream anew from the pain. I nearly succumbed to the sweet darkness but willed myself to stay with him. My fingers were awash with orange-yellow from the Mercurochrome he had already applied. He had snaked cloth between my fingers to keep them separated.

Guessing that my fever had taken over, Hamid tried to calm me down. "What's wrong with you?" he hissed. "Today was unnecessary. I thought we agreed that you'd sign. You think you can outlast these people?"

"*You are one of them.* You sold me out," I sobbed. He stayed quiet for a while.

"Of course I am one of them." As always, he spoke calmly. He got up and fetched the rag. "I have been one of them all my life." He doused the rag in water and twisted it hard, then flattened it back on my brow. "I could accuse you of having been one of 'them' all your life." He spoke lightly, without emphasis. "'Them' is just the group you don't belong to. I never belonged to your group, or you to mine. But here I am, ready to protect you."

"So glad to have had your protection," I croaked, with great difficulty. "I no longer need it. I will sign tomorrow."

He went quiet for a long time. He then stretched out next to me, bringing his head next to my ear. He spoke in a low voice that wasn't a whisper. "Listen to me. This is not about your houses and your money. The old man has let it be known that the Poonaki name is an abomination. As a child of six or seven, he watched some Sheikh hanged in public—the only member of the clergy ever to be executed. *Your grandfather signed the order for this execution.*" He paused while I caught up with him. "I know you don't know what I'm talking about, it was close to seventy years ago. The old man reads the Sheikh's writings to this day. He wants to organize our country according to his vision—and he vowed that no Poonaki descendants should survive him." He stopped again, but I already grasped the message. "You see, you do need me. I convinced them to keep you in this house so that I can stay in charge. Do you think I could visit you every night in Evin prison? If you sign tomorrow, I will go to Jamaran to try to get you out of the country." Jamaran was where Khomeini lived, in the foothills north of Tehran.

"So, whether I sign or not, I am going to be kept here?"

"Yes, unless I can pull some strings. If you don't sign, those two will break you down, even if it takes a month."

"Do they work for you?" I finally got out.

"They are assigned to me," he said. "I inherited them."

As I fell asleep, or passed out, I felt him licking my neck, my ears. I would swear in a court of law, he licked each one of my mutilated fingers.

I signed the documents the next morning, fisting the pen while trying not to touch it. I cried from pain and anger. The two men sat without a word.

It was the morning of the seventh day. Hamid left right away. The two youths used a stretcher to carry me, as they had done for the past two days. The door to my room had been taken off its hinges; two workmen were putting in a metal door. Despite the noise they made, I slept all day and night.

I woke on the morning of the eighth day to discover my two torturers sitting on two folding metal chairs, watching me sleep. Frightened out of my wits, I burst into tears and assured them that I had signed the documents. I had a high fever, my body wracking convulsively every few minutes, and my heart now beating fast with terror. They made me understand that they only wanted to talk to me.

The older man, Habib, began speaking. "Mr. Poonaki, please don't mix us up with this new breed of kids with the new regime. My colleague and I have worked in the old regime for years. If I told you how lucky you are to have had us as interrogators, you would be outraged. We are your first interrogators, are we not?" I nodded yes from my bed.

"Let me tell you, Mr. Poonaki," he began again, as if selling me financial services, "I have worked in this business for more than twenty years, my friend here for five. Both of us have been trained in the United States and Russia. We have taken courses in psychology and medicine at the Tehran University. And we do operate under the Hippocratic rule. Of sorts." He smiled. "My partner and I here have sworn to use only means that do not cause long-term physical injury to the prisoner. Maybe this is not quite the right time, but I assure you that within a month your injuries will heal enough to allow for most normal activities. Within a year, you should not suffer from any of your current injuries, beyond some superficial marks. I am afraid your nails will not grow back, but strictly speaking nails are not necessary for most human activities. We do take some pride in our profession, Mr. Poonaki, and we do not use interrogation methods that maim or destroy citizens."

I spat some blood into a small plastic container next to my bed. "By interrogation methods, you do mean torture?"

The two men exchanged a bemused glance, as if dealing with a naive child. "Mr. Poonaki, I hope you understand, we are not here to apologize. We do not judge the guilt or innocence of the prisoners. We try to minimize the total amount of discomfort for each person." He emphasized this point by chopping one hand into the palm of the other.

"You are an educated man. You will appreciate that we see ourselves as scientists. Our decision to give you the choice of signing the documents only once a day is based on a great deal of work and study, analyzing reams of data." I imagined him giving a presentation to his superiors about the efficiencies gained when a prisoner has a long day of torture staring him in the face. "It is true," he said, "that you might need to invest a day or two up front to convey the message, but overall I can assure you that this method is more humane. It reduces the average time of torture by eliminating some of the few outliers, even though you increase the time spent on the cowardly types. You might ask, why put people—the cowardly type, I mean—through a full day, when they are prepared to talk right away?" The cowardly type clearly disgusted him. He no doubt considered me honored not to be placed in that group. "It turns out that, according to the latest studies, a full day of interrogation encourages even the cowardly to cooperate more freely and for a longer period of time than if they had been allowed to skip the day at the outset."

Stupefied at being part of such a conversation, and still terrified of these two technicians, I asked, with difficulty, what they wanted from me.

Habib hesitated. The lipless one, also hesitant, spoke up. "Mr. Poonaki, please understand that the circumstances of your interrogation have been special. Indeed, you have been special. You lasted seven days of interrogation. Although this is not a record, we consider this a unique opportunity to learn from a subject. Also, the circumstances are unique in that we are in your home, providing a modicum of privacy for this interview."

I doubled up from cramps. He thought I was protesting.

"I know, I know." He raised both hands in a gesture of helplessness. "We could have waited a few more days, but our schedule will be crowded: the times, you know." He shrugged, as if in resignation.

"Perhaps you see no reason to cooperate with us, but I want to persuade you—I mean, by argument." He glanced at Habib, chagrined at his own insensitive choice of words. "Your feedback will allow us to reduce the interrogation time. We seldom get the chance to talk to a prisoner after our work is done."

I was stupefied. I had been targeted for a *customer satisfaction survey*. I would be helping them collect more data. Echoes of the death camps and Doctor Mengele. I groaned from muscle cramps and from the burn scars all over my body. Can I refuse? Not likely, I answered myself.

I nodded weakly. They seemed as excited as a couple of kids. Questions came spilling out.

"Did we make a mistake with the water curing?"

I nodded.

"I told you," Habib said to the lipless one. "You had time to recover, didn't you?"

I nodded again.

"What about the electric shocks?"

"I don't remember," I said.

"You dialed it too high," the lipless one told Habib.

"Same result—*more time to recover*." Habib slapped his forehead, in frustration at his own stupidity.

They questioned me about every detail. How did I feel each night? When did I pass out? How would I rate the pain, on a scale of one to ten? *When* should they use the water cure? On and on they asked questions, mostly to confirm their own hunches. They did need clarification on some points, however.

"Did you swallow too much water during the water cure?"

"Yes."

"Then should we pump the water out like a lifeguard would? Apparently"—an aside—"the Oriental method has people jumping on the stomach of the victim to eject the water." He smiled at the stupidity of the Oriental. "But that is out of the question, if you are concerned with the long-term effects."

They discussed the finer points of my shock treatment. If the shocks had wiped out my memory, then the voltage needed to be reduced. But how could they maintain the proper amount of pain?

Seeing me collapse, they thanked me profusely and assured me that my answers would go a long way to lessen the interrogation time for others. They left me with one disturbing thought.

"Mr. Poonaki," Habib said, "you can see we are professionals. The new generation, set to replace us, is a bunch of brutish peasants. Please take care not to resist them like you did us. They don't understand the difference between inflicting pain and causing damage. We have seen them in action. Many have died at their inexperienced hands. Few survive more than three days. If they do, they live the rest of their lives in wheelchairs—or in the loony bin." He twirled his forefinger at the side of his head. I must have groaned. He approached me to touch my brow, no doubt soothingly, and I winced at seeing his hand. Ms. Vakil, I believe I hurt his feelings.

"You will be good as gold in a few weeks. Make sure you eat the broth," he instructed, like a doctor. They knocked on the metal door. It was opened. The younger one, whose name I never caught, brought in the broth and set it on my bunk. They left me drenched in sweat, gulping air in short, shallow breaths.

The next day, the ninth day, I woke up late in the evening. The keys made clanking sounds on the metal door that woke me every time. I could hear all the doors as they were opened and closed. Hamid came in.

"I am here to tell you that you will be freed from this place tonight." His tone was official. "This gentleman"—he pointed to someone behind him in the corridor—"will take care of everything." I lifted my head to see, but Hamid was blocking the entrance. I studied Hamid's face. Today he looked tired and beaten. I loved him the more for putting so much effort into securing my freedom. He lowered his voice: "You know I loved you both. If you ever see him, tell him so." Hamid turned and left the room.

His companion, a hulk of a man, walked in and greeted me jovially.

"Friend, it looks like they have hurt you in this place," he said. "The pain is over, I promise you. I am here to stop all the pain." He approached me. He had his hands open, facing upward, like a magician showing the audience he had nothing to hide. And in the palm of his right hand was my teardrop-shaped piece of puzzle, its leather strap wrapped around his wrist. He held it out to me, like an offering. In my fever and pain, my eyes full of tears, I swear I noticed a sixth digit dangling on each hand.

Epilogue: A Lawyer's Lies

*Now can you tell me in what verse our
holy Prophet judges the Unbelievers?*

*In this verse: "The Jews say that the
Christians are wrong and the Christians
say that the Jews are wrong, to this extent
both are right."*

— Unknown

Call me Ms. Vakil. I have wanted to write this book since the early years of our Islamic Revolution. This length of time alone justifies the use of the virtual youth serum available to authors: the autobiographical character slyly inserted. Lop off thirty years and thirty pounds with a few sentences, and here is the lovely, creamy Ms. Vakil, working her way through historical manuscripts of the fictional writer.

At 75 years old, I have worked most of my life, not as a historian, but as a human rights lawyer from an office in Azadi square in Tehran. I always had six women volunteers working with me to document human rights cases, with all the risks involved, during both the Shah's regime and the present kleptocracy we call the Islamic Republic. During those years, a few generations of brave students came and went. I still hear from some, I have lost touch with most; a few, I know, have been swallowed into the abysses created by the ever more brutal Islamic Republic of Persiran. For many years, I shuttled back and forth to the United States to see my daughter, then my grandchildren, always returning to the polluted air with more hope than this system deserved. My age, along with the backlash produced by the Green Revolution, ended my legal career in Persiran three years ago, at the age of seventy-two. I will live the rest of my life in Boston, in an apartment exactly like my narrator's apartment. He and I share a love of the movies.

For years, I dreamt of bringing to life on the page the constitutional revolution that is the crowning moment of our modern history. I wanted to write a thickly detailed history, set amid the intrigues of prewar and wartime Europe: *La Belle Époque* of France, the prerevolutionary Russian Empire, the sadomasochistic Weimar Republic, the abject poverty of the war years in Europe, the cynical politics of the English, and the self-righteous volunteerism of the Americans—all imposing their rules on our poverty-stricken country, that understood, better than most, the rules of the game.

All that culling and gathering resulted merely in dozens of gathered and culled notebooks. In a moment of lucidity, well aware of the shortness of the time remaining to me, I ventured to cross the murky border separating fact from fiction.

I created my elaborate scaffolding to use characters strewn across the twentieth century, rather like correspondents covering historical events. My characters had to have gravitas on the world stage, to participate in the unfolding events.

The structure of telling my story over nine nights came to me early. I had always admired the structure of The Book of the Thousand Nights and One Night. When I was no more than four or five years old, my big-breasted *dayeh*, while feeding my younger sister, created excruciating tension by (in narrative) holding the scimitar over Scheherazade's head night after night. Each night after she left, after playfully squirting a quick stream of milk at me from her still-engorged breasts, I tried hard to come up with a story of my own; I always fell asleep before pinning the story down.

I have written a screed against the current mullocracy that has destroyed a country's economy and has wasted at least one generation of its citizens. I have nevertheless taken great care not be accused, like that poor Indian writer, of anti-Islamic sympathies. Years of detailed work, evidence gathering, and witnessing horrible deeds done to individuals are sufficient to demonstrate that the mullahs have created a thoroughly corrupt regime.

I used a pseudonym to write this book mostly for the protection of my family. I am not the Nobel Prize winner Shirin Ebadi, even though our biographies are similar. We did work together, her and me, during the most difficult of times. We worked tirelessly to document the barbaric, pitiless tormentors of innocent individuals. In 2003, when she won the peace prize, I smiled through gritted teeth—but I have come to accept her symbolic role among us, though mixed with a good dose of envy. Unlike Mrs. Ebadi, I never went down the justice department path. After studying law at Tehran University, I set up a small office focused mostly on family law. I practiced without difficulty until the 1979 revolution. When I no longer could practice, I began my work with the human rights organization. It lasted until 1992, when I once again was allowed to practice family law.

Mr. Poonaki did exist. I based his character on a man I visited on one of my humanitarian visits to provide books, underwear, and toiletries to political prisoners. He was a handsome young man with an unexplained facial disfigurement on his right cheek, deformed into a whirl. He already had gray hair; his deep-set eyes had natural bags underneath. He looked like El Greco's suffering John the Baptist. I found out that he was in his early twenties.

That first time I saw him, his pupils jiggered left and right. He scarcely understood why he had been arrested. Most prisoners of the revolution looked for far too long for some cause, some explanation behind their fate. Like many crime victims—and make no mistake, this government is the major criminal organization in the country—Mr. Poonaki was lost in the randomness that follows chaos. I offered him some books and some cigarettes. He lit one right away. He crossed his left arm over his chest and rested the elbow of his cigarette-holding hand on his left palm. Throwing his head up in a feminine way, he took a long drag. He asked me whether I had a religious instruction book. This struck me as out of character. He spoke Farsi with an almost undetectable French lilt. I asked him what religious instruction he needed. Looking right and left, worried about being overheard, he whispered that he needed to learn how to pray.

Most modern, well-to-do young men of pre-revolutionary times never learned or practiced a Muslim's duty to pray five times per day. His plan struck me as a wise survival tactic. He understood what was to come. He no doubt prayed by imitating the actions of others while mouthing nonsense, much like my granddaughter playing air violin in the school orchestra. He feared being caught not knowing the rudiments of his religious duties.

The second time I visited him, he looked beaten up but less scared. I offered to contact his family. He told me that he had none. His name was familiar to me, and I did a light investigation, interviewing a number of friends and acquaintances. Indeed, Mr. Poonaki had lost both parents during his teen years, to modern-day diseases. The parents did not have siblings. He also had lost a twin brother during a skiing accident when only sixteen. The newspaper *Kayhan* reported his heart-wrenching effort, bringing tens of volunteers, to rescue his brother. They found the frozen body; he passed during the helicopter transfer to the hospital.

The next time I visited him in Evin, he was a sight. His hands had swelled. Three fingernails had evidently been wrenched off with pliers; the gross swelling and dried blood clots on his fingertips did not allow a definitive conclusion that the nails were missing, but by this time I had seen enough other prisoners to be familiar with the treatment. In the early days, little attention was paid by either foreign governments or humanitarian organizations.

I asked him, stupidly, how he was doing. He told me that the day before my visit, he had been beaten with cables for a solid day. The modifier *solid* disturbed me and stayed with me for years. It implied continuity. "Solid," he repeated. "I just don't know why. They ask me for nothing. They repeat to me that I deserve every stroke, for the Imam wishes it. *Which* Imam are they talking about?"

Before Khomeini, the Shi'ites recognized the twelve Imams following the Prophet. In taking the mantle of Imam, Khomeini had placed himself among that select group. Mr. Poonaki looked confused and in a great deal of pain, but I detected no more fear. The unknown is fear's greatest ally. Surviving had given him a sense of dignity, maybe even pride.

I asked him how he coped. A painful, peekaboo smile crossed his face fleetingly. "In my head, I live entirely in my ancestral home," he confessed. "I never come out. I have every detail memorized. I look at my cell and see our childhood room: my brother and I, with two of everything. Two identical closets, two soccer balls, two balsa wood model airplanes hanging from the ceiling. We didn't appreciate each other like we should have before he died. Now I long for him." He grew quiet.

The last time I saw Mr. Poonaki, he looked thinner but was in better shape. "They don't let me sleep. They told me why I am here." His voice had a note of satisfaction. "My family has been accused of killing some Ayatollah called Nouri. Who is he?" He shrugged his shoulders and opened his palms as if in prayer.

The killing and torture of the Mujahedeen faction, which was the true and only threat to the Islamic government at that time, went apace. Now I had less time for visiting the overflowing Evin prison. The Islamic government's honeymoon had turned bloody after the bombing of the Islamic Republic Party headquarters, when seventy-two members of the dignitaries were killed. The executions at Evin Prison rose sharply, often carried out in the middle of the night. There were no outside witnesses to the summary executions of hundreds, perhaps thousands, though many surviving eyewitnesses have by now corroborated this account of the government's actions. The death sentences had yet to involve the truly vicious philosophy of later years, requiring the victim to suffer during the execution.

I inquired about Mr. Poonaki's whereabouts a few times. "He is in solitary confinement and cannot receive visitors," they told me. As weeks passed, I began to focus on other prisoners but suffered pangs of guilt. "Could I have done more for him?" I asked myself over and over. I assumed he had been another innocent victim of the waves of killings during those months.

Then, one balmy Friday afternoon in April, as I walked out of Evin Prison, I noticed a fat man—obese, in fact—following me. He had a strange beetle brow that stuck out like a hairy shelf. He would waddle behind me for a few steps but then, as if changing his mind, stop. Then he'd make a head movement, pointing that strange brow forward, and waddle a few more steps, his body following the pointed head. When I had put sufficient distance between me and the vile prison, I stopped around a corner and waited. Taking painful breaths, he passed me and then realized I was no longer in front of him. He did a comic double-take and began to stutter, wiping his brow with a soiled handkerchief.

"Please forgive me, Vakil Khanum," he said. "I should not be seen with you in the streets, but I have crucial information with regard to someone you are interested in." He twitched his eyebrows up and down to convey that we both knew what he was talking about. I had no idea what this sweaty, gelatinous clown had in mind. I told him to come to my office the next day.

There began a series of bizarre meetings. He never volunteered his name; my friends mockingly named him Hekaiatchi, "the storyteller," for he told such outrageous lies. Had it not been for a few nuggets of truth, I would surely have thrown him out. Accompanied by his slatternly, equally overweight wife, he came to my office. When she did not correct every sentence he uttered, it was because she had fallen asleep, snoring like a hippopotamus.

The Hekaiatchis' pecuniary goals quickly became clear. Mr. Hekaiatchi began by telling me that he had been a cellmate of Mr. Poonaki. He shook his head gently, his flabby double chin following in a half beat. "They killed him. I can tell you definitively."

"You saw it?" I challenged.

"Well, not with my own eyes, but they came for him one day. He was in real bad shape. I never saw him again." He threw a sly look at the wife.

"Don't tell her anything more until I hear the jangling of her coins," she said, crude as a piece of ham.

"I am afraid our meeting is concluded," I said. It seemed an obvious hoax. "Zahra," I called to my secretary. "Please see these people out. Thank you. And I am sorry to have put you through the trouble of coming down." I didn't even get up.

Then he uttered one of those nuggets of truth that made me reconsider. He said, "They killed him because his grandfather hanged Ayatollah Nouri."

"They killed him because his grandfather killed someone *a hundred years ago*?" I asked, incredulous. Yet the young man had told the same thing during my last visit.

"Not just someone," Hekaiatchi said. "The Imam considers Nouri his spiritual guide. Rumor says that the Imam witnessed the hanging when he was only six years old. He swore to take vengeance on all the descendants of his killer."

Then he talked about a suitcase of documents that Mr. Poonaki had told him about one night, in the cell they shared. He claimed to have secured it in his possession. "I'd say Mr. Poonaki was a little funny also."

"You mean humorous, or in the head?"

"You know what I mean, ma'am?" He made a ring of his thumb and forefinger while he slid his other index finger back and forth through the ring, accompanied by a breathy whistle.

"That's enough," I said. Handing them cab money, I told them to go home. I said if I found corroborating evidence, I would be willing to pay them more.

"We'll come back Wednesday afternoon," the wife said. "You don't need to worry about contacting us."

I managed in a few days to verify that Mr. Poonaki was indeed a descendant of one of the ten men who sat in judgment of the Sheikh. The story of the young Khomeini's presence at the hanging sounded apocryphal, though his father had certainly witnessed the hanging. And there was no question that the older Khomeini adhered to the Sheikh's vision of an Islamic state.

I paid the couple some more money and sat them down for another interview.

"Please tell me why you had been arrested," I began. "What had you been accused of, to end up in Evin?" All the lies resumed. He claimed he had not been a good Muslim; he had been caught with his hand in the till. He claimed that his father owned a small teahouse that the local mullah had declared a den of sin. I again made up my mind to stop dealing with this useless windbag.

"You must stop lying," I sighed. "The only way you could have ended up in a prison like Evin would have been to be a political agitator, an enemy of the state, or a *taghouti*, a rich boy. I don't see you belonging to any of these groups."

"Tell her," the wife said.

"Tell me what?"

"There is another way for me to end up at Evin," he said with a strange, oily coyness, arching his eyebrows for effect.

"We are not playing twenty questions."

"*I work there*," he announced triumphantly. "I am one of the guards."

After much deliberation with friends, I organized another interview. The discovery that he worked as a guard had many of us excited. At that interview, I offered him double the money I had paid during the previous interview—if he would come without his wife. He looked down, uncomfortable. I made the deal sweeter: I'd pay him in dollars.

"Two *sadis*," the woman interrupted, waving two ringed, fat fingers at me. She required two one-hundred-dollar bills. She knew that no money-changer on Ferdowsi Avenue accepted smaller bills. I insisted on seeing the contents of the suitcase, and then the deal was done. Alone, he would talk more freely, perhaps about other prisoners and their fate.

The last interview began badly. He did bring a suitcase full of papers pertaining to Mr. Poonaki. It contained only an administrative record of the young man's life: birth certificates, a high school degree, and some letters from his father—mostly father-to-son homilies. He had gone to Beaux-Arts of Paris. He had studied art history. That Hekaiatchi had possession of this pitiful suitcase showed clearly that the authorities had no interest in the poor young man.

I started questioning Hekaiatchi about his guard duties, his schedule, and his detailed responsibilities. Again we sank quickly into layers of lies. At some point, I remember shouting at him: all the women in the outside office stopped typing. It had the required effect: he broke down crying and told me that he was only the *ab-pash*, the water boy.

Incredulous, I exclaimed, "Your job is to water the garden?"

He stopped crying as if shutting off a faucet. He pulled out his still-soiled handkerchief and dried his wide, flat face. He looked at me under his beetle brow as if talking to a naive child. "I hose down the *room*," he said, with exaggerated patience. Seeing my childlike incomprehension, he amplified. "I attend the torture room, ma'am," he said. "I wash down the blood when they are finished." He went on. "I saw Poonaki die in front of my eyes. I have seen many die in front of my eyes." Now he broke down again, and this time for real—a catharsis from witnessing horrible deeds inflicted on humans.

Recovering, he told me that they had tortured Poonaki whenever they were not too busy with the hard-core enemies of the state. I asked him how it had ended. He mimed a knot in front of his throat, sticking his tongue out to the side.

Now my heart went out to this storyteller. Some nobody looks for a custodial job. He is hired to wash and clean a torture chamber, ignored like a piece of furniture. He stands in a corner of the room, watching, as horrors are perpetrated on other humans.

I handed him the two hundred dollars as promised. Pledging more Franklins, I asked him to come back. Though he said he would, he never did.

To kill an innocent descendant of one of the signatories of Sheikh Nouri's execution sounds medieval, but the times are such. So amen to all I have set down. You took it and now you can leave it.

Anno Persiranico: Tir 1393.

Vakil.

Made in the USA
Middletown, DE
15 November 2022

15019780R00265